Praise for *The Trea*...

'A gritty and thought-~~...~~
punishment, retributio~~...~~
  David Beckler, auth~~...~~

'Terrifying, topical, totally ~~...~~ — everyone
will be talking about this on~~...~~
  Louise Beech, author of ~~...~~ *Be Brave*

'This is intelligent futuristic thriller writing at its very best.
The central idea is mind blowing and the characters beautifully
realised'
  Victoria Dowd, author of *The Supper Club Murders*

'A high-octane, spine-shivering thriller, in which neuropsycho-
logy, crime, ethics and justice are melded in a mind-stretching
concoction'
  Philippa East, author of *Little White Lies*

'Compelling and complex, but still emotionally charged and
devastating. This is a book you genuinely won't be able to put
down'
  Helen Fields, author of *The Last Girl to Die*

'My favourite kind of thriller: intriguing, intelligent and with
a complex moral question at its core'
  Simon Lelic, author of *The Search Party*

'Smart, shocking, and fearlessly inventive'
  Dan Malakin, author of *The Box*

'*A Clockwork Orange* for the modern cohort. A terrifying near
future imagined perfectly. The book deserves to be huge'
  Imran Mahmood, author of *You Don't Know Me*

'Thoughtful and chilling, *The Treatment* offers a terrifying glimpse into a wholly believable dystopian future. A brilliant crime debut'
Brian McGilloway, author of *Little Girl Lost*

'In *The Treatment*, Sarah Moorhead takes a stunningly original and frighteningly plausible premise of a twisted criminal justice system, and creates a page-turning thriller with characters readers will love and hate. Brilliantly done!'
Guy Morpuss, author of *Five Minds*

'Bold, inventive and one hell of a ride!'
Louise Mumford, author of *Sleepless*

'A terrifying exploration of how far we can push the boundaries of science and criminal justice, to protect others'
Robert Scragg, author of *What Falls Between the Cracks*

'In *The Treatment* Sarah Moorhead has defined hell on earth with her nightmarish vision of future law enforcement. A fabulous concept and a high octane ride with inventive dystopian twists'
Eve Smith, author of *The Waiting Rooms*

'A terrifying glimpse into a darkly dystopian future we hope will never come'
Marion Todd, author of *A Blind Eye*

'What a wonderful novel. Big ideas wrapped in a plot that moves like a freight train. Sarah's got such talent, and it shines through every page'
Stuart Turton, author of *The Seven Deaths of Evelyn Hardcastle*

'A delicious speculative crime thriller that asks some deep and disturbing questions about our justice system!'
Cameron Ward, author of *The Safe House*

The Treatment

Born in Liverpool, Sarah Moorhead has told stories since child-hood and uses writing as bubblegum for her over-active brain — to keep it out of trouble. Fascinated by meaning, motiv-ation and mystery, she studied Theology at university. Over the last twenty five years, apart from teaching in secondary school, Sarah has attained a black belt in kickboxing, worked as a chaplain, established a Justice and Peace youth group, and written articles for newspapers and magazines about her work in education and religion.

THE TREATMENT

SARAH MOORHEAD

CANELO

First published in the United Kingdom in 2023 by

Canelo
Unit 9, 5th Floor
Cargo Works, 1–2 Hatfields
London SE1 9PG
United Kingdom

A CIP catalogue record for this book is available from the British Library.

Print ISBN 978 1 80436 536 6
Ebook ISBN 978 1 80436 537 3

Look for more great books at www.canelo.co

Printed and bound in Great Britain by Clays Ltd, Elcograf S.p.A.

1

For my dad, Terry, who told me 'aim for the stars and you might land on the rooftops'

Love you always X

Is it better for a man to have chosen evil than to have good imposed upon him?

Anthony Burgess, *A Clockwork Orange*

PROLOGUE

Twenty-seven years ago

Grace lay still for a moment, her small body curled up inside her mother's arms, her back against her mum's chest, almost as if she was still in the womb. The grey woollen blanket was scratchy against her skin. She lay half-asleep, thinking about playing in the caged yard later with the other kids. If they were good, they might get permission to go into the vegetable garden. Her seed might have started to grow, its green shoots reaching out of the black earth.

Soon Warden Kane would unlock their door, 'the swishy' as Grace called it, because of the sound it made. Usually her mother was up by now and making a cup of tea with the little kettle that Grace wasn't allowed to touch. When the steam came out of the spout and rose up towards the window, Grace imagined what it would be like to float up into the air, out of the unit, beyond the walls, to see what life was really like out there.

Out There. Too big, too scary, too many people on the other side of the wall. There would be men too. Did all men wear uniform Out There, like the male wardens did?

She could hear Lottie, Remy's mum, singing in the cell next door. She felt safe here with the women, even though they sometimes screamed and shouted, either at each other or at the kids. Sometimes they even fought. The kids could be mean. But not Remy. Remy was never mean.

He'd still be sprawled in the narrow bed next door but it wouldn't be long until they were in class. He'd try to make her laugh and she would tell him to behave. She was only five but she already knew all her letters.

Remy was a year older. He'd be leaving soon. The rule was that if you had nowhere else to go, you could stay with your mother until your seventh birthday. Then they packed you off to state boarding school. But Lottie only had six months left of her sentence, so Remy wouldn't be separated from her.

Grace's mother had reassured her many times that they too would stay together. The idea of being parted from her mum, even for a night, terrified her. It had always been just the two of them. Thick as thieves, her mother would say, and laugh. Sometimes, what choice had they had but to steal? It wasn't wrong, it was survival.

Her mother never sang like Lottie did, but her laughter always made Grace feel happy, like everything was going to be okay.

But things didn't feel okay today. In fact, something felt odd. The room, the bed – everything felt so still.

Grace took a deep breath and turned around to face her mother.

People didn't sleep with their eyes open, did they? They looked weird, too much blue, the pupils tiny black dots.

'Mum...?'

She touched her mother's cheek with her finger and shuddered.

'Mummy, wake up.'

Grace turned to the door as it swished open.

'Morning, pet,' Warden Kane said before halting in her tracks. Without taking her eyes from Grace's mother, she called out 'Lottie!' with a strange lilt to her voice Grace had never heard before.

'Coming, Warden,' Lottie's singsong voice rang out in the corridor, before she turned into the room and stopped dead, her eyes widening.

'Take the child,' commanded Kane quietly.

2

'Remy's been asking for you,' Lottie said, lifting Grace from the bed. Her mother's arm flopped heavily onto the blanket.

But Grace knew that Remy always slept in.

'He has something to show you,' she said, wrapping Grace in her soft, fleshy embrace and moving towards the door. 'It's a spider, Gracie, the biggest one in the block, but you have to hurry or it'll run away.'

Warden Kane began barking into her radio.

Medics? Weren't they the ones who took Jai's mum away when she'd been screaming all night?

Lottie set Grace down in her room and went back out again. Remy lifted his head up from the pillow, his hair ruffled, his face creased like the sheet he lay on.

'What's up?' One of his eyes was still shut. He sat up on the bed with his back against the wall and pulled his knees up towards him.

The alarm was sounding, echoing Lottie's wailing. Through the open door, Grace could see the women congregating in the corridor.

Remy rubbed his face and then patted the bed. Grace clambered up, snuggled next to him, and he wrapped his blanket around the pair of them.

It was when she felt the warmth of his body that it began to dawn on her.

She closed her eyes and tried to close her mind to her worries about her mother, the shouts of the women in the corridor, the silence that fell as the medics – more men in uniform – arrived on the scene.

Sometime later, Grace didn't know if it had been minutes or hours, Lottie came back and knelt down in front of the two children huddling on the bed. 'There's nothing they could do, babe,' she said tearfully. 'Already gone. They couldn't save her.'

Grace looked to Remy for an explanation, his grey eyes wise in his young face.

Instead he said, 'I'll look after you now, Gracie. I'll never let anyone hurt you and you'll never be on your own.'

But all Grace could hear was the words that burned deeply into her mind.

Couldn't save her.

CHAPTER ONE

Present day

This was not the way Brian Corrigan had expected to die.

For a long time, years possibly, at the back of his mind there had been the worry that he'd fade away in hospital from some awful cancer, with ineffective pain relief and pretty nurses who would remind him of what he was leaving behind.

There had once been the possibility that he might die peacefully at home in bed surrounded by his family. But that was never going to happen because Paula had gone before him – he'd been a widower for almost twenty years – and the kids never bloody bothered.

In fact, Brian Corrigan had had years to ponder his own demise. At his age, a ripe old ninety-three – *seven years off a century!* – who wouldn't have wondered how it was going to end? And, of course, after he lost his beloved Paula to heart failure – he could still remember the face of the doctor as he broke the news – death had been something never far from his mind. Something he might even *welcome*.

But not like this, so untidy, so... violent.

He briefly pondered how his body might be found and thought about the indignity of it all – on a blood-soaked pillow in his pale-blue striped pyjamas, the covers turned down on the opposite side of the bed, just like every night since his wedding day – *seventy years ago next year!* – as though Paula would wander up after her programme was finished and get in beside him like she used to, smelling of Shalimar perfume and Aquafresh.

How had it come to this? His failing hearing had not alerted him as the man had broken in, crept up the stairs, entered his bedroom. Brian had woken, confused and afraid, a figure looming over his bed.

How could it be that so suddenly, it seemed, he was no longer the strong young builder with the capacity to kick the fella's arse. Instead, here he was, a frail scarecrow, all that time and strength just drained away like sand in a glass timer.

These had been his thoughts as he'd offered the intruder money, held it out in his gnarled, liver-spotted fist. He always kept some under his mattress. He didn't trust those strange machines and automated bank clerks. Most people only used swipe cards and biochips these days. Surely cash was needed if someone wanted to buy drugs?

But the man wouldn't take the money.

'What do you want? What do you want?' Brian kept asking, until it became a bleating cry of fear. Initially buffered by shock, his musings finally gave way to panic.

'What do you want? I'm an old man! Don't hurt me!'

But the burglar didn't speak at all.

Brian could feel the tears wetting his crinkled cheeks, thankfully blurring the vision of the wooden bat moving towards him. He raised his shrivelled hands, impotent.

He'd found life tough the last few years, being in this frail body, and he'd been drifting with no real purpose since losing Paula. However, at this moment he found some deep instinct wanted to hold on, to grasp what little life he had left, even out of sheer stubbornness that this was not the way he wanted to go, at the hands of some no-mark.

'Why are you doing this? Please don't!'

As the bat hit home with the ease of a spoon crushing a delicate eggshell, Brian Corrigan heard the intruder laugh – a low, cruel chuckle.

It was at that moment that he knew what the man wanted.

Just to watch him die.

11.32 a.m.

I'm outside the offender rehabilitation company, Janus Justice. Crowds of protestors have gathered here this morning angry at the government's decision to give the go-ahead for a controversial treatment called Aversion Therapy, in which criminals are given a taste of their own medicine.

It's been revealed that secret trials of this cutting-edge treatment have been carried out over the last two years, but protestors are riled because it has now become an official court sanction.

Here beside me is Conrad Becker, the founder and CEO of Janus Justice. So Mr Becker, what exactly is Aversion Therapy and why do you think people have an issue with it?

Becker: Well, Dan, let's say it's a way of helping offenders to experience the damage and upset they have caused to others but from their own perspective. Obviously, people are afraid of new technology, but this is a highly tested, highly effective treatment that will very quickly, and very cheaply, rehabilitate criminals, which is our aim at Janus Justice.

Dan: Do you think that people need a Third Tier, Mr Becker? Are Tiers One and Two not effective enough? Is that why you've had to bring in tougher measures?

Becker: No, Tiers One and Two are highly effective for what we designed them for. However, different people have different needs and different reasons to commit crime. For instance, someone might steal bread because they're hungry, or because they were traumatised by not having enough to eat as a child, or they want revenge on the baker for being rude to them. At Janus, we assess the causes of crime and then apply the correct treatment to 'cure' the offender, so to speak.

Dan: But your treatments don't always work and sometimes the criminals relapse, isn't that right, Mr Becker?

Becker: Assessment isn't always straightforward at Tier One and Tier Two. Offenders often straddle the two tiers, therefore from time to time we have an offender who returns to us if their needs weren't met initially. So, for example, at Tier One we deal with people who commit crimes because they lack the basic necessities – food, water, shelter…

Dan: Are you suggesting that the New London Vision – the government's flagship programme of cosy social housing, free schools, excellent healthcare, support for the elderly and infirm, and full employment – has failed? Surely if all these things are provided for people, then there's no reason for them to commit crimes?

Becker: Janus Justice works hand in hand with the New London Vision to provide for and rehabilitate offenders who have somehow managed to slip through the net.

Dan: And what about Tier Two? Do you have many reoffenders?

Becker: Well, let me finish. It may be that we rehabilitate someone at Tier One by meeting their physical needs, but there is the chance they might return to us at Tier Two if their offending is caused by mental health problems, trauma, addiction, or even intellectual capacity. We need to help these people to realise what's on offer for them and how this can transform their lives into one of non-offending.

Dan: And now you're expanding your treatments?

Becker: Offending has dropped over fifty per cent in the last seven years and the government are investing even more money over the next ten years. We're taking that money and creating something revolutionary.

Dan: And will there be reoffending after Tier Three, Mr Becker?

8

Becker: This treatment is effective and lasting. Once an offender has been through Aversion Therapy, they are cured. I guarantee it.

Dan: What about those protestors who say Aversion Therapy is merely a form of revenge?

Becker: An eye for an eye has been a form of justice for thousands of years, hasn't it? I don't see why people are taking exception to it now.

Dan: Thank you for your time, Mr Becker.

This is Dan Gunnarsson reporting for NewsFlex.

JANUS

Disappointment always loomed when an offender returned, not necessarily in the person, but in the circumstances that had brought them back.

Grace sat behind her desk in her bright consultation room overlooking the Thames on the twelfth floor of the Janus Justice building. Her name on the door – *Dr Grace Gunnarsson* in gold lettering, and her various certificates – MB ChB, MRCPsych – in gilt frames on the wall behind her desk embarrassed her sometimes. She worried that they intimidated her clients. No doubt her boss, Conrad, wanted it that way.

'Nikki, you're back.' All four foot eleven of her. 'You've been moved up to Tier Two because you've reoffended. You get that?' Grace asked gently. 'It means we didn't quite get it right in Tier One.' Grace herself had been moved up to Tier Two in a promotion eight years ago, when the managers wanted to put her psychiatry degree and medical training to better use. If there were still problems, the system had to dig deeper. And that was where Grace came in.

Nikki blinked at her, confused.

'You know the way after your first offence we found you somewhere to live, when you were sent to Tier One? That obviously hasn't worked out for some reason. So now we're going to move you up to Tier Two and look at how to help you psychologically.' There was still no recognition in the woman's eyes. 'You know, in your thoughts and your feelings, to work out how we can make your rehab work this time.' Grace nodded, trying to show her that this was a good thing.

Nikki parroted the nod. 'Help me better.'

'Yes, that's right.'

There was suspicion in her eyes. Grace couldn't blame her.

The in-house nickname for the service users at Tier One was 'the Desperate'. Grace never used it, but she recognised its accuracy. These were the people who lived on the streets, who didn't know where the next meal was coming from, who didn't have access to running water or healthcare. Nikki had been desperate when she'd first arrived at Janus, not two miles away from the magistrates' court where she'd been convicted of squatting.

Nikki sat in a chair opposite her, the greasy hood of her coat still covering half her face, her red-raw hands picking at threadbare jeans, her trainers ripped and worn. Grace smoothed the cream linen of her trousers in an unconscious mirroring.

'They're not going to take them off me, are they?' Nikki whined like a sulky teenager, looking at Grace briefly before looking away again.

'The kids? No, I'll make sure they don't. But you're going to have to work with me.'

Grace remembered the police footage of junkies being hauled out of the squat six months previously, when they had found Nikki, the only non-addict in the building, huddled like a stray cat hiding her kittens away – two babies under a blanket. Her pathetic cries as she'd tried to protect her little ones from the intrusion had been heart-rending.

Grace swept her hand over the black glassy surface of her desk and immediately Nikki Paton's life lay in digital documents before her – her physical and psychological health reports, feedback from Tier One, the court documents, even her children's birth certificates. The diagrams from the automatic bio-scan as Nikki had entered the room were displayed also – her heart rate, body temperature, stress levels, and more.

Grace glanced over them, aware of Nikki's trembling lips. What would happen to her now if Grace couldn't solve her problems? Poor, gentle, simple, unlucky Nikki.

'Nikki, love, it's not the end of the world. It's only Tier Two. We're going to sort this out.'

Grace dabbed at her desk and turned up the ambient waves, the emotisonics, in the room in an attempt to soothe her client. Then she cast an assessing eye over her, trying to intuit things a scanner could never find. With her bleached blonde hair and big brown eyes, Nikki might have been pretty if she hadn't had such a haunted look.

'Are you the psycho woman?' Nikki asked tearfully.

Grace couldn't help but smile. 'I'm the psychiatrist, yes. I look at how your brain works and how you're feeling, so that I can help you figure out what you need, and we can get you on the straight and narrow.'

What you need. The nickname for Tier Two users – 'the Needy' – was equally appropriate. Grace assessed offenders and suggested solutions – albeit from a strict menu of government provisions. Her work in this Tier could take many forms, all of which took skills and knowledge to figure out the underlying problem. Already this week, she'd discovered brain damage from a childhood accident on the scan of a violent offender. She'd referred him to the surgery department. It might go some way to curing his violence. She hoped so.

'Let's get your bloods done, see if that gives us any more information.' Grace stood up, took a small metallic bracelet from a nearby cupboard and moved over to Nikki, who shrank back in her seat. 'It's not going to hurt. Only takes a second.'

When Nikki finally held out her arm, Grace placed the bracelet on her slim wrist and immediately it tightened. A second or so later, it released itself. Nikki handed it back and examined the small circle of red dots it had left.

Grace placed the bracelet into an analyser and a few minutes later, the results came up on her desk. She regularly screened her clients for chemical and hormonal imbalances – norepinephrine, dopamine, serotonin, testosterone, for example, which could cause problems, the biological basis of some types of crime. But she suspected Nikki's criminogenic influences were rooted in deep emotional disturbances – neglect or trauma.

She'd seen this too often now. One of the saddest cases was a woman who'd been stealing medicine for her baby, a little boy who'd already been dead for two weeks, but the mother wouldn't let him go. The image never left Grace – the tiny body wrapped in a blue blanket.

If only Nikki Paton could peer beneath Grace's well-maintained facade to see how closely her life had once paralleled her clients' – would she trust her more?

But it was years since Lottie had died and Remy left, and Grace had kept the truth of her background from everyone, even her husband Dan.

Nikki was the lone carer of her children the way Grace's mother had been. But these days they didn't throw the kids into prison and punish them too. No doubt it had been well-intentioned back then, keeping the family unit together. Instead, Grace would send Nikki and her children to the Agrarian Compound, a 'holiday camp for the criminally afflicted' as Dan had described it in one of his more controversial articles for NewsFlex.

How different Grace's life would have been if her mother had been able to access the sort of help that was available now. But her past was also a blessing. Didn't it give her the instincts for knowing what people needed, the desire to analyse the people brought before her so that she could respond and help them to stop offending? *Prevention is better than cure*, Lottie used to say. It seemed the government agreed these days.

The New London Vision was so successful that ministers were prepared to invest billions to roll out similar programmes across the country, starting with Liverpool, Manchester and Newcastle. A huge initial expense that would lead to an exponential return.

Grace pushed the past away, tucked into the dark corner of her mind, and turned her attention to the documents on her screen-desk. *Court-ordered placement at her brother's home in Hackbridge … however, biochip located Ms Paton in Tower Hamlets … broken the conditions of … police found her in another squat … stolen cans of milk, nutripacks, sugar pods…*

'Why didn't you stick to the court order?' Grace asked, as gently as she could.

Nikki shook her head and pressed her lips together.

'Can you tell me why you left your brother's house?'

Maybe a session of hypnotherapy might help to get to the bottom of things.

'Nikki, I want to help, but you have to help yourself too.'

No response.

'You've already been through Tier One and this is probably your only shot at Tier Two. What's going to happen to the kids then, eh?'

Nikki looked up, a fierceness in her eyes.

'You're not taking my kids!'

'Of course I'm not going to take your kids. I'm saying if you don't cooperate, then—'

Nikki jumped up and shouted, 'You're not taking my kids! I'm not staying here! I want my kids now!'

Grace also stood up but spoke calmly. 'The kids are fine, Nikki. They're downstairs in the creche. But you have to cooperate if you're going to make things better… for all of you.'

The bio-scanner reactions burst into colour on Grace's desk as Nikki flew to the door.

'You're not going to take my children!' She pawed at the security panel, wailing, 'Felix! Angel!'

The door opened and a clinic porter blocked the exit – a large, strong-looking Black man in his late fifties. He fixed his hooded eyes on Grace, looking for direction as Nikki pounded futilely against his mass as she tried to exit.

'Hold her,' Grace commanded. In a matter of seconds George had Nikki in a secure grasp, holding her arms across her chest as she faced Grace, who had pulled a nasal sedative spray from a drawer.

'No, don't!' Nikki cried as Grace moved closer. She kicked out with both feet, her dirty trainers making contact with Grace's linen trousers, knocking her backwards. The spray fell from her hand and skittered across the floor.

'Don't worry, Doctor G,' said George. 'I've got one here somewhere.' He kept one huge arm around Nikki and rummaged in his uniform pocket with his free hand. Grace stepped back as Nikki swiped at her.

'Very useful,' he said, smiling as he threw one to Grace, before taking Nikki firmly but gently by both arms again.

Grace applied the nasal spray, and moments later, Nikki stopped struggling and her legs began to give way.

George guided her gently back to the chair and sat her down. 'You'll be okay, honey,' he soothed. 'Doctor G here is the best. She looked after my sister Aleisha, so I know she's going to make it all okay.'

Grace smiled at the memory. She winked at him and he lumbered out of the room.

She knelt down by Nikki, whose face was red, her breathing laboured.

It took a few minutes for her to calm down completely. Once the look in Nikki's eyes had softened, Grace asked, 'Why did you leave your brother's house?'

'He beat me, lots of times, like my dad used to,' she said slowly. 'I was afraid he'd turn on my kids.'

Grace felt her heart sink.

'What did I do to deserve this? My dad, my ex, and then my brother...'

'Oh, Nikki. Why didn't you tell us this before? We could have changed your place of appointment.'

'I was afraid my brother would say I lied. I didn't think anyone would believe me.' She leaned over and put her head in her hands. 'I just can't do this any more.'

'Come on, you can't give up now.' Grace reached forward and patted her on the shoulder. 'I'm not going to let you. I'm going to make sure you and the kids are okay. I promise.'

Nikki breathed a heavy sigh.

'Take report,' Grace said, and immediately a document opened up on her desk and began to transcribe her words. 'Nikki Paton is to be sent to the Agrarian Compound for six months for treatment. Bringing two infants. Therapy and medication to be discussed after orientation. End.'

She rubbed Nikki's back. 'You'll be safe there, plus your kids will love it. There are play areas and classrooms and you'll be taught skills to help you get a job when you leave. I know the manager, Shannon. She'll look after you and I'll be visiting once a week, to see how you're all getting on.'

Nikki's shoulders slumped. She blinked slowly and then smiled at Grace. It changed her whole face.

'Right, then, let's go and fetch the kids from the creche and I'll make the necessary arrangements to get you out there.'

Nikki stood up slowly and made her way to the door, leaning heavily on Grace. George was waiting outside to escort her. She was still an offender, after all.

'Tonight, you'll all have hot meals and clean beds. You'll feel better in the morning, I promise.'

Nikki shuffled out and Grace returned to her desk to fill in various forms. As she did so, the Janus bulletin came up on her screen-desk, including one that caught her eye from the Department of Justice. A familiar name, albeit one she hadn't seen for a long time.

Remy James Wilson.

What the hell has he done now?

What made one person go one way and another person go the other, even when they had the same – or similar –

upbringings? Grace, determined to crawl her way up, had chosen the light. Remy, it seemed, had chosen darkness.

Her finger hovered over the link.

Remy – her foster brother, her protector, her best friend – the love she had for Remy was the purest thing she'd had in her life.

Her thoughts shattered as her boss, Conrad Becker, barged in.

'Grace, I know you're busy but we're short today and it's all hands on deck,' he said, his American accent unchanged by his ten years in the UK.

She looked at him quizzically.

'I need you up on Tier Three.'

Her stomach dropped. 'Conrad, you know what I think of Tier Three. I've got lots of appointments booked here today. I don't think I can—'

'Sorry, Grace, but we need a psych in there, or we can't carry out the procedure. Myriam has called in sick and you're the only qualified person on site today.'

'Can't you reschedule?'

'No, I can't,' he said flatly.

Grace shook her head, staring at him in disbelief. 'I just can't…'

'You know the rules. We need a psych in clinic or the procedure will have to be called off. You don't actually have to do anything, you just have to be there. She's already in the witness room,' he hissed. 'I'm not telling her to come back another day. We can't let her suffer any longer.'

He kept his eyes locked on her until she finally stood up and made her way to the door, resenting him with every step.

Conrad knew Grace's Achilles heel.

CHAPTER TWO

The Old Bailey, London

One month ago

Noah Begbroke was sentenced to Tier Three Aversion Therapy today after an arson attack in which his ex-girlfriend Corrina Saunders suffered extensive burns. 'A cruel act of wanton destruction,' Judge Bamber-O'Malley commented in her concluding remarks, 'intended to punish Corrina Saunders for daring to break free of Begbroke's coercive control.'

It is thought that Miss Saunders will be present to see justice carried out at Janus, which has raised questions about the wider psychological effects on victims as they see their ordeals played out onscreen in a virtual mock-up of the crime. These CGI videos or 'reels' cast the criminal as the victim, but some psychologists suggest it may exacerbate the trauma experienced by the victims nonetheless.

However, Aversion Therapy is not without its supporters. Some government ministers, the right-wing press and many members of the public have shown support, saying that it is an appropriate response and the victims have the choice whether to be present or not.

NewsFlex has tried to talk to a number of victims who have observed Aversion Therapy on their attackers, but they have refused to comment, saying only that they had to sign

–

Grace resisted the urge to run. She knew that what she was about to see could never be unseen.

It was the first time she'd been in the Tier Three Aversion Therapy clinic. Conrad had given her temporary security clearance. The walls of the small room were painted charcoal grey, which added to the feeling of claustrophobia. There was a black reclining chair at the centre which gave the impression that a dental surgeon had decided to oust the usual clinical white and go for something more sinister.

The temperature began to rise and the screen situated in front of the black chair flickered with orange and red pixelated flames. In the semi-darkness, the wavering glow reflected on a large glass window opposite the door – the witness room.

Grace couldn't bring herself to look at the window.

Noah Begbroke couldn't run. A restraining strap across his chest held him tightly in the chair and a nasal spray relaxant had already been administered. However, he was still agitated, his arms twitching. His dark eyes scanned the virtual fire in front of him in small, alarmed circles. He knew what was coming. He'd seen it all once before.

Grace wished she was back in Tier Two on the lower floor. At least down there they were giving people what they needed. That, and healing people, had been her aim when she joined Janus Justice. But this – this was something different altogether.

Was this giving people what they needed?

Her eyes flicked over to the window again. *Maybe it is.*

Some people thought it went too far. The protests outside the clinic and parliament were testament to that.

And then there were those who thought it didn't go far enough, who saw it as an easy way for criminals to get out of a prison sentence.

And at their most extreme were the vigilantes – hidden, masked, lawless.

Begbroke had been found guilty and then screened and assessed at Tier Two. Grace had worked with the team on his case. There was nothing that could be done with him on her Tier: no chemical imbalance, no mental health problems, no childhood trauma. Nothing to explain his actions. The criminogenic factors in Tiers One and Two were usually based on biology and circumstance. Up at Tier Three, morality itself played a bigger part.

It was dark in the witness room, so it was impossible to see anything but shadows. She looked away, grateful. The temperature rose again. If she'd known she'd be working with an arsonist, she wouldn't have worn a jumper and tights.

Bloody Conrad, dragging her into this.

'I don't want to,' Begbroke whined, anxiously staring at the cannula jutting out of the back of his hand. His eyes followed the intravenous tube up to where Abigail, the Tier Three clinical manager, was removing one syringe and attaching another. 'I don't want to,' he repeated. Grace cast an eye over the metal dish nearby containing vials of drugs, some of the brand names of which she didn't recognise.

'Bit late for that, don't you think, Begbroke?' said Abigail.

Abigail was unremarkable – average size, strawberry-blonde hair, not particularly attractive – except for her unusual coloured eyes, the lightest brown Grace had ever seen, flecked with yellow which blazed like amber in the orange light. She felt a fleeting admiration for Abigail, so calm, almost emotionless – quite the opposite of Grace herself.

How did Abigail cope seeing the crimes onscreen day in, day out? It seemed like a punishment not only for the offender.

One of Dan's articles on NewsFlex – the most popular news website – had been titled 'The jailer becomes the jailed'. If only he knew the full truth.

'Can't face up to what you did?' Abigail whispered as she leaned over to check the cannula was secure. Begbroke looked up at Grace imploringly. What did he expect? Words of comfort, after what he'd done? Abigail squeezed the syringe and soon his eyes glazed over and settled lazily on the screen in front of him.

Abigail swiped and stabbed at her handheld shell, the faint green and blue lines of its motherboard visible through the transparent crystal. Bright patterns of data suddenly appeared, lighting up the screen.

Could they really fix an offender with a single treatment? The therapy Grace used could sometimes take months to reach the heart of the problem and get her clients back on their feet as law-abiding citizens. And, of course, it took its toll emotionally on her. Dan had said it was ironic that empaths were often attracted to such work, considering how it might affect them.

He wouldn't be happy if he knew where she was working today. Although the journalist side of him would be curious. The public were well aware of what happened in Tiers One and Two, but Tier Three was a different matter.

Grace was accustomed to using medication, usually the new generation of anxiolytics and antidepressants. In fact, she herself had worked with the pharmacists to develop the types of drugs that would help her clients most effectively. She looked down at the vials again. These must be serious drugs if they had to resort to syringes and cannulas. One she recognised as a relaxant, one she assumed was a psychotropic drug, the other one, she had no idea. But there was so much secrecy about this tier.

She immediately shut down her burgeoning curiosity. There was no need to know, she wasn't coming back here. As though Abigail sensed how she was feeling, she mouthed, 'You okay?'

Grace nodded, but she could feel her body trembling.

There was a cry from the witness room as the face of a young woman appeared on the screen, staring down at Begbroke with shining brown eyes. Her long dark hair was parted in the middle. Her bronzed skin was smooth and flawless except for a single tear-shaped beauty spot on her left cheek. She was smiling, seemingly unaware of the flames lapping around her.

Grace felt a wave of adrenaline. This jarred with her own moral compass. She would have to shut out of her mind all the arguments she had against Aversion Therapy just to get through the next half an hour. Then she would have a go at Conrad for springing this on her. It was written into their contracts, wasn't it, not to go against *what was morally justifiable to the employee*?

What did Abigail find morally justifiable?

Begbroke shook his head from side to side in minute tremors, but his eyes were transfixed in a glassy haze on the woman on the screen who was smiling down at him. Grace knew she wouldn't be smiling if she knew who was looking at her.

'What's your name?' demanded Abigail.

'Noah,' he mumbled, eyes locked onto the screen.

She shook her head. 'He's not fully cooked yet, give it another minute or two.'

Abigail appeared to zone out for a few moments while Grace waited anxiously wondering what was going to happen next.

'He's ready,' Abigail said suddenly. 'The giveaway is in the constriction of the pupils.' She looked back down at her shell and jabbed at it again. A steady stream of smoke began pumping in through the filters into the room. She took two masks from behind one of the panels, passed one to Grace and they put them on.

Begbroke was now under the influence of strong drugs that were going to make him see his crimes from a very different perspective. Part of her couldn't help but feel sorry for him. But then her thoughts turned to Corrina Saunders, who had suffered at his hands. She would have agreed to this punishment, demanded it even. Grace swallowed her feelings – but they writhed inside her.

Abigail locked her amber eyes onto Grace and said, 'I'm turning up the emotisonics.' Therapeutic soundwaves were used everywhere these days – in the gym along with the music to get you going, at hospital to heal you, in school to help you focus and absorb information. But these emotisonics were different – they caused negative emotions to make the therapy even more unpleasant for the offender.

The people behind the window were protected by a fine shield of barely visible mesh embedded in the glass, but here in the clinic they would have to use headbands to block the waves. Abigail passed one to her. Grace put it on, took a few deep breaths and set her body into a defensive stance, as though about to receive a blow.

'This is the usual routine. Wait until the meds kick in and then show the offender preparation reels before the big show.'

Grace tried to swallow, but her mouth was dry.

There was Corrina on a video loop – healthy, cheerful shots interspersed with post-crime photographs. The effect was startling. Begbroke was mesmerised as the images rotated between a happy, smiling woman and a blurred image of brown, red and black that, each time it appeared, felt like a jab to Grace's gut.

Abigail checked the screens that displayed Begbroke's vital signs.

'We can never be too careful,' she said quietly, looking over at the window and back again.

Too careful?

'Maybe don't look. Don't want to upset yourself,' Abigail said kindly.

The jailer becomes the jailed.

But Grace noticed that Abigail didn't turn away.

Grace glanced briefly back at the screen. The image had changed to one of a living room in soft pastel shades, curtains drawn and lamps casting a gentle light. A large mirror above the fireplace reflected the dark-haired woman sitting on the sofa looking down at her shell, maybe reading or watching a programme.

The smoke in the treatment room had covered the floor like a rolling mist and the sound of crackling flames came through the speaker. A distinct change had come over Begbroke. He cowered in the chair, his dry eyes locked to the screen, his mouth hanging open.

'What's your name?' asked Abigail suddenly, loudly, after a few moments, making Grace jump.

'Corrina,' Begbroke whispered. 'Corrina Saunders.'

On the screen, the woman jumped up as the window smashed and a bright missile landed in the middle of the floor. It exploded in a ball of liquid fire, opening up like a huge flower of flames.

'What did Noah Begbroke do to you?' asked Abigail.

After a few moments of groaning as he shielded his face, Begbroke started speaking in a high-pitched voice, one that did not seem to come from him. 'He's my... he was my boyfriend. He was horrible, violent, degrading... I tried to get away from him...'

They knew the details, of course. It had all been played out in court. This wasn't a fact-finding mission. It was a punishment – down to the bad root.

Abigail dabbed at her shell again and the smoke came in thicker and faster. Grace felt as though she was an assistant at a Victorian seance, watching Abigail contacting the spirit of the victim through the offender.

'Yes. I told him we were over, but... he told me... he told me...' Begbroke cleared his throat. 'He told me that no one would want me when he'd finished with me.' He sat forward and gripped the arms of the chair, the veins and sinews in his hands pulsating beneath the dark hairs. He let out an odd yelp and then slumped back, as a medium might relax after the spirit had left, vacant.

Grace could see the freshly inked, dark-blue tattoo that all offenders had etched prior to treatment. It was an image of Janus, the two-headed Roman god, one of his faces pointing to the past, the other to the future, a number three at the centre. It bore a red halo of swelling. The ink would gradually fade over a period after treatment, the length of time depending on the severity of the crime. It served as a warning, a reminder.

'He attacked your house? Is that correct?' Abigail asked disinterestedly, as she checked the cannula in Begbroke's now limp hand. Her manner was calm with a *we're-going-to-get-to-the-bottom-of-this* attitude.

'He'd been in my house, taken my smoke alarms out,' Begbroke said in the soft voice again. 'He thought I'd be asleep in bed... I should have died!' His eyes darted about, his breathing frantic. 'There's fire! The room is on fire!' The computer reacted to his terrified words, the crackling flames became louder, the heat rose, and then came the worst of all – the simulated smell of burning flesh.

Grace gagged and put her hands to her face, reeling even though she wore a mask. Abigail grabbed her arm and dug her nails in. Grace tried to pull herself together for the sake of the watchers behind the glass. Abigail released her grip, took the final vial of drugs from the dish and attached it to Begbroke's cannula.

Moments later, he started jerking in the chair, fighting against his restraints, his eyes wild. He was coughing, panicking. 'I have to get out... I have to get out...' Grace looked in alarm to Abigail, but her face was stony.

Begbroke raised his hands slowly, heavily to his face and screamed.

What the hell had they given him to cause that reaction?

Grace turned to the screen, which showed the beautiful young woman also screaming, the flames encompassing her as she desperately tried to escape the burning house.

Grace couldn't take any more. Horrified, she stumbled towards the clinic door, passing the glass window as she went, and taking in briefly, but fully, the sight of two misshapen hands against the glass, fingers missing or melded together, red-raw with scars, and the melted, burned face of the once beautiful Corrina Saunders watching justice being done.

CHAPTER THREE

Conrad leaned against a wall in the corridor, arms folded, biting his lip. As soon as Grace came out of the bathroom, he uncrossed his arms and moved towards her. She dodged him and headed for the lift.

'I'm sorry,' he began.

She placed her thumb on the scanner, keeping her head down.

'I should have warned you.' He was shorter than her, probably ten years older, but not a grey hair in sight. Her eyes cast down, she could see his expensive ugly leather shoes.

Should have bloody warned her? How dare he put her in such a position!

'Grace, please... Come to my office and we'll have a talk...' He took a step closer to her, his manicured hands outstretched as if trying to placate a frightened animal.

She dabbed the scanner with her thumb again.

'Have a coffee with me. At least let me explain...' he urged.

She sighed heavily, feeling her resolve fading and lifted her head to look at him.

'That was rough, Conrad.'

'I'm sorry, Grace, there's no way to prepare people for it.' He took a step closer. 'You look peaky. Let me get you a glass of water.' He took her by the arm and she let herself be led along the bright white corridor, aware of the silhouettes moving darkly behind the white translucent windows of the offices either side.

The clinical white stopped at the threshold of Conrad's office, replaced by vintage walnut wainscoting, the likes of which she'd seen only on a school trip to a stately home. Wood was so expensive these days. The European governments had been paying to maintain the forests in other parts of the world, mainly South America, for nearly twenty years now – *bribery to protect the lungs of the planet*, Dan had said in one of his reports. Wood import taxes were ridiculous. Maybe it was repurposed? She doubted it, suspecting that Conrad's desire for status would eclipse his concern for the environment.

He nodded towards a chair next to the desk and she reluctantly sat down as he poured her a drink of water from a carafe and put it into her shaking hands. He moved to the other side of his desk, his large leather chair creaking under his weight, and steepled his fingers.

'I know it's not an easy thing to observe,' he began. 'The treatment.'

Treatment? Torture, more like it.

She put the glass to her lips and eyed the brass statue of a racing horse which stood on the desk, as ugly and brutish as the sport itself had been before its prohibition.

'My grandparents had a stud farm in Kentucky,' he explained when he registered her eyeline. 'That's where the money came from to start my research into the rehabilitation of offenders. You think the prison population over here was bad in the 2020s? You should have seen the figures in the US. Janus Justice was so successful back home that the good ol' British government bought my services. We liked your National Health Service, you liked our prisoner rehab, it was a done deal. We built a number of state-of-the-art hospitals and clinics here in the UK and we rent them back to the local health authorities. It's a nice little earner for us and we got to open up the Tier System here. There's quite a bit of money involved.' He chuckled to himself but stopped when Grace remained expressionless. 'I keep it there as a reminder of where I've come from.'

Grace didn't want reminders of where she'd come from.

Avoiding his gaze, she let her eyes travel around the room. A few bound books – rare these days, not just because of the price of paper – sat on the shelf next to an upright display shell showing a series of images of Conrad's family. There was an identical one on the next shelf showing Conrad with various celebrities and government officials. Above his chair hung a painting of a man she recognised as the writer Dostoevsky. A quote underneath it read: 'You can judge any society by how well it treats its prisoners.'

Grace wondered what the treatment she'd seen this morning said about their society.

Conrad swiped at his screen-desk and it immediately lit up. 'Do you like your job in Tier Two?' He looked at her expectantly.

'Yes… yes, I do.'

'You did a good job in Tier One. Promoted quickly. Too easy for you?' He smiled and Grace felt herself blush.

'It's essential to get the basics fixed first,' she said. 'If people don't have food, shelter, income, then crime becomes a necessity to survive. It felt good to be able to help.'

People suffering through unfair life circumstances. There but for the grace of God…

Conrad nodded as he looked at his screen. 'You found accommodation at the home centres for fifty-nine families and ten squatters, employment for thirty-six thieves and shoplifters, you got twenty-four Tier One addicts into rehab… an impressive record for eighteen months on the job.' He swiped at his desk again. 'Moving on to Tier Two… Obviously this is where your education and training are better put to use. Your work developing new generations of medicine to help the traumatised…' He focused his eyes on her, the brown so dark that his irises appeared part of his pupils, and beamed. 'Outstanding.'

She felt uncomfortable at his litany. Wasn't she supposed to have a week's notice before a management performance evaluation?

Grace took another sip of water.

'But your psychometric tests...' He looked down at the screen again.

Grace didn't mind taking the monthly tests. Everyone had done it ever since she could remember – in school, at university, at work – it was part and parcel of the preventative mindset of society, the 'transparent' society as it was often referred to in the press. Since the dawn of the internet, privacy had been gradually eroded until most people accepted that the benefits of the information age far outweighed any damage. Those who disagreed remained technologically unconnected, present-day Luddites.

She was grateful for these tests when it came to her clients – how often had she seen something in the answers which had given her a hint to something the offender couldn't see themselves, couldn't articulate? There were threads she'd pulled that had unravelled and eventually led her into labyrinths of criminogenic cause. Like a dog with a bone, Dan sometimes said.

But she'd taught herself to tailor her own responses. She knew what to say and what to hide, sometimes throwing in a dodgy answer so that her answers didn't seem too perfect, as that in itself would cause alarm bells to ring. She'd learned the hard way, early on, raised eyebrows among teachers that had led to a few sessions with a psychologist. But it was only to be expected, considering her beginnings in life. Thankfully, those records were buried along with her old life, her old self.

'But?' she asked Conrad, turning her wedding ring on her finger.

'I think there's more to come. You have more potential.'

'Why did you really call me up here today, Conrad? To test my potential?'

'No, I told you, Myriam emailed in sick.' He cleared his throat.

'So, you threw me in at the deep end, see if I'd sink or swim?'

'To be honest, Grace, yes. I needed to see if you could hack it in there and I was right about you. You did a good job. Corrina and her family are still in the viewing room with her lawyer and counsellor. I'm giving them a bit of time alone before we reconvene. You can come in with us if you like.'

She shook her head and watched him as he pondered her psychometrics. There was a moment of tension as his eyes flicked up to her and back to his screen again before breaking into a smile.

'Don't look so serious! You've had a great impact on Tier Two. I'm impressed with your professionalism, and obviously your contribution to designing and improving biopsychosocial drugs, especially the self-esteem ones, has been quite extraordinary. You're exactly what we need up here in Tier Three. I want to offer you a promotion.'

Grace felt her mouth fall open.

Conrad sat back looking satisfied. 'I know it was tricky today, but you'll get used to it. Soon it will be second nature.'

Get used to it? She doubted that.

Intelligent, hard-working, maybe overly empathetic – she knew what her tests would say. They certainly didn't suggest this line of work.

She exhaled before she spoke. 'Conrad, I love my job. I'm grateful that I get a chance to help people, people who need it. But this…' She stopped. 'I think you have the wrong person. I'm not cool and calm like Abigail.' How did Abigail shed the trauma she saw every day before returning home?

'Grace, you're exactly what we need. I know it was a baptism by fire, so to speak,' he grimaced, 'but this system is so effective, it's a great opportunity for you. I have a close contact in the Department of Justice who's very interested in what we're doing and wants to support innovation. We're in a very strong position, and with you on the team…'

'I know. I'm not questioning the system.'

'So, what's the problem?' He smiled again but she saw something else in his eyes.

If she gave him a flat-out no, could it affect her present position, or any other future promotions – ones that wouldn't make her feel so out of her depth?

'Look, you know I'm a big advocate of the Tier System, Tiers One and Two, I mean,' she began. 'I wouldn't have chosen a career here if I didn't believe in it. But Tier Three?' Grace shook her head. 'I don't think I'm a good match for the job. I fully believe in Tier One. If a person or a family can't manage, can't provide for themselves, then I think it's only right that we help them out, get them back on their feet. *Any criminal behaviour that is due to citizens not being able to provide for themselves is a fundamental responsibility of the society in which they live...*'

'You're quoting the Department of Justice manifesto to me?' She felt herself blush.

'And Tier Two?' he asked, waving his hand in the air. 'You agree with that because...?'

'It makes me sad, angry, that people offend because they've suffered. Who wouldn't want to help them?'

'Not everyone.' He breathed in and leaned back in his chair, the leather creaking in response. 'But it's certainly where your strengths lie...'

'So then maybe that's where I should stay.'

Conrad drummed his fingers on the glass for a few seconds, but then looked up.

'I need your help, Grace, specifically you, with all that knowledge of psychiatry and biopsychosocial medicine, as well as experience of old school probation officers, someone who is curious about human nature, who wants to tidy up society. Obviously, it's a little more complex than that, but you get the picture.'

'Yes, but there's a marked difference between helping people practically or emotionally and Aversion Therapy, Conrad.'

'It's effective. It's necessary if we want to get on top of offending. It *works*.'

When she didn't reply, Conrad repeated, 'I need your help.' He sighed heavily. 'I'll level with you. Myriam wasn't sick today. She resigned. I don't want this made public.'

Resigned?

'But… why?'

He shrugged. 'Moved on.'

There was clearly more to it that she could tell he wasn't willing to divulge.

'I could really do with you on the team, Grace. I thought you might be getting cabin fever again, might want to move up a Tier… work with Abigail. She's a competent, experienced clinical manager. You'll be her boss. You're ideal for the job.'

Did he think that was a compliment?

'I have zero interest in torturing offenders, Conrad. My contract stipulates quite clearly that I shouldn't do anything that goes against my ethics.'

She wondered if she'd gone too far, but his expression didn't change. He said quietly, 'You can't cure everyone with kindness, Grace. Sometimes you have to be cruel to be kind. It's just the way things are.'

They sat for a few moments in a tense silence.

'The Department of Justice sanctions this treatment, Grace. It's rough, but it works.'

She said nothing.

'Okay, well,' he said after a few moments, his voice light again. 'We'll chat tomorrow, see how you feel.'

She stood, uncertainly and wandered out of the office.

I need your help.

What the hell did that mean?

And how was she going to be able to say no?

33

CHAPTER FOUR

CONTROVERSIAL CLINIC ATTACKED

By Dan Gunnarsson

A Janus Justice clinic in Newcastle has been attacked overnight in the worst such incident since the controversial Aversion Therapy treatment was made public. At least thirty protestors stormed the building, scuffled with staff and caused thousands of pounds' worth of damage.

The number of attacks on Janus have increased in recent weeks, escalating in severity from graffiti and broken windows to arson and bomb threats. Aversion Therapy is under attack from different groups, some who oppose the treatment because, they say, it is brutalising offenders, while others claim it's letting criminals off too lightly.

Conrad Becker, the CEO of the company, downplayed the attack, saying that although some protestors complained the treatment impinged upon human rights, the offenders themselves chose Tier Three Aversion Therapy over being sent to eco-camps for longer sentences.

He concluded by saying this treatment was much cheaper than eco-labour or long-term incarceration and that the safety of his staff was his priority.

–

The light in the office was rapidly dimming, but Sarge liked the dark so the other two said nothing. They didn't even switch on a lamp. They knew better.

Instead, they sat around the desk in the gloom, watching Sarge's heavily lined face, illuminated by his shell, as he stared down at the images of the crime scene. Even from this angle Mal could see the horror.

Finally, he broke the silence and asked cautiously, 'What do you think, boss?'

Bizzy, his dark clothes camouflaged in the shadows, shot him a glance. Mal didn't care. Bizzy looked down on him, but so what? Sarge did too, but Sarge was alpha dog, so he looked down on everyone. *I might be bottom of the pile, but I'm going to be up there one day.*

Shit always floats to the top his dad used to say.

Had Sarge even heard him speak?

Bizzy gave a snide smile.

But then Sarge slowly turned towards Mal. 'This one's a nasty bastard.' There was a glint in his eyes, one that Mal had seen before. He was ready for the hunt. 'It'll test our abilities, lads, but we can do this.' He breathed out slowly through his nose. 'Mal, what do you know?'

'He was treated at Tier Three of Janus Justice on the 16th of last month and was released after assessment four days later.'

'And the treatment was successful?'

Mal nodded. 'According to the manager, it all went to plan.'

'So, there would have been no reason to believe he would offend again.' Sarge nodded thoughtfully. 'We're going to have to work hard to prove it was him. No one will believe that someone who's been through Tier Three has reoffended. It just doesn't happen. The Department of Justice isn't going to like this.'

'Maybe they'll try to sweep it under the carpet,' said Bizzy.

Mal found it hard to hide a smile when Sarge ignored him.

'I've downloaded all the files for you, Sarge,' Mal said, pointing to the shell, 'and I've got the car outside ready to take us to the crime scene.'

Bizzy frowned.

Sarge nodded. 'Have we got DNA?'

'Not yet, but I'll see what I can get from Forensics.'

'Good job, Mal. Right, lads, get your coats. We've got work to do.'

—

Grace had run a bath. She took off every item of clothing she'd worn at the clinic, even her earrings, dropped them on the floor and stepped into the hot water. The smell of synthetic smoke still lingered in her hair so she slipped under the surface until she couldn't stand the temperature any longer. She sat up, water pouring down her face, and took a gulp of air.

Her mind turned to Corrina Saunders, the dry heat engulfing her.

She lay back and rested her arms on the side of the bath.

'Lights down. Emotisonics relaxing, grade four.' The house system wasn't as strong as the one in the clinic but she knew it would soon take the edge off her nerves. The minerals in the pale grey resin that made up the walls, floor, bathtub and sink glittered in the low light.

She thought back, maybe twenty-five years ago, to when Lottie used to drink gin in the bath and tell her and Remy to piss off while they giggled at the door. What would Lottie have made of this bathroom? She'd been a rough diamond, no doubt about it. *A whore with a heart of gold* as someone had referred to her once. Grace hated that cliché. Why did people try to take the sting out of these things? Although there was truth in it. Lottie had been a tom, and a good, loving woman at her core. Not everyone would have taken Grace in.

It had been twenty years too early for Grace to feel the benefits of society's investment in early intervention with families. Now the family was celebrated as the basic building block of society and, as such, the cause and remedy of many of society's problems. What would happen when the effects trickled through and the new generation grew into adulthood? Some would always slip the net. Maybe the nature of their problems would change and so her work would have to adapt. But she'd always been adaptable.

Eventually, she stepped out of the bath and reached for one of the soft, grey, cotton towels. People had always been able to tell she wasn't Lottie's biological child. She was too small and pale with fair hair. But Lottie had never made her feel like anything other than her own. When Lottie had died, nearly fifteen years ago, Grace had felt her loss more keenly, as far as she could remember, than when her own mother had died.

'Hey, love,' Dan shouted, his deep voice echoing through the hallway as he shut the front door. She threw on her robe and made her way downstairs to the kitchen where he was taking two bottles of AltCon out of the fridge. Mood-altering drinks were increasing in popularity and variety after the government ban on alcohol over six years ago. He popped the tops off and handed her one. Even after nine years together, she still sometimes caught her breath when she saw him.

'You look all pink,' he said with a smile.

'Just out of the bath.' She looked at the label before she took a drink. Relax & Reboot. It was deliciously cold. 'So then, Mr NewsFlex, what's new in the world of journalism?' She smiled, leaning back against the counter. He moved close and leaned his body into hers. He was a good thirty centimetres taller and she nuzzled up, feeling his heart beating against her cheek. She breathed him in, an aroma of pine and sandalwood.

'What, apart from my wife working for a company that causes massive protests?' He smiled down at her.

'Hey, that's nothing to do with my Tier.'

'No, but Aversion Therapy certainly keeps me in business. Sometimes I don't know who's for it and who's against it, they're all shouting so much.'

Grace pulled a face and took a drink. She didn't want to think about what she'd seen in the clinic.

'Apart from that, I'm working on something.'

'Ooh, a mystery solved by our favourite roving reporter, Daniel Gunnarsson. Go on, spill the beans.'

'Later. Let's get a food delivery, get cosy on the couch,' he suggested, kissing the top of her head.

'I could do with that,' Grace sighed, as they untangled and carried their drinks into the living room. They relaxed on the long velvet sofa, Grace curling her legs beneath her, Dan stretching his out. He laid his head back and closed his eyes for a moment. She took a sip from her bottle and studied his handsome profile, the strong nose, the fair eyelashes.

'Good day?' He opened his eyes and turned to her when she didn't reply immediately.

'It was a bit of a weird one.'

'Go on.' His aqua blue eyes searched her face.

'I've been offered a promotion.'

'That's good, isn't it?'

'Hmm.' She took another sip from her bottle and felt her muscles begin to relax.

'So, not good?'

She gazed around while trying to put into words how she felt. The living room made her feel calm. It was her safe space with its pale walls, blonde fake wood shelves and coffee table, and a fireplace with clean fuel blocks – retro Scandi chic, to match her husband, she sometimes joked.

Only Grace knew that deep down this design was intended to be as different as possible from Lottie's house. She wanted to distance herself from the dark reds and rich purples of the rugs and drapes, the scarves over the lamps, the chunky, dark-wood upcycled furniture, the golden Arabic vases and pots, the aromas of ylang-ylang and apple tea.

'They want to move me up to Tier Three.'

Dan's jaw tightened. 'How do you feel about that?'

She tried to laugh. 'I thought I was the psychiatrist.'

'Grace, you can't do that to yourself.' He reached over and brushed a lock of damp blonde hair from her forehead. 'One of the reasons I fell in love with you is because you care so much.' He smiled, but it faded quickly. 'But you already bring your work home with you. You're so... open to others, it makes you incredibly vulnerable.'

'What do you mean by that?' Her tone was a little sharp. He hadn't meant it as a criticism, had he? Still, she recognised the truth in it.

How could she accurately portray what she'd seen in the clinic? She didn't want to pollute his mind with that brutal treatment, the once-beautiful melted face...

And she also knew his journalist instincts would kick in and he'd begin to dig for the whole story, and she was too tired to fend off his questions. He was always curious about Janus – who wouldn't be in his position? They'd argued about it in the past, Grace having refused to give him details when he had reported on the Agrarian. He'd had to go through the official channels for that. They'd agreed not to discuss it at home to keep the peace. But if Dan knew what was going on at Tier Three, just how bad it really was, he'd feel duty-bound to tell the public.

The public knew that Aversion Therapy happened. They just didn't know exactly what it was like. Neither had she until today. No wonder Conrad had made her sign a confidentiality agreement. If details got out, who knew how the public might react?

They sat not speaking for a while, the swishing sound of Dan swigging from his bottle puncturing the silence until Grace said, 'I'm not going to take it.'

He sighed heavily. 'Good decision.'

'Conrad wants to see me again tomorrow. Thinks he'll be able to persuade me.'

Dan rolled his eyes. It was no secret how he felt about Conrad.

'Stick to your guns. You're much better off at Tier Two where you're doing something positive and practical. It suits who you are…'

'Dan, I get it.' She held her hand up as if to stop his words reaching her.

'No, listen to me, Grace.' He put his bottle on the table and turned towards her. 'There's something you should know about Tier Three.'

'What about it?' Grace asked, a rumbling anxiety building up inside her.

'It's not safe.'

'Not safe? The treatment is rough, but I'm sure Conrad has all the medical licences.'

'No, I don't mean—'

'If you're talking about the protestors, then the clinic has tough security measures in place.'

'It's not the protestors.' Dan rubbed his face and Grace could hear the faint sound of his stubble against his fingers. 'The story I'm investigating. It's not ready to go yet, but…'

Grace felt a shiver. 'Go on.'

'It looks as though the treatment in Tier Three doesn't always work.'

She shook her head with a half-laugh. 'No, that's not right.'

Dan sat back on the sofa. 'There was a murder last night. It's exactly the same MO as one of the Tier Three offenders who was supposedly cured and discharged about a month ago, a man called Mikey Kilgannon.'

Grace couldn't catch her breath.

'Mikey?' She'd treated him at Tier Two the previous summer. He'd had trouble with addiction which he fed by burgling, but she'd seen an underlying goodness in him, a willingness to help others and a sense of contrition. Although his treatment had seemed successful initially he'd gone on to offend again. It happened every now and then, if they didn't get to the heart of the matter the first time, like with Nikki Paton. Or when they didn't go in hard enough with the addiction treatment at Tier Two.

But there had never been a relapse after Tier Three. They couldn't go in any harder with the treatment.

'What happened?' she asked.

'He was originally convicted of GBH. He was up to his usual tricks, but one of his jobs didn't go as planned. Kilgannon had taken a baseball bat with him, he claimed just to threaten his victim with. The homeowner was an old fella, but he fought back. Kilgannon was high on drugs and got the better of him. The man was hospitalised for weeks and Kilgannon was sentenced to Aversion Therapy and the treatment seemed to be successful.'

'But he did it again?' asked Grace, incredulous.

'Another old man was found dead last night under very similar circumstances, but this time it looked like Kilgannon went too far – the man was found bashed to death with a baseball bat.'

A sudden sadness swept over her. Once someone was a killer, Tier Two was no longer an option.

'Are they certain Mikey did it? It might not have been him.'

Dan shrugged. 'The bat was found at the scene with his DNA on it.'

Was that why Myriam had resigned? Either she'd lost faith in the therapy or else she had somehow messed up Mikey's treatment and Conrad had sacked her. Reoffending wasn't possible after treatment, was it? Surely the post-treatment brain scans would have deemed that he was cured, that he was no longer a threat.

'It's not been made public yet,' Dan said. 'In fact, I think someone in government is deliberately keeping it under wraps. They don't want it to look like their justice system is flawed. My contact in the police says they've been told under pain of death not to say anything.'

'But he told you?'

Dan shrugged. 'I can be pretty persuasive.' He showed his teeth as he smiled.

Grace knew NewsFlex could afford to pay for information. And pay well. The previous year, after a story about a scandal involving the minister in charge of hydroelectricity plants, one of Dan's informers had managed to start a whole new life for herself in Alicante with a huge deposit from NewsFlex in her bank.

'Dan, you're not going to report on this, are you?'

He shrugged, a slight grin on his face. 'Depends what I find out when I get to the bottom of it. I'm not going to break the story yet. I haven't got everything I need. You know me – go big or go home.'

Suddenly, Grace didn't feel like eating. She didn't even want to sit with Dan and let him comfort her after such a difficult day. Her head was filled with questions about Aversion Therapy and images of Noah Begbroke's crime. She put her bottle on the table. If Dan insisted on reporting on this, it was going to cause trouble and she was too tired for a row.

'You look very pale. Are you okay?' Dan asked.

'I'm sorry, I suddenly feel exhausted. It's been an awful day. I just need to get some rest.'

She didn't look back as she left him alone on the sofa and made her way upstairs, wondering exactly what she would see when she closed her eyes to sleep.

CHAPTER FIVE

Agrarian Compound, Essex

Three years ago

In a special NewsFlex report we are here at the Agrarian Compound. This is an extraordinary place where offenders live a life of work and rehabilitation in the Essex countryside, paying off their debt to society and at the same time learning to be healthier, more moral citizens.

After six decades of plastic production, the factory that stood here, NuPoly Plastics, was demolished nine years ago by the Ministry of Reclamation. The Department of Justice fenced off the surrounding land and employed Janus Justice to build the very first Tier Two compound outside of the United States.

Here with me today is Shuggie, originally from Glasgow and one of the first inmates when the compound opened.

Dan: Shuggie, I believe the first residents here actually built the compound. What were conditions like when you first arrived?

Shuggie: Well, we only had tents and buckets initially, but that was okay as many of us here are ex-service men and women, and so it was like being back in Africa but without all the fighting. We were given plenty of materials, such as second-purpose timber and some electricity generators, and told to get on with it. We cleared rubble and dug foundations and built ourselves somewhere to live.

Dan: It's been described as a self-sustaining eco-barracks. Are you proud of what you've built?

Shuggie: It was mainly soldiers that built it, so I suppose we stuck to what we knew and so, yeah, it ended up like barracks. In fact, the whole compound has the look of a military base. It was more a case of accident than design.

Dan: And how do the soldiers feel about being here?

Shuggie: The Cobalt Conflict messed some of us up a bit, and we got into trouble with the police when we came back, drinking and fighting and stuff, so we had to do time somewhere. I've learned since that PTSD can lead to overdoing it on the drink and drugs, you know what I mean, and it was hard for some of us to leave the violence behind. The Agrarian was the perfect place for us to recuperate, both physically and psychologically. We have regular meetings with the psychologists here, and group therapy. And it's nice being out in the country.

Dan: Are there non-military here too?

Shuggie: Oh yeah. The compound is divided into small districts: families, addicts, people with, you know, different psychological problems.

Dan: Do you think that the vast majority of society seems satisfied that offenders are working for their living, not living on taxpayers' money?

Shuggie: I know some people think this is a holiday camp and we lounge around all day, but we do work hard and we work long hours in the cotton fields and mills, sheep-farming, spinning, weaving, and doing land and canal maintenance. All the work we do raises money to sustain the compound and we're nurturing the land and trying to turn our lives around. So yeah, I think people are satisfied.

Thanks, Shuggie. This is Dan Gunnarsson reporting for NewsFlex.

Twice a week Grace made the trip out of London, through the Essex cotton farms, past the wind turbines and solar panels that were dotted around the fields like a spreading techno-forest, to the Agrarian Compound.

Usually the guards transported offenders, but Nikki Paton had got under Grace's skin. She wasn't an escape risk, not with the two sleeping infants in the back of the car. Grace had borrowed the child seats from a colleague, and it had been awkward and time-consuming fitting them.

Nikki had sat silently in the passenger seat most of the way, and to fill the time Grace chatted and pointed out various landmarks. She found herself wittering on about the history of the Tier System, while Nikki stared out of the window wide-eyed or turned back to check on her children.

'We're coming up to the compound now, Nikki, your new home for the next six months or so.' Grace tried to sound as cheerful as possible as she slowed the car and pulled up at the security gate. She turned towards the facial recognition scanner. There was a heavy clunk as the gate began to open slowly.

It was understandable that Nikki would be anxious, but Grace knew she wouldn't recognise herself after a few months out here. Her little family would have safe shelter, hot food, education and fresh air. Nikki would have to work hard, contribute and learn new skills, but how else could they get her back on her feet?

'You okay, Nikki?' Grace asked.

Nikki looked at her, blinked slowly, and then looked back out of the car window, watching the men and women working in the fields in the warm sunshine.

Grace knew the routine and discipline provided many of the soldiers who lived there with the comfort of familiarity. They built campfires at night and took turns to keep watch, but from what threat she couldn't tell. They also policed themselves, so when one of the lads kicked off, they would hold him in loving, disciplined brotherhood until he came back to himself. Shannon's husband had been a soldier, but he hadn't made it back from Africa and she was left to raise their four children alone, another army widow. Grace could sense her affinity with these men and women and she could tell they loved Shannon.

Dan had often reported on the Agrarian. Occasionally, she felt irritated by his privileged attitude. She worried that a return to traditional working skills might also mean a return to traditional class values. Wasn't it always those who were financially worse off who ended up in places like this around the country? Dan's article a few months ago about people offending so that they deliberately got sent to the compound had caused a massive row at home.

However, Grace had some conflicted feelings herself. Certainly, many of the residents of the Agrarian had much better lives here than they could have had in the city. They had jobs and purpose, but was it really any better than the Victorian workhouses that she'd read about as a child? Although the atmosphere was kept as positive as possible, offenders were reminded that they were being punished when they were told what type of work to do and for how long. They were told when to eat and what to eat. They had to attend treatment. There was fresh air and healthy food, but they weren't free to leave. Yes, the residents had a sense of purpose, but they also had a sense of shame. Dan would never be able to relate to that. What would he make of her upbringing if he knew the truth?

She shrugged the feeling off as she rolled up to the compound's office. One of the children had awoken and begun to wail. Nikki, agitated, kept turning back and forth from Grace to the window, to the children, and back again.

Once the car was parked, there was a struggle with seatbelts to get the little ones out and hand them to their mother before a guard led the family into the main office.

'I'll be there in a moment,' Grace shouted after them. She took her bag and phone from the footwell behind her seat and

46

then leaned against the car, gathering herself. The sun shone down on her. The sky stretched blue across fields of white cotton that swayed in the gentle breeze.

Taking a deep breath, she stood and turned to go into the building, but her way was blocked by a group of children – five of them, aged about ten or eleven, arguing over a ball – and her dream from the previous night came back to her.

It hadn't been what she'd expected – Corrina's disfigured face or Begbroke's brutal treatment.

She had dreamt of Remy, a memory of a childhood fight.

What did you say about my mum, you arsehole?'

Remy, scruffy and malnourished, squared up to the biggest boy in the gang who'd followed them down an alley behind the back of the local shops. Grace held back, watching the other two boys behind him, weighing them up. One was about the same size as Remy, although much younger. The other one was chubby, and snarling like an angry Rottweiler. He picked up an empty bottle and fired it over their heads – a warning shot. The bottle broke against a wall behind her. A shard flew up and pierced the skin on her calf. She brushed it out, ignoring the sting and the smudge of blood, and scanned the boys for weapons. It didn't look like they had any, but you could never really be sure.

Remy had taught her that.

'I said your mum's a whore, had most of the fellas in our street.' The big lad looked back at his mates. They smiled but kept their eyes on Remy. 'They had her down this alley. The slag. Took your mum up the back alley.' The three lads laughed, a little too hard.

Grace could always tell when Remy was going to blow. The blood drained from his face and he went very still.

How was he going to manage against three? Remy was usually her protector. What was she supposed to do? She couldn't let him down. Not now.

She braced herself.

Remy suddenly swung his fist at the big lad. The impact must have been hard because for a moment the big lad just stood there, astonished. He reached up to touch his face as if he could remove the stain of Remy having touched him. Then his eyes narrowed.

With a roar he launched himself towards the much smaller Remy, his arms spinning like the sails of a windmill.

Remy took a defensive stance – Grace recognised it from their training. 'Hands up, head down.'

He'd also taught her how to kick. 'Your legs are longer than their arms – don't let them get too close, Grace.'

She watched for a moment, terrified. The big lad was getting some punches in, but he was clumsy, leaning too far forward, off balance. Remy let him get a few hits and then ducked down and belted him in the stomach.

The big lad groaned and leaned over. Although he was winded, he waved his hand and his pals stepped forward: the chubby one looked reluctant, but the little one was smiling, ready for the scrap. As they jumped in, the big lad seemed to get his fight back and the three of them started getting stuck into Remy.

He couldn't beat three of them, but he wasn't looking to her for help. Remy never did. He wanted to protect her.

She took a deep breath and shifted gear. She wasn't going to let him fight alone – he would never let her fight alone. Taking a running jump, she launched herself at the chubby one, feet first. The impact was sudden and violent, jolting the pair of them apart, and both flew backwards. The boy hit a brick wall behind him and went down. As he lay on the ground, Grace struggled to her feet, ran back towards him and dealt him a swift, hard kick to the ribs.

Then she turned to the little one as Remy wrestled the big one. She put her fists up in front of her – southpaw, as Remy had taught her – and bared her teeth as she had seen Remy doing so many times before. The boy's face fell and he ran in the opposite direction.

Remy had taken a couple of hefty knocks but was managing to get the better of the big one, and saw him off with a vicious kick between the legs. When the big lad finally got up from the ground, he shouted something about coming back for them, but Remy replied defiantly: 'You know where to find me!'

Puffing and panting, Grace watched the three boys shuffle off.

Remy hands on hips, bent over double.

'You okay?' she asked, concerned.

But when he stood up straight again, he was laughing, although it obviously hurt as he winced intermittently.

'That could have been worse.' He turned to her and lifted a hand to his face to shield the bright sunlight. 'You did good. You remembered what I taught you.'

A pride spread in her chest. She hadn't let him down after all. She didn't have to be afraid of anything when Remy was with her. And now she'd proved to him that she would always back him up.

Standing by her car in the Essex sunshine, Grace rummaged in her bag, unzipped a hidden pocket and brought out a gaudy plastic keyring photo frame which read 'Funland', each letter a different colour, like a rainbow. There was no key on the ring. It held an image of Grace and Remy, about twelve or thirteen years of age, on a rollercoaster ride, caught by the ride's camera, mid-dip – her cheeks pink with excitement, her blonde hair blown back by the wind, Remy's dark hair cut very short, grey eyes wide – the pair of them laughing, really laughing.

She was brought back to the present, from the street-fighting girl to the grown-up doctor, by her phone ringing and quickly hid the keyring again.

'Dan what's up? Did I forget something?'

She felt strangely guilty that she'd been thinking about Remy.

'You went to bed early and I was fast asleep when you went this morning. Feel like I haven't seen much of you. Just wanted to say hi.'

She'd left him warm and naked under the sheets, lying on his chest, his arms tucked under the pillow as always, those irresistible freckles on his shoulders showing above the duvet. She was a lark, always up and out early to work. He was a night owl, often out late, following some lead or other. Sometimes he came back first thing in the morning after having been out all night. It was a good thing she didn't mind sleeping alone.

The children had obviously solved the issue over the ball and were kicking it away down a nearby field and running after it.

'You at the Agrarian?' He yawned.

She waved her phone around to show him. 'Yep, just pulled up at the office.'

'I'm going to work myself once this coffee kicks in and I've had a shower. I just heard that Mikey Kilgannon's been sent to Tier Four.'

'Oh my God, that's terrible.' Tier Four was presented to the public as being a 'safe space' for those offenders for whom nothing could be done. 'The Incurables' she'd heard them referred to at work. Tier Three might be shrouded in mystery, but Tier Four was a closed book.

She imagined a modern-day psychiatric ward, all strong drugs, pastel colours and therapy groups. Details were vague, however, even for her as an employee. But one thing she did know – when offenders went in, they didn't come back out again.

'He was a vicious, violent thug, Grace. He didn't have any sympathy when he killed that old man with a bat.'

Dan had never even met Mikey.

'Sorry, Dan, I have to go, I've got to sign an offender in.'

'Okay. See you later then. Oh, before you go, can you do something for me?'

She slung her bag over her shoulder and made her way to the office door.

He cleared his throat. 'Can you get me a copy of the files on Kilgannon's treatment?'

She stopped in her tracks and turned away from the main building. She'd expected him to ask her to pick something up from the shop. Not spy on Janus.

'What? Dan, I don't even work in that department,' she whispered, although it was impossible for anyone to overhear.

'Yes, but you treated him at Tier Two. You told me about that, didn't you?'

'That's not the same – I didn't tell you anything that would bring the company into disrepute.'

'Come on, surely you can get some info from Tier Three that might, you know, shed some light on why the treatment didn't work.'

'You want me to risk my job so you can get a scoop for NewsFlex? Are you bloody serious?'

'This is a career-making story, Grace!'

'Apart from being highly unprofessional, it will be so obvious where the information came from. I'd be sacked if I shared that kind of information. In fact, I'd probably be prosecuted. What the hell, Dan?'

'I'm just doing my job, okay?'

'Yes, and I'm just doing mine!'

She cut the call and threw her phone into her bag.

How could he ask that of her? Conrad would know exactly who the leak came from and she was already in his bad books because she'd refused his offer yesterday.

Offer or ultimatum? She was pretty sure people didn't say no to Conrad Becker, CEO of Janus Justice.

Poor Mikey. According to the evidence, he was a killer.

But Tier Four?

It was a life sentence.

CHAPTER SIX

Nikki was sitting on one of the wooden benches in the entrance hall, a writhing, whining infant on her lap and a sullen-faced toddler leaning against her knees, a few cotton sacks containing the family's meagre belongings slumped at her feet.

Shannon emerged from the office in a flowing tie-dyed dress that covered her full figure, her long brown wavy hair tied back.

'Nikki Paton?' Her loud, cheerful voice startled the toddler and made the baby whine even louder.

Alarmed, Nikki turned towards Grace, who reassured her with a nod and a smile.

This was where Grace belonged, not at Tier Three with its dubious methods and complex issues. Here the aim was to meet needs, rehabilitate and reintegrate, and seeing her clients make progress gave her a real sense of satisfaction. Spending time with Shannon also lifted her spirits. She was not just a colleague, but Grace's best friend, who often reminded her of Lottie. Shannon had run the Agrarian for over seven years now and the two women had grown ever closer, not only in their bi-weekly working days, but often spending their free time together too.

'Y'alright, doll?' Shannon said to Grace, having kept her soft Scottish accent despite years in the south of England.

'Nikki, this is Shannon, who runs the compound,' Grace said, her voice low and soothing. 'She'll do your psychometrics like we talked about in the car and get you and the kids settled in. She's a good friend of mine and I trust her.' She looked down at the children. 'Shannon, this is Felix' – the toddler frowned – 'and this is Angel.'

'Aww, look at this gorgeous pair. Shall I give you a hand there, Nikki?' Shannon asked, competent hands lifting the baby from Nikki's grasp, placing her on her ample bosom and patting her back rhythmically. Angel stopped crying and stared up at Shannon, mesmerised. Grace saw Nikki relax. Felix clambered up onto his mother's lap, grabbed her face with both hands and turned it towards him.

'Look at those gorgeous ruddy cheeks,' Shannon said to Angel. 'Are you teething, honey? I have four of my own,' she told Nikki, who blinked up at her as Felix began twirling her hair in his fingers and sucking his thumb. 'They have lessons in the compound school and run wild with the other kids here the rest of the time. Mine're bigger than yours, mind you, but the mums here have a cooperative for the childcare, Compound Kids Club they call it. They take turns when they're not working to look after the littl'uns. There's a good community here. Don't worry, love, you'll soon settle in.'

Nikki looked reassured, as though there was some secret mother code passing between them that Grace was immune to.

'You live here?' she asked.

'Yeah, it's not so bad!' Shannon gave one of her winning smiles. 'Right, let me go and fetch my shell and we'll get you booked in. I've got a lovely cabin you can share with a young mum who has a couple of kids a similar age to yours. It'll be chaos but it'll be fun, won't it, Felix?'

The toddler looked up at hearing his name.

Grace followed Shannon, who held the now sleepy Angel with one arm, as she navigated her way through the security door and into the office. Once in the office, she grabbed Grace into a hug with her free hand.

It felt odd to be so close to a baby.

'She doesn't bite,' Shannon laughed, noticing Grace's expression. 'She hasn't got any teeth. Well, not yet.'

'Dan, he…' She said no more.

'He's on at you about babies again?'

Grace nodded.

'You're going to have to tell him at some point. You can't just lead him on, doll.' Shannon rubbed her back sympathetically.

'I know,' she sighed.

Shannon knew Grace didn't want a baby, but she didn't know the full truth. How could Grace explain her irrational fear that she would leave a child as her mother had left her?

She couldn't, not without unravelling the history she'd spent nearly her whole life concealing. As a psychiatrist she knew that feelings of abandonment as a child could lead to problems. She also knew suppressing feelings was not healthy in the long term. But still, what could she do? And there was more to it as well. But she couldn't face up to that, not now.

Grace let herself relax into her friend's hug.

'You okay after yesterday?' Shannon asked.

After seeing what Noah Begbroke had gone through in the clinic, Grace had been desperate to speak to someone about what she'd seen. When she'd left Dan downstairs the previous night, sleep had evaded her, so she'd called Shannon. Who better to help get things off her chest than her best friend, someone who already worked in the Tier System? Someone who she trusted would keep it to herself. Grace hadn't told her everything. She hadn't wanted to distress her friend. Was a trouble shared a trouble halved?

'I'm okay,' Grace sighed. 'You'll take extra good care of Nikki, won't you? She's, you know… fragile.'

'I know,' Shannon said with a nod, pulling back. 'Right, I'll get the paperwork done and then we'll do the rounds.' She picked up her shell and went back out into the entrance hall with her little passenger.

Grace sat at the desk, the screen in front of her displaying the Janus bulletin. There would only be limited information here, but it might give her some idea of what was going on.

Her fingers trembled as she typed in the name Remy James Wilson. She didn't use the voice search, not only because she didn't want Shannon to hear but because she couldn't bear to say his name out loud, as though somehow it might conjure him up and he'd be standing in front of her.

His image appeared on the screen. He'd filled out, his almost black hair hanging scruffily down to his muscular shoulders and around his strong jawline, his mouth turned down.

She could see the boy in the man's face and was immediately transported back to the past.

'Come on, Remy.' Her knuckles were white as she gripped her kit bag over her shoulder. 'Let's go, the pair of us. There's nothing here for us now.'

Lottie was gone. He had to accept that.

'Just throw some stuff in a bag. Come with me!'

'I don't want to leave London.' For a moment, he sounded like a child, not the young man who stood tall in front of her. 'I'm a London boy through and through. The lads have promised me some work over the next few months. Can't you stay here, instead of going to Newcastle or wherever it is, Gracie? Go to college somewhere closer? I mean, what's so good about university anyway?'

He tried to smile but his grey eyes were sorrowful, as if he already knew he wasn't going to be able to persuade her. In them she saw all the loyalty, support and comfort that she'd known nearly her whole life. What was going to happen when she cut her moorings and drifted?

For a moment she wobbled.

No. She had to be strong. She had to do this. She geared herself up, knowing once the words were out she wouldn't be able to take them back. Once an egg was cracked, Lottie used to say.

'The last thing I want to do, Remy, is to hurt you,' she began, the words burning her lips because she knew that was exactly what she was doing.

His shoulders fell and her heart cramped within her chest.

They rarely had much money, Remy was in trouble with some dodgy people, the city was getting her down. She was tired of the struggle.

'I've worked so hard to get out of the shit, Remy. I have to make a life for myself. I have to do this for me.'

'Without me?' he said, as if the words didn't make sense, as if there could be no 'me' without the 'us'. 'Gracie, please…'

'If you're not going to come with me, then you have to let me go. I don't want to resent you. After all the hard work I put in… two jobs… passing my exams even after losing Lottie…' She saw his face and stopped, dropped her voice to a whisper. 'A place on a degree course! Whoever would've thought that could happen to a person like me? I've got the chance of a new life. Why can't you just be happy for me?'

She'd told him she'd come down to visit him during the holidays, but it was always all or nothing with Remy and she didn't do ultimatums.

So she'd made the hardest decision and let go.

Grace scanned the bulletin. A street fight with a notorious drug dealer had ended in death. That was all the detail she could access. Her clearance stopped at Tier Two files. From what she knew of Remy in the past, he never carried a weapon. Maybe the dealer had died when he banged his head on the pavement. She convinced herself that whatever had happened it had been manslaughter. That meant Remy would go to Tier Three.

It was bad enough seeing Noah Begbroke go through that, regardless of what he'd done, but how would it feel if it was someone she loved?

Love – the idea struck her hard. He was her brother, not in blood, but in bond. What a fool to get himself into trouble like this over a street fight. It must have been an argument that had surged out of control. Had Remy changed so much in the intervening years that he would kill someone? Yes, it was manslaughter, not murder, but still. She knew he wasn't adverse to making money in dodgy ways, or fighting, as she'd seen him do both in the past, but she also knew that Remy hated drugs after seeing what it had done to their mothers.

Grace shut the screen down as soon as Shannon came back into the office.

'Right, Shan, let's get to it.'

–

Shannon and Grace drove around the compound in Shannon's jeep, having settled Nikki and the children into their cabin with a new array of second-hand clothes, bedding and necessities. Grace could tell that Josie, the other mum in cabin 22, had already taken Nikki under her wing, and she began to feel more confident about Nikki's prospects at the compound. They drove through a family area, washing lines full of clean cotton clothes, large and small, drying in the sun, donated toys left strewn around. The older children were in lessons at this time of day but some of the babies and toddlers were sitting on blankets with their mothers.

Shannon slowed the jeep every now and then to wait for the security gates to open. The fences were heavy-duty posts made from recycled plastic, a constant reminder of incarceration. For many residents, the fences gave them security. For others, the notion of freedom was enough to motivate them to get their lives together and get out.

As they drove, Grace checked her shell for brain scans and bio-readings of her scheduled clients. She quizzed Shannon on the progress of offenders and they discussed the competency of the various therapists who worked throughout the day in shifts from seven in the morning until ten o'clock at night.

Progress could be slow at the compound, as no doubt it was at the other, newer compounds around the country. Getting people back on their feet, helping them to build happier, more successful lives, and healing them, chemically and emotionally, took time. Tier Three offered quick, effective results, but this was where Grace's heart lay.

As they drove back through the soldiers' compound, Conrad's offer came into her mind. It didn't surprise her that he would value a swift conveyor belt of profitable cures over the expense and long-term graft of building morally healthy citizens.

'Penny for them, doll?'

Where should she start? Should she tell Shannon that Dan was asking her to spy on Tier Three to find out what had gone wrong? Or say that her childhood friend was in serious trouble and she felt guilty she hadn't been around to keep him on the straight and narrow? She settled for something less difficult.

'Conrad wants me to move up a Tier.'

Shannon briefly released the pressure on the accelerator and the car juddered. 'Really?'

'He asked me yesterday.'

'What did you say?' She kept her eyes on the road.

'I said no.'

Shannon blew out a lungful of air. 'Great, I'd hardly ever see you any more! What would I do without my pal? What did Dan say?'

'He said it would upset me too much.'

'He might have a point.' Shannon pulled up with a jerk and grabbed her shell from the side pocket of the car door. 'I've got to drop something off for one of the therapists. Won't be a minute.'

Grace watched as Shannon stopped to talk to a group of soldiers who were working on physio exercises. Her thoughts turned to Nikki's children. What would her and Remy's life have been like if they'd been in a place like this? She imagined her mum sitting on the grass with the other mothers.

Taking her shell from her bag, she tried to search for more information on Remy, but there wasn't much more she could access other than the bulletin and his photograph.

'I read the case files on him,' Shannon said, suddenly reappearing at the side of the jeep.

'You gave me a fright! Didn't expect you back so soon.'

'Just missed her, the therapist. I'll catch up with her later.' She searched Grace's face. 'Do you know him?'

'Is he getting treated down here, do you know?' Grace asked, deliberately avoiding the question. She imagined him in the London clinic, walking down the corridor towards her, flanked by guards. A fear gripped her that if she saw him in real life, old Grace, *Gracie*, would suddenly come tearing through the fabric of the carefully constructed life she'd built around herself these last fifteen years.

'He was treated up in Manchester,' Shannon said, curiosity evident in her voice.

Treated? Grace relaxed a little. At least his treatment was over and done with. 'That was quick. He only killed the guy three days ago. When did they arrest him?'

'What are you talking about?' Shannon asked. 'They treated him at Tier Three last year.'

'Last year?' Grace couldn't make sense of what she was hearing.

'Yes, up in Manchester. I told you. They sent me the files to look over beforehand because he was ex-forces. He'd had a fight, the other guy pulled a knife and Wilson took it from him and slashed him. Serious but not fatal. In my opinion he had conflict-trauma. I didn't actually meet him,' Shannon added, taking a bottle of water from the drinks holder and slugging from it.

Grace flicked at her shell to look more closely at the details, her heart thumping furiously. 'No, look, he was arrested just a few days ago. Are you sure it was the same offender?'

Shannon looked closer, shielding her eyes against the bright sunlight. 'Yes, Remy Wilson. That's him.' She looked at the date again. 'Wait a minute, you're saying that he offended again, after Tier Three treatment?' Her face was a picture of confusion. 'No, that's not possible.' She shook her head.

Grace thought back to her conversation with Dan the previous night. 'If this gets out to the press…'

'It won't,' Shannon reassured her. 'There's no way Conrad would let it. Anyway, from what I've heard on the grapevine, Conrad's pretty pally with some bigwig in the DoJ. I'm sure he'll put the brakes on a leak.'

Dan's words came to mind. *I can be pretty persuasive.*

'But I don't understand how this could have happened after Aversion Therapy,' Grace said.

'They'll probably scan him for psychopathy. I mean if Aversion Therapy hasn't worked, then he must be pretty messed up. There must be something else wrong with him.'

Grace dug into her memories. Remy wasn't a psychopath. Was he?

Shannon took Grace's shell from her limp hands and typed something. 'Ah, they can't scan him. He's on the run. Good job this isn't in the press. Imagine the public knowing Tier Three wasn't effective. Imagine the hysteria – all those criminals who've been released back into the wild...'

'If they catch him,' Grace began, 'they'll send him to...' Her mouth suddenly dried up, as though her mind wouldn't let her go there.

Shannon said the words she couldn't: 'Tier Four.'

Grace leaned over the side of the jeep and vomited onto the lush, green grass.

CHAPTER SEVEN

Mal and Bizzy stood back and observed as Sarge did his thing. This was his method – absorbing the atmosphere of a crime scene, as though he was psychically connecting with the victim and the criminal.

He was crouched on his haunches, looking across the floor of a living room that was bigger than Mal's whole flat. The carpet, a sign of wealth in itself these days, had already been removed for forensic investigation. The family would have to move out. Who would want to watch a screen in the same room where their husband or father had bled out?

So much blood. Mal stared into the Rorschach stain that had soaked through onto the wood below – images of violence, pain and fear emerging from the red-brown smudges – and felt a quivering in his knees. Extreme cleaners would be sent in, judging by the mess, and a joiner to restore the floorboards. Hell, they'd have to replace most of the floor.

What had passed through the mind of the victim as he lay dying, feeling his life force seeping out, hot and wet, from between his legs? The thought worried and fascinated Mal at the same time.

'Bizzy, what have we got?' asked Sarge, standing up to full height and tucking his shirt into his trousers. Mal knew Biz liked to think of himself as the tech genius and the critical thinker of the operation. He thought more like a copper than Mal did.

But Mal himself wasn't without skills. He was the evidence man, after all, essential to their team mission. He knew more about forensics, DNA and trace evidence than the other two put together, even though neither of them would admit it. All that reading and studying had been worth it, however much of a struggle it had been at the time.

And Sarge – he was their leader, their mentor and so much more. Sarge had shown Mal how to be part of a team, how to be driven to the point of obsession, how to get the sort of results that were essential for success.

Sarge had taught him how to *see*.

'Perps came in through the back door,' Bizzy began. 'The alarm system was disabled. No one home but the victim. In my opinion, the perps will have known this. In previous attacks they'd been stalking their victims for weeks. Not much sign of a struggle.'

Mal hated the word 'perps'.

'Victimology?' asked Sarge.

'He made a lot of money, and I mean a *lot* of money on the Chinese stock exchange and exporting.' Bizzy continued. 'He'd been accused of a number of sexual assaults and rapes. According to my sources, money – and we're talking big amounts – made most of the accusations go away.'

'Yes, but not all,' Mal chipped in.

'He also had influential friends,' added Bizzy, glaring at Mal before turning back to Sarge. 'On the force, and in government.'

'Never convicted,' Sarge said with a sigh.

Bizzy went on. 'The one case that got to court, the evidence was questionable. He claimed consensual, his victim claimed he drugged her, possibly with the same type of drug that was used on him.'

'Toxicology?' Sarge directed this towards Mal but kept his eyes on the bloodstains, as if the victim were still there.

'Neuromuscular blocking agent in the blood,' Mal said. 'It's a clinical paralytic. Would have kept him corpse-still while they castrated him.'

Bizzy winced.

Mal glanced at the bloodstain again, astounded by how a drug that had been designed to prevent damage caused by a scalpel if a patient moved during surgery could have such an insidious use outside of the operating theatre.

'Exsanguination would have taken a little time,' he added. *Exsanguination.* He loved words that made him sound clever. He wrote them down when he studied his books and said them over and over until they became familiar in his mouth. 'Traces of the drug were found in his blood,' Mal went on, 'but only because the pathologist was looking for it, as it had been found in one of the other cases and he considered it odd the victim wasn't restrained but didn't have any defence wounds. It's not the easiest drug to detect – it passes out of the blood so quickly.'

'Which is why there was no evidence that his rape victim had been drugged,' Bizzy interrupted. 'They threw her case out of court.'

He can't stand being out of the limelight for a moment.

Sarge nodded. 'They let him bleed out. Looks as though they didn't trust the Tier System to deliver justice, so they took it into their own hands.'

'Literally,' said Bizzy, with a smirk. Sarge shot him a glance and he frowned.

Mal thought Bizzy was crude and vulgar. He suspected Sarge did too. He liked it when he and Sarge were of the same mind.

'Revenge,' Sarge said with a sigh. 'The greatest reward of all.'

Mal gazed at Sarge in admiration until he looked directly back at him and Mal cast his eyes down. You didn't stare at the alpha.

'Where was the blocking agent sourced?'

'I'll find out,' answered Mal, eyes still averted. It was never *No, Sarge.* It was either *Yes Sarge, Right away, Sarge,* or *I'll find out, Sarge.* Mal looked forward to the day when his own minions would be too afraid to say no to him. It would happen one day.

'What else?' Sarge demanded.

'This is the seventh attack of this nature in as many months,' said Bizzy, taking centre stage again, 'by a very particular set of vigilantes. A number of victims of sexual offences, male and female, have banded together to mete out punishment to their attackers. Call themselves Payback. They take turns to torture and kill the rapists, and the original victim stands by and watches their version of justice being done – the other members of the group do the actual killing. Therefore, it was initially difficult to make the links between the person who died and the killers. This will be the second attack in a week.'

Mal knew from personal experience that the Tier System could never be enough to get revenge for someone you loved.

'Two reoffences in a week?' Sarge said. He unfolded his arms and stretched, yawning loudly before saying, 'Might look like things are getting out of hand.'

Disturbing thoughts had accompanied Grace all the way home from the compound. She'd completed her work in a daze, trying hard to focus on prescribing medication and organising therapy sessions. But her mind had constantly strayed to Remy. Would he have stayed on the straight and narrow if she'd remained with him in London instead of leaving for university? Or would they have gone their separate ways after Lottie died anyway? Maybe it was true that people, however close they were, split when they lost someone. The pain in the other's eyes was a constant reminder of what you yourself had lost. Their little family – as dysfunctional as it might have seemed to the outside – the prostitute mother, the rebel son, the adopted orphan daughter – had been close and loving. It had meant Grace's survival after her mother's death. Love, wherever it came from, kept you rebuilding yourself.

As she closed the front door, she heard Dan singing to himself as he pottered in the kitchen cooking the dinner. The aroma of home cooking and his low-pitched humming soothed the annoyance she'd felt with him that morning.

She leaned against the kitchen doorframe. 'Hi.'

He swivelled around, surprised. 'Oh hi,' he smiled sheepishly. 'I'm sorry about putting you on the spot before.'

Yes, she'd been annoyed with him. But things had changed for Grace since she found out about Remy.

She also knew that Dan wasn't going to give up so easily.

'I get it. You want to solve the puzzle,' she reassured him.

But now she had a puzzle of her own. Information went both ways, didn't it? If Remy had been to Tier Three and the treatment hadn't worked, then maybe Dan could find out something that could explain why. Could they even figure it out together? She smiled briefly. But then Remy's face came to her mind.

She owed him so much. She remembered being seven years old and Lottie had gone missing for a week. Remy had shoplifted all her favourite foods to cheer her up. They had feasted on small marzipan cakes, spicy crisps and brightly coloured fruit juice. When she was fourteen, Remy had taken a beating from Lottie's pimp, protecting Grace from having to join his other women on the street. She didn't want to think about that. And then there had been all the times in between, the fun, the fights, the everydayness of their belonging.

There was no way she could let him go to Tier Four.

'Are you feeling okay? You look really washed out.' His eyes travelled down to her stomach. 'Hey, you haven't got something to tell me, have you?' He looked back up at her questioningly, the hope in his voice triggering her guilt.

'It's something else,' she told him, avoiding his gaze so she didn't have to see his disappointment. She sat down at the kitchen table, and he sat opposite and waited. He laid both hands out in front of him, palms down, his face open, interested.

Grace's mind bubbled like the water in the pan on the hob as she tried to find the words.

'This story about Tier Three not working,' she began. 'Mikey Kilgannon...'

Dan sat up a little straighter.

'Do you think it's true?' she asked. 'I mean, do you think Tier Three is faulty? It's just that there's never been a case of repeat offending after Aversion Therapy.'

Dan's brow creased for a moment. 'Kilgannon killed that old man, Grace. The facts speak for themselves, but the more I'm looking into this, the more I'm starting to see that there's something bigger going on. I've heard from one of my sources that the police suspect an ex-Tier Three offender carried out that attack on the post office in Golders Green a couple of months ago, but it was hushed up.'

She chewed her lip and then said, 'Dan, you can't break this story. If this gets out, if the public find out...'

His expression hardened for a moment before he smiled and said, 'You married a journalist, you know.'

'But what will happen to the clinic if this hits the headlines? There's already a lot of hostility towards the Tier System. You've seen the protestors outside Janus.'

He reached over and patted her hand briefly. 'Look, there might be nothing in it. It might not come to anything. I need more time to investigate, so there's no need to worry about the clinic just yet.'

She didn't feel particularly reassured. 'If Conrad thought anything was wrong with his precious Tier System, then he'd shut that story down, whatever it took.'

'And I bet the DoJ don't want this getting out.'

Grace nodded while scratching at a mark on the white tabletop with a fingernail. Would Dan know anything about Remy from one of his sources? She didn't want to draw his attention to her old friend, but it might be the only way to find out what was going on.

She took a deep breath. 'I saw something in work today,' she said. 'A report about an offender who's on the run. Shannon says he's already been through Tier Three.' She felt her pulse quicken.

'What's his name?'

'Remy Wilson.'

'Remy Wilson,' Dan repeated.

Grace's heart clenched as she heard her husband saying his name, her two worlds colliding – her hidden, painful past, and her settled, successful present.

'I haven't heard anything,' he said.

Disappointment and relief rose in her.

'Anyway, if there's a cover-up at Janus, they won't be able to keep it quiet forever,' he said flatly. He stood up and began stirring the food on the hob. 'And I'm going to make sure that NewsFlex is the first to get the full story.'

Grace felt annoyance at his determination to get a story – even if it meant serious consequences. Yes, it was a great scoop, but what would the backlash be? Dan being silenced by whoever was trying to bury the information? What about her own safety? The clinics would be at greater risk from attacks by the protestors. If she accepted Conrad's offer, then she'd be at risk too.

But on the other hand, if she took the job she'd gain access to information that might get to the heart of the problem and, more importantly, help Remy.

'I don't think I can get hold of Mikey Kilgannon's files,' she said, 'but I think I might know how to get you some information.' *Oh God, am I really going to do this?* 'What if I take Conrad up on his offer of a promotion?' The very idea of it made her insides turn to water.

But it was the only way.

Dan sat back down at the table. She couldn't decipher his reaction.

'But that goes against everything you've ever said about the Tier System,' he said finally.

'I know. But if it meant we found out the truth, it would be worth it, wouldn't it?'

'And what about us?'

'What do you mean? We'd be working together, a team.' She patted his hand uncertainly. 'Cracking the story together.' She tried to smile.

'I mean what about having children.'

She drew her hand back. 'What about it?'

'Grace, Tier Three is very stressful. You said so yourself yesterday. You get upset when one of your Tier Two lot comes back. Tier Three will be much worse. We've been trying for so long. The doctor has said there's no reason we shouldn't get pregnant. Maybe stress is the problem.' His eyes travelled down to her stomach again.

Grace felt a wave of guilt at his ignorance. But then a resentment grew. Why did it always have to come back down to this? Maybe if Dan only knew what she'd been through then he might be more understanding.

That was her fault for not telling him. But how could she?

There were more pressing issues right now. She had to get into Tier Three and see what was going wrong. Maybe Conrad would let her try to fix Remy when the police caught him, instead of sending him up to Tier Four. It was a long shot.

Could she do the job, though? She'd have to toughen up and go against her principles. All those years of trying to help, trying to meet people's needs and assist with their rehabilitation, and now she was going to throw it all away to brutalise offenders with Aversion Therapy.

But if it meant she could solve the puzzle and save Remy it would be worth it.

Wouldn't it?

'Dan, listen to me. I'll take the job just until I can find out what the problem is. We'll be able to figure this out together. You'll get your story and I might even be able to fix whatever's wrong.'

Dan looked uncertain. 'You'll have to get out of Tier Three as soon as the story breaks. It really won't be safe for you there once it's all out in the public domain.' He thought for a moment and then said, 'What if Conrad realises that you're the informant for NewsFlex?'

She'd already considered this. It would be the end of her career in the Tier System altogether. No more helping those who really needed her at Tiers One and Two.

'Then I'll stay home and make Baby Gunnarsson my priority.'

She gritted her teeth. Dan didn't deserve being lied to.

'You'd do that?' The excitement in his eyes made her feel like a traitor.

'Of course,' her lips said.

But her heart said: *No, I'm doing it for Remy.*

CHAPTER EIGHT

Oliver McIntyre sometimes wondered what his victims made of it all. They probably thought it was about his inadequacies, his rage or even just sex. People often assumed these things were about sex, but they weren't, as any good psychologist would tell you.

And he'd seen some good psychologists.

But that was back in the day, when his mother had worried about him and his father had been in denial. They'd given up after a while. Just let him *be himself.* It had been good timing for him, because the particular psychologist he had at the time, Rosemary with her glass beads and her short hair, she'd begun to see him. Really *see* him. He might have only been fourteen, but he knew that the recognition in her eyes meant the game was up. He'd behaved impeccably for the next nine months, which seemed to reassure his parents. Then the psychologists had all gone by the by.

Rosemary had been first on his list, of course, that arrogant bitch, thinking she could suss him out. How dare she challenge him! He smiled as he remembered the sound of the glass beads scattering on the concrete floor of the car park like rain.

There had been a time that he'd tried to fight his urges. Like a reformed smoker, he could go for weeks, months even, without any thought of it, besides the occasional overwhelming cloud of guilt (or whatever emotion it was – he wasn't sure), which had surprised him (what would a psychologist make of that?) Like the poor cow up on the common that time, in the dark, on the scorched earth. She'd been the only one ever to have seen his face because he'd lost his mask in the tussle. He'd been furious with himself, and so overwhelmed by self-preservation that he'd almost strangled her then and there. But the woman had reminded him of his teacher in Year Four, Miss Carlin, one of the few women he'd ever met who'd earned his admiration.

And he'd let her go.

Miss Carlin. Why couldn't he find someone like her to spend his time with, instead of having to dredge the city herd to see if he could find something even close to his expectations?

Miss Carlin.

He wondered how he'd feel about her if he met her now.

What would she make of him?

As he crept along the rain-washed streets, he felt a strange sensation in his chest just thinking of her. He wasn't sure what it was, but it was beginning to soften the edges of his anger. He shook his head. He needed to focus.

Everything was planned precisely. That was his nature, his survival technique. He spent more time and effort plotting and planning than he spent on the actual attack. He wasn't the sort of person to mess up. The lads on his fire crew all looked up to him. He was the *boss*.

NewsFlex referred to him as the Embers Rapist.

He switched his attention back to the woman who was walking along the street and followed her for another few metres, at a distance. He knew the location he was aiming for and his predator's brain, which always took over in times like this, was rapidly figuring out how to get her there if she diverged from the route he'd anticipated.

It gave him a secret pleasure during his working hours to find special places that he knew he could use later to his advantage, places that no one else seemed to notice, where he wouldn't be disturbed in his nocturnal activities, where the light and the space and the situation made a perfect distillery for his ego. Business premises were best, or something out in the industrial parts of the city where there would be less chance of witnesses. Once or twice he'd even considered torching somewhere himself so he could use it later. Being the boss, he was the one who kept the secure keys for the out-of-bounds burnt buildings, so only he had access until the insurance firms got involved. Before that, he would come and go as he pleased, fantasising about his next venture. On the actual night of the attack he would make it look as though there'd been a break-in, but only after the deed had been done.

Sometimes he'd have to wait until the place dried out after the hoses. He'd use his exercise time to run past and check everything was still secure. Often merely the flapping of the Fire Brigade's 'Danger Keep Out' signs or the smell of charred wood made him hard.

Oliver continued to follow his prey as she took the shadowy shortcut – a lazy, foolish risk. He watched as she moved down the empty alley, the tall buildings either side cutting out almost all the light from the streets beyond. He moved quickly and quietly, gaining on her, only four metres away now.

Thinking he heard a sound behind him, he halted and listened, his instincts on overdrive – a superhero with enhanced senses. He turned round to see only stretches of uneven brick wall and shadowy doorways. Reassured, he turned back so he didn't lose sight of his quarry.

She looked in her early thirties, plain enough, her hair dark and long, always good for a bit of leverage. She had wide hips that filled him with a kind of disgust yet served to excite him further. Her scent, cheap and flowery, caught in the wind and reached him, charging his blood with adrenaline.

Two metres away now.

Everything was on track. She was moving in the right direction, he was managing to keep his beast at bay, logic in the driving seat until he could get her right where he wanted her. Then he would unleash, show her what being the boss really meant.

He took a surgical paralysis patch from his pocket and peeled off its adhesive strip, careful of the tiny shards that contained the drug – like the fine hairs of a stinging nettle – ready to pierce her skin and immobilise her in moments. It had been easy to get anything he wanted from some of the nurses he screwed. They were always trying to impress him, even if it meant the possibility of getting into trouble. He demanded people take risks for him.

He rolled his shoulders as he always did just before he struck.

He heard the muffled ringing of a phone. The woman slowed down and began rummaging in her bag. Oliver saw his chance. He had to get to her before she answered. With one long stride he was only a metre away. He leaned forward and went to reach out, the patch ready in his fingers, but his arm wouldn't do what he willed it to, and when he looked down, he saw fingers wrapped around his wrists, and next he felt the strong grip of a hand across his face. He was shoved hard into the doorway of the very building he'd chosen for his attack. His arm was forcibly bent and the patch redirected onto his own skin. There were bee-like stings at his throat and he felt his legs begin to give way beneath him.

There was a moment of hush as three people huddled around him, propping up his increasingly limp body, no doubt so that he didn't fall and get the woman's attention. She began to talk on her phone, her voice becoming quieter as she moved away down the street. The people around him started moving quickly, searching his pockets, taking the keys, opening the door, pushing him into the darkness of the warehouse.

There was a blinding light behind his eyes as something hit Oliver hard in the face. He slid down a wall until he sat slumped on the floor, his back against the damp bricks, his legs splayed out in front of him, his arms useless at his sides, but he was still conscious. A man and a woman stepped forward out of the shadows, athletic bodies clad in black, serious faces. The woman was taller than the man, her shoulder-length hair bright crimson.

The woman outside walked away, never knowing what had nearly befallen her, never experiencing his power. Oliver felt a mixture of outrage that his mission had been interrupted, and fury with his now useless body.

Who the fuck are you?

His mouth would not form the words he intended to speak.

What do you want?

The man got down on his haunches, elbows on his knees. 'We know all about you, Oliver McIntyre.'

How the hell do you know my name?

As if she could read his mind, the woman said, 'We've been watching you.'

His outrage rocketed, obliterating the humiliation of having been stalked without his knowledge.

'Do you know what we do to people like you, Oliver?' the man continued. 'Sex offenders and rapists?'

Oliver tried to tell him he had the wrong man, but his mouth felt as though it was stuffed with cotton wool. The acrid smell of burnt wood and melted plastic filled his nose.

The man stood up and moved out of the way.

Another woman stepped forward out of the shadows. She was small with mousy hair and spectacles. She moved with uncertainty, her hands visibly shaking. It was the woman from the common, the woman who'd reminded him of a long-ago beloved teacher!

Who the hell did she think she was, getting these two morons to kidnap him?

I should have strangled you on the common, you bitch!

He tried to get a grip on his rage. Survival was more important than revenge right now. What were they going to do to him? Maybe leave him naked and humiliated, wandering in the darkness, just as he'd done with the woman in front of him.

They underestimated him if they thought that would stop him.

It was the turn of the red-headed woman to crouch down in front of him now. 'We know all about you, Oliver. We know

74

things the police don't know.' She turned back to the other woman. 'Did you see how his eyes lit up when I mentioned the police?' His victim stood, biting her nails. The redhead turned back to him. 'But we found you before they did.' She gave him a broad grin. 'We got to you first.'

Vigilantes. Oliver's brain rapidly began calculating his chances of getting out of there.

The crimson-haired woman leaned closer. He could feel her hot breath on his face. 'You don't deserve the police and what they'll do to you, Oliver.'

Anger roiled in his guts. Uppity bitch. He'd show her.

'They'd send you to the Tier System, put you into one of their clean, pretty little clinics,' she whispered. 'They'd inject you with their drugs and show you their videos to make you think it was you who'd been raped.' His victim cringed at the word.

How the hell had these people found him? He was too clever to have been caught, too invisible, a respectable Clark Kent during the day. He was a firefighter, a fucking hero!

'But that would be over and done with in a day, your little trip to the clinic.' The crimson-haired woman moved nearer and reached out her hands to his belt buckle. He saw her wedding ring glinting in the semi-darkness as her hands swiftly undid his trousers and with some effort pulled them down to his ankles.

He felt weakened, exposed. How dare she humiliate him like this! It was his role to be in the driving seat.

I'm going to kill you when I get out of this.

'Then you could just walk away,' the woman continued. 'Get on with your life as though nothing had happened. Rehabilitated… put all that behind you…'

She sneered at his exposed groin, pulled a folding knife from her back pocket and flicked it open.

A small sound escaped Oliver's lips as his heart threshed against his ribs.

She leaned into him. 'Do you think that would be enough, Oliver? Do you think that little bullshit act of Aversion Therapy,' she spat the words, 'would really give you an insight into what it was like to be raped – the degradation, the vulnerability, the fear whenever you were alone, the struggle trying to get close to those you love, the medication, therapy for years afterwards, trying to fix yourself after an attack by an evil bastard like you?'

She twirled the point of the knife against his thigh. A bead of blood proved its keen blade.

The man spoke up. 'We don't think the treatment is effective justice. We want you to feel the way your victims feel.' He glanced at the crimson-haired woman but she looked away. 'If only your victims could go and have one brief session of treatment and get on with their lives, eh?'

The mousy woman moved back into the shadows and Oliver could hear her sobbing. Even now, even in this situation where he was clearly the underdog, it gave him pleasure.

They're not going to do anything to me! They're just going to give me a fright, let me go.

The man turned to the mousy woman and said, 'Are you ready?'

The weeping paused, but she remained in the shadows.

You're not really going to do this… you wouldn't…

And then it struck him. He'd read about it in the press.

This was Payback.

And Oliver McIntyre suddenly felt something that he'd never experienced in his whole life.

Fear.

'Don't worry. You'll feel better after this,' the crimson-haired woman told her in soothing tones. 'It won't take long.' Then she turned to the man and nodded. Immediately, he pushed down hard on Oliver's thighs.

Oliver watched in horror, helpless as the blade moved closer to his groin.

'This is for justice,' she said, smiling at him, 'for her, and all your other victims. We're going to make sure you never do it again.'

There was a moment when time seemed to stop, the blade mid-air, his heart mid-beat.

There was a head-splitting crash, the doors flew open and three armed officers in black uniform stormed in.

'Police! Don't move or we'll shoot!'

As his attackers were restrained, the knife fell to the ground between Oliver's thighs with a clatter, the blade revolving quickly, and then slowing down, until it finally stopped, pointing towards his body like a horrifying game of spin the bottle.

Oliver's heart rate took its time to slow down while the police cuffed Payback and took them out, he presumed to a police van. He sat on the ground, furious and humiliated, his buttocks numb against the cold floor. Why the hell weren't they getting him covered up, or calling for medics?

Finally, one of the officers came back in and leaned down. He removed his black helmet, his skin shiny with sweat.

'Are you okay, sir?'

Oliver couldn't respond, but he felt relief flooding his system.

This is so humiliating.

'Don't worry. They'll get what they deserve.'

Cover me up, can't you?

He just wanted to get dressed and get out of there.

'We've been trying to find these people for some time. You are so lucky, sir...'

If the police had arrived a moment later...

Yes, I am a lucky bastard.

It struck him – if the police knew that these were vigilantes, would they also know about his crimes? His powerful survival instinct kicked in. He was confident he could talk his way out of it, persuade them that it was a case of mistaken identity. He was Fire Brigade, they were Police, they had an understanding.

As for the little mousy woman, he would find her and make sure she said nothing to anyone – ever again.

'There was a man recently, sir, not as lucky as you...'

Oliver didn't care about the other man. He just wanted to get out of there. They'd take him to hospital and he might even meet another nurse. Always a silver lining. They'd take his statement and then he'd be back at home relaxing and planning his next attack. He might even get some compensation. He wouldn't let a little thing like this affect him. He was no victim!

What the hell are you doing? Just get me covered up, man!

The officer picked up the blade from between Oliver's thighs with his gloved hand. His face was very close to Oliver's. 'Evidence, always important, don't you think?'

But Oliver recognised something in his eyes. Something that he saw in his own eyes when he looked in the mirror.

And suddenly, Oliver McIntyre wasn't sure if he was a lucky bastard after all.

CHAPTER NINE

She's standing on a sheet of ice, clear but with wisps of opaque white spiralling through it, suspended above deep water. Every muscle in her body is held taut as even a slight movement causes a shift in her foothold.

All around her is calm and cold. The sun shines brightly in a blue sky, but the air is crisp. At a distance, she can see Dan walking along the lakeside. She shouts out to him.

Help me! Help me!

But he just smiles and waves.

Beneath, in the darkness of the lake, she can see movements, a turmoil of memories. Warden Kane's key card, Lottie's bronze tea kettle, her mother's hands. Remy suddenly appears just centimetres beneath the surface, his face bluish-white with cold and terror. He's trapped, the current moving him along, his grey eyes imploring as he bangs against the thick ice, desperate for oxygen.

She falls to her knees, sliding as she hits the solid water with her fists over and over again, but she can't break the surface.

She watches helpless as Remy disappears into the darkness, the last thing she sees are his fingers reaching up towards her.

Grace was roused from sleep by her phone which lit the dark bedroom with a blue glow. It rang off before she could answer. When she swiped at the screen it showed a missed voice call from a street-shell, one of the computer kiosks that were available to the public.

She hadn't received a call from one of them in a long time. An image of Remy, as she used to know him, flashed into her mind from her dream. They used to have a strong connection – would it still be there? They hadn't spoken in years. So why did she suspect it might have been him calling her?

She lay back on the pillow. Dan's side of the bed was cold. He'd texted the previous night to say he was out on a job and might not be back before the morning.

It was early, only half five. In just over two hours, she would be making her way to work. Adrenaline needled her as she saw herself standing in Conrad's office trying to formulate the words. *Deal. Trade-off. Quid pro quo?* She wouldn't be able to get back to sleep now. She got up and made herself a coffee and planned how to convince her boss to let her help a man he didn't know in exchange for a job she didn't want.

–

Conrad looked somehow smaller sitting behind his desk. She sat opposite him, holding her nerve.

'There must be more to all this than you just needing another psychiatrist for the Tier Three clinic, Conrad.' She ran her tongue over dry lips.

'No.' A pause and then he shrugged slightly. 'I just think you'd be perfect for the job.'

He underrated her if he thought a good psychiatrist wouldn't recognise a false smile. She tried to decipher his mood – anxious, embarrassed, manipulative? He wasn't usually on the backfoot. It gave her strength, but she was going to have to be strong to get what she wanted. She was going to have to dig deep – to stop holding herself tense on the slippery surface of a middle-class, married, professional life and break through to the old Grace, the streetwise Gracie, who was ready to take on a fight.

'There's something going wrong with the treatment, isn't there?' Her words sounded brittle.

His expression spun through a roulette wheel of micro-expressions and he settled on what she thought he would consider candid.

He leaned over the desk now, elbows on the glass, placing his chin on his interlaced fingers. 'There have been a few issues, yes.'

'Hmm. And you think I might have the insight to fix it?'

Twenty-four hours ago, she could never have imagined herself talking to the boss of the company like this. But things had changed. Here were two desperate people facing each other.

'Grace, you are the best psychiatrist we've ever had and the therapies that you've developed at Tier Two are absolutely second to none. The synthetic self-esteem drug that you created and trialled was nothing short of miraculous, particularly the amphetamine-based treatment.'

'That was different,' she interrupted. 'Self-esteem is a huge deficiency in our offenders at Tier Two and we only offer that particular treatment as a short-term fix until we can encourage the real thing with our confidence-building therapy. It's the skills we teach at the Agrarian Compound and the relationships the inmates forge that give them the real thing, not the drug. I'd be in over my head here.'

'Don't underestimate yourself, Grace. You have real insight into the human condition.'

She stared at the brass statue of the horse, its bulging eyes and flaring nostrils repulsing her. Did Conrad really respect her abilities, or was he just trying to keep this problem in-house?

'Let's get to the point, Conrad. Did Myriam mess up? Is that why she left?'

He opened his mouth but said nothing. Was he actually going to have the audacity to lie to her again?

'I know about Mikey Kilgannon,' she said.

His face began to flush. 'How the hell did you find out? Dan doesn't know, does he? This *cannot* get out into the public arena, Grace, it just can't.'

'He doesn't know,' she lied. 'One of the Tier Three crew said something that put me onto it. Don't worry. They weren't aware Kilgannon had previous. I put two and two together.'

Conrad looked a little relieved.

'Can I trust you, Grace?'

She didn't answer, but she didn't break his gaze.

'We've had some reoffences,' he said.

'More than just Kilgannon?'

He nodded.

Hadn't Dan said there had been a cover-up at the post office in Golders Green? It was Grace's turn now to lean forward over the desk, still not taking her eyes off him.

'You want me to fix Aversion Therapy for you.' It came out like an accusation.

He nodded again, more slowly this time.

She steeled herself. She needed courage to cope with what she would hear and see in the clinic. She would have to put her conscience aside for a short time for Remy's sake, and be complicit not only in torture, but in deception.

She didn't answer immediately, taking her time, waiting until she saw just enough desperation on his face to know he would agree to her demands.

A slight twitch in his left cheek.

She sat back in the chair and crossed her arms. 'I'll take the job on two conditions.'

Conrad perked up, but there was suspicion in his eyes. 'Go on.'

'Firstly, I will not commit anyone to Tier Four. If we scan a Tier Three offender and it becomes clear that there's nothing we can do for them at Tier Three, then it's not going to be my name on the forms.' She knew her limitations. 'I don't want to be responsible for placing someone in a psych ward for the rest of their life.'

Conrad didn't look surprised, he just nodded. 'No problem, Abigail can do that. And the second condition?'

She cleared her throat. 'If I come up with a way to make Aversion Therapy fool proof, then I want to trial it on an offender of my choosing' – she emphasised the last two words – 'whom I consider, as an expert, to be the best chance of proving that it's a secure and reliable treatment.' She held her breath and tried not to think about Remy, as though somehow Conrad would pick up on something in her if she did.

'Okay, that sounds reasonable,' he began.

'And,' she jumped in, 'I want your solemn word that this offender will be freed if I cure him… or her…' Remy hadn't even been caught yet. He might never be. Was she going to put herself through this for a chance that might never come? But then what of the other offenders, like Mikey Kilgannon and Noah Begbroke. If she couldn't help Remy, maybe she could help *someone*.

Conrad was weighing her up.

She refused to look away.

He gave her a slight nod.

'Say it, or I want no part.'

'Yes,' he said quietly but firmly. 'You fix the therapy, you can pick your guinea pig.'

'And have them freed if the treatment is successful?'

'Yes, and I will personally sign the release papers.'

'Then it's a deal.' She felt herself relax a little.

'But…'

She caught her breath.

Conrad continued '…not a word of this to Dan. This stays off NewsFlex. You'll have to sign an additional confidentiality agreement.'

Grace exhaled. 'Of course.'

He stood up and put his hand out to her. She followed suit, hoping he wouldn't feel her tremble, and they shook.

'I'll let Abigail know.'

Five minutes later, Abigail slunk into the room like a cat. Her amber-coloured eyes glanced briefly at Grace and then rested on Conrad.

'Abigail, Grace is replacing Myriam.'

'I said I can sort this, Conrad,' Abigail said.

'No, you can't,' he said firmly. 'I've made my decision. You're only a technician, Abigail, a damn good one, but a technician nonetheless. You need a psych and the treatment needs a thorough investigation. It's above your capabilities.'

Abigail opened her mouth as if to protest.

'But you can still have responsibility for the scans and the paperwork for Tier Four.'

She looked momentarily placated but then said, 'I really think I can do it—'

'No, you damn well can't!' he shouted.

Grace had never heard Conrad raise his voice before.

'There was another one last night,' he told her, more quietly.

Abigail let out a small gasp.

Like Dan, Conrad had his contacts. It probably came straight from his contact in the DoJ.

He gave Abigail a hard stare. 'Payback have attacked again. A firefighter in one of the cotton warehouses off Penhaligon Road. I don't know all the details yet.'

'That's not possible!' Abigail whispered. 'There are other members of the Payback group. It might not have been the ones we treated. It could have been some of the others.'

Grace saw beneath Abigail's professional veneer and felt a little sorry for her. It was natural to feel threatened by having someone new coming to work alongside her, someone who was more qualified, more senior in status, especially in a crisis. But Grace didn't see it like that. Abigail had the experience, knew the day-to-day routine in the clinic, and knew how to program and use all the kit. Abigail would have to show her the ropes. They'd be a team, wouldn't they?

'We'll find out, once they're apprehended,' said Conrad.

'You mean no one's been arrested yet?' asked Abigail. 'So we don't know if we treated them or not?'

Conrad shook his head.

'What will happen to them then?' asked Grace. 'Will they come to Tier Three?' She shuddered to think what she'd see on the screen for that therapy.

Conrad shook his head. 'Either way, they'll go to Tier Four. The first time we treated some of the Payback lot, we didn't realise they were a gang. We thought it was just a one-off, someone getting revenge. Now we know who they are – what they do – it's straight to Tier Four.'

'What do they do to them in Tier Four?' asked Grace, then immediately wished she hadn't.

Neither answered. Instead, Abigail asked Conrad, 'But what if they've been to Tier Three already and Myriam messed up the treatment, or misdiagnosed them?'

'It'll make the system looked flawed,' Conrad said, his face pale. 'If this gets out, then my business is screwed. If doubt is cast on our methods, then the whole Tier System is going to be called into question. Every single case. Imagine the lawsuits we'll have to face!'

'If the protestors get wind of this…' began Grace.

'They'll up their game,' Conrad said. 'We have to be on our guard. I won't stand for another attack like the one last year.' He slumped back his chair.

Grace and Abigail looked at each other and then back to Conrad, who suddenly sat up straight. He swiped at his desk. 'Call Deacon Security.'

He looked at the women with a serious expression as the call was put through. As soon as he started talking, he looked away, his expression as jovial as his voice. 'Gary, hi, yes, it's Conrad Becker. We're looking into developing our security, you know, tightening things up… No, no problems, but it's always better to be safe than sorry.' He cleared his throat. 'Maybe you could do me a deal…'

Abigail pulled at Grace's arm.

'Right, we'll get on, then,' she said, but Conrad ignored her.

In the corridor, Grace said, 'Payback took a massive risk – knowing they'd go to Tier Four if they were caught.'

'Maybe they thought their version of justice was worth taking risks for,' Abigail said bluntly.

Remy's face beneath the ice flashed into her mind and a cold feeling gripped her.

Abigail suddenly turned to her with an expression of panic. 'I didn't make mistakes in the clinic. I did everything by the book. I'm not to blame!'

'Abigail, it's okay,' Grace said kindly, briefly laying a hand on her arm. 'I'm not judging you and I certainly don't blame anyone. I just want to figure out what's going wrong so that we can make it right.'

Abigail blinked a few times and then nodded. 'Sorry. I, you know, just don't want you thinking I'm not good at my job.'

'Of course I don't think that. We're a team now. We're going to sort this.'

Abigail seemed reassured. 'I'll take you to Tier Three, show you the ropes.'

As they passed the bathroom Grace excused herself, saying she'd catch up with Abigail in a few minutes, and watched her walk away down the corridor towards the clinic.

Once in the cubicle, she called Dan.

'Do you know anything about an attack by Payback last night?' she asked in a whisper.

'Where?'

'At a cotton warehouse near Penhaligon Road. They're trying to keep it hush-hush.'

'Thanks for the tip-off. I'll get onto it right away.'

Grace put her shell in her bag and came out of the cubicle to see Abigail standing at the sink, her hand on the tap. She caught Grace's reflection in the mirror and smiled.

CHAPTER TEN

WESTMINISTER

7.46 a.m.

I'm here outside Parliament where protestors have spent the night demonstrating against Aversion Therapy. As you can see behind me, there's a large police presence keeping the crowd under control.

Robyn Cooper, a thirty-two-year-old from Bromley, was sentenced to the controversial treatment yesterday afternoon, for stealing ten genetically enhanced cryo-preserved foetuses from the CRYOGEN laboratory where she worked as a technician.

Unable to conceive a healthy child naturally, Cooper alleged she was promised one of the foetuses by a gang who planned to sell them on the black market. Her role in the theft was to give the gang access to the secure labs where the foetuses were kept.

The illegal trade in genetically enhanced babies has grown over the last two decades as effective screening highlights a vast array of potential problems. Many would-be parents use genetic modification to correct these problems, but some issues cannot be solved with therapy, taking away any chance of having a healthy child.

In mitigation, Cooper's barristers said that, as a technician, she would never be able to afford the fees for gene therapy if she wished to have her own child. Many people in a similar situation live with the knowledge that their baby would be at a disadvantage to other genetically enhanced children, and some even choose sterilisation, as they feel their potential offspring's chances to be too meagre.

Unlike Cooper, the gang members were not offered the option of Aversion Therapy and were sentenced to eco-labour for twenty years. Some were sent to the now defunct oil rigs in the North Sea which have been repurposed as part-prison, part-recycling plant. Inmates there collect swathes of plastic from the sea in huge metal nets and then gather it into bales which are then sent to the eco-stations on land to be recycled into building bricks. Others were sent to the landfill camps to endure painstaking sorting and separation of landfills, 'detritus archaeology' as the head of the Department of Justice recently referred to it, in an attempt to prevent the planet being smothered by waste.

As the gang members settle to the next two decades of incarceration, there's outrage that Cooper will be released at the end of the week. A large number of protestors gathered late yesterday afternoon in Parliament Square to demand proper punishment. They've clashed with demon-strators on Cooper's side who are asking for leniency. Both groups appear to be against Aversion Therapy, but for very different reasons. Many people are carrying plac-ards displaying phrases such as STATE SANCTIONED TORTURE and FIGHT FOR HUMAN RIGHTS, while others are demanding a return to the old-fashioned prison system, particularly whole-life tariffs for more serious crimes.

The Department of Justice has refused to comment on Cooper's case.

As yet, there's no sign of the crowds dispersing, and clashes are expected to get worse as the day goes on.

This is Dan Gunnarsson reporting for NewsFlex.

The clinic was very different from the day of Noah Begbroke's treatment. The temperature was cool, the blackout electro-chromic glass in the windows switched off to let in the morning light, softening the dark grey of the walls. It was simple, minim-alist, and could have been any other clinic in the building, except for the chair that sat in the centre of the room – empty, innocent – but a reminder of what Grace had seen and could not forget.

The bio-scanners picked up on her anxiety immediately and she felt the buzz in her bag as the readings came up on her shell. She didn't need to look to know what it would show.

If Abigail had heard her conversation with Dan, she hadn't said anything. Now she moved briskly around the room, pushing at various wall panels which opened to reveal the tech kit necessary to carry out Aversion Therapy.

'So here we have the main emotisonic wave controls. We programme it here before treatment and then use the shell to adjust, but I'm sure you're familiar with all that.'

'Yes, we use them in the Tier Two clinics,' Grace replied, 'but it's usually to reassure or calm our clients.'

'Here we use waves that elicit a negative reaction, as you saw with Begbroke. The therapy is more effective if we agitate their emotions to make them feel less at ease.'

Had that been one of the reasons that Grace had felt so unsettled at Begbroke's treatment? The very atmosphere had been created to be uncomfortable. Even as the idea crossed her mind, she knew there was much more to it than emotisonics.

Abigail pressed another panel, her long fingers pale against the grey. The push-catch clicked as the cupboard slid open to reveal a defibrillator. 'Just in case. No one has ever had a heart attack as far as I know, but with this sort of therapy, I suppose it could happen.'

'My main concern is for the psychological health of the offenders.'

'You saw yourself with Begbroke, he was a little shaken, but nothing to be concerned about.'

'I'll see where he's up to at his post-treatment appointment.'

Abigail looked at her, bemused. 'Myriam didn't do follow-ups.'

Grace felt her brow crease. 'Did someone else do them?'

Abigail shook her head. 'Conrad said they weren't necessary, money was better spent on drugs.'

'Really?' Grace's instinct was to turn round, march back to Conrad's office and confront him.

But then she remembered. She wasn't going to be here long. It wasn't her problem. Right now, she had enough to deal with.

'Has any offender ever had a psychotic episode in clinic?'

'No. The worst we see is anxiety before the treatment, or distress afterwards, but it's to be expected.'

'And the relaxant, what do you use?'

'One that doesn't cause any mental impairment or affect memory. We want the offender to be physically impeded, but cerebrally sharp so that the treatment really hits home.'

'Is that what this is?' Grace pointed to vials still in the dish from Begbroke's treatment.

'Oh, I was meant to clear that away. No, that's something else.' She busied herself taking the vials and placing them behind one of the panels. 'We use nasal spray for a relaxant because it enters the body very quickly.'

'Have you worked here long, Abigail?'

'Just over a year. I was head-hunted from another clinic up north.' She flicked at her hair with her hand.

Up north. Vague. There were clinics in many of the big cities around the country.

'Conrad has a high opinion of you.' Grace wasn't sure that was true, but if she was going to be working alongside Abigail, she had to try to get on the right side of her. It didn't take a degree in psychiatry to work that out.

She looked at Grace warily before saying, 'Really?'

'He told me that you're highly competent.'

She seemed pleased by this and started to loosen up a little. 'I used to work at Newcastle, and Bradford before that. Nowadays, I sometimes go to other clinics to give training – Manchester, Bristol and other places.'

Grace nodded in approval. 'I'm a willing student. I need to be if we're going to get to the bottom of this problem.'

'We?' Abigail turned her attention to a workstation with a triptych of screens.

'I'm going to need your expertise, Abigail. I can't do this on my own.'

Even as the words left her lips, Grace felt conflicted. Yes, she was trying to gain Abigail's trust, to lower herself so the other felt elevated, as she so often had – a survival technique learned way back. But the pre-university Gracie would have scoffed at this attempt to ingratiate herself.

Abigail placed her hand on a palm-reader and immediately the three screens burst into life. 'Myriam's already been removed from the security system.'

Removed. Like a cancer cut out.

'Abigail Hawesthorne.' She spoke clearly into the voice recognition mic as the scanner scrutinised one of her golden-orange irises.

'Heavy security,' Grace mused.

'Look into the reader,' Abigail commanded. 'Needs to be heavy, we had protestors break in last summer. Some of the photos they took ended up on the media websites. They tried to make out we were torturing offenders.'

'I heard about that.' The iris scanner left a lingering red dot swimming in Grace's vision. She blinked a few times. 'Looks like Conrad's stepping up security again. There'll be new guards starting this week.'

'Better to be safe than sorry. Handprint,' Abigail said, pointing at the palm-reader. 'At any one time you'll need two of the three identity markers to get in. We've had hackers try to get into the system as well. We can't be too careful.'

That phrase again.

She watched Abigail's fingers fly over the keyboard as she readjusted the security settings.

'Okay, now say your name.'

'Grace Gunnarsson.'

'And again.' Her eyes moved from scanner to screen and back again.

'Grace Gunnarsson.'

'One more time.'

'Grace Gunnarsson.'

'Okay, you're in.'

The central screen was a dashboard of information about the clinic – who was present, a video monitor of the witness room and various update reports. The bio-analysis reader for the chair was currently flatlining. Grace could see her own readings, her heart rate a little high.

She felt transparent, like a scientific specimen.

Abigail's did not appear to be responding.

'Obs can be deactivated?' Grace asked. Sharing biological information might have become second nature, but she began to worry that her stats might give something away.

Abigail nodded. 'Look at the settings menu under your name.'

The screen to the left showed the dark blue logo of Janus Justice, the head of a Roman god with two faces looking in opposite directions. Janus – the god of transitions, duality, beginnings and endings. The gateway god who looked to the past and the future at the same time. Conrad's idea, no doubt, a tinpot god in his own little cosmos.

'So here we have the clinic log,' Abigail said, shifting her attention to the screen on the right. 'As you can see, tomorrow we have Robyn Cooper in for Aversion Therapy. The various windows show all the information about this offender and her case.' She moved her finger across the screen. 'Here are the details of the crime. And here's her background information, medical history, and her pre-treatment assessments. This is the reel that she'll see tomorrow during treatment, the emotisonics programme and the drugs we'll use. Myriam already prescribed these at Cooper's previous assessment. You'll be prescribing for the next offender.'

Grace felt a wave of uncertainty. As if reading her mind, Abigail said, 'All the information is here on the screen, the types of drugs and doses that we use. You'll be able to figure it all out. You can readjust your screen to add in other windows, but these are the main ones. Cooper will come here tomorrow straight from hypnotherapy.'

'Hypnotherapy?' asked Grace. It was something they also used in Tier Two but, but like the emotisonics, here she was sure it would be in a negative way.

'It reinforces the illusion that the criminal is now the victim.'

'The video of Corrina. It was… disturbing to say the least. Who makes the reels?'

Abigail flicked at her hair again. 'As the main technician on this floor, that's my job.'

'Where does the information come from?'

'Police records, court cases, audio and video, and witness statements, including the victim, if possible.' The words hung in the air.

Grace imagined her trawling through hours of digital files, crime scenes and police interviews. 'How do you feel about making them? I mean, it can't be easy.'

God, now she really sounded like a psychiatrist.

Abigail's eyes narrowed. 'It's essential to the success of the treatment. I take that part of the job very seriously.'

'I just meant, it must be… difficult to see the files.'

After a pause, Abigail said, 'Mood drinks help… Lots of them.'

Was that a smile?

Abigail turned away with a shrug and picked up a shell from the workstation. 'Here, take this home. It's got all the Tier

Three info on it. You can read up on the case and the meds, so you have everything you need before tomorrow.' She thrust the shell into Grace's hands.

All the information she needed about Mikey Kilgannon, and more importantly Remy, was accessible to Grace now. Her fingers seemed to crackle with static as she wiped them across the crystal. She eyed the screen, hoping her heart monitor on the main screen didn't draw Abigail's attention, and made a mental note to disable her observations as soon as possible.

'Thanks.'

Abigail turned her attention back to the screen. 'There. I've given you security clearance on that shell too. Just be very careful with that – Myriam took the up-to-date clinic shell with her. This one hasn't got an iris scanner on it, so make sure you use a very strong password. I know you're learning on the job, but I'll be here and it will all become clear in practice.'

Grace leaned in to take a closer look at Robyn Cooper's information.

'Stealing a foetus?'

'Helping to steal ten from a laboratory for a black-market trader.' Abigail brought up a document on the screen. 'This is the legal documentation from the court that gives us the power to carry out the sentence. She couldn't have a genetically healthy baby naturally, so she stole one.'

Grace caught her breath.

She knew all too well the ticking time bomb of something within waiting for a trigger to trip the gene. Problems that might lead to a clinic like this.

A stolen foetus, however, implanted into the womb by any number of shady doctors looking for extra cash, could make it appear that you had your own perfectly healthy child.

'At least Cooper had the choice of eco-camp or Aversion Therapy,' said Abigail.

'That sounds like a tough choice.'

'I guess so.' She turned to face Grace. 'People choose this treatment for all sorts of reasons, usually because they don't realise how distressing it's going to be. They want to get their punishment over and done with and move on as quickly as possible. Cooper miscarried, so destruction of property was an added charge.'

'God, that's terrible!'

'Yes, the government want to make an example of her. Stop this kind of thing.'

'I didn't mean that. I meant that poor woman can't have a healthy child, and then loses the baby and has to go through this too. Surely she needs compassion, not punishment?'

'She took her chances.' Abigail shrugged.

Curious about Abigail, Grace asked her a question that was frequently thrown about in bars on a Friday night. 'What would you choose? A quick, painful fix of Aversion Therapy, or a longer, more drawn-out punishment of eco-labour?'

From a distance, Grace had often seen the yellow hazmat-suited convicts swarming over the disposal sites as she drove to and from the Agrarian Compound.

Abigail didn't answer the question, but instead said, 'At least it's a choice. Imagine the attacks we'd get if it was forced. Many people think it's an appropriate punishment. Although a lot of people seem to trust a long haul in an eco-prison more than Aversion Therapy.'

Grace could understand why people might not trust the treatment. It seemed so quick, and most people could never really imagine what took place, so they probably didn't see it as much of a punishment. She herself hadn't realised until yesterday just how distressing it was. As a psychiatrist, she would have more insight than most about how traumatic such a process might be. She could also see that psychologically some people would want to choose eco-labour, where the penitent offender was seen to be redeemed.

'But the results speak for themselves,' Abigail said. 'It's cheaper than long-term incarceration, quicker, and highly effective.'

And what would the general population think if they knew that sometimes it didn't work? No wonder Conrad is worried.

'And those people therapy can't fix?' asked Grace. 'What do you do with them?'

'I'll show you.'

CHAPTER ELEVEN

Westminster

10.53 a.m.

Protests outside Parliament are intensifying this morning, following recent questions raised about Aversion Therapy, as attention turns to what Tier Four might have in store for offenders. This tier has long been the subject of speculation by conspiracy theorists, and the lack of information from Janus Justice has only served to fan the flames. Demonstrators, already agitated by the Robyn Cooper case, have been demanding answers.

Glossed over in government reports as a 'safe space' for those who cannot be rehabilitated, little is known about this tier, which is reserved only for those who cannot be cured lower down the system, including psychopaths and serial killers. A Minister for Justice has described it only as 'a secure unit for those who cannot be trusted with freedom, to protect the safety of our citizens'. When pressed, the minister refused to say more.

It's rumoured that criminals who participate in serial crimes but who have not been through Tier Three may also be sent there. Conrad Becker, CEO of Janus Justice, went some way to clarify this, saying: 'Offenders who take part in premeditated murder or serial crime may well be sentenced to Tier Four. They know what they're doing. The lower levels of the Tier System are designed for those who want a

chance to change. These people don't want to change, so
they end up at the final destination.'

This is Dan Gunnarsson reporting for NewsFlex

Tier Four – the Incurables.

Only those with the highest security clearance were allowed
on this floor. Grace assumed it was because the inmates here
were so dangerous. It was reserved for the worst of the worst –
murderers, terrorists, serial criminals – people who Tier Two
could not heal and Tier Three could not rehabilitate. She'd
assumed it was some kind of secure unit where offenders wore
slippers and watched TV in a communal sitting room, jeering
or cowering at the occasional fight between one of their fellow
residents and the guards.

Now she was going to find out the truth.

Abigail scanned her eye and palm on the digital panel and
the lift door opened onto a brightly lit, white corridor where
George was standing talking to another clinic porter.

'Hi Abigail. Hi Doctor G. Don't usually see you up here.'

The other porter entered the lift pushing a cart of linen and
the doors shut behind him.

'Just doing a quick tour,' Abigail said, looking down the
corridor.

'Promotion, huh?' he said to Grace pleasantly.

'Something like that, George,' she replied, unable to return
his smile. They usually made time to talk. Grace would ask
about his three school-age children. George would update her
on how his sister was doing. But today, her mind was on other
things.

The two women made their way through yet another
security door.

Grace's senses were on high alert as Abigail ushered her in.

98

It was not what Grace had expected at all.

The room was huge, white and clinical, the lights dimmed, the air still. Row upon row of inmates lay in beds that lined either side of the room like a hospital ward. Their prone bodies, covered up to the neck with white sheets, were all motionless. It was difficult to tell which were male or female. Their heads were shaved. Each of them wore a headset which covered their ears and eyes, metallic bands criss-crossing their shiny or downy skulls.

Grace felt as though she was standing in a mortuary. It was deathly quiet apart from the occasional rolling of the ergonomic mattresses making a sound like the sea crashing onto shingle.

'What is this?' Grace's words came out in a shocked whisper.

Abigail studied her face.

'We call it the Siberia ward. Biostasis, chemically induced locked-in syndrome.'

Siberia – the pure white, the sensory deprivation, the internal exile – an apt nickname.

Grace had read about locked-in syndrome as a student and it had terrified her then. Now here it was, laid out before her, in all its horror.

These people were fully conscious, alive and awake, but unable to move or communicate. They could think and reason, but could not express any need or desire. There were no choices for these offenders. And no escape.

The body had become the prison. Who knew where the mind would go in such a situation?

Grace imagined lying still, paralysed, naked and vulnerable, as people washed her, shaved her head and catheterised her. The thought made her skin crawl. Death seemed preferable, but they would keep her alive – force-feed her through tubes, pump her full of antibiotics. There would be no relief.

Next to each bed was a white post containing the liquid, feeding and waste tubes which came out at the top and ran under the sheets. At the top of each post a shell flashed away, projecting a bright rectangle of information onto the wall above the inmate's head – name, number, vital stats, reminders, and other information necessary to maintain life in this most meagre of ways.

'Who knows about this?' Grace asked in a hushed voice.

'They can't hear you,' Abigail replied, pointing to the earphones on the headsets. Her words echoed around the clinic.

'Who knows?' Grace asked again, her voice louder but tremulous.

Abigail shrugged. 'Obviously Conrad and the hand-picked staff who work here. We have a minister in the Department of Justice who's aware, and now you.'

So this wasn't just a crazy project of Conrad's. The government actually knew about this.

'Is this the only clinic like this in the country?'

'For now. We're running the trials, and if it's agreed with the Department of Justice then it will be rolled out over the next five years.'

'How long do they stay like this?' asked Grace, unable to absorb what she was hearing.

Abigail didn't answer. Instead, she moved towards the nearest bed and raised the wrist of the occupant. 'Here,' she said, showing Grace a tiny ribbed fan under the skin of the inside lower arm. 'The bioplastic implants break down over time, to maintain sedation, and we use this,' she turned the hand over to show a cannula, 'to inject psychotropic drugs that make up part of the treatment. It's intravenous so we can adjust it depending on the efficacy of the dose.'

Grace wondered how efficacy might be measured in this situation.

Her eyes travelled along the arm until they reached a familiar tattoo, the Janus Justice logo with a number 3 beneath, still unfaded. She looked up at the display and read the name Mikey Kilgannon. The last time she'd seen him, he'd been mowing lawns at the Agrarian. He'd smiled and waved at her in the sunshine. She could smell the cut grass now.

'Why are these people here? Are you trying to cure them?'

Abigail tucked Mikey's arm back under the sheet. 'I think that was Conrad's intention initially, but to be frank, I think he bit off more than he could chew. As if anyone can cure a psychopath.'

'So they're going to stay here – until they die?'

'Until natural death. Yes.'

'But that could be years! And Mikey? Why is he here?'

'He's a reoffender. We don't know what else to do with him just yet.' She touched his temple gently. 'Maybe he is a psychopath, which would explain why Aversion Therapy didn't succeed, because…'

'…they don't have the emotions to make it an effective treatment,' Grace finished for her.

'That's right. It would have been water off a duck's back.'

'So why don't you scan him and find out for sure?'

'Doesn't really matter now. Because it's an unusual case, he has to stay here until Conrad figures out what to do with him.'

Grace glanced at Mikey. It hurt her heart to look at him for too long. She remembered him telling her a stupid joke and laughing like a kid. Her heart ached for him.

'I treated him at Tier Two, you know, after he burgled a social club and punched one of the workers when they tried to stop him getting away with some expensive kit. I didn't pick up on any signs of psychopathy, though.'

Abigail raised her eyebrows slightly. It felt like a judgement.

'We did our best for him, but…' Grace began. From birth Kilgannon had been steeped in crime, raised in a notorious family. 'It's not that easy with the violence gene. Sometimes we manage to retrain behaviour and thought patterns. But I guess we just couldn't get through to him.' Had they missed something at Tier Two?

'That's what Tier Three is for,' Abigail said, tapping at the shell screen. 'You deal with the sad and mad, we get the bad.'

The mad? At least those who committed crimes out of insanity didn't have to come here. They were safely tucked away in the secure hospitals. Weren't they?

But how trustworthy was the Department of Justice if it condoned this?

'But Tier Three wasn't successful either,' Grace countered. Abigail kept her eyes on the screen. This was her chance to glean some information for Dan's investigation and to help Remy. 'Is there any reason you think Mikey might have offended again? I mean, you might expect a Tier One or Two to reoffend because sometimes we need to dig deeper to get to the root of the matter, but Tier Three – it's a different type of treatment altogether.'

'It is,' agreed Abigail. 'We're not pandering to people's needs but cauterising the cause of crime.'

Grace ignored this. Probably another one of Conrad's sound bites. 'So why did it fail? Why did no one recognise that Mikey is a psychopath, if that's what's going on here?' She pointed vaguely towards the bed.

Abigail's orange eyes flared briefly at Grace's deliberately chosen 'fail', a trigger word for perfectionists. Grace was hoping it might provoke some clarity.

'It must be because Myriam didn't read the scans properly before she treated him,' Abigail said, smoothing the sheet that covered Mikey's body.

'What did the brain scans say?'

'I don't know. I can't find them.'

'Can't find them?' *What's going on here?*

'Maybe Myriam deleted them before she left. She might have realised her mistake and tried to cover it up,' Abigail said.

'But it was you who scanned Mikey's brain?'

'That's the usual routine. I did the scanning but I left it to Myriam to read them. She was the expert, after all.'

Grace turned her attention back to the man in the bed.

'So they just lie here, stuck in their own worlds, thinking about God knows what?'

She imagined Mikey feeling hungry, or having an itch, or worrying about his mum, or being bored or desperate to die… Her chest tightened and she felt breathless. She watched the rhythmic thud of his carotid artery against the skin on his neck. His lips were moving slightly as though in silent prayer.

'They're thinking about their crimes. All the inmates here have their own personal reel, like the one you saw used with Noah Begbroke. The only difference here is that it's on a loop.'

'What?' Grace was sure she'd misheard.

'You know, like a prolonged version of Tier Three treatment.'

Grace's mind went back to the images that Noah Begbroke had been prescribed. It had been horrific – overwhelming and suffocating.

And it had only been played the once.

'You mean, they actually watch the reels over and over again?' asked Grace, appalled by the idea of continual misery and mental anguish.

This was way beyond torture.

She looked down at poor, daft, troublesome Mikey and tried to get her head around what was happening to him.

Oh Mikey, I'm so sorry. I should have fixed you. I should have made you better!

'See here,' said Abigail, as she touched the shell and the stats display above the bed was replaced with video footage. A silhouette of a man with a bat appeared to be leaning over the viewer. 'This is what Kilgannon sees – as if he was the victim.'

The bat came crashing down.

Mikey's arms twitched slightly.

'They have audio as well, of course,' Abigail added. 'And the drugs make it seem like it's really happening.' She appeared unmoved.

Grace felt a rising nausea. She pressed her hand to her mouth.

'It's not as bad as some of them,' Abigail insisted. 'Bed six over there, she's a serial killer, tied men up and shot them at close range. Bed nine, he did the terrorist attack on the kids' hospital. And don't even ask about bed fifteen.'

A personal video loop of the darkest deeds they committed, replayed over and over, but with them as the victim, intensified with psychotropic drugs and emotisonics? *Death is too good*. She wondered what the public would think if they found out.

Her stomach lurched.

'This is… this is horrendous,' she whispered. 'You can't do this to people! The government can't…'

Abigail turned her feline gaze towards Grace with curiosity.

'No worse than what they do to their victims, if you think about it. These people would reoffend ad infinitum. This is best for everyone. They're getting punished. Their victims are getting justice. Society is safe.'

'But don't their relatives try to stop it? What must it be like to have a brother, a sister, a son or daughter go through this?'

Abigail shrugged. 'Most of them don't know what's going on in here. Lots of families think they deserve punishment. Usually disown them.'

'They don't get any visitors?'

'What would be the point?' Abigail laughed and Grace felt her cheeks burn. She was glad that none of her bio-readings were visible.

Abigail put her hand on Grace's shoulder to steer her out of the clinic. 'It's a lot to take in, a bit of a shock first time.' She took her hand away as they came to the door and said, 'Think about some of the horrendous things these people, these criminals, have done, Grace. It's the balance of justice.'

Grace took one last look behind her, trying to remember every tiny detail as if somehow to convince herself that this was really happening.

This wasn't justice. This was vengeance.

–

'Grace, don't question yourself,' said Shannon on the other end of the line. 'We always do our best, doll. You go above and beyond for all our residents.'

It was mid-afternoon and Grace was standing outside the herbalist on the street corner, the warm summer air mingling with the smells of fennel and thyme wafting from the shop's open door.

'I feel like Abigail's analysing everything I do. Maybe she's keeping an eye on me for Conrad. Am I being paranoid? I mean, I get it, she's going to resent me because she thinks I'm taking over. And I'm horrified by—'

She stopped herself.

'By what?'

Part of Grace wanted to blurt out everything she'd seen on the upper floor of the Janus building. But how could she put it into words? What she'd seen was so distressing that it had burrowed deep down into her, like a parasite.

She didn't want to burden Shannon with thoughts of Siberia. Plus, she'd signed the extra confidentiality agreements. If it got out that she had told someone, she'd be out of Janus in a heartbeat. There'd be no helping Remy then.

Instead, she said, 'So you don't think we messed up with Mikey, that it's our responsibility he's here?'

'Don't beat yourself up,' Shannon said. 'We did our best for him. Don't let that cat-eyed bitch knock your confidence. It's all bloody mind games. Abigail's pissed off because you're on her patch, so she's trying to wobble you. No wonder Myriam fucked off. Maybe she left because Aversion Therapy is so… horrible. Maybe she was just sick of seeing the worst things a person could see, day in, day out.'

'But that's the thing. Abigail seems to think that it was Myriam who messed up, didn't read the brain scans properly, and that's why Mikey reoffended. It wasn't because the tech was faulty, but because he wasn't assessed properly. And now the scans are missing.'

'Missing?'

'Disappeared. No record on the whole system.'

'Sounds like someone's hiding something,' Shannon said. 'Do you think Abigail's covering up her own mistakes by trying to blame us in Tier Two, suggesting we could have spotted something earlier? We're not bloody fortune tellers.'

'When offenders come to us, it's usually obvious what the problem is. We don't even scan for psychopathy.'

'There's no point. Our clients don't commit the sorts of crimes that psychopaths are known for,' Shannon interrupted. 'So why does she think Mikey is a psychopath?'

'Because he kept on offending, even after going through Aversion Therapy. It's ineffective with them because of the way their brains work – no empathy, no reaction to fear and a totally selfish obsession with getting what they want. Psychopaths don't stop, Shan. That's the problem.'

'But if, as you say, Aversion Therapy is so distressing, how can it not affect them?'

'Because psychopaths don't see those images as horrible and upsetting, but as *interesting*, so it's obvious that reels, even with them in the starring role of those little horror films, aren't going to cure them.'

'So they get dumped up in Tier Four because they can't be fixed?'

Grace didn't reply, imagining Remy lying in Siberia, the human version of a toxic waste dump, and her disgust and anger grew.

'I'll have another look at the data we've got on Mikey and send the file over to you, doll, but as far as I remember he was in good shape when he left us. He certainly wasn't psychopathic. Plus, we're always very thorough.' She sighed and said sadly, 'I liked Mikey.'

'Yeah, so did I. Thanks, Shan.'

'No problem. Speak soon.'

'Bye.'

Grace stood for a moment in the street watching the people go by, wondering how many of them were psychopaths. One per cent of society so the text books said – but they weren't all homicidal criminals. Many were highly functioning members of society.

Her phone rang in her hand. She brought it up to her ear. 'Don't tell me, Shan, you think I deserve to go out and drink lots with you on Friday night.'

'Grace?'

It was a man's voice, one she didn't immediately recognise. She looked down at the caller ID – a street-shell.

She put the phone back to her ear. 'Hello?'

'Gracie…'

The whole street around her seemed to come to a standstill like a paused reel, the sounds muted, the faces blurred. She knew this voice but it was deeper and tinged with fear, something she'd never heard there before. A surge of dammed-up memories was released.

'Remy…' she whispered.

'I'm in trouble. I need your help.'

An automated message declared credit was out.

'Remy… Remy?' She pulled the phone from her ear to see the display but there was no caller ID. She put it back to her ear. 'Remy?'

The action in the street started up again, a light rain began, and Grace was left standing on the pavement saying his name over and over again, but there was just silence on the other end of the line.

CHAPTER TWELVE

Mal couldn't deny that he was still on a high. Pride swelled in his chest remembering the previous night and the apprehension of Payback. The Embers Rapist had thought he'd got away with it. It had been a double whammy. Imagine if the lads from the station could have seen him. They hardly ever saw him, rather they looked through him, as if he wasn't there at all.

But he also knew there was a darker, more substantial reason why he felt satisfied. It was times like this when he could open that small, painful box inside his chest and examine his treasured memories – her beautiful smiling face, the way he felt happy and sad at the same time when she used to sing, the way she held his hand in the dark as though it wasn't her who was afraid, but she was trying to comfort him instead.

He'd met Layla at a gig when they were both fifteen.

His first love.

His only love, really. She was the first person to ever make him feel better than the shit on someone's shoe. The first person to have seen the good in him. The first person to tell him that she loved him.

Yes, there had been women since, if he got lucky, but nothing serious. No one came close to Layla. And they never would. She was enshrined in perfection, as those who died young often were.

He tried to keep it that way. That's why he kept the box so tightly shut, to keep the bad memories out, so that nothing could hurt her any more. She'd been perfect before those animals had got her, and brutally torn away her goodness, her beauty, her joy.

His beautiful Layla would never have left him, if they hadn't...

He couldn't bring himself to even think of the word.

They'd promised to be together for ever, but after what happened it wasn't possible. He understood that now, although he'd fought hard at the time. That's why he forgave her for leaving him.

Sometimes people just couldn't go on.

When the gang who'd destroyed her were convicted, they'd been sentenced to Aversion Therapy. This was in the early days, before gangs were sent to eco-labour. It hadn't seemed like much of a punishment to Mal, but Layla insisted on trying to put everything behind them and moving on.

A few months later, Mal and Layla had been having a quiet drink in an old-fashioned beer-and-crisps pub in the East End when one of the men walked in.

He didn't even recognise Layla, looked right through her as she froze in fear.

They watched him having a pint with his mates, laughing, getting on with his life.

It was then that Mal realised that justice hadn't been done.

A week later, Layla was dead.

The 'arrest' at the warehouse last night had been satisfying because, although he might never get justice for Layla, he could get justice for other victims. That was why he'd joined up, wasn't it? Because he knew how it felt.

While Sarge and Bizzy had been wrestling with Payback, Mal had been sent for the recce, as was his role. He'd been securing the scene and gone into one of the old offices.

That was where he'd found the terrified woman, curled up on the floor against a wall in the shadows, her hands over her head. He'd tried to comfort her, and when she finally uncovered her face, he recognised her from the rape report files.

She wasn't anything like his Layla.

Layla had been so small and yet so full of life. Colour and light seemed to surround her constantly – her hair, her clothes, the very air about her, were vibrant with vitality, until the end, when all her colour was drained, washed away in the murky water of the Thames.

The woman in the warehouse the previous night had been a pale ghost. But Mal had seen in her the darkness that had eaten away at Layla. When she looked up at him, her face morphed and all he could see were Layla's big, sorrowful eyes.

She'd been through enough. So he made a decision, one that Sarge would not have approved of.

He'd let her go.

He knew he wasn't following protocol when he'd hurried her out of one of the windows at the back of the warehouse. She didn't need to suffer any more than she already had. The other two hadn't even seen her. He didn't blame them, of course, they were so wrapped up in the action.

Once she disappeared, there was a brief moment when he felt something unfamiliar, as though he had purpose or was somehow redeemed.

But that was soon replaced with a surge of panic when he heard the others return. He rushed back in and told them all was secure. Then the usual routine commenced and he hadn't let himself think about the woman until he went to bed in the morning after the night shift. He'd hardly slept, still buzzing with the adrenaline, feeling as though he'd done something important, as though somehow part of Layla had escaped too. He closed his eyes and saw her face in his mind's eye, her heart-breaking smile, and it calmed him.

No, Layla would never have left him, would never have thrown herself from that bridge, if she'd been able to get the justice she deserved.

The door of the office flew open, disturbing his thoughts, and Sarge strode in, followed by Bizzy.

'Well done, lads. Good job last night,' Sarge began. 'But it's a new shift now and we have another crime to think about, another arrest to plan.'

It was always like this, as if Sarge didn't take the time to appreciate what they'd just done, to savour it. Always on to the next thing as though their achievements didn't mean anything.

Mal wondered if Sarge had just seen too much in his long career of dealing with evil and become desensitised to it. Mal sensed that Sarge had been changing recently, although he couldn't quite put his finger on it. Was it something to worry about? A tiny bud of fear bloomed – what if Sarge was getting ready to retire? For so long he'd been like a surrogate father to Mal, better than his own shit of a bio-dad. He looked to Sarge to teach him the ways of the job, to show him how to be in the world. And what would happen to him and Bizzy if Sarge left? Without him, without his skills, his attention to detail, his drive, they'd flounder.

It was funny how sometimes, due to circumstances, you could be at the fork of a road and it was merely the toss of a coin as to which way you went. After Layla, Mal had been left with an impotent anger. It had got him into trouble a few times, and he could have gone the wrong way altogether. But then Sarge found him. Now he knew exactly which road he was on.

Sarge stood in front of them, his shell projecting a video onto the flaky plaster of the wall behind him – the paused, blurred image of a tall red-headed man. 'This is our next target.' Mal felt a surge of energy, motivated by the determination in Sarge's expression as he spoke. 'We need to get this right because we're dealing with a right tricky bastard here. We can't let him get away with his crimes.'

Bizzy nodded as he listened.

'Our suspect is controlling and manipulative. He clearly chose this woman because she was vulnerable, as domestic violence perpetrators often do. He would have portrayed himself as charming and sensitive but then gone on to gaslight and gradually dominate his victim until she was totally under his power. We believe he killed her pet cat as a punishment for trying to contact her mother. This is classic coercive control.'

Mal marvelled at Sarge's insight into both the perpetrator and the victim. There was so much to learn from his mentor. He could tell Bizzy was awestruck too. How often had he taken the piss out of Mal for hero-worshipping Sarge, and yet there he was, lapping up every word.

'This video will give you an understanding of what we're dealing with.' Sarge turned to the projected image. The footage played out as the three men watched in silence. Mal tried to remain expressionless.

When it ended, Sarge continued. 'This guy thinks he's got away with it. We know differently, as do the vigilantes, and we need to get to him before they do.' Sarge's jaw tightened and Mal could hear his teeth gritting together. 'We can't let him walk away from this.'

Sarge stood silently for a moment, his shoulders dropped, head down. Mal and Bizzy shuffled uncomfortably until he looked up at them and said slowly, 'We are going to get this' – he lifted his fingers and made an O between finger and thumb to emphasise his last two words – 'spot on.'

It was the thing that Mal most admired in his boss, the desire to get everything just right. Sarge was like an artist almost, trying to replicate perfectly the crime that had been committed so that he could see as the criminal had seen, delve into their psychology to get to the heart of the matter.

'Bizzy, I want you to go over that report again to see anything that we might have missed. Mal, we're going to need more evidence.'

'Yes, Sarge,' they chimed together.

Sarge's shell pinged and he glanced at it briefly before looking back at them with a broad grin. 'We've located him, boys!'

The two men followed Sarge out of the office, ready to see real justice done.

CHAPTER THIRTEEN

The evening light was fading as Grace arrived home from work. Finding Dan was out, she took the opportunity to study the files on her work shell. She knew she had to prepare for the next day, but Remy's voice was still ringing in her ears. She still hadn't set a password. She made a mental note to do it later.

Sitting upright on the edge of the sofa, she typed his name with trembling hands. She needed to find out what had happened the first time he had been arrested.

Her breath caught in her throat when his police mugshot came up on the screen. He'd been sent to Tier Three for a violent assault the previous year – on a man called Alfie Bullock.

Grace immediately recognised the name but he was more commonly known as 'Bulldog'. He was a pimp and a drug-dealer, exactly the same type of man who had been responsible for Lottie's death – although not directly responsible – Remy's mother hadn't died by her pimp's own hands, but as a result of the drugs that he'd forced on her in an effort to make her vulnerable so he could control her.

From a quick scan of Bulldog's records, Grace could tell he manipulated women in the same way. Was that why Remy had attacked Bulldog?

Why the hell hadn't Remy claimed mitigation? If the court had known about his background, then he might have been sent to Tier Two to deal with his childhood trauma and the loss of his mother. But there was no record of his past in his case notes.

Remy's bio-results showed nothing out of the ordinary: no high levels of testosterone, no PTSD, no drugs, prescribed or otherwise. His chemicals were balanced, no neurological damage, so there was nothing they could do at Tier Two to help, heal or rehabilitate.

More recently, it appeared that he'd viciously attacked a drug dealer in a transaction gone wrong. The dealer had died. Remy had already been through Tier Three and so was heading for Tier Four.

He'd made a run for it.

It didn't make sense to Grace. Why would Remy deal in drugs, something that had killed both their mothers, something that they both detested? Yes, street fighting and occasional stealing had been part of his repertoire, but never drugs.

But Grace knew herself how much could change in fifteen years.

She scrolled down and saw Remy's brain scan that had been done during his treatment at Tier Three.

It wasn't a clear image, but certain areas were lit up that suggested psychopathy.

She stared at it for some moments, a cloud of shock and denial crossing her mind.

Remy – a psychopath?

She was getting tired, and she needed to prepare for the next day, so she turned her attention to the case of Robyn Cooper.

Stealing foetuses.

Whatever she did, Grace had to hold it together tomorrow in the clinic. She didn't want to be under Abigail's scrutiny any more than she already was. She couldn't afford to let her complex feelings about babies be triggered out in the open. It was too personal, too painful. She'd worked very hard to protect herself, building veneer upon veneer of shielding – education, money, marriage – all the things that would bury her past deeper with each layer.

Robyn Cooper wanted a child but couldn't keep it.

It was too close to the bone for Grace.

In the spring after she and Dan had married, she'd suspected she was pregnant. Used to being independent for so long, she'd said nothing to Dan and gone to have her scans alone, telling herself it was so she could present Dan with the good news in the knowledge that all was well.

But the genetic screening had told a different story.

Her baby boy carried two key genes which combined could lead to a violent and aggressive nature. A very high chance the doctor told her. After tests, she found out the genes were from her side. She hadn't known her father. Had he been violent? Her mother had never spoken of him and when she'd asked Lottie it had been a dead end.

Grace had seen the effects of this genetic cocktail in her work and in her own life – what happened to people who couldn't control their violent instincts. She'd seen them giving and taking beatings, controlling girls on the streets, thriving in organised crime, dying in street fights.

She knew that genes could lie dormant. The life she could give a child would be very different to the life she'd grown up in. But she also knew that genes could be triggered by events that would be beyond her control; random, unexpected events, which might have led to her boy hurting someone – or worse, killing someone – and ending up in the Tier System. The gun loaded the genes, but the environment pulled the trigger.

Like Remy.

The moment she'd found out, all her experiences and anxieties crowded her like journalists outside a courtroom, and she knew she couldn't face the what-ifs.

The doctor's advice merely reflected the attitude of society: get rid of violence before it becomes a problem. So many women in her position did the same, for the benefit of all, they were assured.

Out of fear, and under pressure, Grace had terminated the pregnancy, choosing to protect her son by never letting him live, curing violence in society with violence in the womb.

It had broken her heart and she'd pushed it deep down with all her other sorrows.

Now, she was afraid she'd never escape the hand her genes had dealt her. Yes, she knew they'd made leaps and bounds in genetic treatments, but they still struggled with certain problems. There would be risks, and personal cost, and the probability of losing more children.

She couldn't face it. She lied to Dan about not being able to get pregnant, shut down her desire for a child and paid the price in guilt and loss.

Just as this thought crossed her mind, Dan came in.

Grace grabbed one of the mustard yellow cushions from the sofa and clasped it to her chest.

'I'm glad you're still up.' He leaned over and kissed her on the forehead before flopping onto the sofa next to her. 'Any info about Kilgannon?'

'I've spent this evening going through his files.' That was partially true. She held out the shell as though she was holding a holy book and about to swear an oath. 'I can't find anything unusual about the treatment they gave him at Tier Three. It's all there. The right amount of psychotropics, the visual-audio therapy, the emotisonics, the usual drugs in the usual doses, although I'm looking into those in more detail as there's some I'm not familiar with. According to the records, everything was in place for a successful treatment.'

He looked disappointed. 'So what went wrong?'

'Abigail seems to think Myriam messed up, possibly misread a brain scan. Maybe Mikey was an incurable after all.'

'That doesn't explain the post office attackers reoffending. Unless Myriam misread those scans too. Are you sure she knew what she was doing?'

'She seemed really competent. Did you find anything on the Payback attack?' Had Abigail said anything to Conrad after she heard Grace talk to Dan on the phone in the bathroom? If she had, he hadn't pulled her up on it.

Dan became animated again. 'You were right. One of my police informants told me the gang had a guy tied up in one of the old warehouses on Penhaligon Road.'

After the day she'd had, Grace wasn't sure she wanted to hear this.

'Did the police get to him in time?'

Dan shook his head. 'Castrated, bled out, like the other victims.'

'Oh my God.' She sat up straight.

'Get this – it was a married couple who did it. The police think the wife was attacked years ago and that's how they got into the gang.'

'A married couple? How do you know? Have they been caught already?'

Dan nodded. 'They found her phone at the scene.'

'Stupid mistake, to leave something like that behind,' Grace said.

'I thought the same.'

'Do you know if they'd already been treated at Tier Three?'

'Police say there's no record of it. It's the leading story on the NewsFlex website.' His eyes were shining.

'That's so sad. That poor woman. I mean, I don't agree with what she did, obviously, but to have been raped and then do something like that, and then to be sent to Tier Four.'

'They're not going to Tier Four.'

She snapped her head round to look at him. 'But they've been knowingly part of a serial crime. Offenders who get involved with serial crime are automatically sent to Tier Four.'

'They were found dead this morning in their car, down by the river. Suicide pact. Rumour has it Payback hack into police websites and communications. Maybe they knew the police were onto them.'

It all seemed so fast, so over and done with.

'And they killed themselves rather than going to Tier Four,' Grace said, more to herself than Dan.

'Yeah, I don't get that one either. I can't imagine Tier Four is so bad that it's worth killing yourself over. Although if you listen to the conspiracy theories…'

If she didn't do something, Remy would be in one of those white beds, a place where death seemed preferential. Hearing his voice on the phone earlier had shaken her, threatening to fracture the layer of ice beneath which she kept her old life hidden. For a split second, she felt that the whole of her history – Remy, Lottie, the street life – was going to spill out and she would tell Dan everything, her history transparent.

But she couldn't tell him about Remy and her past. It would be too strange to bring it all up now. He would know she'd deliberately hidden it from him. There would be too many questions.

And she couldn't even tell him about her present – the new confidentiality agreement Conrad had made her sign, and the fact she would lose her job loomed. But worse still, if she told Dan about Tier Four and the horror of what she'd seen, then it would be all over NewsFlex, and then what would happen to Janus? To all the good work done there at Tier One and Two?

No, the only way she could help Remy, if she could help him at all, was to keep all that she'd seen and heard and felt in Siberia to herself – bide her time until Remy was found and brought to Janus and she could somehow intervene before he was put into biostasis.

Was it possible? Could she get to him first, help him somehow?

'Are you okay?' Dan asked, concern knitting his brow.

'Yeah, yeah, fine.'

Dan began to chat about one of his leads, but the words weren't going into her brain.

Instead Grace's mind was swamped with the images and sights from Siberia, the sexless, corpse-like bodies, the tubes and screens and the faint antiseptic smell. A permanent chemically induced sleep with their own horror stories being pumped into their brains 24/7. Maybe the death penalty was better than what they were going through. At least if they were dead they'd get some peace.

She remembered Mikey Kilgannon's lips moving as he lay in cerebral torment, his body as tranquil as at a chapel of rest.

The emotion suddenly clawed at her and she gave an involuntary sob.

Dan stopped talking and put his hand on her arm. 'Look, I know something's not right. What's going on?'

She coughed and shook her head. 'I'm fine, I just… I've had a tough day. Conrad's on my case. I'm sad about Mikey, just seeing him lying there with the others…'

Shit. It had just slipped out.

He homed in on her now.

'What, you saw Kilgannon? But he's in Tier Four! What the hell were you doing there? It's not safe… all those violent and homicidal criminals.'

How was she going to get out of this now? He would hound her until he had the truth. He suddenly stopped talking as if to give himself a moment to rewind what she'd said.

'Hold on a minute. What do you mean, *lying* there with the others?'

'Oh, just leave it, Dan. I don't want to talk about it.'

'What are you saying? We've all seen the footage,' he insisted. 'The inmates exercising in the yard, tutors in the library, pottery classes, for goodness' sake…'

For a moment she wavered between telling him everything and telling him nothing.

'I didn't mean that – it was just a slip of the tongue.' But she could tell from his expression that he didn't believe her.

'You'd tell me, Grace, wouldn't you?'

Would she?

'There were rumours that something weird was going on, but I wasn't sure if they were coming from people who wanted to bring the Tier System into disrepute. It's just like any other secure prison, isn't it?' he asked, his eyes narrowed.

Her thoughts turned to the child that should have been, how maybe, at some point in the future, he might have ended up at Tier Four. And Remy – what might happen if word got out about Siberia? Those who were looking for tougher punishments might approve but the human rights crowd would be outraged.

'Yeah, of course, just like any other secure prison.' She could hear the weariness in her own voice.

Dan lay back on the sofa, staring at the ceiling, his mouth slightly open – in full journalist mode.

He sat up suddenly and turned to her. 'If there's anything going on, Grace, the public needs to know.'

'There's nothing to tell.'

'I know when you're holding back.'

'Do you?' she said offhandedly.

'Look, just tell me. You said you were going to leave work anyway. This is as good a time as any.'

'Dan, just leave it!' she snapped. 'I've signed confidentiality forms. I don't want to lose my job. I'll walk away when I'm ready. I'm not going to be a sacrificial lamb for your career.'

'Jesus, Grace!' Dan sat upright and ran his fingers through his hair. 'You think you're better than me because you're a bloody psychiatrist and I'm just some hack. My career is important too, whatever you think.'

'What the hell? Where's this coming from?'

This seemed to enrage him further. 'We agreed you're going to leave work anyway to have a baby, so what's the problem? My job is just as important as yours.'

She stood up and hurled the cushion back onto the sofa.

'You'd be happy for me to lose my job so you look good, wouldn't you?' Dan and his bloody ego. 'Selfish bastard.'

Dan laughed. 'Oh, I'm the selfish one?'

She walked out, ignoring his protests, and headed up the stairs.

Once in the bedroom, she sat on the edge of the bed for some time contemplating the road ahead of her. If she ignored Dan's demands, would it cause a small tremor in their foundations, or a greater quake which would throw their relationship off the rails?

If she told him, it would be the highpoint of his career.

If she kept her mouth shut she might have some time and space to help Remy.

Or she could tell Dan everything, let him have his glory, lose her job, and let Remy undergo biostasis.

There was a choice to be made – Dan or Remy?

CHAPTER FOURTEEN

Noah Begbroke stared at the digital menu above the bar for some time before he finally made his choice. At the Altered Consciousness Bar, or AltCon as the pink retro neon sign outside proudly displayed, there were so many concoctions to choose from. The spectrum ran from mellow to confident through to ecstatic, with various grades in between. There was even some kind of serotonin boost you could take home to replenish you the morning after.

He ordered Chilled & Confident mixed with grapefruit and mandarin juice. He'd decided his next drink would be the same but flavoured with aniseed and blackcurrant instead. It didn't have to be fruit juice, of course. Many people drank the legal substances mixed with fruit teas, carbonated drinks, or even just water.

The bartender placed the glass down with a smile. The place was packed, the music low and soothing, the lights soft and welcoming. Hung around the walls were huge canvases of what Begbroke supposed were artists' interpretations of different moods. His favourite was one of calm blues and purples in a swirling pattern. He couldn't bring himself to look at the orange and red one. Everyone in there seemed to be smiling. It was exactly what he needed. He took a long drink and after a few minutes could already feel the AltCon doing its magic.

There had been great debate in the press about making alcohol legal again, but no one wanted to go back to his parents' generation of hangovers and street fights. The government certainly didn't want the huge costs of healthcare and crime it caused. There was still a call for it among older people in hidden corners of the city. Alcohol, apart from being toxic and addictive, had a roulette wheel of moods, but Begbroke much preferred to be able to choose how he felt and not suffer for it the next day.

He'd chosen a drink to take the edge of the vulnerability that had plagued him ever since the Aversion Therapy, an unfamiliar emotion for him. He turned his back to the bar and leaned against it, waiting for the effects to kick in further. When it did, it was powerful and welcome.

Maybe his grandma had been right and penance was good for the soul.

He didn't recognise the man that he'd been when he'd launched that bottle of burning fuel through Corrina's window. Whatever had motivated him was completely gone. He supposed it had been anger, jealousy, and if he admitted it… control. There was still work to be done on the causes of that behaviour. He quite looked forward to the group therapy with other men in his position, all trying to find a new way of being. To see there were others like him made him feel less of a monster.

Lost in his thoughts, he was surprised when the woman approached him. She was slim and attractive, wearing a pale blue dress. He usually went for brunettes, but tonight he wasn't bothered. He recognised her straight away, but this was very different to the last time they'd met. He was a different man now.

'Do you want to buy me a drink?' she asked, brushing her hair back from her face.

He paused, uncertain. Another new emotion. She ran her fingers over the Tier Three tattoo on his wrist. It was still raw and stung under her touch.

'I'm surprised you're okay with that. Chatting up an ex-con.'

The woman smiled and relief washed over him. Maybe his post-Tier life was going to be okay after all.

He called the bartender over and pointed at the woman.

'I'll have Bold & Sassy with orange and passionfruit, please,' she said. Before treatment he would never have gone for a woman who'd approached him, a brazen, assertive type. When he'd met her previously he'd considered her attractive enough, but now she really appealed to him. Was that another effect of his treatment?

'How was it?' she asked.

He shrugged. 'You know.'

'Better than going to one of those eco-rigs.'

'My brother Lucas is on the rigs,' he said.

She nodded solemnly and leaned against the bar, glass in hand.

'Didn't want anyone messing with his mind,' he said. Worried that it would affect his virility. Kept his machismo intact and now he's hand-peeling shrink-wrapped plastic and fishing for bottles in the North Sea for the next twenty years.'

'Fair play to him.' She raised her eyebrows. 'But you're the one with your freedom.'

'I didn't think you'd want anything to do with me after… you know.' He looked down at his tattoo again.

'Most women like to change men. The hard work's already been done for me,' she said and smiled again.

Pointing over to a small table that had just become vacant, she said, 'Why don't you go and get those seats for us and I'll bring over more drinks. You've nearly finished yours already.'

An hour later, Begbroke felt as though a whole new life had begun. He was free, a changed man, having a great conversation with a gorgeous woman. He didn't even have to hide what he'd been through. Who would have thought after the last few months that things could turn around so quickly?

His head was swimming a little, but he could feel positivity flowing through him and he didn't know or care if it was the drinks or just his circumstances. There was clearly physical chemistry, so it was no surprise when she cocked her head to one side and said, 'Do you want to come back to mine?'

This was what he needed, to get back into his stride, to feel like a man again. Tonight, he would draw a line under his old life. He would begin again, his blue tattoo a reminder of what he'd left behind and what his new post-therapy life could offer him – the two-faced god Janus looking both to the past and to the future.

They took a cab back to hers. The lights of the city swum past in a haze as they chatted and laughed flirtatiously. Begbroke couldn't ever remember AltCon having ever had such a good effect on him. He was lightheaded and more than a little woozy. Twenty minutes later, they pulled up at the house.

She fumbled with the key in the lock and he wondered if her hands were trembling because she was as excited as he was. Once in the kitchen, she took two bottles out of the fridge, pressed one into his hand and said, 'Don't drink it yet. Wait until we're upstairs. Give me two minutes and then come up. Bedroom at the back.'

He watched her as she left the room, admiring her figure wrapped tightly in the soft blue material.

A few moments later, he moved clumsily up the stairs, feeling giddy and inebriated. His legs felt weak, he could hear his blood rushing in his ears. Holding the bottle in one hand, he reached out to push the bedroom door open with the other. His vision was slightly blurred now and he misjudged the distance, pawing at the air before finally making contact with the wood of the door.

She was already lying in bed, the covers right over her head. The blue dress was on the floor. Was this part of the fun? He pulled the cover back.

The woman was naked and still. Maybe she'd overdone it with the drink? She'd bought quite a few rounds. Disappointment reared. Maybe they'd be able to go out another night. Her hair looked a bit darker in the shadows.

He looked closer. This wasn't the woman he had met in the bar.

He threw the cover over her again, his head fuzzy and confused. He went to take a swig from the bottle he was holding. But when he brought it close to his face he smelled something pungent, familiar, undrinkable.

Still inebriated from the AltCon, he leaned over the woman in the bed and prodded her clumsily. There was no response.

Something sinister was going on here and he needed to get out fast.

He stumbled towards the door to make his exit, but a police officer appeared from nowhere and blocked the way, pointing a semi-automatic at his chest. He was older than Begbroke, with silver hair and pale eyes. Behind him was a tall, dark-haired officer, leaning casually against the doorframe, arms folded.

'We've been keeping an eye on you, Begbroke,' the pale-eyed officer said. 'Ever since you left Janus. And now we've had a call from a woman who said you threatened to kill her.'

'No… no…' Begbroke mumbled.

The woman who had brought him here had disappeared. He was beginning to doubt it was her house.

'She told us you threatened to cremate her in her bed,' the officer went on, nodding towards the prone woman.

'I wouldn't…' Begbroke breathed, starting to feel nauseous, uncertain if his words were audible. 'I've changed… I've *been* changed.'

The officer leaning against the door unfolded his arms, reached out and took the bottle from Begbroke's hand. 'I'll take that.' He held it carefully at the top with gloved hands and sniffed it, waved it under his colleague's nose. 'Smells flammable to me.'

Begbroke's whole body began to shake, his heart felt as though it was beating in his head, a slow rhythmic toll. 'It's just a bottle of AltCon.'

The woman in the bed wasn't the woman who'd brought him here. He looked back at her lying flat out in the bed. Was she even alive? Suddenly she turned her head and sighed deeply. Her eyes rolled in her head. Had she taken something? He could see her face now and recognition slowly burrowed though his dazed state. Lexi! This was the woman he'd dated before Corrina. What was she doing here? Was this her new place? What the hell was going on?

Begbroke turned back to see the dark-haired copper now standing closer to him, still holding the bottle, which now had a rag inserted into the neck. The man pulled a lighter from his pocket with his gloved hand and lit the rag, slowly returning the lighter to his pocket as he waited for the flames to get going.

'No... no!' Begbroke cried, shaking his head. His body felt beyond his control, as though his brain was sending the messages but they just weren't reaching his muscles. He lurched forward, but the officer threw the bottle onto the bed then grabbed hold of Begbroke, his fingertips biting into the flesh of Begbroke's arms.

The bottle bounced twice on top of the soft covers before the burning fuel came leaking out and soon there was a blanket of dancing flames covering the woman. She opened her eyes and started to wail, but appeared unable to move. The officer pushed Begbroke further into the bedroom and stepped back behind the other man who still had the gun trained on him.

Begbroke cowered and whimpered. The Aversion Therapy had done its job: his new-found fear of fire and whatever the other woman had put in his drink – *where is she?* – rendered him unable to run.

'Help me,' he cried, holding out his shaking hands, but the officers stood still and watched as the flames grew in intensity.

'Help her...' he whispered.

He looked back to Lexi, who was staring at him, terrified but motionless as the flames finally reached her.

'What did you give her?' he slurred and tried, in his fug, to reach out, but then pulled back as the flames suddenly engulfed her.

Soon, there was a revolting smell of melting hair and crisping skin which made him gag. The dark-haired officer suddenly dealt him a brutal punch to the temple and Begbroke fell across the bed, momentarily knocked out. The flames licked at him before gathering strength.

Mal ambled up the stairs and entered the bedroom, arm shielding his face against the rapidly growing heat.

'You've planted the bottle, Bizzy?' Mal asked. 'I mean, they'll know it's him, but the more evidence the better.'

'I know, I know!' Bizzy said, irritated. 'It fell off the bed, not broken, should be okay.'

'Shall we go, Sarge?' asked Mal.

'Just wait, a few minutes more. Won't be good if either of them survives.'

'Them?' asked Mal. 'I thought she'd left already?'

'I mean the other woman,' Bizzy said.

'There's a fine line, lads, in waiting until we know for sure the fire has caught and waiting until the firefighters turn up,' Sarge said. 'And we definitely don't want to be here when the real police arrive, do we?'

He grinned and Bizzy laughed.

Begbroke regained consciousness, his face close to Lexi's charred and blistered one, just in time to feel the flames swallow him up.

'I hope his screaming doesn't wake the neighbours,' Sarge tutted.

Mal looked at the bodies on the bed, but not for long as the heat hurt his eyes. For a split second he felt something he hadn't felt before while he'd been with Diros – the name Sarge had given their gang: a flicker of doubt. More than a flicker. This should have been about Begbroke's crime and arson – no one else should have been involved.

The trio stood watching until they could no longer take the temperature, and Sarge said, 'Right, that'll do. Some busybody neighbour will be phoning the emergency services now. Time to go, boys.'

And for the second time that week, Noah Begbroke experienced what it was like to burn.

But this time, it was for real.

CHAPTER FIFTEEN

The Tube train pulled grudgingly to a halt at a station. Grace held tightly onto a pole in the already packed carriage, dreading the crowd of travellers ready to board. Dan had insisted he needed the car for his investigations that day. He didn't usually take the car. Was this his petty way of punishing her for withholding information? Did he really think she felt superior to him because of her job? No wonder he would be happy for her to give up work and stay at home as a child-rearer. Resentment curdled inside her.

There was a moment of stillness before the doors opened and people began squashing on. She gripped the metal tighter, her eyes lazily sweeping the faces on the other side of the glass, a blur of flesh-toned ovals, until they rested on one that she recognised.

Remy.

His eyes bored into her and she began to fight her way towards the door, struggling against the hot tide of bodies. He stood still on the other side of the glass, staring back at her, arms by his sides, making no effort to board the train.

She squeezed past the other passengers who were blocking her way, but when she could see the window again, she struggled to locate him in the crowd. She found herself on the platform just as the train doors shut behind her.

Remy was nowhere to be seen.

Had it really been him?

Her head spun with questions as she searched the faces of the people remaining on the platform. She frantically scanned the windows to see if he'd boarded the carriage. The train lurched forward and pulled out of the station.

Remy had disappeared.

–

The clinic was lit in hues of blue and pink, soft lullaby music playing through the speaker system. Knowing what was to come, Grace's stomach tightened.

'Ah, you're here,' Abigail said cheerfully, her eyes lit by the screen at the workstation.

'Sorry, I missed the train.' Grace put her coat and bag in the small storeroom at the back of the clinic and then composed herself, building up her mental armour, ready to face the punishment reel of Robyn Cooper, the baby stealer.

'I'm just checking the drugs that Myriam prescribed,' Abigail told her as she approached the workstation. 'It'll be you prescribing the next time, so you may want to see this.' Grace moved closer to the screen. 'They're pretty standard. We use the same types of drug in most of the procedures. I've double-checked dosage against weight and made sure they're ready to be given – either by nasal spray or intravenously.'

Grace had found herself wondering about the other psychiatrist while she'd read over the preliminary reports written prior to Myriam's departure. The two had met a few times at in-house training and the odd social, and, although pleasant, Myriam had seemed self-contained. She had the habit, which Grace used often in her own professional life, of being able to remain silent, as if to provoke the other into filling in the silence, maybe give something away. Grace had liked her. She'd appeared to be more than competent. Had Myriam been scapegoated for something inherently wrong with the treatment? Maybe today would give her some clues as to what was going on.

'Which drugs are we using?'

Abigail picked up a spray from a dish on the workstation. 'As you know, this is a relaxant. We have a few extra ready here just in case the offender gets antsy, but we also administer before treatment begins so the offender will slow down and absorb what's going on. Cooper's already been given a psychotropic, which works really well with the hypnotherapy and will make her more open to believing the reel is actually happening to her, but we have some more here to top her up.'

'Is Robyn in hypnotherapy now?'

'Yes, she's already had a few sessions but she'll be brought straight to us in a hypno-state.'

'And what about this one?' Grace picked up a small glass vial.

'That stimulates parts of the brain that make the treatment highly effective.'

'Which parts of the brain?'

Abigail paused. 'I don't really know. *Above my capabilities*,' she quoted Conrad with more than a hint of spite. 'I just know the name and the dose. I don't know how it works exactly, but I do know it's fast acting, so we do that one last, mid-treatment.'

'You didn't ask Myriam?'

Abigail shrugged. 'All the information's here on the screen.'

Grace moved closer and read on the screen 'TIMORAD-MINISTREN'.

'We call it Timorax,' said Abigail.

Grace had never heard of it. Bloody Conrad! Typical of him to arrogantly use an experimental drug, quackery, to make a name for himself. Her instinct told her that this was a more likely scenario for the treatment failing than Myriam messing up. Had Conrad sacked her to cover his own back?

She was about to collect her shell from the storeroom to research the drug, but the clinic door opened and George gently guided Robyn in. She moved slowly, her eyes unfocused, carrying a baby doll wrapped in a pink blanket which trailed on the floor.

Grace was struck by how ordinary she looked – pale and plump, no trace of the villainous caricature that her crime might conjure. She was reminded instead of the many women who passed through her care at Tier Two – careworn, unfortunate, and lacking the sort of support that might have prevented her from getting into the situation she was in.

George helped Robyn into the clinic chair, strapping her in like a father might secure a child in a buggy, and stood back.

Abigail turned on the emotisonics and increased the volume of the lullaby music. She administered the relaxant with two brief sprays, one in each of the nostrils, which seemed to simultaneously startle and amuse Robyn. Once George was satisfied that Robyn was under control, he nodded sadly at Grace and left.

'What?' Robyn said, once Abigail had inserted a cannula to her hand and begun to administer a syringe of colourless fluid. 'What?' she repeated, her voice thick.

'Don't worry,' Abigail said, in a surprisingly kind tone. 'These are the nano-scanners, Robyn. We'll inject them and use that machine to get them into the right place in your brain. They'll pass out of your body when we're done. You won't even notice them.'

Robyn's gaze slid from the needle to the long metallic arm of the powerful magnet which Abigail extended from its moorings on the wall behind the clinic chair and positioned so that it was touching Robyn's skull. It reminded Grace of the X-ray machine at the dentist's when she was a child.

'Hurt?' asked Robyn, heavy-eyed. She clutched the baby doll protectively.

'No, no, you won't feel them,' Abigail reassured her. 'They send images back to our screen so we can see what's going on inside your brain.'

Robyn looked nonplussed.

Abigail checked Robyn's stats on the screen. Grace's breathing became increasingly laboured as she waited for the therapy to begin.

Had the other foetuses been returned or sold on? How would the parents feel – having their children stolen and out there in the world somewhere, children they would never be able to find.

'Mummy loves you… Mummy loves you…' Robyn whispered to the doll's expressionless face.

Finally, the punishment reel began to play – sounds and images of a labour ward, women crying in pain, babies wailing.

Grace's heart went out to Robyn. *The government sees this as a crime of property. The rich can make their perfect babies, but the rest of us go without or have to face our 'responsibility'.* She'd seen the records from Tier Two. Robyn had been screened there to see if there were any mitigating circumstances, but there were no mental health problems nor any hormonal imbalances that might make her do these things, just a desire to have a baby of her own to love.

There was no cure for that.

Dan came to mind and guilt pricked her conscience.

She couldn't bear to watch the wall-screen. Instead, she turned to the three screens of the main computer and brought up the real-time brain scans sent by the nano-scanners. She could see areas of the brain lit up by the psychotropic drugs, as she'd expected. What would happen when the Timorax was put into the mix?

But moments after Abigail squeezed the syringe adding the unfamiliar drug via the cannula, changes began to show on Robyn's brain and bio-scans – in the amygdala, then the hypo-thalamus. Robyn's heart rate jumped up, adrenaline and cortisol were released. Her breathing quickened and her hippocampus and frontal lobes blazed on the screen.

The moment she began screaming and thrashing against her restraints in the chair, Grace recognised what was going on.

Abigail had just injected Robyn with synthetic fear.

–

'What the hell is wrong with you, Mal? You were happy when we got the Embers bastard, but now you're moping about like a kid whose sweets have been nicked.'

Bizzy punched him on his upper arm and then threw himself down into one of the chairs in the office, leaned back and put his feet on the desk in front of him.

'She was innocent. I didn't think we were going to kill her,' Mal said, tapping away at his shell pretending to look for information on their next job. 'Begbroke didn't kill his victim.'

'He might as well have done. She's a real mess. Anyway, where's your conscience suddenly come from? The Embers Rapist didn't kill his victims either. You didn't moan about that. In fact, you seemed quite enthusiastic about that fucker's demise.'

'That's different,' Mal mumbled.

'How?' Bizzy threw his hands open. 'How is that different?'

Mal said nothing. He wasn't going to tell Bizzy about Layla. *Don't cast your pearls before swine* he remembered a street preacher shouting when he was living rough. Now he knew what it meant. God knows what he would do to Bizzy if he ridiculed her precious memory. Probably kill him, and what would happen to the gang then?

'I need to get on with this before Sarge gets back.' Mal indicated his shell.

'You chickenshit!' Bizzy sneered. 'You're scared, aren't you? Afraid of Tier Four if they catch us, eh? Wait till the boss hears this. He won't like it!'

It was true, Sarge didn't like people questioning his methods. And he often said there was nothing worse than a coward. *Cowards let the team down.*

Am I a coward? Mal wondered. His father would have thought so.

'He might even chuck you out of the gang if he finds out. And you know what that means.'

Mal did know.

His mind switched immediately to another lad who had once been part of the gang, Josh.

He watched as Bizzy drew a finger across his throat.

'Fuck off, Biz.'

'You fuck off! You've always got your nose up his arse, trying to impress him. What's he going to think of you now, eh? He'll see you for what you are, a chickenshit who cleans a police station for a living!'

Mal felt his hackles rise. 'Yeah, a cleaner who's got a key for the forensics department. You'd be lost without me. Where else would you get all the evidence to pin these crimes on the original offenders?'

Bizzy just grinned, incensing Mal further.

'You wouldn't have any evidence!' Mal spat. 'Who would have known that the police had an AltCon bottle with Begbroke's fingerprints on, one that we replicated? Who could have got hold of Kilgannon's baseball bat, DNA of the other jobs, all the other stuff? This gang needs me.'

'Needs you!' snorted Bizzy.

'At least I don't believe I'm a real copper, like you do. Anyway, what the fuck do you do? Dick about on a computer and play dress-up bobby!'

But Bizzy's comments had hit the mark. *Sarge must have seen something in me, something more than just the fact that I work as a cleaner in the police headquarters, surely?*

'Begbroke had to go, Mal. And as for the woman, she was just collateral. Imagine if either of them had survived and told the police about our little gang. You'd better get your head straight or I'll have to let the boss know you're having doubts.'

'Don't tell him, Biz.' Mal cringed as he heard himself say it.

'Don't tell me what?'

Andrew Sargeant, or 'Sarge' as he was nicknamed, strutted into the room. He was an imposing figure, broad-shouldered and muscular, with a buzz cut and a scar on one arm – both visible reminders of his time in the forces. He stood straight-backed with his hands at his sides.

Bizzy immediately took his feet off the desk and stood. 'Mal here's having a flash of conscience.'

Mal froze under Sarge's stare.

'You don't have the luxury of a conscience,' Sarge said calmly. 'We've got a job to do, lads. There's no room for second thoughts.'

'I told him that, Sarge.'

'Shut up, Biz,' Sarge barked. 'Mal?' His pale blue eyes settled on Mal.

'It's all good, boss. A misunderstanding, that's all,' Mal said.

'Glad to hear it. Nothing, and I mean nothing, is going to spoil our mission.'

Diros – a name meaning terrifying, but also enlightened. Even the name gave Mal a sense of vocation. Whatever his doubts, Mal needed this troop. It had saved his life – given him direction after he'd lost perspective when Layla had died. Given him a way to cope with his anger and frustration. There was no way he was going to end up back on the streets with the filthy losers.

'Just remember our mission,' Sarge said. 'If the justice system can't deliver proper punishment, then it's up to people like us to do it. At ease.'

Bizzy sat down again and Mal perched on the edge of the desk, his shell still in his hand.

'When I came back from Africa, damaged but not broken' – he indicated his arm – 'I found my purpose in continuing to fight the enemy, but the enemy had changed. We can't allow these criminals to get away with a flash-in-the-pan bullshit treatment as punishment. It's just not acceptable.'

'Mal here doesn't like people dying,' Bizzy said.

'I just thought,' stammered Mal, 'that we were trying to show the flaws of the system.'

'Every good cause needs sacrifices, son.' Sarge slapped Mal on the back and relief flooded his body. 'Just remember, this is our mission – part of the bigger plan. We're going to destroy

Janus so that criminals get proper punishment and victims get true justice. And the sacrifices,' he turned and pointed to Mal as if to emphasis what he had said previously, 'the things we do in a good cause, however… difficult… are all leading to this mission being successful. Things are going our way, boys. The plan is unfolding.

'However, we've got another problem – a new psych at Tier Three, some busybody who might put an end to our mission if we don't deal with her. She's married to a journalist who's already put an article on the web about our work at the cotton warehouse.' He took Mal's shell from his hands and moments later showed them an image of Grace. 'It's only a matter of time before the pair of them put two and two together.' He let that hang in the air for a moment. 'Bizzy, I need you to get the lowdown on this journo. Get as much information as you can.'

'Yes, Sarge,' Bizzy said. He sat at the desk, picked up another shell and got to work immediately.

'Mal, I want you on obs. Follow this Gunnarsson woman, at work, at home, at the weekend. See where she goes, what she's up to. If it gets tricky then we'll know where to find her.'

'Yes, Sarge.'

'What's her first name again?' Sarge asked Bizzy, who tapped his shell.

'Grace, Sarge.'

'Grace,' Sarge repeated.

As Mal went to open the office door, Sarge called his name quietly.

Mal's fingers shook as he held the doorknob. He turned around, hands by his sides again.

'If you question me again, you know what will happen, don't you?'

CHAPTER SIXTEEN

'Have you any idea how Aversion Therapy might affect someone, particularly someone who is as vulnerable as Robyn Cooper?' asked Grace angrily.

She stood, hands on hips, in front of Conrad's desk. She'd managed to stay in the clinic until the treatment had concluded, but only for Robyn's sake.

'Lower your voice,' Conrad said with a mix of curiosity and disdain. 'There's been no evidence of any psychiatric fallout after Aversion Therapy. None whatsoever.'

'No, you probably covered that up too… that was if you even did the follow-up appointments. But apparently the money for that was diverted to some experimental drugs.'

He didn't respond.

'And what about the emotional effects? They are human beings, Conrad, you can't just—'

'We're not here to pander to people's emotions, Grace.'

'It's not ethical!' she snapped back.

'The government seems to think the treatment is ethical enough,' he said calmly, reaching over to the carafe on his desk and pouring himself some water.

'The whole government or just your crony in the Department of Justice?' She raised her eyebrows.

He briefly stopped mid-pour.

'If the government thinks the treatment is ethical, as you claim, then why is there so much secrecy about it? I mean, how can *synthetic fear* be an ethical treatment?'

He fell silent for a moment, drinking his water but keeping his eyes fixed on her. She could hear him swallowing.

'Don't treat me like an idiot, Conrad. What, you didn't think I'd figure it out?'

Finally, he put the glass down. 'I don't know what you mean. Maybe Myriam came up with—'

'No!' She slapped his glass desktop with her palms. 'The buck stops with you. Don't blame Myriam for this.' She paused. 'Is that why she left?'

'I don't know why she left,' he said, his voice a little too high-pitched. 'She emailed an immediate resignation and I haven't seen or heard from her since.'

'You should have told me. If I'm going to work in this clinic then I need to know the whole story. Instead I have to find out what you're doing from interpreting brain scans and prescriptions.' She took a deep breath. 'Have you even looked at these offenders post-treatment? The likelihood of depression, breakdowns, suicide attempts? Christ, Conrad!'

'This treatment is what they deserve.' He stood up now. 'It's highly effective and it gets the job done.'

'And that's your attitude, is it? It's effective, so it doesn't matter if you're actually *torturing* people, because that's what this is…'

'Torturing,' he said with a sneer.

'Is this drug even licensed? Where the hell did it come from?'

'That doesn't matter.' He swirled the water around his glass as though it was single malt and stared into it as he said, 'If you're going to keep working with us, then you need to get on board.'

She could still feel Abigail's patronising arm rub as George had wheeled Robyn Cooper out of the clinic, screaming for the baby doll that had been torn from her grasp. She could still see George's expression of deep concern.

'And biostasis?'

'You've been in the Siberia ward?' he said in astonishment. He lowered the glass to the desk. 'I hope Abigail got you to sign another confidentiality agreement.'

She turned away from him, trying to calm her breathing. After a few moments, she looked back and said more quietly, 'No wonder the public don't know about this.'

'The public don't *want* to know. They just want to be *safe*,' he said. 'You'd better watch yourself, Grace.'

'Oh, *I'd* better watch myself? What you're doing is unethical, never mind illegal.'

His expression became flinty. 'Don't think I haven't seen your *husband's article* about Payback reoffending.'

'That article had nothing to do with me.'

Had Abigail told him about the phone call to Dan?

'If I believe for one minute you're a *mole*, Grace, then it's not just about losing your job. I'll take you to court and you won't work ever again. You signed contracts and confidentiality agreements. Your loyalty is to me, not to NewsFlex. If I even *think* you've divulged information—'

'And will Myriam keep quiet?' she interrupted.

Conrad sighed heavily before running his hands over his face. Finally he looked up at her. 'Maybe you're right and that's why she left – she didn't have the balls for the job.'

'You can't cure criminals by frightening them, Conrad. It's a plaster on a laceration. You'll only suppress what's inside them.'

'And what do you suggest? That we cure them by being fucking *nice* to them?'

He took a moment to calm himself. 'I'm sorry. It's been a very stressful time.' He pointed to the chair. 'Please, sit down. Let's talk about this sensibly.'

She hesitated for a moment, but then sat, still trembling with anger.

'Look, I know you're an empathetic soul, Grace, and no doubt being kind works for many of the offenders at the lower Tiers. But the type of criminal we have in Tier Three, they're a different kettle of fish altogether. They always have to be in control, they enjoy exerting power, and they hurt other people. Aversion Therapy is effective because they're at the receiving end for once.'

'A taste of their own medicine,' Grace said flatly.

He didn't seem to notice her venom. 'Yes, we're redeeming them and that may well take... questionable methods. We're being cruel to be kind.'

'Kind!' she spat. 'But obviously it doesn't work, or Mikey Kilgannon and Payback wouldn't be reoffending.'

'Yes, something's gone wrong, but in general it's working and the real emotions are there.'

'Fear wears off, Conrad, once the threat is gone. What happens when the desire to offend outweighs the fear of Aversion Therapy? It's the basic pleasure pain principle. No wonder it doesn't work for psychopaths.'

He looked up at her with narrowed eyes. 'What do you mean?'

'Psychopaths don't feel afraid. They don't feel empathy. They don't care that they're hurting others. That's why they can do those awful things without regret or guilt. I'm not sure your *Siberia* is even a punishment for them. They're probably just lying there watching curiously or even, God forbid, *enjoying* it. The idea that you can fix people by fear is so bloody misguided.'

'But you really think you can fix them with kindness?' There was no trace of anger now, just curiosity.

Kindness, was it such a bad quality? Conrad had seen this as her weakness, her Achilles heel. But could it actually be a strength? Could kindness be more powerful than cruelty or fear? Maybe she *could* use kindness, or more specifically, empathy.

Not kindness *towards* them, but kindness *within* them.

Her heart began to race as the possibility of not only preventing such torment, but also providing a cure began to surface. If she could encourage the offenders to feel empathy, create a real response to the victims of their crime, not just a temporary one, then maybe she could create a more humane, more effective treatment.

'When I work with offenders at Tier Two we look at how their actions affect other people,' Grace told him, her anger dissipating and excitement growing in the pit of her stomach. 'Sometimes we've used restorative justice and they've had to meet their victims face to face. Do you know what one of the hardest things for an offender is? Accepting responsibility, seeing how their victim really feels, to be confronted with it and let it sink in. Many of my offenders have told me that this is what messes them up the most, it's what crystallises their road to recovery. There's no reason why Tier Three can't use the same technique.'

'And how are we supposed to do that? How do we get them to feel what their victims really felt so that we can cure them?'

It went against every fibre in her being to help this man, and for a split second she considered going home and telling Dan the whole story, including the horror she'd seen at Tier Four, let him put the whole unpalatable truth all over the news, whatever the consequences.

But there were the offenders to think of, people who needed a chance, a change – people like Remy.

'Maybe I can't cure them by being kind, but maybe I can cure them by making *them* kind. They don't need synthetic fear,' Grace said. 'They need something far more painful, something that hits home more than being scared that what they do could happen to them, something that hurts them more.'

'And what might that be?' asked Conrad, sounding cynical, but she could see the eagerness to find a solution in his face.

'They need empathy.'

–

It was dark when Grace made her way from the Tube station towards home, tired and frustrated after a day's unsuccessful research. It was going to take time.

Conrad was urging her on. He didn't care about kindness – only anything that might get him out of trouble.

Grace was focusing on anything to get Remy out of trouble.

She took her phone from her bag and called Shannon.

'Ah, Shan, I just needed to see a friendly face.' Grace held the phone in front of her and walked along carefully.

'Where are you, doll? Looks pretty dark. I can hardly see you.'

'Just making my way home from the clinic.'

'It's nearly eleven o'clock! I know you're not afraid of putting the hours in, but is there something special going on?'

If Grace was honest with herself she was hoping to avoid Dan.

'Everything okay?' Shannon was in bed, her face make-up free, her brown wavy hair loose.

Timorax, Siberia, Dan, Conrad, Remy – all these things were tumbling about Grace's brain. Where to start?

'Shan, things in the clinic are… I mean, I went to Tier Three yesterday, and…' Grace checked for traffic as she stepped off the kerb and crossed the road. Once on the other side, she continued speaking. 'It was just awful. You want to see what they—'

Her words were interrupted by a growl at the other end of the line, and Grace heard Shannon scream, then she disappeared from view.

'Oh my God, are you okay? Shan?' Grace stood still on the pavement staring at the screen. 'What's happening?'

She heard Shannon shriek but could still see nothing but the ceiling of Shannon's bedroom. What if one of the residents had broken into her home on the compound and… Oh God, it didn't bear thinking about.

'Shan, please!' Her voice cracked with anxiety. One or two passers-by turned around to stare at her.

Suddenly she heard raucous laughter, and Shannon reappeared, this time with a stocky, bearded man lying next to her on the pillows. They were both smiling and the man had his arms around her. Grace stared at the screen, not immediately comprehending what she was seeing.

'This big bear has just grabbed me!' Shannon wheezed, her face pink. 'Grace, this is Shuggie. Shuggie, this is my best pal, Grace.'

Grace sighed heavily, relieved. 'I thought you were being attacked, Shan!'

'She will be when this call ends,' said Shuggie in his gruff Scottish accent, and then belted out a laugh.

Grace recognised him as one of the recovering soldiers from the Agrarian. It was against the rules to be intimate with any of the residents, but Shannon had been so lonely since her husband had died in the African conflict, Grace could hardly blame her. She'd been raising her four children alone and working on the residential site without much of a chance to meet anyone else.

Shannon had asked her a few weeks ago to delay signing Shuggie's release forms.

Now she knew why.

There was no judgement between the two women. A flash of disappointment that Shannon hadn't been able to trust her, but then she remembered Remy and understood.

Some things needed time and space.

Shuggie grabbed the phone from Shannon and his face filled the screen. 'Now, don't you worry, hen. I'm gonnae look after this girl here. I'm sound now, all well. I'm a new man. I'm gonnae take care of them weans too.'

'I'm glad to hear it, Shuggie. Don't you let her down,' Grace warned him sternly before she felt a smile soften her features.

'I won't,' he replied gently.

Grace started walking along the street again.

Shuggie's big cheerful face was replaced by Shannon's and Grace saw something she hadn't seen there for a long time – joy.

Whatever Shuggie's background, he made her friend happy.

People could change. She knew that from her work and from personal experience, didn't she?

Shannon didn't speak, just gave her a wink.

'Right then, you two, have fun,' Grace laughed, momentarily forgetting her own problems. 'Shan, I'll see you at the end of the week. You can fill me in with all the gossip then.'

She put the phone back in her bag and turned into a side street as a shortcut home. Wide, bow-fronted semis stood in established gardens, surrounded by half-brick walls topped with wooden fences and overhanging bushes. Chinks of light escaped from drawn curtains illuminating the short, dark pathways from the pavement to the houses.

Grace felt a warmth spreading through her because of Shannon's new relationship. Dan and her used to be happy like that, didn't they? All the stress, the talk of a baby, the jostling for who had the best job, had taken its toll and left Grace feeling anxious about the state of their relationship.

A sound behind her gave her a start. She turned to see a cat had knocked an empty drinks can off a garden wall and onto the pavement below. Its eyes flashed yellow, briefly reflecting the light from a nearby house, before it strode off into the night. There was a rustling in a bush in one of the front gardens, probably birds agitated by the cat's presence.

She hoped Dan would be asleep when she got in. She was too tired for conflict at home as well as work.

Her ears pricked up as she heard a movement behind her. Was that another cat? She moved away towards the kerb.

She remembered when she'd fallen in love with Dan and it was new and exciting, like Shannon and Shuggie. The fleeting question in her mind – *do you still love him?* – frightened her, shook her stability. They'd be able to find their way back to each other, wouldn't they?

Footsteps behind her – the hairs on the back of her neck stood up. She pulled her bag tight against her shoulder and quickened her pace.

'Grace!' came a whisper.

She stopped dead in the street and turned around, her heart beating fast.

She could see no one.

'Remy?' she called quietly.

A shape appeared from behind one of the bushes at the gate of a house, a man dressed in dark clothes, his hood pulled over his head.

'Remy?' she said, now trembling, taking a step forward. 'Is it really you?' It *had* been him at the train station that morning! He stood stock-still as she moved forward a little more, feeling the muscles in her face relaxing and forming into a smile. Whatever he'd done, whatever trouble he was in, this was her friend, her brother. Now he was here she could help him, couldn't she?

She loosened her grip on her bag, opened her arms and moved forward again.

'I've missed you!'

But as the light from a nearby porch caught his features, she realised it wasn't Remy.

The man lunged at her. Grace reared back in fright but he was suddenly on her and hit her once, hard, across the face. She fell to the ground, banging her elbow and her hip, the shock of impact giving rise to nausea.

'This is your only warning!' the stranger growled. He bent over her as she writhed on the ground, trying to escape from him, and grabbed her face hard. 'Get out of Tier Three!' His breath smelled bitter. She could feel her face speckled with his saliva. 'Don't touch that fucking therapy or I'll come back for you. And next time, you won't survive!'

Dazed and sickened by the blow, Grace lay on the damp pavement as the man ran away into the night.

CHAPTER SEVENTEEN

The swelling on Grace's face throbbed as Dan pressed a cold, wet cloth to it. Her hip and elbow were swollen and bruised. She sat uncomfortably on the sofa, hoping the painkillers would work fast. She'd run to a nearby house after the attack and waited there until Dan had come for her.

'You've got actual nail marks on your face! What the hell were you thinking, taking a shortcut that time of night? Putting yourself at risk...' he said, his voice tight.

A brief flare-up of resentment pulsated alongside her injuries. Was he really suggesting it was her fault that a man had jumped out of the shadows and attacked her? How many times had she heard that from the police officers when Lottie had taken one of the street girls to them after a punter went too far?

He must have seen the look in her eyes, and recoiled.

'You had the car, remember,' she said flatly.

He lifted her hand and placed it on the cloth to hold it in place, then moved over to the armchair on the other side of the room.

'I'm sorry. I'm just worried about you.'

'It must have been one of the protestors. They're outside the clinic most days now. If I don't take the car, I sneak out the back, but one of them must have seen me leave, maybe followed me.'

He didn't reply but went out to the kitchen and brought back two AltCon drinks, Sweet & Soothing. He handed one to her. It was pineapple flavour with a hint of coconut.

'Did you get a look at him?' he asked, sitting down again.

She took a sip from the bottle, still holding the cloth to her face. 'Not really… dressed all in black, hood over his head.'

'Tell me what he said again.'

'No, he threatened me about the clinic – "Get out of Tier Three, or next time, you won't survive."'

Repeating her attacker's words refreshed her fear. She shivered as though still lying on the cold pavement. 'How did he know I work in Tier Three?'

'Maybe he just guessed? I don't see why you won't call the police and report it.'

'I'm already in enough trouble with Conrad, and Janus doesn't need any more negative publicity.' She put both bottle and cloth down and went to reach for her phone. 'Talking of Conrad, I'd better ring him.' She stopped when she saw Dan's expression.

'What's wrong?'

'Before you do, there's something you should know. There's been another case of reoffending. Noah Begbroke. I wasn't going to say anything, seeing as we're not exactly swapping information… But in the interests of safety, you should know.'

She put her phone down.

'Another arson attack,' he said. 'Killed an ex-girlfriend last night. Torched her in bed.'

'Oh my God, I was there when they treated him. Have the police got him?'

'Yes, well, no.'

'What does that mean?'

'They have his body. He died in the fire.'

'That's just horrible, I can't believe…' Dan was still staring at her. 'There's something else, isn't there?'

He sighed heavily and ran his hand through his hair.

'For God's sake, what is it?' Grace asked, alarmed now. 'Just tell me.'

'Myriam Kyriacou was also found dead last night, at her flat. Someone killed her.'

Grace half stood, caught her breath and swallowed hard before sitting back down.

She couldn't face 'how', so instead she asked 'When?' It came out as a whisper.

'A few days ago.'

'But Conrad said she resigned, sent an email.'

Dan shook his head. 'She was strangled. Anyone could have sent that email.'

'Any suspects?' It could have been a protestor, or someone who'd been through Aversion Therapy and wanted revenge.

Next time, you won't survive.

Maybe the man who attacked her was the same man who had killed Myriam.

'Police think vigilantes killed her – in their minds she was supporting a flawed system, letting criminals off with a rap on the knuckles,' he said.

Then something occurred to Grace. 'Dan, tell me you didn't put this report out already? The story about Myriam and the stuff about Begbroke reoffending.'

He shrugged. 'Went out this afternoon.'

Grace felt the blood rushing in her head.

'I thought you were going to wait until you had more information.'

'If I didn't report on it, then someone else would have.'

Anger overwhelmed the fear and shock from her attack. 'And what about Payback? Have you reported on that yet? Or Mikey Kilgannon reoffending?'

When Dan didn't answer she grabbed her shell and brought up NewsFlex with its familiar yellow and black logo.

The headline: TWO-FACED JANUS – AVERSION THERAPY LIES!

She scrolled down – it was all there:

mistakes made … cover-up … Mikey Kilgannon's treatment unsuccessful … does Aversion Therapy work? … post office Golders Green … murdered staff psychiatrist … efficacy …

denied at highest levels in government ... millionaire Becker
... claims of lasting effects ... an eye for an eye ... 'They
are cured, I can guarantee' ... Noah Begbroke treated only
a few days ago ... protestors justified...

'I begged you not to put this story out!' Rage engulfed Grace.
'You're worried about me, you say? So worried that you went
ahead and published this information – without so much as a
warning, without thinking about the impact it might have on
me?'

'You're not seriously blaming me for this, are you?' he asked
indignantly, pointing to her bruised face.

When she didn't reply, he said, 'If it's so dangerous, then I
don't think you should work there. Tell Conrad to stick his job.
The article's out.'

'Oh, so *now* you don't think I should work there?' Sarcasm
emerged from the shock and horror. 'You were more than
happy for me to go there when you wanted me to get information for you!'

'You need to leave. It's too dangerous now.'

'Yes, and whose fault is that? I make my own decisions,
Dan. I'm not leaving just because you say I should! And what
about the treatment? I can't give up now! I need to sort out the
problem with the therapy.'

'You're not seriously going to—'

'You've told the world that Aversion Therapy is flawed, so
now the whole system will be called into question, even Tiers
One and Two. All that important, life-changing work, will be
washed away in a flood of outrage about bloody Tier Three. I
can't let that happen!'

'Christ, Grace, maybe people *should* be calling this system
into question! Don't tell me that you're starting to support
Aversion Therapy?'

'No, but I need to prove it works so that I can clean up this
mess! I might be able to fix it. I need to help those people.
Who's going to save them if I don't?'

He stared at her, incredulous.

'Listen to yourself! Who do you think you are? Grace Gunnarsson, saviour of the wretched? Some people can't be saved!'

'That's not for you to decide!'

Couldn't save her... a grey, scratchy woollen blanket, *a spider, Gracie... the biggest in the block!*

Her thoughts turned to Remy and her head swirled. She was back on thin ice again, a cracking sound ripping through her brain as the brittle membrane between her two worlds became even more fragile.

She scrabbled to find her shoes on the floor, stood up and grabbed her coat and bag from the arm of the sofa where she'd dumped them. 'I'm going out.' She didn't look at him.

Dan stood too. 'No, you're not! At this time of night, after what's happened...'

Grace thrust her arms angrily into the sleeves of her coat and pulled it up over her shoulders.

Anxiety mellowed Dan's features. 'Please, Grace, love, don't go out now. You've had a fright, let's sit down, have another drink...'

But the front door slammed behind her as he was still talking.

—

Grace's hands were still shaking as she turned the steering wheel and pulled up in front of a small row of shops half a mile from her house. At this late hour, the shops were shut, the main road quiet. She turned off the engine and sat in the shadows, feeling safe in the bubble of her car.

She took her shell out of her bag and reread the NewsFlex reports on Janus. Too wrapped up in her work, she had missed them before.

DOCTOR FOUND DEAD

By Dan Gunnarsson

Myriam Kyriacou, a psychiatrist at Janus Justice, was found dead at home last night. Ms Kyriacou lived alone in a flat in Belsize Park and had not been in touch with friends for a few days, which was described as 'unusual'. Police have asked for anyone with information to speak directly to them, and to avoid speculating on social media.

Speaking from the Headquarters of Janus Justice, CEO and pioneer of the Justice Tier System, Conrad Becker, said that Ms Kyriacou had emailed her resignation with immediate effect. 'It wasn't clear what her reasons were for leaving us so abruptly,' Mr Becker said. 'She was an integral part of our team here at Janus Justice and a trailblazer in criminal rehabilitation. Her loss will be sorely felt. She was irreplaceable.'

What a hypocrite Conrad was!

Another article on Noah Begbroke read:

Begbroke had recently been treated with Aversion Therapy at Janus Justice for a firebomb attack on his ex-partner's home. During the attack, Corrina Saunders suffered extensive burns.

She scrolled down.

His body was found at the scene of another arson attack in which another previous partner, Lexi Woods, was also found dead. Identification was made using dental records…

…This case, and a recent possible reoffence by the vigilante group Payback, raises questions about the efficacy of Aversion Therapy, something which vigilantes and protestors have been conflicted about since the Tier System was implemented over ten years ago…

Grace's eye caught a movement outside the car. A man walking his dog paused briefly nearby as the dog relieved itself on a clump of weeds. She felt herself tense until he moved away.

Grace's chest felt tight, her mind raced. Things were only going to get worse now that the public knew they were having problems at Janus. The protestors would up their game, there was no doubt about it. The Department of Justice was going to be all over the clinic. They'd carry out an investigation and then who knew what would happen?

She had to find Remy and treat him before the clinic was taken over by the authorities. It was only a matter of time. Once they were under investigation, how would she be able to get him the right treatment? Would the authorities even allow her to try? She had to find him, fix him and free him. Was it even possible?

She flinched as a jogger ran by her window, his grey hoodie flapping as he passed, the zip catching the wing mirror with a clicking sound. She cursed him under her breath as she watched him move away down the quiet street, bouncing rhythmically across the eco-tarmac, past the recycling deposit units at the end of the row of shops, towards the park. His hood reminded her of the man who'd attacked her. She checked the doors were locked.

She picked up her phone ready to call Shannon and tell her everything – the attack, Dan's attitude, she would even tell her about Remy. She could trust Shannon. Shannon would know what to do.

But then she threw her phone back down on the seat and rested her forehead on the steering wheel. If Shannon knew about Remy, then she might be found culpable if everything came out. There was too much to lose.

A few moments later, her phone rang. It would be Dan, telling her to come home, but her anger refused to let her answer.

The ringing stopped and almost instantly started again. She put it to her ear.

'Dan, I—'

'Gracie…'

Her heart leapt into her mouth. 'Remy?'

'Yeah, it's me.' He sounded out of breath.

She opened her mouth and closed it.

'Gracie?' he said again.

'Yes, I'm here. It's nearly one in the morning.'

'I've just run past your car.'

She twisted and turned in her seat, trying to catch a glimpse of him.

'Have you been following me?' There was no sign of the jogger in the grey hoodie. 'Where are you?'

'It doesn't matter. I need your help. I'm in trouble.'

'I know! I've seen the reports, at work. Remy, what were you thinking? Killing a drug dealer… what the hell?'

'I didn't do it, Gracie. I swear I didn't.'

She sighed heavily. He would see it as a betrayal if she questioned his innocence, so instead she said, 'You have no idea what they do to people who have reoffended.' The image of the bodies under white sheets in Siberia ward flashed into her mind.

'I need to get out of the country, Gracie… to get away from them.'

'From who?'

He didn't answer.

'I need a biochip to get through airports…'

'You can't go to an airport! The police are looking for you.'

'It's not the police I'm worried about.'

She looked out of the car windows again. Was he nearby? Maybe behind the recycling deposit units, watching her?

'Who are you trying to get away from?'

'You don't need to know.'

'We're not kids anymore, Remy, I don't need you to protect me, for God's sake! How am I supposed to help you if you don't even tell me what the problem is?'

Silence.

She looked down at the display – a street-shell.

'Have you got a phone? Give me your number. Let's talk…'

'No, Gracie, you don't understand. If they get me – *when* they get me – I can't let them have any way of getting to you.'

'What do you want me to do?' she asked desperately.

His last words before the line went dead were: 'You know where to find me.'

CHAPTER EIGHTEEN

Mal stood by the small window in the office. It was pitch black outside. The only light in the room came from the naked bulb of a lamp on top of an empty, rusted filing cabinet. The office was the back room of what had once been an electricals shop. With online shopping and various new streaming technologies, many small businesses like this had long since become defunct and their premises turned into low-rent accommodation.

He'd not long arrived and Sarge wasn't there.

'You're late.' Bizzy said. 'He's gone to see a man about a dog.'

Mal suspected 'dog' meant 'gun'.

Life must be easy for Bizzy. He had his army pension and regular work in the food waste recycling plant during the day. As a manager, Bizzy didn't even actually have to be in the room when the trucks full of rotting, stinking food were processed. He probably sat in his office and ordered the lower echelons of workers to pour it into the vats of cockroaches which devoured tons of leftovers every day. He was in charge of the breeding rooms, and when the new batch of roaches reached maturity he would order his staff to grind up the old ones and feed them to the poultry housed on the other side of the plant. How hard could that be?

Mal, on the other hand, was used to getting his hands dirty. He didn't mind his cleaning job at the police station. It was early in the morning, he worked on his own and it was fairly easy. He also had access to things that Diros needed. The other part of his paid employment – cleaning crime scenes – was more unpredictable, and occasionally he didn't make it to the office on time.

He picked up a shell and started scrolling. 'Tier Three, Tier Three,' he was saying as he moved his fingers. He'd better find something for Sarge to make up for his tardiness.

'Jesus, Mal, can you stop saying that? It's driving me nuts.'

'There's a fella got done for drug-driving,' Mal suggested, ignoring his comment. 'Caught a student under his wheels. Treated last August.'

'Hmm…' Bizzy murmured. He leaned back in his chair, feet on the desk, staring at nothing in particular. 'Hit and run… no close physical contact. You know what Sarge will say – not much skill involved. We need something good now all our work is hitting the headlines. We need a good case just to push the protestors over the edge. Make them really flip out. Hurry up. He'll be back soon.'

Mal needed to find something good in the Aversion Therapy files or else there'd be trouble. This was it – *the crescendo*, Sarge had called it – although Mal wasn't really sure what that meant.

'Oh, what about this one…' Mal said. 'A woman poisoned a water tank to get back at her ex's new woman. Made a whole apartment block sick.'

'Boring. You're going to have to come up with something better,' Bizzy said.

'You find something then!' Mal snapped. He turned and kicked the filing cabinet hard, and the metallic rumbling sound echoed around the room.

Bizzy grinned at Mal. 'Oooh! Getting cranky are we?' he mocked, but then his mood turned surly. 'I can't wait until this mission is over and we can just spend the night hunting paedos.'

It sounded like Bizzy would enjoy that sort of thing, a light-hearted night out for a sadist like Biz, like joyriding but for killers. But there was no way Sarge would let Bizzy out to play – well, not unless Biz found a vigilante gang who were already killing paedos to hide behind.

Too base and barbaric, Sarge had said when they'd suggested it in the past. *Too visceral. No art to it.*

Mal had pondered his words for some time.

'I don't think Sarge would be too impressed by that suggestion. He likes something meaningful that he can replicate perfectly.'

'What, you're an expert on the boss now?' Bizzy barked, leaning over the desk. 'I learned more about that man in Africa than you ever will know. You think just because you bring him tidbits from the police station that you *know* him? You fucking moron.'

Mal shrugged. He was used to Bizzy now. So what, he'd been in Africa with Sarge? He'd heard all their stories – too many times. And maybe Bizzy was right. Mal knew he wasn't the sharpest tool in the box, but at least he had a good reason for doing the work they did. Layla would be proud of him.

But she wouldn't have liked that woman dying in the fire.

Not at all.

'You'd better find something good, Mal. He's in one of his moods and that's partly your bloody fault for questioning his methods,' Bizzy snapped.

It was true. There had been some discussion late the previous night about the death of the woman in the fire with Begbroke.

Mal could easily have ended up one of those people Sarge despised, who lived on the streets and died on drugs. Sarge had found him kicking an old man to death – someone who'd been outed as a sex offender, who'd made advances to a few of the very young street dwellers that Mal knew. Instead of grassing on him, Sarge had helped him hide the body and taken Mal under his wing.

He owed Sarge. But how had he repaid him? He'd questioned the death of Begbroke's ex, questioned the mission.

Insubordination, Sarge had said.

Maybe Mal should have kept his mouth shut, but he hadn't signed up to Diros to kill innocent people. He'd joined to get justice. The previous night he hadn't been able to sleep, wondering what might happen to him if he showed doubt in front of Sarge again. He decided for the time being he'd keep his mouth shut and stay under Sarge's radar.

'I still don't understand why he's so angry,' Mal said. 'I thought he'd be made up that the plan's finally coming together. That's what he wanted, wasn't it? And now it's even in the news.'

But Bizzy didn't have a chance to answer as the door flew open and Sarge walked in. Bizzy jumped to his feet. Sarge placed a handgun on the desk and then sat down in the chair that Bizzy had just vacated. His folded his arms.

'Have you found our next task?' he asked, putting his feet up on the desk and crossing them at the ankle.

'No, Sarge, I'm working on it.' Mal could hear his voice tremble.

Sarge launched himself out of his chair, tore the shell from Mal's hands and flung it across the room. It nearly hit Bizzy, who pulled his arms up protectively. 'When I came back from Africa, I didn't expect to have to fight here as well,' he snarled, spittle flying. His minions cowered. 'Look what we have to put up with! Scumbags! Rats! Everywhere. People who lack discipline, who don't follow rules! I didn't survive out there just to come back and turn to drugs and end up sleeping on the streets like so many of my army brothers. Don't you get it?'

Mal and Bizzy nodded.

'I survived for a reason, a mission. We have *work* to do, lads. Now find me something worth doing!'

He stormed out again, leaving Mal and Bizzy staring at the door.

That poor woman who'd died in the fiery bedroom. Was that part of the mission? Something in Sarge had changed. Mal was sure of that now. And he didn't like it.

'Isn't he happy that Janus is all over the news?'

'You don't even know what's up with him, do you?' Bizzy sneered.

Mal didn't reply.

'Remy Wilson is out and about,' Bizzy said, looking miserable. 'If you'd been here on time tonight, then you'd have known.'

Mal had repeatedly heard the stories about Sarge and Remy serving with the British army. They'd been trying to prevent conflicts over minerals used in tech production while keeping the flow coming to the West. Sarge had saved Remy's life in an ambush, and then Remy had, for a short time, joined Diros. Remy was another man who owed Sarge, although it looked as though Remy wasn't paying up.

'The police haven't caught him yet?' asked Mal. 'But we put all the evidence in place. What's the problem?'

Bizzy frowned. 'Oh no, we set him up perfectly. The police got him, but he did a runner.'

The usual routine was to ensure the criminal they were copying either died at the scene, like Noah Begbroke and Oliver McIntyre, or else they made sure it was easy for the police to catch them, like Mikey Kilgannon. But Remy Wilson was a whole different kettle of fish.

'Slippery bastard,' Bizzy said bitterly.

Mal often wondered about Remy.

They'd been a strong team in the beginning. They'd started out as bounty hunters – collecting offenders for the authorities and getting well paid for it. *Money and justice*, Remy used to say, *what's not to like?*

But when things started to change, when *Sarge* had started to change, putting a stop to their bounty hunting, calling the team Diros and moving into something darker, then Remy lost his enthusiasm. He told Mal that Sarge's mission wasn't aligned with his own any more.

Sarge began to focus on Janus, pouring all his anger and frustration about the things that had happened in Africa, and the crimes of the fugitives they'd caught, into a campaign against the company – which Sarge believed was a traitor to justice. He saw himself as a crusader.

And then people started dying.

But Mal and Bizzy – they'd just gone along with Sarge.

Mal because he had nowhere else to go, no one else to go to. And if he was really honest, he could never avenge Layla's death, but this was damned close.

And Bizzy did it because he enjoyed what they did.

Maybe Remy had been right about Bizzy too – cruelty for cruelty's sake.

It was only Remy who had questioned the new mission.

And Sarge couldn't have anyone questioning his authority. Of course, by then, Remy knew too much. It could only have ended badly.

One evening, Mal turned up late to the office after a particularly difficult post-crime clean, and Remy was there alone. He told Mal he was leaving soon and asked him to come along. Said he had a plan, somewhere to sleep, the possibility of a job. Mal had refused – out of loyalty to Sarge, or had it been fear? Regret overwhelmed him when he remembered telling Sarge what Remy had said. That night, they killed a drug dealer, and Sarge had framed Remy, not only leaving his jacket covered in the dealer's blood at the scene, but also giving handfuls of the dealer's drugs to the local addicts in exchange for them describing Remy in great detail to the police.

Mal still felt bad about it. It was a shame, really, he'd liked Remy. He'd always spoken to Mal as though he was his equal, with a little respect even, which was more than Sarge and Bizzy ever did. But their priority was to protect Diros at all costs. *Loyalty is the key* Sarge often said.

'No wonder the boss is pissed off.' Bizzy sniffed loudly and then hawked a gob of phlegm into the rusted metal bin. 'Remy's the only weakness in our armour. We should have got rid of him when we had the chance. If the police get to Remy first, then he's going to tell them everything.'

Remy should have kept quiet. Asking questions was where the trouble started. Mal knew that only too well. *Mouth shut, eyes open* his dad used to say.

Maybe Mal could find out where Remy was and get on the right side of the boss. But he'd make sure not to tell Bizzy, so he couldn't take the credit as he always did. Mal would keep his eyes wide open and his mouth firmly shut.

—

Grace's arms are pinned in place by a sheet wrapped around her, so tight that she can hardly breathe, her lungs only taking in tiny amounts of oxygen, starving her brain and giving rise to panic.

There are sounds of footsteps around her, whispers.

She tries to move, but her body won't respond. She can feel her fingers, her legs, her arms, but no matter how much she wills them to shift, they remain static. She can feel people pawing at her, and the sting of a sharp needle as it punctures her skin. And then a woozy sensation, like slipping into a hot bath, and the sound of her own heartbeat getting louder and louder until it becomes a thudding, throbbing vibration that seems to fill the whole room.

Her eyes won't open, there's something holding them shut, smothering her face, but somehow she can still see.

And what she sees and feels is horrifying.

Her mother's lifeless body, clamped around her, clawing into her, eyes open, staring, blue irises surrounded by bloodshot sclerae, her lips blue, mouth slightly open…

Grace can't even scream.

She fights against her restraints and finally manages to free her arms. Raising her hands, she feels a metal band across her face and, with some difficulty, pulls it away. Her eyes blurred, she can see shadows moving around her.

As her vision comes back into focus, she sees Siberia ward. She feels the soft bristle of her shaved head. Above her, a screen. She looks down to see her arm punctured by a cannula.

In the bed next to hers, head shaved and dead to the world, lies Remy.

Grace sat up in bed, the sound of her rapid breathing loud in the dark. She instinctively reached out for Dan but he wasn't there.

She was in a single bed.

Then she remembered she was in the spare room. When she'd got home the night before, after talking to Remy, Dan was already fast asleep in their room.

So much for being worried about her.

Still shaken from her dream, she got out of bed and stood in the hall, listening to Dan sighing in his sleep. She pushed the door open and in the faint light of the approaching dawn she cast her eyes over him.

For a moment, the near decade they'd been together, the good times, the holidays, the cosy nights in all swam in her mind. She considered his warmth and charm, his dedication to his career, his desire for a family.

As angry as she was with him for the news reports, she realised that Dan was perfect – but perfect for the Grace she'd conjured, the Grace with the amazing job, the magazine-photo home, the lifestyle that many would envy.

But what would *Gracie* want? Remy coming back into her mind had brought something out of her that she'd tried to suppress for so long. Gracie was back, and she was questioning everything.

You know where to find me.

After she'd gone to university in Durham, their phone calls and messages had become fewer and more difficult. He became more taciturn, she more resentful, as his feelings of abandonment suffocated their bond. But now he was back.

Where are you, Remy?

Maybe at Lottie's place, the two-up two-down in the East End? That was the last place she'd seen him. Had he inherited it after Lottie died? She wasn't Lottie's biological daughter, didn't have any claim to it, and even if she had, she'd heard nothing from solicitors. But then how could she have? Gracie had moved, changed her name, covered her tracks.

Dan sighed in his sleep again – deep and slow. What would she lose if she let the past thaw? Was it worth the sacrifice?

She crept back into the spare room, but stopped before climbing into the still-warm bed. The sheets reminded her of her dream and the prone bodies of the offenders at Tier Four. Her mind had abandoned sleep and turned itself to considering the problem and searching for a solution.

She'd already developed a synthetic self-esteem drug at Tier Two. It had taken the best part of five years, with the drug trials and licensing and all sorts of other hoop-jumping.

She didn't have that sort of time.

In fact, she didn't have any time at all.

She picked up her phone from beside the bed.

5.27 a.m.

She had to prove to Conrad that she could fix the therapy before the police arrested Remy, or worse still when *they* got to him, whoever *they* were.

She would get up, get herself a coffee and get to the clinic.

There was work to be done.

CHAPTER NINETEEN

BROTHERS JAILED

By Dan Gunnarsson

There has been yet another domestic armed robbery in Basingstoke, the sixth one in as many months. Last week brothers Kevin and Marvin Lofthouse, were caught red-handed by police when they assaulted homeowners and demanded they open a safe, before taking an estimated £10,000 worth of jewellery. As this was their first provable offence, the brothers were sentenced to Aversion Therapy at Tier Three. Afterwards, as the law requires, they will have to repay all costs plus compensation.

—

Mal liked this time of day. The sun was just coming up over a sleepy London, the light catching the glass prisms of the skyline. He turned away from his view of the British Ecological Headquarters and the newly opened Cotton Exchange and swept his sonic mop in rhythmic motions across the floor of the police headquarters, his lanyard swinging in time with his movements.

Unlike the other hygiene operatives he didn't listen to music on his phone, although he wore his earpiece so as not to look odd. This was his time of day for thinking and planning. While his body was fully immersed in the choreographed movements of cleaning, his mind percolated plans that Diros had been discussing – the bringing down of Janus Justice once and for all.

By the time Sarge had returned to the office the previous night, Bizzy had come up with another Tier Three project and Sarge, his frustration having abated somewhat, had accepted their meagre offering with some reticence.

Mal swept in and out of the computerised communication booths, thinking about the crime Diros was about to emulate. The crime itself seemed straightforward. At least no one would get killed. He'd been ambivalent about Begbroke's death, but the woman… He hadn't even known she was there until the burning-pork smell hit him as he'd climbed the stairs to check Bizzy hadn't messed up the evidence. He'd felt a certain sense of shame that he'd been involved somehow, even though he hadn't realised until it was too late.

Mal felt uncertain. It was easy to feel buoyed, inspired even, when Sarge built them up with strong words about mission and brotherhood and justice. But that poor woman who died, cremated in her own bed, that wasn't justice. Bizzy hadn't even seemed fazed by it. Before Remy left, he'd told Mal that Bizzy liked to do bad stuff for the sake of it. Maybe that was true. Something darker was emerging from Diros, something that scared Mal.

It seemed too big a problem for him to solve right now. He shook his head. A moral wobble, Layla would have called it. He would focus on the job in hand. Try to make sense of it later.

Mal took a spray bottle from the large pocket of his heavy-duty cotton apron and squirted it on a stain. He continued making his way slowly over to the corridor which led to the evidence room, the mop guiding him like a blind person's stick. There were ten minutes to go before handover, so he'd have to act now, when there were less people around, less chance of getting caught. He paused in the corridor, leaning against the window for a moment as the last of the officers left to go downstairs to the briefing. He looked out across the Thames from the fifteenth floor, where the barges moved along the river like colourful toys, the people mere pixels, the glass and metal buildings shining like gold in the morning sun.

–

Grace walked along the embankment, watching the barges as they ferried early morning deliveries before the shops opened. A cool breeze swept across from the Thames carrying with it the smell of manure that lay in steaming piles on the road from the horses that pulled the wagons loaded with cargo from the barges. A collector with his shovel and cart moved along, sweeping up what the horses had left behind ready to be sent to the agricultural compounds. Nothing seemed wasted these days. The collector passed her, singing loudly to a song only he could hear in his earpiece. Moments later, she heard the clip clop of another horse as it pulled its cargo cart, dumping more manure in its wake.

Her mind oscillated between wondering where Remy was and figuring out how to fix Aversion Therapy. Creating empathy, chemically or otherwise, felt like a feat above her proficiency, but she had to keep faith that she could do it. Conrad's team had created synthetic fear, hadn't they?

It would take months, years even, to create a new drug from scratch, including research, trials and licensing. She'd have to swerve the usual procedures, but obviously Conrad didn't always take the legal route. Remy would be caught sooner rather than later and it was imperative that she had treatment ready.

She decided her only option was to adapt the treatment that was already in place, try to turn it to her purpose. Building on an already shaky foundation didn't give her much hope that the new treatment would be a hundred per cent effective, or even long-term for that matter.

She couldn't worry about that right now.

Then she would have to prove her new treatment worked so that she could get Remy off the hook. Whatever happened after that… Well, she'd have to think about that later.

-

Mal looked around one last time and, seeing no one, swiped the door with his card and quietly slipped in. The hairs on his arms stood upright. It was like Christmas – a room full of evidence, some of which had been used already to prove an offender's guilt, some waiting to be used to catch criminals, and some which, if you had the nous, could be used to frame others. It was like picking a suit from a rack in a fancy-dress shop. *Who do you want to be today?*

All the white boxes stacked up in the room were portals into other worlds of crime. Mal felt himself relax a little, his doubts melting away. Sarge was a genius – he'd have to be to have come up with something like this.

He studied his phone to double-check the information Bizzy had given him about exactly what to look for in the evidence room. If Sarge was the artist, Biz was the planner, and even though he pissed Mal off on a regular basis, Mal had to admit he knew his stuff. Biz had spent the previous night route-finding, alarm-checking, security system-hacking, and finding the best possible target.

Mal was aware of his place in the pecking order, but it didn't detract from the excitement he felt being in this secret treasure trove. He smiled softly to himself, enjoying the knowledge that Bizzy couldn't come here. Mal wasn't as disposable as Bizzy sometimes suggested.

He found the number he was looking for. He took a pair of disposable gloves from his apron pocket and put them on. The books he'd read had taught him what would be the best thing to take, and sure enough, he opened the box and found hair samples and already-chewed gum in small plastic bags. He shoved them into the large pocket of his apron, replaced the box carefully and hurried out of the evidence room, mop in hand.

–

The Janus Justice building was almost empty apart from one or two eager interns and a few hygiene operatives. Deacon Security guards were positioned at the doors and a couple were doing the rounds outside. George passed a tin to Grace as he said goodbye after a nightshift. 'My wife's walnut, date and honey cake, Doc G,' he said with a grin. 'Always grateful.'

'Your gratitude is going to end up on my hips, George!' Grace said with a laugh. 'You tell Louise thank you.'

He gave her a wave as he left.

The mood of the Aversion Therapy clinic seemed to change with the shifting light of the day – and whatever activity was going on in there. The sun had come up fully now and the early morning cast a cool light across the grey surfaces, giving a calm ambience. Grace had brought an organic vegan roll and a coffee from the bakery on the way to work, but both remained untouched on the workstation.

She turned her attention back to a set of brain scans in front of her. Flicking between screens automatically, the images already as familiar to her as her own reflection in the mirror, she felt a growing anxiety. She'd broken down the Aversion Therapy so that she could try to replicate and adapt it. An idea occurred to her. She didn't even know if it would work. But that didn't matter. She just had to convince Conrad that it would.

Emotions were caused by the body's chemistry reacting to an external stimulus. Aversion Therapy worked by tricking the brain into feeling fear by getting the body to replicate the feelings, adrenaline, palpitations, nausea, shaking, sweating. Sensory information – the smell of fire, the sounds of screaming, the images on the screen – all caused the brain to begin transferring information, triggering autonomic

171

responses. It was clear from the scan that the therapy had the required effect, because the amygdala and the hypothalamus were lit up. The Timorax drug, the hypnotherapy and the emotisonics all contributed to a symphony of fear so distressing that it induced trauma in the offender, which in turn prevented them from wanting to reoffend.

How the hell was she going to be able to produce a better therapy? At least with fear there were clear indicators to the body that something was wrong, and so those indicators could be reproduced. Fear was so much more automatic, so biological. How was she supposed to recreate empathy? Could she somehow bypass the real emotion and stimulate it in brain and body using chemistry? And if so, would that cause changes in the brain that would be visible on the scan, so she could prove it worked?

Her notes were rough, scribbled in a frenzy of study.

Empathy – UMBRELLA TERM!
Four types:
1) cognitive – understanding how the other feels – psychopaths HAVE THIS ONE – they use it to manipulate feelings in others – psychopaths HIGHLY manipulative. Usually the only type of empathy they have. There is NO EMOTION here. Theory of mind – seeing things from the other person's viewpoint. Helps them predict how the person might react to their manipulation
2) emotional – feeling sorry for someone – you can feel the feelings they are experiencing
3) compassionate – you feel motivated to help the one suffering
4) somatic – mirror neurons – gives you a sensation in your body that you can understand – physically feeling something someone else might be feeling – like when someone stubs their toe – you can imagine it – THIS ONE!!!
All on a spectrum in each individual like a graphic equaliser

She knew she couldn't recreate all four types.

She didn't need to.

She didn't have the time or the knowledge to reconstruct a person to that degree. She'd have to stick to what she could actually manage to prove – it wasn't going to be long-term and comprehensive. She just needed to show that a change had taken place in Remy's brain and then Conrad would let him go.

There was a growing seed, a memory of a time she and Remy had tried an empathogenic recreational drug as teenagers. She couldn't even remember the street name for it now, bunnies, maybe? That had given her strong feelings of empathy, hadn't it? Was it possible to start the chain reaction in the brain so that, like with Timorax, they could produce a chemical shortcut to the real emotion? Or even just cause some reaction in the brain so that if she couldn't actually cure Remy for good, it might look as though she had?

There was no doubt Aversion Therapy worked initially, but did it maintain the change long-term in the brains of offenders? Possibly for some, but not for others. That might explain why Begbroke and a few of the others had reoffended. If Conrad had followed procedure and the post-therapy follow-ups had been completed, Grace would know for certain. Maybe she could rescan the offenders and see for herself what had changed after the treatment. She turned to the computer and called up the records.

A few minutes later, Grace stood staring at the screens, a feeling of dread overcoming her. She wouldn't be able to do follow-ups.

All the reoffenders were dead – the post office gang, the Payback members, Begbroke. Myriam had been murdered. Even Mikey Kilgannon would never wake again.

It looked as though they had all been silenced.

CHAPTER TWENTY

Exhausted but not wanting to go home, Grace ambled along the Thames in the gentle evening sunlight. The barges on the water had been emptied of their commercial cargo and were collecting refuse instead.

She'd made progress at the clinic but not enough to convince Conrad yet. Remy's words on the phone echoed in her mind. *You know where to find me.*

Disappointment mingled with tiredness. It would be better if she could go to Remy with a definite plan, tell him that she had an agreement with Conrad that she would fix the therapy in return for his freedom. But she couldn't wait any longer. She needed to see him.

She turned swiftly on her heels and took a left down a side road, a sudden spring in her step. She didn't notice a shadowy figure behind her who also changed direction rapidly.

The Tube train was already at the station, doors open, as if waiting for her to step on board. It was past rush hour. She'd lost track of time. On the train she texted Dan to tell him she was working late – no kiss or kind words.

No reply.

Arriving at the familiar East End station, she felt as though she was split into two – Grace and Gracie – at once feeling at home and alien. On the surface, things appeared very different from the last time she'd been here. Coming out of the station, she moved along the pavement and looked more closely. There was so much hidden beneath the veneer of the new, and she started to recognise things, as if they were markers on a map drawing her back to her old life: a wall where she and Remy had once scrawled their names, the lamp post under which Lottie had claimed her patch, the local shop from which they'd nick the odd item when times were hard.

She turned down a street, past the old gasworks, which was now an air purifying station. Veering around the corner into the alleyway that led to Lottie's, the small two-up two-down where Grace had spent much of her childhood, her knuckles caught on the rough wall, grazing the skin. Ghostly echoes seemed to bounce off the brickwork: the shouts of the kids they used to play with, a twelve-year-old Remy laughing as he ran to escape the police after shoplifting sweets, the grunts of a punter leaning up against Lottie, Gracie and Remy puking after drinking too much alcohol before it was made illegal. 'Last round at the bar!' Remy had said over and over as she'd splattered the pavement with bile.

At the end of the alleyway, Grace gasped. All the old terraces had been demolished, obliterated, and replaced with neat cream-coloured houses with solar panels on the roofs and rainwater butts in the front gardens.

Where would she find Remy now?

She stood for a moment looking up and down the street, uncertain where to go.

–

Mal felt a little sorry for Grace Gunnarsson. She wasn't what he'd expected. She was petite and fair, not unlike his Layla in some ways. He still felt bad for hitting her in the street a few nights ago. Sarge had told him to frighten her off. Biz had goaded Mal before he left the office, full of adrenaline: *You won't hit her. You're chickenshit!* He'd tried to impress Sarge and prove Bizzy wrong, but he was overwhelmed with guilt. He hoped that the attack might have made her give up on Tier Three so that things wouldn't have to get nasty.

Mal had lain awake that night, thinking of how disappointed in him Layla would be, hitting a woman. In his mind he could still see Grace's terrified expression when he'd leaned over her on the pavement. Bizzy would have enjoyed that, but not Mal. They were chalk and cheese.

Looking at her now, he couldn't understand why Sarge considered her so much of a threat to Diros. He thought back to Sarge's words – *Could bring our whole company down … stop us having any more projects … prevent our mission … No one, no one is going to spoil the work we're doing, not that bitch from Janus, and certainly not that fucking Remy Wilson.*

He watched her finally turn and move off down the street. Why couldn't she have just taken the hint and left Janus? The other one hadn't though, had she? Sarge had sent Biz to 'deal with her'. Bizzy hadn't told him what he'd done to her and Mal hadn't asked.

He hadn't wanted to know.

Something really bad would happen to Grace too if he didn't try harder to warn her off. He knew what Sarge was like – he'd stop at nothing to protect Diros. If Mal couldn't persuade her to give up interfering in Aversion Therapy, then Bizzy would be sent to deal with her. Mal wasn't sure exactly what Biz would do to her, but he couldn't bear to think about it.

–

Grace didn't want to go home yet. She sat in a small, cheap and cheerful bar, with strings of coloured lights criss-crossing the ceiling and plastic tables and chairs that were moulded and painted to look like wood. A few customers sat around in pairs or small groups, but Grace remained alone on one of the stools at the bar. She stared at the AltCon menu then finally settled on a coffee. While she waited for it, she took out her phone and called Shannon.

Shannon was lying in bed. 'What's the emergency, doll?' she asked, her eyes half-closed.

On the screen from this angle, Grace could see that her shoulders were naked and an arm rested across her, dark hairs and a military tattoo of a dagger and rose with words in Latin that she didn't understand.

'God, sorry, I've disturbed you!'

'Don't worry about him,' she smiled. 'He sleeps like the dead now that he takes the meds to get over the PTSD.'

'Why didn't you bloody tell me sooner!' Grace whispered, as though the man in bed with Shannon might hear.

'I was just waiting to see if it went anywhere. Got to have some good points about living on the compound.'

'I'm so pleased for you,' Grace said, and she meant it, but then anxiety reared. 'Who else knows?'

'The lads all know, but they won't say anything, band of brothers and all that. And the kids love him. The youngest two don't even remember their dad, so it's a big novelty for them having a man around the place.' Shannon rubbed her eyes, smudging her mascara. 'What's happened to your face?'

'It's a bruise. I'll explain later. Are you sure you're okay to talk?'

'Of course.'

'That job Conrad offered me at Tier Three. I've got to take it. I don't want to, but it's the only way I can...' She heard a waver in her voice, felt her lip begin to tremble. A single teardrop splashed on the bar top.

Shannon didn't reply but lifted the man's arm gently from her. The image on the shell screen showed the ceiling for a moment, and when Shannon came back into view, she was in the bathroom leaning against the door, wearing a peach-coloured satin robe.

'What's this about, Grace? You and Dan are on good money aren't you?'

'It's not about the money,' she replied, sniffing and keeping her head down to prevent anyone in the bar seeing her cry.

'Then what is it about? Any time we've ever talked about Tier Three you've never had a good word to say about it.

"Brutal torture", I think were the last words you used.' The phrase emphasised Shannon's rolling 'r's and the sound stuck in Grace's mind.

Shannon pursed her lips and waited, but when Grace didn't reply she said, 'What's going on, doll? It's not just the job, is it? Your reaction the other day, in the car. That man, the one on the run. Is he something to do with all this? What's his name, Remy Watson?'

'Remy Wilson,' Grace corrected her.

She recognised that Shannon had picked up on something but had given her time and space. There weren't exactly secrets between them, but a trust that they would tell each other things in their own time.

'You know the Tier Three clients that have reoffended? One of them… that man… Remy Wilson… he's my friend, well, more than my friend.'

Shannon looked puzzled.

'You've never said anything before.'

'We haven't been in touch for a while,' Grace admitted.

'Looks like I've not been the only one keeping secrets.' Shannon smiled sympathetically.

'Aversion Therapy, it's not working properly. They're using synthetic fear to try to stop criminals offending, but…'

'They're reoffending,' said Shannon, her face serious again. 'I saw the reports.'

'Yeah, Dan and I have had a massive row because he thinks it's too dangerous for me to work there, but it's okay for him to splash it all over NewsFlex. He's put me at risk and now he's spooked because I was attacked in the street…'

'The bruise! Oh my God, are you okay?'

'I'm fine. But they know I work there. What if they come for me again?'

'Maybe Dan's right, Grace. Come back to Tier Two.'

'I want to! But you see, I have to stay working there, otherwise Remy will…' She sniffed hard and wiped her face with her sleeve as the bartender placed her coffee in front of her.

'God, you've got yourself into a right mess, doll,' said Shannon, kindly.

'I could really do with one of your hugs right now.' Grace tried to smile.

'This fella, Remy,' Shannon said. 'I mean, I'm not one to judge, but are you sure you're not playing with fire? Don't do anything to hurt Dan. He's a good man. He loves you. I know there are things you have to work through, but…'

Did Dan love her? He'd put his work before her safety. She wasn't convinced. Not like she once had been – only a few days ago. So much had changed.

'It's not like that, Shan. Remy's like a brother to me. I owe him. He always looked after me when I was a kid. I can't let him down now.' She kept her voice low as she said, 'He's on the run and if they catch him they're going to send him to Tier Four.' Her voice cracked. 'I can't even begin to describe what it's like in there. I can't tell you… it's awful… I had to sign a special confidentiality agreement. Conrad must have had one of his cronies in government give it the green light, because he got the money and the permission from somewhere. But it's all experimental…'

She sobbed.

Shannon remained in silent solidarity until Grace's anguish and frustration had calmed. Finally, she said, 'Okay, so what's your plan?'

That was what Grace needed to hear – an inkling of hope that there was a way forward. She sniffed hard and said, 'I've told Conrad I'm going to fix his therapy in exchange for being able to use it on an offender of my choice.'

'Is it even possible?'

Grace jumped as a man slammed an empty glass down onto the bar next to her. She stared at it. AltCon wouldn't be strong enough to use for what she had in mind. She'd have to get something on the street if she was going to make this work. There wasn't enough time to order anything from pharma without having to go through metres of red tape, and she didn't want to face difficult questions.

'Can you do it, doll? Can you fix the therapy?' asked Shannon.

Could she? Her mind wandered back to the alleyway, the portal between her past and her present, and she remembered a friend of Lottie's who was a small-time dealer. A plan began to form in her mind.

'I'm not sure, but I'm going to give it a good go,' she said, sounding suddenly brighter. 'Wish me luck.'

'I only hope you know what you're doing.'

'Oh God, so do I.'

When they ended the call Grace drained her coffee and made her way out of the bar.

Mal stood at the bar, pretending to sip his drink. He couldn't piece together the entire conversation, but he was beginning to understand why Sarge was worried.

The main thought going through his mind as he left the bar was that Grace knew Remy Wilson. *Wait until Sarge hears this!*

CHAPTER TWENTY-ONE

Grace waited by the alleyway for Harry the Box. He'd agreed to meet her at nine p.m. It hadn't been difficult to find his details. She'd logged into Janus on her shell and found him easily enough – a few arrests for possession and dealing of soft drugs, enough to create a record. Harry could get his hands on exactly the sort of drug she needed. Of course, it had taken some persuasion to convince him that it was Lottie's little Gracie from Morgan Street before he agreed to meet her.

Walking through the alleyway the previous night had cracked a wall of ice inside Grace that had hidden so much from her – it was like going back in time. Thankfully, Harry the Box was one of the memories that had thawed. He'd been a friend of Lottie's, a hangover from the nineties and rave culture. He was known for carrying around a huge weird-looking metal box that played outdated music. He wore a tie-dye T-shirt that read 'Love the Love' and sold marijuana and ecstasy. Back in the day, Lottie had described him as a 'good dealer' – he didn't do it for the money. He just wanted to spread a bit of happiness. The local kids threw stones at him.

Grace found it impossible to believe dealers like Harry existed in the present climate. AltCon drinks contained legal soft drugs, but the hardcore stuff that the government considered harmful was peddled by career dealers, people who cynically exploited those with weaknesses and addictions to line their own pockets. Nothing made Grace happier than when they were caught and sent to the eco-camps for a twenty-year stretch. She'd had to deal with so many addicts at Tier Two that she had first-hand insight into the suffering those people caused.

Her phone said five to nine. It was a balmy evening and the street was quiet. The buildings either side of the alley entrance had once been shops but were now converted into flats. Grace smiled at a memory of buying huge bags of sweets there when Lottie was flush and sharing the sugar rush with the gang of kids from the estate, Remy handing them out to the grasping little hands, his tongue between his lips as he concentrated on sharing them out fairly.

You know where to find me.

She smiled to herself, thinking how ironic it was that the key to helping Remy was not in a psychology book or a pristine clinic, but on the streets.

Could she help him? She didn't remember any evidence of him being a psychopath, but back then she hadn't known what to look for. As children they'd seen all sorts of behaviour that might have been described as psychopathic, but much of it could have just been survival.

Where are you, Remy?

Grace looked again at her phone. Two minutes to nine. A car drove slowly down the street but didn't stop. She felt nervous about seeing someone from her past, as though it would let something out of the strongbox that her heart had become, something she wouldn't be able to put back in. But what choice did she have? Harry had told her on the phone that he could get the very best, strong and unadulterated.

One minute to nine. As she waited, something caught her eye, a scrawl on the bricks, faded with time, almost camouflaged by the rest of the graffiti. She bent over and leaned closer. It was a small square with a triangle drawn roughly on top like a little house. Next to it were numbers. She stared at them, trying to decipher a meaning. A phone number? No… it was a time and date. But what did the shapes signify?

Still pondering, she stood up straight and was startled by a figure standing next to her.

'Jesus, Gracie, is that you? I didn't mean to frighten you.'

Harry the Box looked totally different. Gone was his music, the whistles and light-up bangles, the tie-dye T-shirt, the yellow smiley faces and the round glasses with the blue lenses. He looked like a little old man in grey slacks and a brown jumper, colourless glasses, an old-fashioned baseball cap and trainers.

'Harry, I didn't recognise you.' Her heart was still thumping.

'I could say the same for you. You're not the Gracie I remember.' His grin was the same though, one crooked front tooth darker than the rest.

'No, I'm not.' She returned his smile. 'Thanks so much for agreeing to help me.'

Mal watched from his car nearby, through the screen of his shell as he took a few photos. He wondered why Grace would be meeting an old man in a dark alleyway. His eyes flicked to the clock on his dash and he realised if he didn't get a move on he'd be late again and with the mood Sarge was in, he really couldn't risk it.

—

'Don't hurt my children!'

Mal couldn't look at the woman, her last words still ringing around his head as Bizzy pulled out the roll of duct tape and stretched it around her eyes and mouth.

Her husband, tied to the elegantly carved wooden chair identical to the one his wife was tied to, hung his head. He'd already taken a beating. Blood dripped from his nose and mouth onto his burgundy coloured trousers. Bizzy covered his eyes too.

Now that the couple couldn't see, Mal lowered the gun while Sarge and Bizzy went off to look for the safe. He lifted his mask above his forehead so he could breathe easier.

Hurt her children – what sort of people did she think they were? Mal himself had checked the kids and locked the doors so they couldn't get out. He didn't want them to see this. They were only tiny, so he knew they were no threat. Couldn't even use a phone. They'd probably sleep through the whole thing, he told himself. He prided himself on only ever hurting people who hurt others.

But things were changing. Sarge had compromised Mal's moral code after he sent him to find the Gunnarsson woman. She hadn't hurt anyone to his knowledge. But she would be able to do Diros damage because she knew too much. Did that count? And then there had been the woman in the bed…

Mal studied the man. He appeared strong, well built, maybe the same age as Mal, but taller, fitter, better fed. It didn't seem fair that one man should have so much. But did he deserve this?

The woman began crying louder, the noise wet and muffled through the duct-tape gag. Mal tried to distract himself by imagining that this was his home. He let his eyes travel around the room, taking in everything like a hungry man eyeing a feast, ignoring the husband's grunting as he wrestled with his restraints.

There was no denying that the 'big house', as Diros had referred to it in their plans, was a luxurious home. The carpet was a rich, deep blue. He could feel his feet sinking into it as he moved. The velvet couch wouldn't have fit into any rooms that Mal had ever lived in. There were actual paintings on the wall, thick with layers of oil that showed the artist's brushstrokes. Mal couldn't understand the appeal. He couldn't even work out what most of them were supposed to be. He preferred the glazed screens that most people had on their walls these days, with images that could be changed with the flick of a switch when you became bored of them.

He still hadn't told Sarge what he'd found out about Grace. He hadn't had the chance yet. He'd only just made it in time. Everything was planned meticulously by the clock, but if Mal had left the bar in the middle of her conversation on the phone, he'd have missed the crucial piece of information. *She knows Remy Wilson!* More than that – she was trying to help him! Sarge was going to flip when he heard that one.

Mal rarely held the power. He was going to enjoy it for a little longer, knowing things that the others didn't.

Sarge and Bizzy came back into the room again, empty-handed, frustrated.

Mal felt his stomach dip and began to feel sorry for the couple. He didn't understand why people didn't just give it up. They had to make it so hard for themselves. But he supposed people like this didn't reckon on someone like Sarge, who wouldn't stop until he got what he wanted, nor someone like Bizzy who didn't mind the use of violence, who revelled in it.

Sarge nodded to Bizzy, who gave the man a sudden, brutal punch in the face.

Mal flinched.

'Where's the fucking safe?' Bizzy yelled. He took a bowie knife from his belt and cut the tape from the man's mouth, leaving a rivulet of blood on his cheek.

'We don't have… a… safe…'

Bizzy punched him again and he groaned.

'Just tell us where the diamonds are and we'll go,' Bizzy said in a mock-pleasant tone.

'We don't have anything here. It's all in the bank…'

Bizzy hit him again and the man's head dropped.

The woman started crying louder. Mal hated the sound.

Bizzy took the gun from Mal and then flung himself onto the sofa, his legs spread wide, staring at the woman and pointing the gun towards her from his crotch.

Mal's anxiety about the way this was going was rising, but he had a job to do. He took a small plastic bag out of his pocket that contained the hairs and chewing gum, not much evidence, but he knew it would be enough to convince the police that the Lofthouse brothers had been up to their old tricks again.

Give a dog a bad name his dad used to say.

'Do you have to sit there?' he said to Bizzy. 'What if you leave evidence traces?'

He looked over to Sarge for back-up, but Sarge was poring over a book he'd pulled from the bookcase as though he was standing in a library deciding his next read.

'You really think you're a forensic support officer, don't you?' said Bizzy.

'At least I'm not taking any risks,' Mal replied. 'If they find something on that sofa...'

Bizzy stood now and came up close to Mal, chest pushed forward. He was a full six inches taller than Mal. 'The police will find the stuff from the evidence room and jump straight to the conclusion that it was the brothers.' He jabbed Mal in the chest, hard, and sat back down again. 'They won't be looking for anyone else. That's the bloody point.'

Bizzy didn't have to be such a prick to him all the time. Mal was about to reply when Sarge said, 'First edition of *The Time Machine*.' He sounded impressed but then dropped it onto a pile of other books on the floor and turned his attention back to the man.

He knelt down in front of him and said very quietly, 'If you won't tell me then I'm sure your wife will.'

The man strained against the tape, the veins in his neck bulging. 'Don't touch her!' he yelled, saliva flying from his mouth.

Mal looked from Sarge to Bizzy and back again. His unease grew. Something just didn't feel right tonight.

'Biz,' said Sarge.

As if understanding his unspoken command, Bizzy stood up and moved over to the woman. He tucked the gun into his belt, took out his bowie knife and cut her restraints swiftly. She gave a strange yelp in her throat.

'I think he's telling the truth,' Mal said.

They both ignored him.

With a nasty grin Bizzy sniffed at her hair and then licked her neck. The woman went silent and began visibly trembling. Bizzy dragged her out of the room. The husband began freaking out, screeching, 'Leave her alone! Leave her alone!' He thrashed against the chair like a snorting bull.

One swift punch from Sarge's powerful right hand and the man was unconscious.

'Sarge,' Mal began. 'Aren't we going to get the goodies and get out? This wasn't in the plan.'

Sarge turned his back on him and began looking at the paintings as though he was in an art gallery, standing at each one for a few moments before moving around the room to the next.

Minutes later, Mal could hear the woman shouting 'No! No!' from the room next door. Bizzy must have taken off her tape. It was not a good sign.

They never usually deviated from the original crime. Had Sarge and Biz agreed this sort of behaviour when he hadn't been there? When he was running from the Tube station to the office, late as usual?

'The Lofthouse brothers didn't do this sort of thing, Sarge,' he whispered. 'We can't change the MO.'

'Shut up!' Sarge snapped. 'I told you not to use any names!'

'But the brothers never—'

'According to Biz, they did once.'

Mal shook his head. 'He told you that so he could get away with it.'

'What do you care?' asked Sarge coldly. 'If you've got a problem, speak to him.' He turned back to the books and continued to pull them out, one at a time, and briefly regard them before dropping them onto the ever-growing pile on the carpet.

Mal made his way into the hall, pulled on his mask and paused before he opened the door to the front room.

The woman lay on her back on the floor, her clothes slashed open, the tape ripped from her face, her mouth a grotesque cave. Bizzy had pulled his trousers down, his buttocks exposed, kneeling over her.

Mal felt a rage building up in him. What would Layla think of this?

'What the fuck are you doing?' Mal yelled.

Bizzy turned his head towards Mal. 'What does it look like?' he said with a laugh.

'My children,' the woman said, pleading, as though she sensed Mal would help her.

'You're just as bad as the Embers Rapist! What is wrong with you, Bizzy?'

'Shut the fuck up and get the fuck out.' He turned back to the woman.

Mal left the room, the sounds of the woman crying about her children ringing in his ears. He stood on the other side of the door feeling weak and pathetic. What if it had been his Layla in there with an animal like Biz? Hadn't Mal joined the group to get revenge on people exactly like Biz, people who callously took what they wanted and never faced justice?

He thought about the husband in the other room.

He remembered the months and months after Layla's death, the agony of her loss, the anger and frustration at her attackers, and pressure began building up in him.

Blinded by rage, Mal kicked the door open and with an animalistic roar he launched himself at Bizzy. They both fell across the woman and onto the floor. They grappled for a moment until Bizzy, the stronger of the two, threw Mal off. Mal rolled over and hit a sofa. Bizzy stood up, pulled up his trousers and kicked Mal as he tried to get up.

The impact took his breath away.

'You fucking little prick. I'm going to kill you!' Bizzy yelled.

The woman began to move away from them, shuffling to a corner of the room, her hands, still taped together, over her face as the two men threw punches at each other. The force of one of Bizzy's blows knocked Mal crashing into a glass cabinet, shards showering around him. He regained his foothold and launched himself back at Bizzy, pulling off his mask as they fought.

'That's enough!' shouted Sarge from the doorway.

The two men, grasping each other's clothes, faces pale and blood-smeared, stood still, breathing heavily.

'Enough is enough!'

Sarge closed his eyes as if he found the view distasteful.

Mal and Bizzy let go of each other.

'She's seen your face,' Sarge said to Bizzy in a whisper.

The woman was whimpering, her body squeezed up against a wall, her face turned away from the men.

When Sarge opened his eyes again, he said, 'One of you has to go.'

Fear clenched Mal's guts. Josh had had to go — another member of Diros who hadn't made the grade. Josh had ended up in the foundations of a building. A concrete coffin. They had never spoken of him again, but his ghost was a constant reminder.

Sarge stood pointing his finger at them and then began to wave it between the two as if playing a game of eenie-meenie-miney-mo, his eyes dull, emotionless.

Finally, he stopped at Mal. 'I don't know if you have the guts for this. Too emotional. It's interfering with our work. Bizzy, make it look like the husband shot him and then kill the couple.' He turned towards the door. The woman was whimpering loudly now.

Was that it? After the last few years of brotherhood, their work together, their *bond*, now Sarge could just turn around and order him dead?

'Wait! Wait! I know something!' Mal shouted after him.

Sarge didn't even stop.

Bizzy pulled the gun from the back of his belt and aimed it in his direction. Mal ducked and ran into the hall after Sarge.

'You can't kill me!' shouted Mal, as Bizzy caught up with him, threw him against a wall and pressed the gun hard into Mal's face.

Sarge turned around and sneered. 'Oh yeah? And why's that?'

'Because I know how to find Remy Wilson.'

CHAPTER TWENTY-TWO

Conrad leaned against the door of the witness room in the Tier Three clinic, as far away from the offender, Penny Lithgow, as possible. Penny sat in the treatment chair and looked up at Abigail who was adjusting the arm of the magnet, extending it to reach Penny's skull.

'What's she done?' Conrad pointed a finger vaguely in Penny's direction but kept his eyes firmly on Grace.

'She's been convicted of helping her paedo boyfriend secure minors for high-paying punters,' said Grace.

Minors. It somehow seemed less painful than saying children. She could see how Penny might seem unthreatening to her victims. She was petite, smaller than Grace, the fringe of her dark bob trailing over her large brown eyes. She looked like a child herself.

'What about the boyfriend?' asked Conrad.

'Nasty bastard. He's up in Tier Four,' replied Abigail.

It didn't seem fair that, once caught, Remy would be put in the same ward, classified with the likes of Penny's boyfriend.

The sedative had kicked in and Penny gazed around vacantly.

'She's already been committed to Tier Four by the Neuro-court in Essex,' Abigail told him.

'But we have a small window of opportunity to trial my new therapy,' Grace added. 'Once she's in Tier Four it would be impossible to get her out and do this. You know the legalities.'

Abigail stepped away from the chair and nodded to Grace.

'Should we be having this conversation in front of her?' asked Conrad.

'She's going to Tier Four anyway after this,' Abigail said flatly. 'She's not going to be talking to anyone.'

'Just for clarity, Conrad,' Grace said, 'this is for preliminary trials and tests. This is not my chosen subject.' Remy's face flashed into her mind. 'I need time to get the correct treatment into place, make sure it's successful. If I can get this right, it's the least you owe me.'

She paused, waiting for his response. He nodded reluctantly.

She looked back at Penny, whose face, now slack with drugs and indifference retained a youthful, almost angelic glow. Grace felt deeply anxious having to work with such an offender. It was hard to see past the heartless cruelty and the damage that such a criminal could cause – especially to those who were so weak and vulnerable. But she reminded herself this was a means to an end. She couldn't think now about the heinous crimes this woman had contributed to, the devastation of lives, and young, innocent lives at that. Grace had to focus on the task in hand. Once Remy was in Tier Four, there would be nothing she could do for him.

She had to make this work.

'What we have here is a classic psychopath,' Grace said, 'which is why we aren't using emotisonics, as they'd have no effect. Abigail has already injected the nano-scanners, so in a matter of minutes, we should be able to see' – she looked up at the screen – 'there we go… exactly what's going on in Penny's brain.' Grace checked the nano-magnets were in place. 'She scores very highly on the psychopathy scale on her psychometrics, so she's the perfect test subject to see what we can achieve here.'

'There's a lot of people who score highly on the scale,' Abigail said, 'but they live productive, lawful lives. Psychopathy doesn't always have to mean serial killer, you know.'

Grace found herself smiling, feeling a sense of camaraderie with Abigail against Conrad, who now looked at her questioningly.

She nodded. 'It's true. Psychopathy has its… upside, if you can call it that. Difficult decisions can be made without being swayed by emotions, useful for bankers and financiers,' Grace said. 'A CEO, for example, who can make a rational decision that would save millions of pounds even though it puts people out of jobs. Good for the company, if not good for the employees. You'd want a surgeon with a steady hand in a life-or-death situation, wouldn't you? Someone who had the total self-belief that they could do the job, regardless of the odds?'

'You'd think it would be easy to spot them,' Conrad said.

'Psychopaths can be charming,' Abigail told him. 'You might be one and not know it.' She smiled at Grace and then turned back to her screen. 'It's a spectrum. It's not just black or white.'

A spectrum. Grace had seen Remy make quick and brutal decisions in the past which she'd thought at the time were based on survival, but had there been more to it than that? She didn't remember him being heartless or narcissistic. Or had he managed to hide it from her? Manipulation was the psychopath's superpower.

Grace felt her phone buzz once in her pocket.

'However, psychopaths are callous and lack remorse,' said Grace. 'So if they want something, then they're just going to go for it. In this case, little Penny here wanted a lot of money and didn't care if it meant selling kids to her sick boyfriend's associates.'

On hearing her name, Penny swivelled her eyes slowly to Grace, stared at her disinterestedly for a moment, and then looked back to the blank screen in front of her.

Grace beckoned Conrad over to the workstation, and he moved past Penny at a wider than necessary angle. 'On this brain scan here you can see the brain at rest. As I told you, fear won't cure a psychopath. The problem is the psychopathic brain itself.'

Grace turned to Abigail. 'Are all Tier Three offenders scanned for psychopathy?'

'Not always. Depends if there are obvious traits.'

'And if you find high levels of psychopathy?'

'We send them up to Tier Four,' Abigail replied. 'As you said yourself, the treatment that we use presently isn't going to make a difference. It's for the best.'

From his safe distance Conrad nodded in agreement.

So that was it, relegated to biostasis.

'But offenders don't know that, right?' Grace looked to Abigail and Conrad. 'I mean, they know when they get into Tier Three that they can choose eco-labour or Aversion Therapy, but they don't know before they're scanned that there's a possibility they can be sent to Tier Four?'

'We can't fix them,' Conrad said indignantly. 'Plus a diagnosis of psychopathy is an aggravating factor. They're highly likely to offend again.'

So he did know something about psychopathy after all, but it was only logistics.

'And at what point, Conrad, do you tell them that actually Tier Four isn't a nice, comfortable secure home for the criminally insane, but Siberia?'

He didn't answer.

Grace felt her phone vibrate once again. She nodded to Abigail, who fired up the reel on the viewing screen. Images of puppies playing appeared, five beautiful golden retrievers with short, cute snouts and big liquid eyes. The sounds of their whining and yapping tugged at Grace's heart.

'When the majority of people watch a video like this, you'd expect some activity in these parts of the brain.' She pointed to the images relayed from the nano-scanners. 'See here, the nucleus accumbens, or the ventral tegmental area, or even the amygdala, because most people would find it pleasurable watching these adorable puppies playing.' She turned to him. 'But as you can see on the scans here, Penny's brain does not respond in that manner. However' – she used the remote to move the video on and lowered her voice so Penny couldn't hear – 'watch this. For the record, this is CGI, not a real film, but she doesn't know that.'

Grace looked away from the screen as a larger dog, snarling with saliva-covered jaws, came onto the screen and moved towards the puppies, but the sounds turned her stomach. Synthesised or not, they were distressing to hear. She watched Conrad's response. He grimaced and directed his gaze to Penny.

'She doesn't even blink!' Conrad sounded amazed.

'Abigail, can you put headphones on her,' said Grace before turning to Conrad and saying, 'Probably fascinated by what she's seeing, doesn't want to miss anything.'

Once the horrible noises were only within Penny's hearing, Grace turned to her screen again. 'In a healthy subject, we'd expect to see these areas lit up...' She pointed to the scan: 'the anterior midcingulate cortex, the somatosensory cortex and the right amygdala – all areas involved in empathy, because most people would find viewing this sort of footage distressing. They feel sorry for the puppies.'

Abigail turned from the screen to look at the scans.

'However, look at the areas that have just lit up in Penny's brain,' Grace said, pointing to a curved shape near the centre of the scan.

'Which areas are those?' asked Conrad.

'Ventral striatum,' said Grace.

'The reward centres,' Abigail said, amazed.

It took Conrad a moment.

'You mean she's enjoying this?' he asked horrified.

Grace nodded solemnly.

'Reward?' he repeated as if he could not comprehend.

'She made money out of seeing children suffer,' Grace said. 'It was a win-win for her.'

Penny sat in the chair gazing at the screen, no outward sign that she was any different to the other people in the clinic.

'Why?' asked Conrad simply.

'It's the way she's wired,' Grace replied.

'Her heart rate has remained consistent throughout the test,' said Abigail. She moved closer to Penny and put a blood sampling bracelet on her, clearly fascinated.

Grace's phone went off again but the continuous vibration told her it was a call this time. She slipped it out of her pocket and took a quick look. Dan. His friends were over for dinner tonight. So wrapped up in her work, she'd forgotten. If she didn't get home in time, things were only going to get worse than they already were. She cut the call.

'There appears to be abnormal connectivity between the insula and ventromedial cortex,' Grace said, slipping her phone back in her pocket and pointing at the screen. 'This area is important for empathetic decision making. It's another sign of psychopathy.'

She nodded at Abigail, who injected Penny while Grace used the remote to change the video. 'Okay, Conrad, so Abigail has just administered Timorax. Should kick in pretty quickly.'

'Now watch this,' Grace told Conrad as she started the reel.

Penny's gaze intensified as she regarded the screen – CGI of Penny herself, looking much younger, being abducted by two large men. After a few minutes, Penny became agitated and distressed.

'Is this working?' asked Conrad, looking confused. 'Surely this is upsetting her?'

'Yes, but the part of the brain which registers empathy is still unaffected.' She turned away from the scan to face Conrad. 'Which proves to me that your therapy, Timorax, helps offenders to recognise that they don't want this to happen to them, but they still don't care if it happens to others.'

'Afraid, but not empathetic,' said Conrad.

'Exactly,' said Grace. 'The treatment isn't thorough enough. It doesn't get to the heart of the matter, which could be why it works in the clinic but doesn't always seem to have long-lasting effects after treatment. This is, I'm assuming, why some people who have had Aversion Therapy are reoffending. To really cure them, we need to see that the empathy areas of the brain are lit up, that they're registering just how terrible the victim's experience is, how awful, terrifying, degrading...'

Conrad folded his arms, staring intently at the screen before turning to Grace with an expectant expression.

'So, what I am proposing,' said Grace, 'is that we keep the therapy as it is in the main, but instead of using Timorax, we stimulate other parts of the brain instead, such as...'

'Can it be done?' he interrupted.

'I'm going to give it my best shot.' Grace hoped he didn't hear the wobble in her voice. 'I'm going to use the basic approach of Aversion Therapy – hypnotherapy, relaxant drugs and some kind of stimulus, minus the emotisonics. The important difference is that we need to change the focus from creating fear to creating empathy, targeting a different part of the brain. I'm going to dose her up with an empathogen...'

'Is it legal? I don't want the company getting into any trouble,' he began.

'It's only as illegal as anything you've already done, Conrad,' she replied coldly.

'Aren't they going to have to take it long-term to maintain—' Abigail began.

'We can think about that later,' Grace interrupted, still looking at Conrad. 'You're just going to have to trust me that we can sort this mess out.' She held her breath and looked him straight in the eye.

He opened his mouth to speak and at that moment his phone rang. Irritated, he looked at the screen. A light sweat shone on his forehead.

'I've got to take this.' He walked out of the clinic.

'Probably his pal in the DoJ,' Abigail sneered.

Grace looked at the time on the screen. She was cutting it fine to get home on time, even if she left right away.

Abigail leaned against a counter, took her phone from her pocket and began tapping. Grace wondered what her life was like outside the clinic. They only ever talked about work. Did Abigail have a partner, a family? What would Abigail make of her now she knew Grace could obtain illegal drugs?

'How long until the Timorax wears off?'

'Not sure, another half-hour or so?' said Abigail.

Grace's phone buzzed again. She took it out of her pocket and read the message.

Where the hell are you?

Bloody hell! If she didn't turn up, it might prove to be the straw that broke the camel's back with Dan.

'Abigail, I'm really sorry, but I've got to pop out for a while. I know this is extremely important, but there's something I must deal with at home.'

Grace teetered on the edge of her decision. She should be here, working on the therapy, saving Remy, not at some bloody dinner party with Dan's friends. But she needed to maintain the domestic status quo for now, even if just for her own sanity.

Abigail lowered her phone. 'Hey, no worries. I've no plans for tonight. What do I need to do?'

'We can't inject the new drug until the Timorax is out of Penny's system or we won't get a clear reading on its effects. She should already be in Tier Four, we're running out of time. Please, it would really be great if you could—'

'Wait until her system's clear and then give her a shot of the new stuff?'

Grace felt uncertain for a moment – something so crucial, was she really going to leave it to someone else to deal with? But then she reminded herself: what was important was the results. She'd be back in a couple of hours when the new drug would be taking effect and she could read the brain scans to see if her treatment had worked. That was the important thing.

She stood for a moment, desperate to stay. But she knew that the thread between her and Dan was so fine, at breaking point, that to not go home now would be a decision she wasn't sure she could return from.

'Yes, it's this one in the vial here.' She lifted one of the silver trays and then put it back on the work surface.

'No problem.' Abigail put her phone on the counter and turned to face her. 'Look, Grace, I'm more than happy to help. But are you sure this is going to work?'

Don't do this now…

'I think there's a good chance that it might,' Grace said, teeth gritted.

'It's just that, well, I know I'm only the technician, but I've been doing Aversion Therapy for a few years. I've given training on it in Newcastle, Brighton, Manchester. I know this treatment inside and out.'

'Look, Abigail, if you and Myriam made mistakes, then—'

'I know you really want to fix this, to do your best for Conrad, to make it right for our offenders, and I really admire that, I do… but surely a drug isn't enough to make someone feel empathy? Most people know about basic psychology – attachment theory, life experience, personality even, surely those things are what make up an empathetic person, not just some chemicals.'

Grace felt herself bristling.

'I mean there's lacking empathy,' Abigail went on, 'and then there's being a psychopath.'

Grace turned towards the workstation screen, her cheeks burning.

'I knew a kid at school who suffered severe neglect,' Abigail went on, not taking the hint. 'I think she lived in a cupboard or something until the authorities put her in one of those homes. How could she "feel" empathy – even artificially – if she'd never had the experience of it from loving relationships? Or from the usual emotional scaffolding that comes with lived experience? Isn't it a bit like taking antidepressants without working on the wider issues?'

'Look, what you're saying makes sense, but the brain's neural circuitry is malleable – it can be rewired through neuroplasticity. If a person practises imagining oneself in someone else's shoes there's a possibility that might reinforce the neural networks that enable us to put others' feelings first. It's possible for victims of neglect to go back to an earlier part of their development and work on what was missing, build up their foundations – it's not impossible.'

But there just wasn't the time. There was no time to rebuild emotional structures, or nurture someone through that learning process, or give their neuroplasticity a good workout, or rewire a neurodiverse brain. Maybe at some point in the future this was something they could work on, throw in some behavioural genetics once it was up and running – think of all the problems that could be solved.

What if these things had been available to my child? That sort of intervention, plus the love and nurturing I would have given him…

'Are you sure you want me to do this?' asked Abigail, shaking her head as though the trial was already a failure.

Grace's phone buzzed in her pocket again.

'Yes, I want you to do this, Abigail,' Grace snapped. 'I'm your line manager and I'm directing you to complete this trial. Your opinion of whether or not it will be successful is irrelevant. All the kit is set out. You'll have to record the scans for me so I can analyse them as soon as I get back. Make sure they don't' get *lost.'*

She sighed heavily. 'Look, I'll explain it all to you tomorrow. I've got to go. Can you text me to let me know how things are going?'

Abigail nodded, eyes cast down.

Under pressure and resentful about Dan's insistence that she return home, Grace fetched her bag and coat from the storeroom. She had to get Conrad to agree to let her treat Remy. And to do that she had to convince him that she could make Penny Lithgow feel something that she lacked, something crucial, something that would make her more human and less of the monster she was.

CHAPTER TWENTY-THREE

'Sorry, I didn't hear the question,' Grace said, looking at Elliott's earnest face. Her mind was back in the clinic, anxious about what Abigail might be seeing on Penny's brain scans. Her fingers twitched towards her phone. Any second a message or an image might come through. She'd linked her phone and her shell so that she didn't miss any information from Janus, particularly the Tier Three bulletins. She knew this was a security risk, but what if Remy was caught? She'd need to know immediately.

The four of them, Grace, Dan, and his friends Elliott and Caro, sat around the large table in the dining room. Dan had scowled when Grace had come in halfway through the main course and downed half a glass of AltCon before even removing her coat.

'I was just asking how your work was going. You know, anything interesting? That's why you were late, I take it?' Elliott probed.

Dan was chatting to Caro, one of his oldest friends and colleagues. They had cut their teeth together as young cyber-journalists and when Caro had met Elliott, also a journalist, he quickly became Dan's friend too. Grace liked Caro. She was good company. It was a shame Grace's resentment prevented her from enjoying it this evening.

Dan collected a stack of plates and took them into the kitchen.

'I'm developing a therapy that might be a little more humane than Aversion Therapy,' Grace said, hearing the tiredness in her own voice.

Elliott's ears pricked up at that. His eyes, a little piggy, narrowed and searched her face. 'Interesting!' He sipped his drink.

Why had she opened her mouth? He wouldn't let it go now.

What she wouldn't give to go back to the clinic and see with her own eyes what was going on.

'Go on,' said Elliott. 'Dish the dirt.'

'Dan!' called Caro, laughing. 'Elliott's grilling Grace!'

'Don't even think about it, Elliott!' Dan said, bringing a tray of colourful fruit and pastry desserts into the room. He placed it on the table and served the women before handing a dish to Elliott. 'I'm the husband, I get first dibs on any scoops. Don't be trying to wheedle out the information when I'm out of the room!'

'Fair play,' said Elliott, sipping from his glass again, looking disappointed. He turned back to Grace. 'So go on, off the record.'

'I think there's a less brutal way of approaching the therapy.' She wondered what Abigail would be seeing at that moment; the nano-scanners should have picked up on some brain activity by now, surely. She took her phone from her pocket and had a quick glance. There was a message from a street-shell.

'Brutal?' Elliott asked, his interest piqued further. 'Do tell us about the mysterious world of Tier Three.'

'Sorry, work,' she said, standing up and going into the kitchen.

Can we meet?

There was no name but she knew it was Remy. Her guts turned to water.

Where? she typed.

203

> You know where I am. Where we always used to go.

>   ???

How did he expect her to remember after all this time?

Dan came into the kitchen. She slipped her phone into her pocket quickly. He came up behind her and put his hands around her waist. She felt herself tensing up, and she knew he could feel it too. Had he had too much AltCon or was he just spying on her?

'Anything interesting?'

'Just work. Waiting to see if there's any change in an offender's brain.'

He let go of her and turned her round to face him.

His smell was so familiar and comforting. A feeling of deep loss overwhelmed her.

'Does it look like things are going to work out?' He searched her face and for a moment she wondered if he meant their relationship.

'No news yet. Although something should have changed by now.' They moved apart and she felt herself close down as she prepared a pot of coffee and he fetched mugs from the cupboard, both of them moving around the kitchen in a dance of avoidance. He carried the tray into the dining room and she checked her phone again.

Nothing else from Remy. Nothing from Abigail. She followed Dan back into the dining room and tried to focus on her guests.

'So how are things?' she asked Caro.

'Oh you know, baby Lu isn't sleeping. Mum has her tonight, so I might even get a lie-in.' Grace let her chat on for a minute, nodding at the appropriate times. She was almost relieved when Elliott interrupted.

'It's a shame what happened to your predecessor. Did you know her?'

'I met her a few times,' Grace said.

'The murder rate is really going up around here.' Elliott raised his eyebrows. 'First Myriam Kyriacou, and then the Payback couple...'

'No, that was suicide,' Grace clarified. 'They didn't want to go to Tier Four, they left a note...'

Elliott looked to Dan, who closed his eyes a fraction of a second too long.

'You haven't told her yet, Dan?' He slurped his coffee. 'The post-mortem suggests it wasn't suicide after all. Police say the man was holding the gun in his right hand, but he's left-handed. Foul play. People are getting picked off all around.' He licked his lips.

'Elliott!' Caro admonished.

'You should have told me, Dan,' Grace said coldly.

'You were late, I didn't get a chance... Plus it's not exactly the sort of news you want to receive at a dinner party, is it?' He glared at Elliott.

'All sounds a bit dangerous at the clinic,' Elliott banged on. 'I'm surprised Danny boy here lets you do such a dangerous job.' He laughed. No one else did.

'Yes, well, it's not about "letting" me, Elliott. I don't need permission to go to work,' Grace said.

'Now, come on,' Caro said in her pleasant but firm way, putting her hand on Elliott's arm. 'We were having a nice time...'

'It's not a dangerous job. We do a lot of good at Janus, taking care of people's needs and rehabilitation.' Grace felt herself getting hot.

'Bloody rehabilitation! What happened to good old punishment? Retribution?' Elliott, the smiling provocateur. It was always the same when they were together. 'You do the crime, you should do the time. I don't know why all these protestors get so agitated by it. Human rights, my arse! If you break the law then you must expect to suffer the consequences. It's as simple as that. I don't think it goes far enough, to be honest.'

'Elliott, she doesn't want to talk about work on her night off.' Caro grimaced and looked apologetically at Grace.

Dan, on the other hand, sat back in his chair, picked up his glass and nodded. 'So, go on then, Elliott. How far would you go?'

Dan had given him the green light. Elliott leaned in. 'Lex talionis.' He nodded and winked at the same time. 'If you injure someone you should be penalised to the same degree as the injured party. You should take from others what was taken from you.'

'Lex talionis means that you receive the estimated value of the injury in compensation, not the exact same injury,' Grace said. 'So who decides the value of what was taken?'

'Surely that should be the authorities?' Caro suggested, interested now, but keeping a wary eye on Elliott.

'Would they be able to really understand what was lost?' asked Dan. 'The Department of Justice would merely introduce blanket compensation for categories of crime, when in reality two people who have suffered the same crime might feel very differently about what was done to them.'

'So you're saying it should be the person who's been injured who decides the punishment?' Grace asked.

'But would they be thinking straight?' asked Caro. 'Balance and perspective would go out of the window. If someone hurt my Lu, it wouldn't just be an eye for an eye. I don't think I'd be able to stop.'

'I think the vigilantes have the right idea,' Elliott said. 'Certainly with the Embers Rapist.'

'Well, that's not an eye for an eye, is it?' Dan said, turning to face him. 'Should they have killed him, if he only raped them?'

'Only raped?' said Elliott. 'Sounds harsh, Danny.'

'Some women might think death was preferable, depending on their suffering,' suggested Caro.

'You know what I mean, though,' said Dan. 'The Payback vigilantes were just trying to compensate the victims. If your idea of eye for an eye is relevant here, then surely they should have done something comparable…'

'Such as what? It's not exactly the same for a man.' Caro sounded irritated.

'I didn't say it was. I'm just suggesting something comparable.'

'And castration isn't comparable?' asked Elliott.

'But it wasn't just castration, was it? He died,' Dan said. 'You can't leave these things to vigilantes. Maybe Caro is right and the Department of Justice should be sorting out compensation—'

'But that's the problem,' said Grace. 'Justice is a blunt instrument.'

It riled her how he could sit there and make theoretical judgements. What about the woman who helped the gang steal the foetuses? As wrong as her actions might have been, Grace still felt some empathy for her.

'But what about people who commit crime for what seems to them to be a good reason?' Grace asked. 'Stealing food to survive, for instance. What would you suggest as punishment for that? Let them starve to death?'

'Well, that's not going to happen,' Elliott said. 'The government don't let people starve to death any more. It's not Victorian Britain.'

'Don't they?' Caro asked, but her words were lost in his bombastic rant.

'Giving the offenders a drug-induced fantasy and a slap on the wrist isn't justice if you ask me,' he went on. 'It's not even an eye for an eye. It's no punishment at all.'

'I think eye for an eye was meant to actually *limit* the amount of compensation that the injured party could take,' Caro clarified. 'So they didn't go *too far*.' She raised her eyebrows at Elliott. 'So that the compensation didn't go beyond the instigating crime. It would be all too easy to lose control…'

'I treated a woman recently who helped a gang steal foetuses because it was the only way she could give birth to a healthy child,' Grace said. She saw Dan's face fall. 'She wasn't evil. She didn't do those things to hurt others or to be cruel, but because she was suffering. She couldn't have her own child. How would you suggest she be punished?'

Elliott didn't have an answer.

'An eye for an eye leaves everyone blind,' said Caro.

Elliott pondered her words for a moment, then took a deep breath and said brightly, 'Anyway, judging by what Dan has told me, it all sounds pretty dangerous. Maybe you should give up… get on with having children. It's the best thing we ever did, isn't it, love?'

Caro smiled and nodded, but immediately looked at Dan anxiously. Grace felt a heat rising in her cheeks.

Not unexpectedly, the evening quickly drew to a close after that.

—

'You told Caro?' Grace asked as Dan loaded the dishwasher after their guests had left.

'We've been friends for years. It helped to have another woman's perspective on the situation.' He pushed the full rack into the machine and closed the door.

'You didn't need another woman's perspective. You've got *my* perspective.' Grace folded her arms.

He turned to face her. 'I need support too. You've got Shannon to talk to. Don't you think this is hard on me?'

'Hard on you, Dan? You have no bloody idea!'

'Anyway, don't be coming across like you're all innocent.'

He took hold of a towel and began wiping his hands.

'What's that supposed to mean?' She felt her cheeks flush again.

'Who was texting you?' asked Dan.

'What?'

'You were fast enough to hide your phone when I came into the kitchen. Should I be worried?' It sounded like a vulnerable question, but there was a hard glint in his bright blue eyes.

She turned away from him, picked up a cloth and began half-heartedly wiping down a surface. 'I told you it was to do with work. You're not the only one who has a stressful job. There's a hell of a lot riding on this therapy I'm working on.'

'Oh yeah, like what?' Sarcasm laced his words.

What was she risking? A loving, stable marriage, a good job – things that she'd worked hard for, that she'd needed after her difficult start in life. And for what? A stranger from a troubled childhood, who might even turn out to be dangerous.

What the hell was she doing?

The ground beneath her seemed to shake, a seismic crack as the ice began to dissolve. It wouldn't be long before her past broke through her protective barrier and then there would be no going back.

'What's the real reason you don't want a baby?'

'I never said I don't want a baby.'

'You don't have to say it,' he almost shouted. 'It's true, isn't it? The secret text messages, being out late, saying you're out with Shannon when you could be anywhere...' His voice cracked. 'I know you're seeing someone else, Grace.'

'No, no, you've got it all wrong.'

But he wasn't listening.

'I'm going to bed,' he said without looking at her. She listened as he went upstairs and closed the bedroom door, something that they rarely did.

She stood for a moment in the silence of the kitchen, aware that her next move might change the course of her life.

She could go upstairs and try to reconnect with Dan, try to reassure him that he was the only one for her, that she loved him and things were going to be fine.

Or she could go back to the clinic, find out how the trial went, and then get on with trying to save Remy.

She went into the hall. She put her hand on the banister and peered into the darkness above.

A few minutes later, she was in her car driving back to Janus Justice.

CHAPTER TWENTY-FOUR

Abigail's expression told her everything she needed to know.

'Thanks for staying so late.' Grace dumped her coat and bag on the grey work surface and moved over to look at the scans, hoping to discover something Abigail hadn't, something that would give her hope that the therapy had worked.

'Shit,' Grace said finally.

'I'm sorry. I thought there might be better news,' Abigail said, 'but it wasn't a complete failure.' She swiped at the screen with her pale fingers. 'Here's the pre and the post images from the nano-scanners.' A fan of various images of the brain spread out like a deck of cards and Grace began flicking through them as though trying to find the ace.

During the treatment the empathy centres of Penny's brain had lit up to some degree, but not nearly enough to effect the change Grace had hoped for, and the change hadn't lasted. At one point, there had been a weak glow in the supramarginal gyrus, but it had faded like dying embers. If she couldn't show a clear and definite change, then how could she prove that the treatment had worked?

'Is Conrad around? Have you told him?'

Abigail shook her head. 'You should be the one to do it.'

She reached out and rubbed Grace's arm, whether in consolation or pity, Grace couldn't tell. It was the first time they'd had physical contact and her skin prickled beneath her sleeve. Was Abigail trying to apologise for questioning Grace earlier? Maybe she was making the point that the treatment wasn't going to work.

'It looked as though something was beginning to happen,' Abigail said, the bright images from the screen reflected in her marmalade eyes.

'Yeah, something, but just not enough.' Grace sighed.

'Not enough to convince the Department of Justice that we got it right,' Abigail added.

Grace couldn't decipher her tone. Disappointment? Or did she feel sorry for Grace that the experiment failed?

Grace couldn't care less about the Department of Justice. Her priority was curing Remy.

'Do you want a coffee? Help you stay alert?' Abigail offered. Another first.

'Er... yes, please.' Grace hoped she didn't sound too surprised.

Abigail smiled and Grace found herself smiling back. Maybe it wasn't pity, but Grace's fallibility meant Abigail could relax, let her guard down.

The thought depressed Grace further.

She perched on the stool that Abigail had vacated and studied the screen.

Not enough to convince the Department of Justice...

Then it struck her. She didn't need to convince them, only Conrad. Could she lie to him, tell him she'd solved the problem, even if she hadn't? If Conrad believed that Grace had found a cure, surely he'd sign the papers to release Remy?

And if Grace could convince Remy that Conrad was going to get him off the hook with the authorities, then she could persuade him to come to the clinic and go through the motions, couldn't she?

Convincing Conrad that she had a cure wouldn't be too difficult. He was full of himself, too interested in his own ego to think about the small details. He just wanted to win, to make money, to boost his reputation. He couldn't care less about the offenders. He'd shown himself to be someone who'd ignore protocol, take hefty risks, use unlicensed drugs and condone

Tier Four. Surely it would be easy to fool a man like this, a man whose own ambition blinded him.

But what would she do after Remy was freed and then Conrad expected her to fix others? What would happen to her job then? Could she say Remy's cure was a one-off and then go back to Tier Two?

And how would she be able to convince Abigail to go along with her plan? Unless she somehow faked the results and convinced her? Although hadn't Abigail said herself that she didn't exactly know how to read the scans? Grace would be able to lie about the results.

Maybe she couldn't save Penny, or Mikey, or anyone else in Tier Four. She might have to cut her losses, accept her limitations and just try to save Remy alone, leave behind those in Siberia. Frustration burned in her.

A click heralded a message on her work shell and her phone pinged at the same time. She picked it up, her mind immediately distracted, but also acutely aware of Abigail's presence as she returned to the desk with two cups. Grace still hadn't set her password. Abigail wouldn't be impressed if she found out.

Was it Remy, decoding the cryptic venue he'd suggested in his last message? Why was he afraid to come out with it? Was he paranoid about surveillance?

She rode a brief wave of adrenaline before it crashed when she saw the email icon. Abigail placed the two cups on a nearby surface and Grace stood up to be out of her eyeline as she opened the email.

The title read *HACKED!* The sender name was a series of letters and symbols.

Grace scrolled down to the message.

> We know what you're doing you torturing bastards!!! We've hacked this computer and we're in your system. We've seen all the confidential files and we're going to go public with them! Desist!

> Your treatment of these people is wrong and evil!!
> They are humans and should be treated like it.
> We can see what you are doing in your torture
> lab and we will stop at nothing to make sure that
> EVERYONE knows!

'Are you okay?' Abigail asked.

'Look at this.' Grace pushed her shell towards Abigail. 'Protestors. They're going to go public.'

Abigail put her hand to her mouth.

'Call Conrad's personal line,' Grace told her, as she flicked through the emails to see if anything else had been sent. Nothing.

Abigail picked up her phone. 'Conrad, you need to see this, right away,' she said as soon as he'd answered. 'A security breach, email.'

Grace couldn't hear his reply.

'Sent it already... Okay... will do.'

She ended the call and dialled again. 'He's coming back now. I need to speak to the head of IT. Conrad wants to shut down the main computer immediately until we know if it's a genuine threat.'

As the screen went blank, Grace felt like screaming. It was yet another obstacle in the way of helping Remy.

—

Mal felt as though the whole world was closing in on him.

This wasn't what he'd signed up for. This was not who he was, what he did, was it? The parameters had all shifted in the last few hazy, horrifying hours.

Bizzy, on the other hand, seemed to be almost happy about what had finally transpired at the big house. Lance Corporal Jackson Bizant of some battalion or other, called to serve his country, decorated in the Cobalt Conflict for heroism in the Democratic Republic of Congo, was really just a rapist with a taste for violence. Mal wondered if Biz had got that taste in the Congo, or was it something that war had brought out in him.

But it was Sarge who worried Mal the most.

Sarge, who had taken him, poor Malachi Peterson, off the streets and given him a home, stability, a mission. Sarge – of whom Biz spoke in reverential whispers and regaled tales of his bravery and the care he showed for his men when they were still in the army.

Sarge's actual rank was only a corporal, but his ego had relished the nickname. Had there always been something dark underlying his apparent goodness? Had he taken Mal off the streets only to give him a false sense of security and then groom him into becoming a killer?

Mal had fallen for it. Thinking he was doing something *noble* by delivering justice to those who'd evaded it. But the woman in the big house, she'd been innocent. And he'd been there, he'd been a part of that.

'How was your shift this afternoon?' Bizzy asked, snapping Mal out of his anxious thoughts.

'What do you care?'

Biz looked up from the screen he was working at and scowled. 'Who's pissed on your fire?'

'Sorry, just had a tough shift on a crime clean-up.' He immediately regretted apologising but after what had happened at the big house, he was trying to keep the peace.

'Yeah?' Bizzy focused on him. 'Anything interesting?'

'No, unless you call the blood-spattered living room of a young mother killed by her partner "interesting".' The woman from the big house came to mind and Mal felt a wave of despair.

Bizzy shrugged and turned his attention back to the screen.

Mal had been shaken up at the scene. One of the other cleaners had asked him if was he okay, and he'd been furious with himself. It was that sort of weakness that got you noticed, made people suspicious.

But he'd been shaken up all right. Not because he'd never seen a body before, nor a murder scene, nor blood – so much blood – but because it had reminded him of the woman from the big house. If it hadn't been for him, she would never have seen their faces, heard them talking, heard him say Bizzy's name.

It was his fault she was dead.

Sarge hadn't spoken to Mal, looked at him even, since that job. If Mal hadn't found a connection between Grace and Remy – his insurance – who knows where he'd be buried now? Maybe under a building like Josh. Or alongside that poor mother. Mal had been the one to bury her. His punishment, Sarge had told him, and he'd wept until the last shovelful of soil. If he'd let Bizzy have his way then maybe she would still be alive.

He couldn't bear to think of her children, but the memory of them crushed his chest: the blonde hair, the cartoon pyjamas on the older one, the dummy and the baby-gro on the little one, obediently, innocently lying down, when the strange man told them to, when he told them their mummy and daddy would be okay, they were just having a cup of tea…

Him and Layla had talked about having kids, a boy and a girl, the names they'd give them, the places they'd take them.

How could he ever be a father now after what he'd done?

And even though Sarge had said one of them had to go, Bizzy was still here. Maybe Sarge realised he needed both of them to complete the mission. Then what would happen to them?

'Lofthouse brothers have been arrested,' Bizzy said, looking at his shell.

They'd be done for murder – another thing weighing heavily on Mal's conscience.

'Look, Sarge doesn't want us scrapping,' Bizzy said reluctantly. 'We've just got to get on and make the best of…' He waved his two index fingers between the two of them.

Mal decided he should go away for a while. Try and make a life without them, like Remy had. But for now, he would just have to play ball, keep under the radar. His father's voice echoed in the back of his mind: *You never stick with anything! You're a loser, Malachi!*

'What are we going to do about Grace?' asked Mal. 'She's not going to die, is she?'

Bizzy's eyes switched to Mal. 'You got a soft spot for her? You shouldn't get so attached, you idiot.'

Mal shrugged. 'I was just wondering.'

'Yeah, well you'd better make good on that promise that you can find where Remy is, or you know what will happen.'

Mal knew all right. It would be a toss-up between the two of them – him and Grace. Either he kept his mouth shut and Sarge and Mal would kill him, or he told them where she was and another innocent woman would die.

CHAPTER TWENTY-FIVE

'But did they actually give you any proof that they'd hacked the system? I mean, did they mention any *specifics*?'

It was nearly midnight. The IT security team had taken over at Grace's workstation just as Conrad swept in and they'd been there for thirty minutes, analysing the system to see what had been going on.

Conrad had been grilling Grace for most of that time. 'But why did they send the email to you?' He was anxious and sweating. She'd never seen him so out of sorts.

'I don't know,' she said as he read the email over again, as though he might be able to decipher some hidden meaning behind the words.

'But they don't actually give any details' – he directed this to one of the IT team. 'I mean, they don't seem to actually know anything about the confidential files, do they?' He turned back to Abigail and Grace and whispered, 'This information is highly sensitive. If it gets out then I am *fucked*! This company is fucked!'

The IT technician carried on tapping away, impervious to Conrad's vexation.

'We need more security on these computers.' Conrad was leaning over the desk, practically shouting in the technician's face. 'This should have been done months ago! What the hell am I paying your company for?'

He turned back to Grace. 'My brief from the department is to get the number of offenders down, and I've done that. This is the most successful penal programme ever seen. Maybe we use some unorthodox methods, but it works.'

'What do you want me to say, Conrad?' said Grace.

But he didn't seem to hear her. Instead, he said, 'I'll have to ring the Department.'

Abigail yawned as Conrad disappeared with his phone.

No one wanted the coffee Grace offered.

Conrad came back ten minutes later and looked somewhat relieved when the technician said that he couldn't find any security breaches on confidential files, but he wouldn't be certain until more tests were run.

Maybe the so-called hackers had lied just to cause trouble.

They'd have to wait and see.

Exhausted, Grace said she'd see them tomorrow, took the lift down to the underground car park and got into her car. She closed her eyes for a moment and leaned back against the headrest.

Shannon would probably be asleep or with Shuggie, but she needed to hear a friendly voice. She drove around until she found a public communication shell.

'The treatment – it didn't work,' she said, as soon as she heard Shannon's sleepy hello.

'Ach, doll, I'm so sorry.' Her face came closer to the screen. 'Are you calling from a street-shell?'

'Yes. Looks like the clinic computer's been hacked. I've linked my shell to my phone, so I'm not sure if my phone is safe or not. They're threatening to go public.' Tears burned behind her eyes. 'Which means the press will be all over us, and some of the treatments… Conrad hasn't exactly used legal methods.'

'There'll be an investigation if this gets out?' Shannon asked.

'For sure. The protestors are going to go ballistic when they know what really goes on in there.' Grace sniffed and then said, 'I really thought my treatment was going to work, there were some changes in Penny's brain, but not enough.'

'Did she seem any different afterwards, in herself, I mean?'

'She's a pathological liar, so who knows? Abigail recorded her reactions. Penny cried buckets, said she was completely devastated now that she realised what she'd done to those kids, even swore she was going to start up a charity to help victims of sexual abuse. She was totally plausible, Shan, but the scans told the truth.'

'Classic psychopathy, manipulative to the end,' said Shannon.

'Exactly.'

'What did Conrad say? About the failed therapy, I mean?'

The word 'failed' sounded worse coming from a friend.

'He doesn't care if offenders get fixed or not. He was too wound up about the computer system.'

'It won't be safe to work there, Grace. It's bad enough already.'

'If this goes public then Conrad's on his own. There's no way a government minister is going to put their name to scandalous treatments of offenders or experimental trials, regardless of whether he condoned it or not. What happens to my work if the clinic gets shut down? If the police find Remy, what will happen to him then?'

Shannon stifled a yawn.

'God, I'm sorry. It's so late. I'll let you go.'

'Look, Grace, none of this can be sorted tonight. Get some sleep. You must be exhausted. Speak tomorrow when we have a better idea of what's gone on with the computer.'

'Yeah, sorry to wake you. Thanks, Shan. Night.'

Grace closed the screen then hurried back to her car in the dark, empty street. Once in, she locked the doors, let her hands slide to her lap and sighed deeply, gearing herself up for the drive home. After a few moments, she put her thumb to the dashboard ignition pad and the electric engine started up with its quiet hum. The graze on her knuckles caught her eye as she placed her hands on the steering wheel. She remembered when she'd caught her hand on the wall in the alleyway by Lottie's, and the symbol on the wall popped into her head – a square with a triangle on top and numbers, a symbol that she knew had been important when she'd been a kid. It was just out of reach, somewhere at the back of her mind...

And suddenly she remembered. It wasn't a triangle, but a crude drawing of an open book, face down, and the numbers represented the time. Her head exploded with memories of leaving secret messages on the wall – meetings, times, dates... their secret hideout.

You know where to find me.

Twenty minutes later, she was back in the area where she'd grown up. She left her car outside a hypermarket and made her way to the large corrugated iron perimeter fence behind the shop, which separated the car park from the railway embankment beyond. Behind the fence lay the small, derelict community library, obscured and forgotten in the no-man's land between the fence and the trees that muffled the sounds of the trains. It was a neat, squat 1960s building with beige pebble-dashed walls and a row of narrow windows that ran around the top just below the roof. It had been abandoned long before the rise of digital books and the price of paper had put the final nail in the coffin of codices, and had provided their gang with a fort the other kids were envious of. Grace had an image of herself standing on the roof in her wellies throwing stones at would-be invaders.

She made her way around the building through the weeds and accumulated rubbish. Bushes had grown up over the years, making it more difficult to access the rear, but eventually, she found the back door, a large metal affair, covered in graffiti and bent up at the bottom corner where they had wrestled to get access as kids.

Grace pulled at the handle and simultaneously used her foot to pull at the bottom of the door, her body remembering. There was a scraping sound as the metal cried out against the concrete beneath it, and then she stepped into the darkness and stood for a moment in the silence.

Hearing nothing, she moved forward, her feet rustling through pages torn from old books strewn on the floor like autumn leaves. She switched on the light from her phone but it was feeble against the blackness that filled the corners and the spaces between the nearly empty bookshelves.

She heard the scrape of steel against concrete again and her whole body tensed, frozen, unable to move.

'You found me, then.'

It was his voice, older, deeper, but it was Remy.

She swivelled round and there he was, his hood up, holding a cotton bag from the hypermarket, wincing against her light. She pointed it down and stood in the thick darkness for a moment. A match made a tiny explosion in the dark as Remy lit it, and then the soft glow of an ancient oil lamp, an artefact of their gang days, illuminated the librarian's reception desk.

He pulled back his hood to reveal his face, pale like when he was about to go into a fight as a boy, his hair long, still raven dark, his jawline that of a man's.

'Remy... Look at you...' He was dishevelled: black cargo pants, scuffed black trainers and a battered old army jacket. He looked like one of the many veterans who lived on the streets, used up and worn out.

'Look at *you*,' he replied, his voice low and quiet. 'You look like that teacher in senior school, the one we used to drive mad making the humming sound.' A smile flickered across his face, a hint of the old Remy, and she began to relax a little.

He was her friend, her brother, but was he also a psychopath? Was he guilty of those things that the justice system wanted to punish him for? Grace said *Maybe*, Gracie said *No*. Gracie won out and moments later she was in his embrace. Regardless of his tatty clothes, he smelled like soap. He felt solid, substantial, no longer the wiry boy she'd said goodbye to when she left for university.

'The army fed you well.' She was glad he was thriving, but also aware of his brute strength.

Whatever dam had been holding back her memories for the last fifteen years suddenly broke and she was awash with a rising tide of emotion. Her breath felt torn from her as she sobbed.

'Hey, hey. It's okay...' He pulled back and looked at her, concerned, his eyes the same sea-grey she remembered.

'I'm sorry, I'm just overwhelmed seeing you. What are you doing here? What's been going on? Have you got any money, enough to eat?'

'Slow down, slow down!' He took her by the hand and led her behind the reception desk where there was a small back room. She felt as though he was leading her back into the past. Flashes of memories from twenty years ago jolted her brain as they made their way into what had once been the den headquarters. Remy had set up a small camp behind two floor-to-ceiling bookshelves: an army regulation sleeping pod, an army backpack, some clothes folded in a neat pile on a lower shelf, alongside a wind-up army lamp, a few bags from the supermarket and a small stack of books from the main library. He nodded to a couple of chairs in the corner as he sat down on the pod, but she remained standing.

'I was out with the army in Africa for a while.'

She raised her eyebrows. 'I didn't think you were the type for discipline.'

'It gave me somewhere to be.'

'Running away from someone?'

'Something like that.'

There was still graffiti on the walls from way back. She ran her fingers along the hieroglyphs of their childhood and smiled, feeling a rising nostalgia. Her wedding ring caught the light and he nodded towards it. 'I didn't think you were the type for discipline either.'

Dan. He would be worried, however pissed off with her he was at the moment.

'Give me a minute. I'd better message home.' She took out her phone, typing instead of dictating so that Remy wouldn't hear, ashamed somehow. Maybe her two worlds would collide, but she was determined to keep Dan and Remy apart as long as possible.

At work. There's been a security breach at the
clinic. Hackers in the system. I'll get back asap.
Sorry.

Remy pulled two bottles of water from the bag he was holding
and held one out to her. She took it, brought a chair over and
sat down.

'You said you needed help. Do you need money?' she asked.

He shook his head. 'Mum left me money.' His face fell. 'I
should have shared it with you, but I was so angry when you
went. You look as though you've been doing okay… Your house
is pretty nice.'

'You followed me?' She shook herself. This was Remy, not
some serial killer.

He shrugged. 'Had to check you were okay.'

She pulled her jacket tighter around her.

'Your husband, he's tall, eh?' He grinned but then turned
more serious. 'A journalist?'

Embarrassed, she said, 'I don't think you came here to talk
about my husband.'

He nodded and then said, 'Can you get me a bio-passport
to get me out of the country? As I said, money's not the issue.
I just can't get out without the ID.'

'If you've been through Tier Three then you'll already have
a probation chip under your skin. They put them in when they
do the tattoos. So when they scan you at the airport your image
and all your details will come up. They'll know exactly who you
are.'

Most people only used bio-passports temporarily when they
went on holiday as they were impossible to lose and could also
be used for bank transactions, but there was still huge debate
about government surveillance and civil freedom. Those happy
with the transparent society retained theirs as ID cards and
received huge tax breaks for doing so.

'I managed to escape before they put the bio-chip in.'

'Why doesn't that surprise me?'

'I was hoping you could get me one with a fake name.'

'No, Remy, I don't have access to biochips. I don't do that kind of work and I'm certainly not going to commit fraud for you.'

He shrugged. 'Never mind, it was a long shot. Anyway, I'll probably never get through security with this.' He pulled up his sleeve to reveal his Janus tattoo. 'It'll be ages before it wears off.' He looked resigned. Then he said, 'So what does your work entail?'

'I used to rehabilitate offenders at Tier Two. People who are in need, homeless, troubled, men and women who came back from Africa.'

How 'troubled' was this man in front of her?

'Used to?' He grabbed the shopping bag and pulled out a packet of sandwiches which he tore open and began to devour. Halfway through it he looked up and paused, mouth full, and held the remaining sandwich out to her.

She shook her head.

'Now I… I work in Tier Three.'

He lowered the sandwich and a piece of cucumber fell to the grimy floor. 'Really?' The disappointment in his voice burned her.

'I was promoted recently.' She cleared her throat. 'Look, the thing is, Rem…' She blushed, his nickname rolling off her tongue automatically, but feeling too intimate. 'I've done a deal with my boss. You must have seen in the press that Aversion Therapy isn't as effective as previously thought. He's agreed that if I can make Aversion Therapy foolproof then I can use it to fix you and get you off the police wanted list.'

'What?'

'So you can be free.'

His expression darkened.

'I told you the sort of help I need. I don't need any bullshit therapy.'

'Well, clearly you do as it didn't work the first time, otherwise you wouldn't have been arrested for the same crime twice.' She was irritated now. He was judging her for trying to help when he was the one in trouble?

'You actually choose to work there, even though you know what they do in Tier Three?'

'Never mind me, have you got any idea what they're going to do to you if they catch you and you go to Tier Four?' Her voice cracked.

'I didn't do it, Gracie…'

Lying – one of the most obvious psychopathic traits. How had she missed this? What other traits had she not seen as they were growing up? She stood up, pulled her coat around her.

'Oh my God, do you know how many times I've heard that?'

'But I didn't do it! I was set up.'

'Remy, the police are looking for you. You killed a drug dealer, a deal gone wrong they said, for God's sake. What the hell were you thinking, doing deals with drug scum? Didn't Lottie's death – my mother's death – mean anything to you?' A loud gasp escaped her lips and she covered her mouth with her hand. She felt raw and exposed. Her mum, that moment in the bed in the prison block, was a memory that she hadn't allowed herself to dwell on for years.

'It's not like that,' Remy said.

But she didn't want to hear. 'Lottie would still be alive if it hadn't been for that pimp and his drugs, and you've been working with people like those bastards who killed our mothers?'

She remembered Harry the Box and suddenly felt guilty about buying drugs from him. It wasn't the same, though, was it?

'Have you wondered why all of a sudden it looks as though Aversion Therapy doesn't work?' Remy said. 'It's because there's a gang of men called Diros and they're—'

She was too tired for his excuses. 'Look, Remy, whatever's happened, you've been convicted of a serious crime and the only way you can get out of this is if you let me cure you properly, with a new therapy.'

'But I haven't done—'

A noise from the main body of the library startled them.

Grace's ears pricked up and her whole body tensed.

Remy stood and put a finger to his lips. He picked up a thick wooden window pole which lay along one of the dusty shelves and made his way silently out of the office. Grace hovered around the door listening. Who should she fear more – whoever was in the library, or the man who'd gone out to look?

It wasn't me, Gracie.

Psychopaths could be manipulative to serve their own needs. Was he playing her just to get something that would get him out of trouble? Christ, what was she doing here with someone she hadn't seen since she was a kid? Someone who had killed twice! He could say it was a set-up all he wanted, but she'd seen his scan.

And scans didn't lie.

CHAPTER TWENTY-SIX

It was him or Grace. Only one of them would survive.

Mal stood on an ancient recycling bin, its lid half chewed away by a long-cooled fire, as he continued his surveillance of Grace through the high library window, his breath fogging the dirty glass.

He wasn't going to let her out of his sight now.

His life depended upon it.

But how could he let them kill her and then go on living himself?

A movement inside the library distracted him. There was someone else in there with her. Mal felt adrenaline radiate through his limbs. She was too small and fragile to be able to protect herself. He ought to do something. But then his cowardice got the better of him and he remained, ashamed, standing on top of the bin. What was the point of trying to save her if Sarge was only going to kill her anyway?

Why was this woman messing with his mind?

Chickenshit! Biz taunted him inside his head.

The man began to speak and Mal immediately recognised his voice.

Remy.

Mal ducked down briefly afraid his old comrade might see him, but as the conversation developed, curiosity got the better of him and he peeped through the broken window again. He absorbed everything they said: Remy's desire to escape, Grace's intention to help him, Remy's belief that he'd been set up by Diros. The cat was out of the bag. Sarge had been right. Grace was a threat, not only because of her work at Tier Three, but because now she knew too much.

As he shifted position, mentally preparing his report for Sarge, his foot slipped on the bin. Remy suddenly stopped talking and moved towards the door.

Mal panicked. He hopped down to the concrete below, slipped through a gap in the fence and ran towards the hyper-market.

As soon as he got to the lights of the shop, he looked back. To his relief there was no one following him. He immediately called Sarge and informed him both the targets were together – *no they hadn't seen him, yes they were still there, yes she knows everything* – and after giving directions was given a 'good man' instead of a goodbye from Sarge.

A feeling of relief cooled his nerves. He was out of the doghouse with the boss for the time being. He leaned against the wall of the hypermarket and took a few deep breaths. The late-night food redistribution truck pulled up nearby to collect stock that was hitting its sell-by date to take to those in need at Tier One. He recalled a packaged sandwich donated to him when he'd been living rough – rye bread, beef, Emmental cheese, mustard, pickle. It had been the most delicious food he'd eaten in months. The taste memory tantalised his tongue.

Had it been worth it – leaving the streets for the lifestyle he had now?

Had he sold his soul for a roof over his head?

One phone call had put Grace's life at risk – another inno-cent death on his hands. He let out an anguished yelp, startling a woman who swerved her trolley away from him. He slapped his face, hard, once on the left cheek and once on the right cheek, trying to sharpen his wits and disperse the maelstrom in his mind.

What choice did he have? Either he offered up Grace to Sarge, or Sarge would kill him. He was a coward, that was true, and his survival instinct was strong as a cockroach's, as Biz had once said. And Biz knew about cockroaches. Mal had just signed Grace's death warrant to save his own skin. Shame and frustration burned in him. He was worthless, his whole life had never amounted to anything. The only noble thing he'd ever done was loving Layla, and that was only because, for some ridiculous, unfathomable reason, she'd loved him first.

And look where that had got him.

He'd felt a strange twinge when Grace had embraced Remy. Mal wasn't altogether sure what the feeling was, but he squashed it down.

'Layla, Layla, it's not the same as me and you…' he prayed, guilt overwhelming him.

They'd be here soon. Sarge would want Remy alive to find out if he'd told anyone else about Diros. Damage limitation. He pushed thoughts of Grace out of his mind.

Focus on the positive. Because of Mal's discovery, they'd be able to eliminate the threat to Diros. Bizzy would be so jealous. It would be like killing two birds with a single stone.

He thought again about Remy and Grace.

Two birds.

One stone.

—

'I think it might have been a rat. All quiet now.' Remy came back into the room, as though the library door was a wormhole and he'd just returned from their childhood.

He sat down on the sleeping pod and they started speaking simultaneously.

'Remy, I don't know what—'

'Grace, I didn't do it.'

An awkward silence.

'You can't blame me for being suspicious.' She sat back down on the chair. 'You weren't exactly on the straight and narrow when we were young.'

His eyes dimmed with disappointment. 'It's been a long time.'

'I'm sorry for leaving you,' she began. 'When I went to uni…' but he held up a hand to stop her, shaking his head.

'Water under the bridge.'

'Maybe you wouldn't have gone off the rails so much if I'd stayed.'

'Off the rails?' He sounded offended.

'Remy, you're a wanted man…'

'Yes, but not by the people you think… you've got to believe me.' He hung his head and a swathe of dark hair covered his face. He took her by the hand and she let him hold it for a moment before pulling away. He was convincing, there was no doubt about that, but she'd learned too much along the way to be fooled.

'Honestly, Gracie,' he said. She felt a brief wave of reassurance as he said her name, but then she remembered. She braced herself, it was time to face the facts.

'You were treated in Tier Three, up in Manchester the first time you were arrested,' she said. 'I've seen the files and they clearly show that there's something wrong, something I think I can fix…'

'There's nothing wrong with me!' he snarled and she pulled back from him.

'I've see the scan with my own eyes. I've seen the fault in your brain…'

'The fault in my brain?' he scoffed angrily. 'Someone's messed with the scans.'

'How could they? The scans are relayed right to the computer. There's nowhere in between for someone to mess with them.'

'There's nothing wrong with me!' he yelled.

She looked at him aghast.

'I'm sorry,' Remy said, shaking his head. 'I'm just very, very tired.' He lay back on the sleeping pod, with an arm across his face.

She was running out of energy and time. If she could persuade him to come to the clinic and keep him safe for another few days, she might be able to get the synthetic empathy to work. Anything to save him from Siberia.

'The second time you were arrested you'd done the same thing again, attacked a dealer after he ripped you off according to the reports, but this time he died. And this was *after* you'd had Aversion Therapy.'

'I didn't do it.'

'No, but the police say you did. There's evidence to say it was you. And it wasn't just a fight gone wrong this time. It wasn't manslaughter.' She'd found out that the dealer had been stabbed to death. Remy had brought a knife. It had been premeditated. It was a Tier Four offence.

'I was set up. I know I'm not a psycho, so when they scanned me and said that I was — I knew that *they* had done it to get me out of the way.' He paused. 'I just don't know *how* they got into the files at Janus.'

'Remy, if the police rearrest you then you're going to end up at Tier Four and you have no idea what it's like… It's not a place I would want anyone I love—' She stopped. 'I want you to come with me. So I can help you.'

'If *they* find me, then I'm going to end up dead, so it's a lose-lose situation.' He sat up and began poking his fingers into the various pockets of his army jacket.

'They? Who are you talking about?'

'I've been trying to tell you.' He pulled out a crumpled printout of a photograph and passed it to her. Three men in desert camouflage stood outside a tent, smiling, arms across each other's shoulders. Remy was in the middle, between a tall dark-haired man and a baby-faced soldier who couldn't have been more than twenty. Next to them was a thick-set older man with silver-grey hair. He stood apart, arms folded, unsmiling. Remy pointed to the photo. 'There's another one too, who wasn't in the army. They call themselves Diros. They research crimes and then try to copy them.'

232

'Diros? Copy crimes? Why would they do that?' She passed the photograph back and rubbed her fingertips as though it had left a residue.

He put it back in his pocket. 'I used to be one of them,' he replied quietly, his words chilling her to the bone.

She leapt from the chair and tried to get to the door, but he was on her. He grabbed her by the shoulders and turned her to face him.

'I don't want any part of this,' she cried, scrambling to get away from him. 'I thought you were in trouble. I didn't think you were a killer!'

'Gracie!' He grabbed hold of her and shook her.

She stood still.

'I swear to God I haven't killed anyone... not like that.' His grey eyes told her he was telling the truth. 'Yes, in Africa, but I was a soldier. That was different. Please, listen to me.' He loosened his grip. 'Just give me five minutes to explain and then you can walk out of my life forever, and never look back, but give me an opportunity to at least tell someone the truth before... before...' He didn't finish the sentence.

She nodded reluctantly, her heart beating madly. Did she owe it to her childhood friendship to stay and listen? They stood in an uneasy truce as he began to speak. She listened, but her eyes roamed the room, looking for a way out. One of the windows behind him was bigger than the ones in the main library and waist height, probably just about big enough. He was still holding her by the arms.

'When I came back from Africa,' he began, 'I had nowhere to stay. Lottie's place had gone. I had some money, but I wanted to start a new life somewhere and I just needed a little time to think about what to do. One of those men, Sarge, offered me his sofa. He'd been our outfit leader over in Congo and I guess he was our leader back here too. I bunked down with him for a while, but things took a strange turn.'

'What's that supposed to mean?'

He released her and sat back down on the pod.

Was the window locked?

'We were bounty hunters,' he continued. 'The government were looking for reliable, well-trained people to clean up the streets to make the new justice system appear as efficient as possible. I guess they didn't want a whole new raft of problems caused by ex-army coming home with conflict trauma. Most of the ex-service people I knew ended up either collecting criminals or going to one of the Tier Two compounds themselves.

'I wanted a regular income after Africa and there were plenty of veterans needing work. We were in a gang of five. We used to collect all sorts of criminals. Got a good price for some of them. I'll be honest, I also wanted excitement. I'd been on three tours for Cobalt and when I got back it was just... boring. It was a good life at first, getting paid to catch bad men, and women too sometimes, and we partied hard at the weekends.

'But then things started to change. I wasn't getting the same high for each catch. Sarge saw himself as on a mission to do justice or some shit, and when Janus started letting people off with "day-trip treatments" as he called them, he set himself up as some sort of vigilante, finding people who'd been through Tier Three and punishing them. Then he got the idea that if he made it look as though Aversion Therapy was faulty, they could get it shut down altogether, have people going back to prison for long stretches instead.' He rubbed his hands over his face. 'Anyway, suddenly they were calling themselves Diros and' – he shook his head – 'they turned on one of the gang, a young fella called Josh. He'd started questioning Sarge. Josh couldn't keep his mouth shut, began criticising some of the things we were doing and refused to get involved in some of the cases...' Remy paused. 'And rightly so.'

'Why didn't you go to the police?'

'They were like a family to me. We'd bonded in the army. Unless you've been through that, you don't know what it means. Where else was I to go? Plus, I was hardly innocent.

I'd used unnecessary violence, overlooked some of the things the others did. If they'd gone down, they'd have taken me with them. Sarge accused Josh of insubordination and then, one night, Josh didn't come back. Biz said he'd gone to live with his sister, but Josh had told me out in the Congo that he only had brothers.'

Remy blew out a steady stream of breath. Were those tears in his eyes? Grace had never seen him cry, even when his mother died. Remy sniffed hard and went on.

'That was when I realised just how bad things were. I'd already made plans to move on and it seemed more urgent than ever to get away. I asked one of the lads, Malachi – we called him Mal – to come with me. He was young, like Josh, wasn't army, though. He didn't seem as bad as the others, but he refused to leave. I don't think he believed me that the other two had got rid of Josh. Anyway, Sarge began finding out the names and details of people who'd recently been through Tier Three. He suggested we could copy the crime using the same MO and plant evidence so that it looked like the original offender did it. They even managed to get their hands on evidence to convince the police. Sarge said it was the perfect crime and no one would ever catch us, no one would ever suspect that anyone else was involved.'

The people who had been silenced – Noah Begbroke, the post office robbers, Mikey Kilgannon. They bore testimony to what Remy was saying.

'But why?'

'Sarge wanted to destroy Janus because they were letting people get away with stuff. But Biz, he was just an animal, loved the violence. Used to get a kick out of hiding a crime within a crime, he said. Mal – I really don't know why he stayed.' He sighed. 'We were so messed up after the things we saw in Africa. Maybe that had an effect on us.'

'How did they find out about the Tier Three crimes?' asked Grace.

'One of them, Bizzy, was an experienced hacker, but I think there was someone who worked there, an insider, who gave them information.'

An insider?

'Oh my God,' Grace said, shocked. 'Myriam!' Had the mild-mannered professional given Diros information? Forced or willingly?

'I don't know who it was.'

'They killed her,' said Grace slowly. Had she known too much, or refused to cooperate?

Remy nodded gravely. 'Doesn't surprise me.'

'Conrad gave me her job.'

'What?'

'I'm the new psychiatrist at Tier Three.'

She saw that look on his face, the one he used to give her when they were kids, the one that said he was going to protect her. But how could he protect her against this?

'I can imagine you working at Tier Two,' he said. 'You always liked to help people in need.' His face fell again. 'But Tier Three?'

She didn't answer but glanced down at his Tier Three tattoo, deep navy against his pale skin. She wondered how he'd escaped arrest.

'You know, Africa was… traumatic… awful at times, some of the things I saw, but I chose to go there, I was doing a job. But it was nothing compared to what they do in that clinic. Going through that therapy, especially when I hadn't even done the crime…' He shook his head. 'You're not living the sort of life I expected, Gracie.'

'What's that supposed to mean? You thought I'd end up on the game because of Lottie?'

'No,' he said.

'And look at you. You're living exactly the sort of life I thought you'd live, sleeping rough, in trouble with the law and gangsters. When are you going to grow up, Remy?'

An uneasy silence. Finally she stood up. 'I took a job at Tier Three because it was the only way I could help you. Do you think I wanted to put offenders through that torture? At least I'm trying to do something positive, change the therapy for the better so that it actually works...'

'Don't you see? The therapy *does* work!' Remy said. 'It's what Diros are doing that makes it look as though it doesn't.'

'So why don't you just tell the Department of Justice? Tell them what you told me. Then they'll let you go and Diros will be their problem.'

He smiled sadly and shook his head.

'As if they would believe someone like me.'

'Remy, I want you to come with me. My car's by the hyper-market. You've got to hand yourself in. That's the only way I can legitimately get you off the hook.'

'Get me off the hook with who? Do you think I care about the authorities?' He stood up to meet her eye to eye. 'You have no idea how dangerous Diros are. They're the ones in control here, hiding behind offenders who've already paid the price. A crime is committed in exactly the same way and then they plant the evidence to make the police believe that the original criminals have reoffended. Diros are destroying people's chances to start again and literally getting away with murder. And you think they're going to let us just walk away? They'll silence us like they silenced the others.'

'Us?' said Grace, fear creeping through her.

'You can't save me, Gracie. How can you, when there's nothing wrong with me and the authorities aren't going to listen to a word I say? I don't have any evidence. It's my word against compelling physical evidence that I'm lying. And once they see those falsified scans...'

There was no evidence for Diros's existence, but there was plenty of evidence for Remy's flawed brain. What did her instincts tell her? Who was she, right now? Grace who trusted science or Gracie who trusted her instincts?

'You've known me since we were tiny,' Remy said. 'Don't you think you'd have known by now if I was a bloody psycho?'

'It doesn't matter whether you are or not. Unless we do something, then either the police will get you or Diros will. You can't just sit here and wait for it to happen.'

'I thought out of anyone in the world, you would believe me.' He sounded resigned, like a man who knew he'd taken a losing bet. 'And you're right, I'm not going to sit here and wait for it to happen.'

He pulled his hood up. 'I'm sorry I dragged you into this. Just… just forget it. I shouldn't have asked.' He looked up at her one last time, disappointment and rejection in his sea-grey eyes. 'Bye, Gracie.'

And he was gone.

CHAPTER TWENTY-SEVEN

Grace stood by the window in the back room and watched until Remy had disappeared into the trees behind the library. He'd come back. He'd see sense and realise that her plan was the only way of dealing with his problem. Even if he was a psychopath, he'd figure out his best chances of survival rested with her, and psychopaths always took their best chances of survival.

She switched her phone light on, the only light in the back office other than the small army lamp that sat by Remy's army pack. She couldn't resist so she sat on the pod and lifted the flap on the pack. There wasn't much, mainly army issue, a small shower and shave kit, food rations, a health pack and supplements, some underwear. Lottie would be sad if she could see her boy living such a meagre existence.

In one of the front pockets, she felt something hard and flat. When she took it out, she saw it was a brightly coloured plastic 'Funland' keyring with a photo of the two of them, identical to the one she always carried in the zipped pocket in her bag.

He had kept it all this time.

She held the photo between her fingers and smiled sadly at the image of the two of them laughing on the rollercoaster. There had been so many good times. They had meant so much to each other. If he was psychopathic, he wouldn't have shown so much care for her, would he? Unless he was getting something out of their friendship that she couldn't see. He was still her friend, the only family she had.

She was so confused. Had everything he'd told her been true? Or had he just been manipulating her?

She'd done this the wrong way – she could see that now. If he wasn't a psychopath then he would be offended by her attitude. If he was a psychopath, then what was the point of telling him that he needed to be cured? He wouldn't care! What she had to do was to somehow come up with a plan to persuade him to come with her, that it would all be to his advantage. If he was cunning and manipulative, then she would have to match him.

She heard a shuffling in the main library and quickly shoved everything back in the pack, except for the keyring she was still holding.

She stood up, ready to work on him.

'Remy, I'm sorry,' she called out. 'Come on. Let's talk it over.'

The shuffling outside stopped.

She sighed heavily. He'd been stubborn and unrepentant as a kid. She couldn't imagine that having changed. She put her head around the door to the main library. It was dark and shadowy beyond the weak light of the oil lamp.

Grace moved forward, trying to avoid slipping on the pages of abandoned books. She came out of the back room and stood behind the counter. She could see his outline by the door, but her eyes were still adjusting to the dark. He moved a little closer to her but didn't speak.

'Look, I'm sorry, I've got no right to march back into your life after fifteen years and try to tell you what to do,' she began. 'Maybe I can get you a biochip somehow...'

She felt guilty, knowing she was manipulating him. But it was for his own good. She would persuade him to come with her to Janus to get a chip, and then what? She would decide as she went along. All she needed to do now was just get him in her car.

First things first.

He stood still by the door. God, was she going to have to beg him? He hadn't lost his stubborn streak, then.

Her phone beeped. *Where are you?* Had Dan not got her last message? *I just rang your work. I know you're not there.*

Bloody hell. She was in for it now.

There was a shuffling by the door. He moved a bit closer. Why was he being like this? She was exhausted and now dreading going home and having to come up with something to tell Dan. She didn't need Remy having a strop.

'I'm too tired for this right now. I'll come back tomorrow and we'll talk then. Hopefully you'll see sense and I'll be able to help you get away from…'

A bright light burst on, blinding her. She put her hand up to shield her eyes.

'Jesus, Remy, switch it off!'

He said nothing and the light stayed on.

'Get that out of my face, Rem!'

She heard a noise to her left and began to feel afraid. Was there more than one person there?

The light swivelled upwards and as her vision readjusted she could see silhouettes of people moving around.

Three people.

She felt as though she'd just drunk a freezing cold glass of water.

It had only been a matter of time before the protestors found her. They must have followed her straight from Janus.

Streetwise Gracie tried to talk her way out of it. 'Look, I don't agree with Aversion Therapy either,' she began. 'I don't even want to work in Tier Three, I'm only doing it so that I can… I'm only in there to get information for NewsFlex so they can throw it open. I'm one of you. I swear—'

Two more torches burst into life and Grace knew she was in trouble.

She could see them now – a tall, lean, dark-haired man held a gun pointed in her direction, leering at her. Another man, smaller, shuffled by the door, facing away. But the man in front of her, holding his torch against his cheek so that his face was lit up like a terrifying mask – he was the one who frightened her the most.

He wasn't particularly tall but he was broad, the outline of his muscles neat beneath his tight black top. His grey hair was almost white at the temples. He stood almost perfectly still, his lips hinting at a smile, his ice-blue eyes locked on Grace.

'Shut up,' said the leader. He spoke calmly, quietly, almost *pleasantly*.

Grace's blood ran cold. He was the man from the photograph that Remy had shown her. They weren't protestors. They were after Remy.

The smaller man twitched and moved closer to the door.

'Stay!' commanded the leader, without looking back at him.

The man froze and then slowly turned back.

The tall one, on the other hand, didn't move his eyes from her body, taking in every detail from her head to her feet and then back up again.

Grace pulled her jacket tighter around her. The men stood between her and the main door. They'd catch her before she could get to the back door. The windows were too small and too high up in this part of the library for her to get out of. Where was Remy when she needed him? Gone off in a bad mood because he hadn't got what he wanted!

She could see no escape.

The leader took a step towards her and said, 'You need to tell us where Remy is… right now.'

Mal hadn't thought things through. His father had often told him he hadn't the brains to understand consequences.

She was prettier this close up and somehow that made it worse. He regretted not waiting for her to leave before he'd called the others. All he'd been thinking of at the time was to save his own skin. He knew better than anyone how cruel Sarge could be.

Mal longed for an alternate universe in which he'd gone with Remy six months ago, instead of standing here as a dog in Sarge's hunting pack, about to attack this poor woman.

If only he'd kept his big mouth shut! He could sense Bizzy's interest in her. His mind travelled back to the woman in the warehouse with the Embers Rapist. If only he could let Grace out of the back door like her, shuffle her away from whatever the hell was about to be unleashed.

'Look, I don't know who you are...' Grace lied.

'We know who you are, Grace Gunnarsson.' Sarge took another step towards her and Mal could see her eyes widen, her body tense. 'And we know that you're trying to fix Aversion Therapy.'

'Diros,' she said quietly.

'Ah, you've heard of us,' Sarge said. 'But, you see, Grace, here's the thing.' He took another step towards her. Mal felt his chest tighten, his breaths shortening. 'You're a threat to our mission.'

Our mission.

Mal knew he wasn't one of them. Not any more. It was no longer about bounty hunting or vigilantism. Their darkness was growing rapidly, feeding off their deeds. Cruelty for cruelty's sake.

'And Remy... well, he's been disloyal.'

Mal shifted uncomfortably.

'We're going to deal with you, Grace, and we're going to wait here for Remy, and then we're going to deal with him too.' Sarge chuckled to himself and hung his head for a moment. When he looked up he directed his gaze towards Mal. 'Disloyalty breaks down trust. No trust, no brotherhood.'

Mal turned away.

'We've had serious breaches of loyalty before,' Sarge said. 'What do we do if someone's been disloyal, Biz?' Bizzy was still looking the woman up and down. His attention snapped towards Sarge but it was clear to Mal that he hadn't heard the question.

For a moment no one spoke.

'We give them an opportunity for redemption, or we make them pay,' Mal said slowly, uneasy with the silence.

'Which is it going to be?' asked Sarge, turning towards Mal. 'Do you want an opportunity to make up for your disloyalty after that fuck-up at the big house? Or do you want to pay?'

When he didn't answer Sarge said, 'It's you or her, Mal.'

'But she hasn't done anything wrong.' Mal stammered. 'We punish people who get away with things... not the innocent.'

'Justice,' Sarge said quietly, 'guilt, innocence. What does it matter?'

Sarge reached to the back of his belt and pulled out a gun, took off the safety catch. He held it out. Mal's tongue felt rough in his mouth.

Time slowed, the blood rushed in Mal's head, his heart beating out a rhythmic countdown to a terrible, inescapable fate.

Grace let out a little cry and he stole a glance at her, ashamed.

It's you or her, cockroach.

Sarge still held the gun out, as he unwrapped a pellet chewing gum with his free hand and put it in his mouth.

If Mal didn't prove his loyalty he'd end up like poor Josh, whose mum would always be left wondering what had happened to her boy.

He took an uncertain step towards Sarge.

Grace cried out, 'Don't... please!'

He took hold of the gun. It was heavier than he expected, and warm from Sarge's grip. He swallowed hard and lifted his arm, pointed the snub-nose at her. It was self-preservation, wasn't it? *You or her, cockroach...*

'Please don't,' she whispered, tears running down her cheeks.

Bizzy watched, eyes wide with excitement.

The sting of sweat broke out on Mal's forehead as placed his trembling finger on the trigger and tried to slow his breathing. A wisp of light caught his eye behind one of the dilapidated shelves to his right. Was it Layla, drifting between the remnants of the books, her expression one of sorrow at what he had become?

All eyes were on him; Grace terrified, Bizzy excited, Sarge expressionless.

'I can't,' he stammered, lowering the gun slightly.

The words shattered the tension.

'Fucking chickenshit,' Bizzy spat. 'I *knew* he wouldn't do it, boss!'

Sarge sighed heavily and Mal knew he'd failed the test. The gun hung from his trigger finger, flaccid. He reached out to return it to Sarge, a man who hated weakness more than anything.

'You give me no choice,' sighed Sarge.

Mal looked over to where Layla's spectre moved between the shelves. *We'll be together soon, my love.* She would forgive him for being weak. She would forgive him, too, for having feelings for Grace. They were nothing like what he felt for Layla, of course. She would understand.

He closed his eyes and braced himself, waiting for the bang, Layla filling his mind. She was all around him, trying to reassure him, tell him it would be over quickly.

But there was only silence.

When Mal finally opened his eyes, Sarge had tucked the gun away and was flicking through the pages of one of the ancient books as though nothing had happened.

His hopes rose, but he'd seen Sarge in action too many times.

There would be worse to come.

'I've got a better idea,' Sarge said, chewing his gum loudly. He pulled out a wad of cash from inside a zipped-up trouser pocket and thrust it towards Mal. 'Call Thumbs. Tell him I want a fuck-load of heroin. Take the car. We'll wait until Remy gets back, make it look like he killed her – drug deal gone wrong.' He grinned at Grace. 'Remy's got form.'

Two birds, one stone.

Mal reluctantly took the money and turned towards the door, knowing it was only a matter of time before he was dealt with too. The plastic money felt slippery between his fingers. He could make a run for it. But where would he go? He had nothing, no one, besides Diros.

As he pushed the door open, he heard Bizzy chatting like an excited puppy. 'Can I have a go, Sarge?'

Mal turned back, horrified.

'Whatever,' Sarge said, without looking at him as he turned his attention to the few books remaining on the shelves.

'Biz, what the hell?' Mal said, his hand on the door.

'Mal's fallen for you,' Biz said with a laugh, as he grabbed Grace by the arm. 'But I'll show you what a real man does.' He stared at Mal with an evil grin and pushed Grace towards the back room.

Fury raged through Mal's body. He stood rooted to the ground, his position in the pack too precarious to challenge Bizzy. If only he'd been there when those animals attacked his Layla.

But he knew he didn't have it in him.

Biz was right. He was chickenshit.

'Just get the drugs, yeah?' said Sarge, as though he was talking about buying a pint of milk from the corner shop.

Mal pushed open the door and stood at the threshold for a moment, the cold breeze on his face cooling his burning guilt, listening to Grace's howls as she was ushered into the storeroom.

He didn't leave, but instead turned back and shouted hopelessly, 'Biz, you don't have to do this!'

CHAPTER TWENTY-EIGHT

'You don't have to do this,' Grace parroted, the words bouncing off the walls of the small room. The reply was a brutal slap across the face. Her mouth felt numb, her ears rang with the impact. His hands travelled down her body. She retched.

Biz stood in front of her with the arrogant stance of a man who knew he was about to take something the other didn't want to give.

There was no point screaming, they were too far away from the hypermarket for anyone to hear. Words were useless. How was Dan going to feel when they found her body – dumped, violated and lifeless? *If* her body was ever found.

'I'm going to enjoy this.' He smiled and slid his belt off.

Gracie would be fighting like a wildcat and yet here was Grace, her body rigid with fear, as Bizzy grabbed her roughly and licked her face and neck again.

Bizzy's hands moved lower, roughly pulling at her clothes, mauling her.

Fight back, come on, Gracie, where are you?

He bit hard on her breast and she cried out in pain.

'Don't worry, love, you'll start enjoying it when I really get going,' Bizzy said as he ripped her top. She tried to push him away, but her arms felt too heavy and her feeble attempt only amused him.

'Ooh, a bit of fight left in you?' he goaded, somehow playful and menacing at the same time. 'Go, on, resist! It will make it more fun for me.'

The flash of a memory suddenly ignited in Grace's brain, something that she'd never allowed to float to the surface of her consciousness before: her bedroom at Lottie's place in the small hours of the morning, a man – much bigger than her, touching her, an equilibrium of fear and revulsion – just like this moment.

But Remy wasn't here to rescue her this time.

Bizzy was struggling with his zip, which appeared to be jammed. During the brief respite, outrage and anger began to bloom in Grace. The feelings grew rapidly, overtaking the fear until Gracie took the driving seat. As he was looking down, she grabbed the army lamp from the shelf. All the trauma of Gracie's past, the strength of Grace's adult body, the frustrations of trying to help Remy, and the anger and fear about what he was about to do to her came crashing down on Bizzy's head in one swift motion.

He was stunned.

Before he could gather himself, she hit him again, hard and swift, across the side of the skull. He fell back on the pod, groaning and grasping his head, and she took her opportunity to scramble towards the small window.

The old plastic frame was stuck fast, melted near the base, where it looked as though someone had let a candle get out of control. She banged at it with heel of her hand but it didn't budge.

Bizzy sat up slowly, shock and fury emerging in his expression.

She banged at the window again.

She hopped up onto the chair and began to kick at it. The whole frame gave way as her leg bashed painfully against the edge of the surrounding wall.

Bizzy was trying to get up now. 'Get back here, you fucking bitch!' His words were slurred, but she knew it would only be a matter of time before he was alert.

Terrified that he would signal the other two, Grace quickly jumped off the chair and scrambled through the gap, grateful now for the difference in size between them. There was no way he'd be able to follow her.

She landed in the scrub outside, catching her hand on a broken bottle, the adrenaline providing pain relief, but the blood beginning to run freely. She heard Bizzy shouting and the others responding to him.

Her mind was racing as she pulled her sleeve down to cover her hand in an attempt to mop up the blood. In a few minutes, they were going to be outside and they would catch her. What would they do to her then? A hundred metres away, the lights shone from the hypermarket.

But they'd get to her before she even reached the perimeter fence.

She hopped up onto a recycling bin, scrambled onto the roof and then lay flat, trying hard to calm her breathing, the sleeve of her top darkening with blood.

The rear exit of the library burst open and the three men ran around the building, the sound of their feet kicking through the cans and broken glass jangling her nerves.

'Go and look in the trees, Mal.' Sarge's deep voice, hardly a whisper. 'I'll go to the car park. Biz, stay here and see if Remy comes back.'

Ten, twenty minutes later, she wasn't sure, they reconvened.

'Nothing,' she heard Mal say, sounding out of breath.

'Me neither,' said Bizzy. She would know his voice anywhere now.

'Don't worry, we'll get the bitch at the clinic,' Sarge said.

'Do you think she'll send the cops here, boss?' Mal's voice again.

'No chance if she thinks Remy is coming back. There's no way she'd risk him getting caught. Let's go back in and wait for him. There's time to deal with her later.'

'Fucking little whore,' Bizzy said. She heard him spit. Her skin crawled.

All her instincts told her that as soon as the fire door banged shut she should run.

But whatever trouble he was in, Remy had always been there for her.

It was time to repay him.

If she wasn't there to warn him on his return, he'd die at the hands of the men who moved around beneath her.

She gently pushed herself up onto her knees and crawled across the roof to look out for Remy through the trees. He'd return, she could feel it instinctively. Getting back in touch with her old self had reignited their connection.

There was only one thing she could do now to save him.

And he wasn't going to like it.

She took out her phone, relieved to see it was on silent, and rang the security department at Janus.

'It's Doctor Gunnarsson. I'm transporting an offender. I'll be there within the next hour,' she said quietly. She held the phone with her left hand, conscious of her injury.

'Do you need us to come to you and help bring him in?' asked the guard.

'No, no. If he sees anyone else, he'll run. He doesn't suspect anything so he should come with me willingly. I can get him into the car park, but when he sees you lot, he's going to fight it.'

'We'll be ready,' came the reply.

She lay in wait, her heartbeat the only marker of time.

Finally, she heard someone moving through the trees by the railway line. She was about to climb down when the scrape of the metal door signalled one of the men had come out. Grace ducked and then she heard someone relieving themselves against a wall. When they had finished, she peeked over the edge of the roof to see Mal standing alone. Inside, the other two men were laughing.

'Fuckers,' he mumbled.

Remy was moving towards the library, she could see him through the trees, hands in his pockets. Her throat strained with the desire to shout out. *Remy, stay there! Don't come any closer!* But it would be suicide.

She saw Mal turn his head swiftly in the direction of the railway embankment.

Blood rushed furiously in Grace's head as Remy moved closer.

Mal stood still for a moment and then went back into the library.

Quiet as a cat, limbs trembling, Grace hopped down from the roof onto the bin and ran towards Remy.

He looked up, startled. 'Are you still here? Go away, Gracie... I don't need...'

She put her hand across his mouth and he pulled back, confused. 'They're here,' she whispered.

He bobbed down, hands in front of him as though he expected an immediate attack, eyes locked onto the library.

'My car...' she whispered, and pointed before grabbing his hand and pulling him towards a gap in the fence.

This time, she was rescuing him.

Once on the other side, she let go and started running, Remy close behind. The car park was empty but for a few vehicles pooled in light near the hypermarket entrance. Her car stood alone. Seconds later, the three men appeared and began running towards them, yelling.

A shot rang out across the car park.

Out of the corner of her eye, Grace saw Remy duck and come up again, before the pair of them made it to the car. Her heart was beating fast and her hand shook as she reached out to the thumbprint recognition pad.

Another shot rang out and the rear windscreen shattered.

The central locking systems clicked, Grace yanked open the door and threw herself in. She slammed the door hard as Remy scurried round to the passenger's side. Two more shots fired in quick succession and pinged off the bodywork.

Through the glass, she could see Sarge, Bizzy and Mal as they hurtled towards the car, pushing a startled late-night shopper out of the way. Her trolley hit the ground, its contents bouncing and smashing on the tarmac as the men ran.

Remy fumbled with the handle and finally opened the door.

'Get in! Get in!' Grace screamed.

Remy hurled himself in and quickly pulled the door shut.

Bizzy slammed against the car.

The engine fired up and Grace screeched off in reverse.

Mal, driving another car, skidded to a halt next to Sarge and Bizzy and they jumped in.

Grace swung her car around so it faced the exit and shot off through the gates and onto the main road.

Remy held onto the dash, his fingers spread wide, white at the tips. He turned around to see where the others were.

'Faster, Grace! Go on!'

'I'm going full whack!'

'They're behind us!' he barked, even though she could see in the rear-view mirror.

The one with the silver hair was driving. The one who'd tried to attack her was leaning out of the window, a gun in his hand.

A plan came to Grace's mind, and she slowed down a little and skirted into a side road leading to a warren of streets that had been their stomping ground as kids.

'We'll lose them down here,' she told Remy confidently, squeezing the brakes to take another corner fast.

'They're still there!'

She took a few turns, trying to shake them off, and when they disappeared momentarily, leaving the street behind a black void, she swerved down an alleyway where she cut the lights and the engine.

Seconds later, the other car sped past the entrance to the alley.

Grace and Remy sat in the darkness for some time until their breathing had calmed and they were sure they were gone. Grace started the engine and reversed out onto the main road.

'Where are we going?' Remy asked.

'I know somewhere safe.'

He nodded at her briefly but kept scanning the road and turning round to make sure no one was following. After ten minutes of driving in silence, he visibly relaxed. In contrast, she felt herself gear up for what she knew was coming.

'We lost them,' he said, exhaling.

'Good,' she replied, tight-lipped.

'Where are you taking me?'

'I've changed my mind about getting you that biochip. I'm going to stop off at work on the way and get one for you.'

'Oh, Gracie!' he sighed. 'Thank you!' He leaned back against the headrest and closed his eyes. 'I'm so tired. I feel like I haven't slept for weeks.'

His response exacerbated her guilt further.

By the time Grace had parked in the underground car park of the Janus Justice building, Remy was in a deep sleep.

The guards, armed with strong sedatives, didn't have much of a struggle.

CHAPTER TWENTY-NINE

Grace stood alone in the semi-darkness of the foyer of the Janus Justice building, waiting for the lift. She stared into space, seeing only Remy's face, a mask of resentment and betrayal, as the guards had escorted him to a secure room, the soles of his trainers squeaking against the white lino.

Her last words to him had been 'This is for the best, Remy.'

The responsibility was crushing. If she didn't make this therapy work – and in the next forty-eight hours – then she would have betrayed him for nothing.

Time was of the essence. It wouldn't be long before other employees started asking questions and the authorities would find out there was a Tier Four offender in Tier Three.

It wouldn't be long, she also suspected, before the authorities or the protestors would be banging down the doors of Janus, and it would be game over.

One of the clinic technicians had cleaned and sutured her injured hand. It throbbed beneath the white bandage as she raised her hand to the scanner to call the lift.

When it arrived, she stepped in and the confined space took her back to the small, stuffy office in the library, Bizzy standing in front of her. A wave of rage briefly submerged the trauma, but all too soon it ebbed away, leaving her fear exposed like wet sand, cold and unstable.

Bizzy's threat had pulled at the sinews of her childhood, causing physical and emotional involuntary reactions, drawing Grace and Gracie ever closer together, and suddenly, all the flight or fight gone, she began to sob. The lift doors opened and she shuffled into the darkness of the clinic and sat with her head on one of the grey work surfaces until she'd cried herself out.

Finally, after a trip to the bathroom to wash her face, she took two bottles of stimulating AltCon from the staffroom fridge and a sandwich someone had left from the previous day, and headed to her workspace. She checked her phone – nearly half three in the morning. Dan hadn't messaged her.

Turning her attention to her work on the screen – specifically Penny Lithgow's brain scans – Grace realised that something important, irreversible, had happened in that small room at the library with her would-be attacker. Gracie had fully broken through into her present and had melded with Grace.

With Grace's knowledge and experience and Gracie's determination and survival instincts, she had survived Diros – for now. Could she extend those abilities and pit them against psychopathy itself?

Penny's scans sat side by side in digital clarity. Abigail had been right, something had changed – the empathy centres of the brain had responded – but not enough to make the treatment work. Something else was needed.

Her eyes rested on the screen, but her mind wandered back to the library… *I'm going to enjoy this…* Bizzy too close, the smell of sweat, the movement of trees blowing in the breeze outside the window… the words of the small, dark-haired man, shouted from the main body of the library as the door behind her began to close…

'Biz, you don't have to do this!'

You don't have to do this…

And then it occurred to her – she'd been looking in the wrong part of the brain.

-

'You're in early,' Abigail said as she hung her coat in the storeroom.

Grace nodded in reply, not taking her eyes from the screens in front of her.

Abigail came to a standstill next to her and put a hand on the back of her chair. 'I'm sorry things didn't work out with Penny,' she began. Grace felt herself bristle.

'I'm onto something else, something that will be more effective,' Grace said, sounding more certain than she felt. Excitement and exhaustion battled within her. Could she actually do this, revolutionise the treatment? Then she wouldn't have to lie to Conrad about fixing criminal brains. She could keep her job. God, she might even be able to help some of those poor souls in Siberia ward. Not disembodied souls but de-souled bodies, bodies with the core removed, empty shells. Since her visit to that terrible ward, she'd often dreamt of the spirits of the offenders in biostasis, hovering above their former hosts, lost and afraid, wandering in technological nightmares.

Could she save them?

'What's the plan?' Abigail asked, snapping her back to the present.

'I'm going to activate the empathy switch so that we can *control* psychopathic impulses.'

Abigail's expression didn't change, but Grace felt a shift of energy in the space between their bodies. It caused the hairs on her arms to rise.

'The empathy switch?' Abigail asked.

'It's a myth that psychopaths can't feel anything. To some degree they can, they just choose not to. I mean, psychopathy is a spectrum, and we're dealing with the extreme cases here, but...'

Abigail shook her head very slightly as though she didn't understand or some part of her was rejecting the idea.

'Put it this way, psychopaths only feel empathy when they want to. It's not their default position. It benefits them to, at times, put themselves in someone else's shoes.'

'Why?'

'Because they're highly manipulative and what better way to manipulate their victims than to relate to and emulate their emotions? It means they can show kindness and consideration, which instils confidence and loyalty in their *prey*.'

Bizzy's face and words were on the edge of her consciousness. She pushed them away. 'However, they can choose to shut it down so they don't let emotions interfere with their... activities.'

'Selective empathy? So they can get what they want?' Abigail's expression was one of intense concentration now.

'It's not exactly a conscious decision, more like something that happens in the brain,' Grace nodded. 'But I'm going to make it so that they can't switch it off, so that they won't be able to shut it down. So they can't avoid feeling.'

'How, though?' asked Abigail, sounding astonished.

Grace looked down at her notes.

> By DEFAULT – in psychopath the region of the brain associated with pain has REDUCED ACTIVITY.
>
> It CAN BE ACTIVATED!
>
> Only when ASKED to imagine the pain of their victims did the MIRROR SYSTEM fire up as it did in control subjects (non-psychopaths) – not sure if they feel the same things as non-psychs.
>
> Use MDMA or other empathy drug and STIMULATE mirror neurons – so that they can actually feel/imagine to SOME DEGREE the pain of their victims.
>
> NEVER going to be able to make them want to HELP victim – just make them want to STOP HURTING THEM.

'Administer the synthetic empathy drug, as it was useful to some degree. Then I intend to stimulate their mirror neurons and then finally, and this is the big one, use electromagnetic pulses on this part of the brain here...'

Grace pointed to an area just above the ear on Penny's scan.

'The temporoparietal junction,' said Abigail.

'Yes, I'm going to use electromagnetic therapy to stimu-late...'

'No.' Abigail shook her head. 'That's not going to work. Any disruption of the TPJ is just going to cause adverse effects. All the studies have shown that, if anything, it makes a person less moral. I read about people inducing psychopathic behaviour by disrupting it.'

'Not if we do it my way,' Grace said decisively. 'This treat-ment needs to reinforce the self-other distinction, and we need the TPJ to do that. This part of the brain is just too important in moral decision-making for us not to try.' Grace looked back at the screen. She had to keep total faith in the success of her experiment until proved otherwise. 'The treatment will also stimulate the mirror neurons so that they can relate to the other person's experience and be more in tune with how it must feel for their victim. If the patient...'

'Offender,' said Abigail quickly.

'Offender... can understand the pain they themselves would feel if this was happening to them...'

'Then they'd be less likely to do it to others,' finished Abigail.

Grace nodded. 'Exactly.'

'Sounds like psychopathic bromide to me,' Abigail said and gave one of her rare smiles.

Grace felt relieved. It looked as though Abigail was in her corner.

'Will they need to stay on the treatment for life, though?'

Grace nodded.

'And obviously someone will monitor them – like chemical probation?'

'Yes, although it's more than just chemical. They'll need a small implant at the back of the skull to take readings and to send a regular pulse to keep the nano-particles in the brain stimulated.'

'This sounds like it could actually work,' said Abigail.

And for a moment, Grace allowed herself to hope.

Two days later, Conrad stood in the clinic, clearly excited by the prospect of launching a cutting-edge technological treatment for offenders and, Grace was certain, the money that would come with it.

She just wanted to patch Remy up and get him somewhere safe.

She'd gone to bed the previous morning at ten o'clock after pulling her all-nighter at the clinic. She hadn't spoken to Dan – just gone upstairs to the spare room and straight to sleep. Before she'd left the clinic, she'd given Abigail the instructions to organise the necessary kit for the therapy and do preliminary tests on Penny. Grace had slept like the dead, woken at midnight and returned to the clinic. She'd been there ever since. It was nearly two o'clock in the afternoon. There'd be time to be tired later.

Even though she'd been given a strong relaxant, Conrad gave Penny Lithgow a wide berth, skirting around the edge of the clinic wall. Penny sat in the chair, gazing curiously at the other humans in the room as an owl might lazily observe a mouse just after it had eaten.

'The synthetic empathy just wasn't effective enough for our needs,' Grace told him. 'As you will have read in my report that I sent this morning.'

Conrad nodded.

'Have you any questions?' Grace asked.

'Not at this stage, no. I just want to know that it works.'

Abigail had been quiet so far. Was she annoyed because Grace wanted total control over her own trial, and had therefore taken over most of Abigail's usual tasks, such as injecting the nano-particles?

'So here... this is the part of the brain that we're targeting.' Grace pointed to the screen and Conrad leaned in a little closer. 'In a moment or two you should see... ah, there we go.' A tiny constellation of blue lights appeared on the scan. They watched for a moment as the pinpricks of light positioned themselves. 'These little beauties are the magnetic nano-particles that, if all goes well, are going to make this therapy successful. Something similar is already used in neurosurgery to help damaged nerves and relieve extreme pain. They'll not only direct the electrical impulses to this part of the brain, but they're also scanners and they'll relay all the information we need back to the computer.'

Grace lifted Penny's dark hair to show a miniature bio-chip at the side of her skull.

'It can be read by any shell or hypernet device with a quick swipe,' said Grace. 'The readings will show exactly how effective the treatment is at all times. It also generates and sends the electrical impulses.'

'That has to be surgically implanted?' asked Conrad.

'Yes, but it's not a big operation,' said Grace. 'It's on the offender at all times and can be scanned by authorities, or even family members who are trying to support the offender's rehabilitation.'

'So they can check if the kit's still working and if the offender poses a threat?' Abigail asked.

Grace nodded.

'And, tell me again, how does this work?' Conrad asked, looking as though he was stirring an imaginary cup of tea with his forefinger.

'It works by stimulating the empathy switch…' Grace began.

'It's not an actual switch, is it?' Conrad laughed as though he'd made a joke, but he looked uncertain.

'No, it's an activation point in the brain which allows people to understand how it feels when other people are hurt. It seems to be switched off in psychopaths by default, as it is here in Penny's brain. We're going to give it constant stimulation, so that she'll react to other people's pain and suffering in a more neurotypical way.'

'And what way is that?' asked Conrad.

'She should find it disturbing, as she'll be able to imagine how that pain would feel if it was being inflicted on her. She'll suffer vicariously – the feeling of compassion for someone who's in pain will be spontaneous, as it is in most people, and so hopefully, she won't want to hurt anyone else. We hope that after this trial, Penny will be back on the mainstream spectrum of empathy.' Grace took in Penny's blank expression and, for a brief moment, wondered what it would be like to not feel for others.

'Okay,' said Conrad happily.

'Abigail, do you want to tell Conrad about yesterday?'

Abigail's expression brightened.

'I ran a few trials yesterday while Grace was busy and I showed Penny the reel from the first experiment, the one with the dogs. The reactions after this new treatment were much more extreme than with the synthetic empathy alone.' Abigail brought up more scans on the screens. 'So this one is after synthemp.' A faint glow at the brain's centre showed where the neurons were working hard. 'But this one is with the new treatment.'

Penny's brain was lit up like cities on an aerial map at night-time, showing activity in all the areas that Grace had hoped.

Grace had, of course, seen these scans immediately upon her return to the clinic, but now she wanted to prove it for her own peace of mind. Once could have been a fluke. Now it was time for the final hurdle.

She put on a reel made from footage submitted at Penny's trial, and simulated hints and suggestions of the sort of unnameable acts that Penny had been involved with and convicted of.

'I'm not watching this,' Conrad stated, turning his back to the screen.

'That's okay, you don't need to. I'm not going to either,' said Grace.

How could Abigail make those kinds of reels without it driving her mad? Those poor police officers who had to go through hours and hours of this sort of footage to find the culprits.

But if Grace wanted to find out whether this offender might ever be safe enough to be in public again, in places where children lived, played – then she had to run this test, and that included playing the reel, however abhorrent it was.

They'd run the reel that morning without the treatment, and Penny and her brain had reacted in the way a psychopath's would be expected to in the face of children's suffering – as though she was watching a cartoon.

Abigail placed headphones on Penny to contain the sounds.

'You're going to hear a number of beeps indicating markers that I've already set up so we can correlate what Penny's watching with how she's reacting,' Abigail told Conrad.

'So we don't have to watch the footage,' Grace explained.

'This screen here,' Grace pointed to a set of images on the left, 'shows the scans from this morning when Penny watched this exact same reel without the treatment. See these numbers here? These correspond with the beeps, so we can map the changes in reaction to the exact same scenes before and after the new treatment.'

The reel was ready, the nano-particles were injected, the synthetic empathy had been administered and the electric currents were live.

All that was left was to dim the lights and hit play.

Grace took a deep breath, pressed Enter on the computer and turned away from the reel so she wouldn't have those images imprinted on her mind's eye. She momentarily locked eyes with Abigail, who looked nervous, the first time Grace had ever seen that emotion in her.

Five minutes later, Penny Lithgow began to scream and didn't stop until the second dose of tranquilliser hit her blood-stream.

CHAPTER THIRTY

The clinic was silent. Conrad stood, hands in pockets, Abigail perched on the clinic chair as Grace came back in.

'She's in a secure room, heavily sedated. I've told George to make sure someone's with her at all times.'

Conrad looked at her questioningly.

'Suicide watch,' Grace said. 'When the sedatives wear off her emotions are going to be all over the place and she'll realise she's still going to Tier Four.'

'That treatment was something else,' Conrad said.

Grace didn't reply but went back to the workstation to scrutinise the brain scans. Whether the changes in Penny's brain were partial or full, long-term or needed constant monitoring, time would tell.

But Grace had done it! She wouldn't have to fake scans and lie to get Remy out. She was going to be able to save him. She imagined waking Mikey Kilgannon from his Siberia sleep. The future seemed to open up before her, a future where she could make a real difference in the lives of offenders but also keep other people, potential victims, safe too. For the first time in weeks, Grace felt a sense of hope. She wondered if this even extended to Dan. Where would they be after all this was over? Was there any hope for them?

'Grace, you're a genius!' Conrad exclaimed. 'My contact in the government is going to be thrilled. This treatment means reassurance that the reoffending problem is dealt with, saving money from not having to house Tier Four offenders. And' –

he sighed heavily, clearly relieved – 'it will get the press off our backs.'

What other revelations had Dan been broadcasting over the last forty-eight hours? Consumed by her work, she hadn't looked at NewsFlex in days.

'I knew you were right for this job.' Conrad folded his arms across his chest.

Abigail rolled her eyes.

'It's not a miracle cure, Conrad,' Grace told him. 'This is going to take years of testing and licensing before it's accepted by the Department of Justice and legally allowed in the Neuro-courts. You know that, right?'

He didn't reply.

'It's going to need thorough research,' she went on, 'and I insist you put into place rigorous post-release checks. That's essential if you want to get out of the mess you're in. You can't take shortcuts this time,' she added sternly.

Conrad unfolded his arms and waved his hands as if swatting away her concerns. 'I'm going to tell my minister the good news, ask him to get his spin doctors onto it, before the reoffending story gains any more traction. Good job, Grace!'

He moved towards the door and Grace followed.

'You agreed, Conrad,' she said quietly, aware of Abigail.

He raised his chin, brow furrowed.

How could he not remember?

'You said after initial rounds, if it was successful, I could choose an offender to run my own trial on,' she said. 'I want to run a trial on Remy Wilson.'

He gave her a hard stare and then nodded briefly before moving through the doors.

Relieved, she turned to Abigail.

'Can you bring Remy Wilson to the clinic, please. He's in the secure room, next to Penny Lithgow.'

'What do you want him for? We only needed one trial. Wilson's already been through Tier Three, hasn't he?' Abigail said. 'Anyway, can't George or one of the guards bring him?'

'Abigail, what's the problem? He's not dangerous. He'll still be under sedation from having his bio-chip fitted.'

'So why is he…?'

Abigail was going to be assisting with the treatment – she might as well know. 'Not that it's your business,' said Grace, 'but Conrad said I could choose an offender and use the new therapy on them. And I chose Remy.'

'But why him?'

'What's that to do with you?' Grace snapped. 'Just do your bloody job.'

The orange eyes narrowed.

'I'm sorry, I didn't mean to snap. I haven't slept much lately and this is an important case… for my career…'

Abigail continued to stare.

'It's just that Remy has… an interesting brain. If I can fix him, then I can fix anyone.'

Abigail didn't break her gaze.

'Don't you get it, Abigail? This is a win-win. We provide a far superior therapy, the government approves our treatment and therefore releases offenders from biostasis, and then the protestors will be happier because it's a more humane way of treating these people.'

Why was she even explaining herself?

'Apology accepted,' Abigail said and turned on her heel.

What the hell had got into her? Gracie reared her head – *What the hell did you apologise to her for?*

While she was gone, Grace organised all the kit necessary for the procedure. There was no footage from the Neurocourt, as Remy had done a runner before the trial, but she'd downloaded the reel from the first time he'd been tried. It was the same type of crime – drug dealing and grievous bodily harm – so it would do.

The thought struck her momentarily. The second time, the victim died, but it was the same crime, the same set of circumstances, a drug dealer, a transaction gone wrong, a blade…

The same crime.

She knew most offenders were one-trick ponies, but something didn't quite sit right. What Remy had said about Diros recreating crimes came back to her.

Everything was ready but Abigail was taking her time. Grace picked up her shell while she waited and had a quick look at NewsFlex. Dan's face came up on the screen above the yellow and black logo and the ticker tape breaking news, his handsome features showing no distress whatsoever, unlike Grace whose skin felt paper-thin, whose eyes were red-rimmed and circled with darkness.

'…a large crowd has gathered outside the Janus Justice building.' Dan was straining to make his voice heard over chanting. 'It's believed that Remy Wilson is being held here…' The clock on the screen told her this was happening in real time. She moved over to the window and when she opened it, she could hear shouting below. How the hell had they found out?

Flicking back to other reports from the last few days, she saw that Dan had led the reporting on Remy's capture. He'd known about Remy's arrest and escape. He knew about Remy's previous crimes and his original treatment at Tier Three. Maybe Dan had an insider at the police, but how did he have information from the clinic?

Anger reared as she realised he must have been looking at her shell while she slept. How else could he have found out?

Where the hell was Abigail? She'd better not be whingeing to Conrad. Remy was prepped and ready to go, she didn't have time for histrionics. The faster she completed his treatment, the faster she could get him out of there. Conrad would have to deal with the police or the Department of Justice if questions were asked.

Conrad had *promised*.

Where was she?

The door opened and a guard appeared, pushing Remy in a wheelchair. Remy's shoulders were slumped, his head a little to one side, his hands in his lap. He was sedated but she could tell he was angry. His eyes locked on her. She focused on the task – to fix him and free him.

He'll thank me later.

'If you see Abigail, will you tell her to hurry, please,' she said to the guard, but he merely shrugged as he helped Grace get Remy into the chair and strapped in before leaving the clinic.

After injecting Remy with the nano-scanners, she used the magnet to move them into place so that she'd be able to see exactly what was going on in his brain.

She geared herself up. It was time to face facts. Her heart went out to her old friend who didn't realise how sick he was. She projected the images of his scans onto the main viewing screen so he could see. Would that make him come to his senses?

'Remy, look,' she said, leaning down to speak into his ear. 'Look at the screen.' She moved his chin with her hand. 'These are your scans from Manchester, when you went through your Aversion Therapy last time. Look.'

His eyes were downcast.

'Look!' she hissed.

His eyes travelled slowly up to the screen.

'These prove that you're suffering from psychopathy, and the only way to help you is to treat you with the new therapy.'

He blinked slowly – hell, how much sedative had he been given? – and slurred a single word, 'Diros.'

'Remy!' she barked through gritted teeth. 'You're just going to have to trust me. I'm going to fix you and get you away from those people. Any minute now, you're going to see your brain, in real time, and you'll see that it's messed up. But I'm going to make it right, you'll see…'

The graphics came up on the display, a real-time image of Remy's brain, and Grace stopped speaking, stood up straight, eyes riveted to the screen.

Remy's brain did not resemble the scans from his treatment in Manchester.

Not at all.

She was looking at two different brains.

The doors to the clinic flew open and three protestors burst in, yelling loudly. Shocked, Grace couldn't make out the words. Behind them, a man dressed in black combats, his face covered with a balaclava with shaded eye panels, dragged a screaming Abigail in, one arm around her neck. Grace backed herself into a corner as far away from them as she could manage.

The man in black threw Abigail to the floor, and her head caught the corner of a metal trolley as she fell. The guard who had brought Remy in moments before ran in and the man in black flung his arm out violently, catching the guard on the throat, and he went down to the floor, choking.

The other protestors were not like the man in black – they were teenagers, dressed in colourful sweatshirts with cartoon characters, wearing beanie hats and scarves around their faces. One froze, looking at the guard on the ground in shock, before he pulled an aerosol can from his backpack, jumped up onto one of the workstations and began spraying words in black on the wall.

The alarms started howling as the other two started opening cupboards and drawers and throwing the contents around the clinic. One kicked the glass doors of the drugs cabinet. Another was hitting the viewing screen with a metal dish.

The man in black grabbed the wheelchair that Remy had been brought in on, pulled it towards the clinic chair, unstrapped Remy and bent to lift him.

Grace launched herself at the man but he shoved her hard and she flew back, skidding across the clinic floor and hitting a wall. She got back to her feet and braced herself. The man had got Remy into the chair now.

One of the youngsters had opened a can of fizzy drink and was about to pour it over the main computer. Grace ran towards him and shouldered him out of the way with a shout. The can flew across the room, bright orange liquid splashing on the floor. Startled, he made a run for the door and escaped.

Grace grabbed a stool, ran towards the man in black and hit him as hard as she could across the back with it. It seemed to have little impact, as he ignored her and swivelled the wheelchair to face the door, Remy sitting in it, helpless.

Jumping on the intruder's back, Grace tried to gouge his eyes, memories of street fights and their instinctive movements flooding back to her. He somehow smelled... familiar. He let go of the chair and swatted blindly at her, but she held fast, digging her fingers into his face.

The guard had managed to get to his feet, his hand to his throat, and he called for help on his radio before tackling one of the kids to the ground.

'Take Remy!' Grace instructed Abigail, who was cowering beneath the trolley. 'Get him somewhere safe!' Looking slightly dazed, Abigail nodded, clambered up and pushed the chair out of the clinic. 'Hurry!' Grace shouted as she continued to struggle with the man in black, trying to keep him from going after Remy.

The guard had one of the youngsters on the floor now, face down, and was zip-tying his wrists together. The boy's companion stood wide-eyed, spray-can in hand, as George and another guard, a new one Grace didn't recognise, ran in.

'Help me!' Grace shouted as the man jumped backwards, crushing her between his powerful body and the wall. It knocked the air from her lungs and she fell to the floor gasping for breath. As he made a run for the door, George tried to tackle him, but the man dodged him and disappeared into the corridor.

'I'll get him,' the new guard shouted and ran after him as George regained his balance and pulled the remaining kid down from the worktop.

Grace crawled over to the clinic chair and hauled herself up onto it. Her legs were shaking, her heart thumping, her breath coming in staggered, painful pants. She looked around at the devastation of the clinic as George and the other guard restrained the protestors.

'Did they get him, George?'

He shook his head. 'He'll be around somewhere. They'll find him.'

God, she hoped Abigail had got Remy somewhere safe.

Two sweaty-faced kids, hands bound behind them, their backpacks open on a worktop, lay face down on the floor, their slogan on the wall behind them:

TIER THREE IS TORTURE! HUMAN RIGHTS FOR OFFENDERS!

CHAPTER THIRTY-ONE

'And get that damned CCTV looked at!' Conrad barged out of the witness room followed by two of the Deacon Security team who shuffled out of the clinic after him.

The teenage protestors were locked in secure rooms. The man in black was nowhere to be found. A cleaner was attempting to scrub the black paint off the wall. Drips marked the workstation below like definitive full stops.

George was leaning over Grace. 'You sure you're okay? Are you hurt anywhere?'

Outrage had provided a strong anaesthetic but now it was beginning to wear off. Her back felt bruised and the cut on her hand from the library had opened up and her bandage was sodden. 'I'm okay. Do you know where Remy Wilson is? The offender I was treating?' She winced as she moved. 'Is he okay?'

George shook his head and shrugged. 'Do you want some painkillers, Doctor G? I got some in my pocket.'

'Grace, I need you in my office,' Conrad said.

'I'm fine, Conrad, thank you for asking,' Grace said.

'Sorry. Are you okay?'

When she shook her head he said, 'We're waiting on the police. Will you come to my office when you're ready?'

'Yes, of course.'

Moments after he left, Abigail came in, looking pale. Grace turned to her. 'Abigail! Where have you been? Are you okay? You've been gone for ages. I didn't know what had happened to you!'

A trickle of blood ran down Abigail's face.

'Let's get that seen to,' Grace said, standing up. She pointed to the clinic chair and Abigail sat down. There was a small gash on her scalp and her hair was sticky with blood. George looked concerned.

'I don't think it needs a stitch but let me just clean it and have a closer look.' Grace looked around at the ruined clinic. Bottles were smashed, panels had been pushed back, cupboard doors kicked off, items spilled out onto the floor. Glass crunched beneath her feet and the orange drink pooled on the floor. Thankfully, she'd saved the computer just in time. She hoped the vials and drugs she needed for Remy's treatment were okay. She didn't have time to order more.

But then she remembered – he didn't need fixing.

There was nothing wrong with his brain.

Her stomach gave an excited flip.

'Is Remy okay?' she asked, but Abigail just groaned.

'George, can you pass me that kit?' She pointed to a first-aid box that lay half-open beneath the magnet arm.

'Sure thing.' He nodded towards her hand. 'And make sure you take care of that too.'

He brought it over and watched with interest as Grace used an antiseptic wipe to clean the area around the laceration. Abigail winced. She looked like a little girl on a visit to the school nurse.

'You put up a good fight,' she said.

Grace felt as though she had revealed a hidden side to herself and a feeling of vulnerability overcame her.

'Did they get the man?' Abigail asked George, who had begun picking up items from the floor and putting them on the trolley next to the chair.

Grace dabbed at her scalp again and Abigail let out a little sound.

'Don't worry. We've got the team searching the building. He's probably been caught already,' George said reassuringly.

'You'll have to be careful when you wash your hair,' Grace told her. Then she added, as casually as possible, 'Is Remy okay?'

'Yes, I put him somewhere safe.' Before Grace had time to find out where, Abigail asked George, 'How did they get in?'

Grace unwrapped her bandage and began to clean her wound. She'd have to get it seen to properly. But that would have to wait.

'Had a guard with them. Wasn't one of our fellas, but they had one of our uniforms. Sounds like a well-planned attack.' He looked up at the cleaners, struggling to remove the spray paint. 'But there's something odd here...'

'What?' Grace asked, applying a pad and beginning to wrap a fresh bandage around her hand.

'You sure you don't want help with that?' George asked, hovering as Grace held the loose end of the bandage in her teeth.

She nodded and he tied it for her.

'Thanks. So what was odd?' she asked.

Abigail turned her attention to George.

'The kids had a lot of money in their backpacks, and I mean a lot of money. Some guy in the crowd of protestors gave it to them, they said, told them to cause as much chaos as possible. Said he could get them in posing as a guard. He was able to bypass security scanners and everything.'

'Do you think they're the same people who said they hacked us?' asked Grace.

George shrugged.

'Can the kids identify him?' asked Abigail.

'They'd never seen him before.'

There was more to this than ordinary protestors. The kids had just been a distraction. The man in black had been trying to kidnap Remy. But how could she tell the guard that without drawing attention to Remy himself?

'Did they find the fake guard?' She imagined him wheeling Remy's chair down to the underground car park, unchallenged. Thank God Abigail got him away in time!

George shook his head again. 'I don't know how the hell they got in or out. Ghosts.'

Not ghosts, but Diros. She was sure of it. The intruder all in black – she remembered where she'd smelled his odour before – in the back room at the library. She'd been too panicked in the clinic to pinpoint it. They'd said they were going to come for her at the clinic, and instead they'd come for Remy. Or maybe they'd just come for Remy *first*.

She shivered.

Maybe they were still in the building. If they'd bypassed security then they could get to Remy. She wanted to see him immediately, check he was safe, warn him that Diros had been in the building, may still be in the building, and tell him that he'd been right all along – they could get to him wherever he was.

She also needed to tell him that she believed him. Remy was no psychopath.

How was she going to be able to gain his trust again?

First things first. Once they knew the coast was clear, she would have to *pretend* to conduct his treatment. It was the only way she was going to get Conrad to sign the release papers. At least she knew now that the post-treatment scans would be perfect. It would look as though the therapy was highly effective.

But now she had a new set of problems. Who had swapped Remy's scans and why? How were they going to get away from Diros? And with the story all over the press, it was only a matter of time before the authorities were alerted. They would insist Remy was sent to Tier Four and there would be nothing she could do for him then.

And it would have been her fault. She'd brought him to the clinic and Diros knew she worked there.

'I'm going to go and see Remy, check he's okay,' she said brightly, moving towards the door. 'He's in one of the secure rooms?'

Abigail was touching her scalp gingerly, and looked up. 'What?'

'Where did you take Remy? Which one of the secure rooms?'

'I… I…' She winced.

It was a simple question. Was she still in shock?

'Where's Remy?' Grace asked more urgently. 'Where did you take him?'

'He's safe. He's in one of the secure rooms, no one can get to him,' Abigail stammered.

Grace felt herself relax a little. 'Okay, I'll just go and…'

Conrad stormed into the clinic.

'Grace, I need a word.' His elation when she'd shown him the new treatment had completely disappeared and now there was only stress, and something else – anger.

'I've an urgent matter to see to. Can it wait?' She began to move away but he caught her by the arm. She looked down at his hand. 'Look, Conrad, I know you must be angry with these arseholes for what they did, but it's not the end of the world. We can fix the clinic up. There's no lasting harm done…'

'I'm not angry with the offenders!' he bellowed. 'I'm bloody angry with you!'

Grace took a step backwards, pulling her arm out of his grip.

'Angry with me? What the hell have I done?'

He waved his shell in her face, a photograph of a younger Remy in crisp pixels, his long dark hair pushed back, a police mugshot, the black and yellow NewsFlex logo in the bottom right-hand corner.

'This is your husband's fault! He's standing outside right now spouting off about Remy Wilson to the entire world – telling everyone that he's in here, that he's already been through Tier Three, which, incidentally, you failed to mention when you asked for a test subject. Nor did you tell me that his Tier Three treatment failed—'

'If you had more knowledge about the offenders we're dealing with, instead of just focusing on the money, Conrad, you'd know that Remy had already—'

He cut her off. 'What else did you tell your hack of a husband, Grace? *Why* did you tell him? You've broken every rule on confidentiality!'

'I didn't tell Dan anything!' Had he been listening in on her conversations with Shannon?

'It's all over the goddamned hypernet. This is gross misconduct, Grace, spying on the company, informing the press. I blame you for this whole fiasco today.' He stabbed his finger through the air. 'This company, *my company*, looks like a complete failure.'

'I didn't tell him anything,' Grace insisted. Abigail eyed her silently and the conversation with Dan about the Embers Rapist that Abigail had overheard in the bathroom sprang to mind.

There was a tense silence. Grace was going to have to take the bull by the horns. 'There's only one thing that we can do to fix this – get Remy and use the new treatment on him. We have to come clean and say there was a problem with the original Aversion Therapy and now we have something better in place. Hell, it might even be good PR.'

She bit her lip.

'No,' Conrad said finally.

'No, what?' she asked with a growing anxiety.

'No. We can't treat Wilson.'

'No, Conrad. You promised me!' Her voice rose in pitch, echoing her heart rate.

He didn't answer, just shook his head.

'You said I could use an offender of my choosing. We agreed!'

'Yes, that was before you put my company on the line!' he roared.

'I didn't tell Dan anything!' she yelled back.

'You expect me to believe that? And you choose a high-profile offender, one who the whole country has their eyes on? What were you thinking? The deal is off the table. You can forget it.'

'We had an *agreement*. I fixed your bloody treatment for you, saved your reputation, didn't I? You can't go back on it now. You're lucky I haven't talked to the press yet, Conrad. God knows there's plenty I could tell them—' she spat angrily.

'I don't have any choice, Grace! How's it going to look if I free Remy Wilson, huh?' He came up close to her, his face twisted and menacing. 'My contract with the Department of Justice will be in jeopardy. The general public will think Wilson has got away with murder. The protestors will think it's unfair that he's been released and riot or attack the clinics around the country. I'm not losing my business because, for whatever reason, you insist this particular offender is worth treating. We'll use Penny Lithgow's results to cover our asses. You can forget about Remy Wilson.'

Abigail's gaze swung between the two, with obvious curiosity.

'Please, Conrad.'

'The minister is furious. We look like idiots! I'm going to have to spend a fortune to boost security *again* because of this.' He looked Grace in the eye. 'You're done here.'

'What?' she asked, stunned.

'Yes, you're done here. You've broken your contract and your non-disclosure agreement. It's gross misconduct, Grace. In fact, you'll be lucky if I don't take legal action.' He rubbed his hand over his face. Then he snarled, 'If you tell anyone about Siberia, there'll be more to worry about than just legal action…'

'Are you threatening me?' Grace said. She got a grip on her anger and tried a different approach. 'Come on, Conrad. What about all those others in Tier Four? Are you just going to leave them to rot when I can help them? I can save them from—'

'I've got what I need. Abigail can help the others.'

On hearing her name, Abigail winced.

'That's my therapy!' yelled Grace.

'You made your choices.' His voice was quiet now, controlled.

'You haven't heard the last of this, Conrad,' she said bitterly.

But he didn't appear to hear her as he left the room.

Grace's mind raced.

Screw Conrad. Remy didn't need therapy. He didn't need fixing. The sedatives would have started to wear off now and he'd probably be able to walk. She would go and fetch him from the secure room, get him down to the car park, into her car and then drive. She didn't even know where. She couldn't think that far, she just had to get him out.

'I want to see Remy before I go. Where is he?'

Abigail didn't answer straight away.

'Abigail! Just tell me which secure room he's in.'

'He's not in a secure room.' Her face was angled down but she looked up at Grace from under her fringe. 'The rooms were all full. The guards put the protestors in there, so I took him…'

'*Where?*' Grace wanted to shake her.

'I had to get him somewhere safe. It's the most secure place in the building… he's in Siberia.'

CHAPTER THIRTY-TWO

Grace's heart threshed against her ribs as she entered Siberia ward and its permanent twilight. She saw him immediately, recognisable by his long dark hair – there obviously hadn't been time to shave him.

She observed his stats, his heart beating firm and strong, his body chemistry that of a man in his prime. He looked pale, his muscles well defined beneath the cotton. That wouldn't last long. Soon, he would be eaten away, no more than a living corpse.

Grace flung herself across him, sobbing heavily.

He didn't flinch. He had no idea she was there, and no idea where he was.

She removed the metal eye screen and clasped his face in her hands.

'Remy! Remy!' she wept, trying to wake him.

She could see his eyeballs moving from side to side beneath the lids.

The display above his bed burst into colour, and she could see, in all its horrific detail, what Remy would see for the rest of his life – over and over again.

It was from his perspective. He was in an alleyway at night, rain beating down, splashing the puddles that gathered in the troughs of the uneven pavements.

A stranger approached – Grace couldn't see his face clearly, but the knife he held was in sharp focus.

A sudden movement, the man slashing out with the blade again and again.

Grace could see hands covered in blood, so much blood, a man's wailing, crying for help, and then everything went dark.

A moment later… an alleyway, the rain beating down…

'No, no…' She gave a broken, weary cry. She leaned over him and whispered, 'It wasn't meant to be like this. I was trying to help…' even though she knew he wouldn't hear. A single tear fell onto his closed eyes.

A pair of guards approached and stood either side of her. One of them replaced the eye screen. The other took her by the arm.

There was no way she could help Remy now.

Conrad appeared by the door. 'Time to go.'

'No, please, Conrad, no…'

But he ignored her and nodded to the guards.

The second guard took her other arm now and the two of them began to guide her away from the bed but she resisted.

'Remy!'

They pulled her harder now, grabbing her upper arms forcefully as she tried to squirm away from them, twisting her body as they dragged her towards the door. She dragged her feet along the floor, and then began kicking out and screaming.

Remy's words from the prison block rang in her mind: *I'll never let anyone hurt you and you'll never be on your own.*

'Remy!' she screamed over and over again.

She was leaving him on his own and in the worst place imaginable.

The next thing she knew, she had been dumped on the pavement outside Janus. She crumpled to the ground, exhausted and hollowed-out, knowing that part of her would always lie with Remy in his death-sleep.

–

When Grace arrived home, she was met by the rich aroma of garlic and herbs. Dan was playing music in the kitchen and humming as he cooked.

He plated up. There was only enough food for one.

He poured himself a glass of AltCon and sat down at the table with his bowl of stir-fry, added a dash of soy sauce and began to eat. Grace suddenly realised how hungry she was, how much food symbolised the comfort of their home.

'I thought you'd be outside Janus whipping the protestors up to a frenzy,' she said bitterly.

'I came home for a quick bite to eat. They'll still be there when I go back in a bit.' He didn't look at her.

'Your articles, your news reports,' Grace said, her voice controlled. 'You just lost me my job...' *And so much more than that*. Tears built behind her eyes and she clenched her jaw. She'd learned as a child to hide her feelings, especially from those who could hurt her most.

He ignored her and took a sip from his glass.

'Did you sabotage my career on purpose?'

Dan didn't reply but took another mouthful.

'Was this your way of forcing my hand?' she persisted. 'You'd get me sacked and I'd what... settle down and give you a child?' He wouldn't look at her. 'Like some bloody baby machine?'

As the fork rose to his mouth again, she swiped his plate from the table and flung it at the wall. Dan sat mouth open in shock as the food, still steaming, slid down the white wall in a viscous mess.

'What the hell?'

She leaned over and gripped the sides of the table, her face close to his.

'You threw me under the bus! Conrad thinks I'm a spy for NewsFlex and now my career is fucked.'

He stood up, knocking his chair backwards and jabbed a finger towards her. 'We'd agreed the plan!'

'No, you *decided*. And you changed the plan! You want to punish me over Remy Wilson.'

'I wondered when you'd finally mention him,' Dan said quietly.

'You did this on purpose because you assumed I was having an affair with Remy. You're jealous and you wanted to lash out – is that what all this is about?'

'Stop right there! The other night when you told me you were at work to help with some emergency… it was a lie. I rang your clinic and I rang Shannon – she didn't know what I was talking about.'

'It's not like that!' she shrieked.

'You expect me to believe you?'

'I was working! You work long hours, Dan. I've never accused you of having an affair.'

'Yes, but I never lie about where I am.'

'I was in charge of a major project, revolutionary, but none of that matters now because you, selfish bastard that you are, decided to report on something sensitive and confidential, and my boss thinks I gave you all the information to write it, and now all that hard work has just gone down the drain because of your ego!' She had to know. 'Where did you get the information from?'

'You,' he said smugly.

'I've told you nothing!'

He went to her bag, pulled out her work shell and held it up to her face. 'You really should use a password.'

She grabbed it from his hand. Her fears had been confirmed.

'You've looked at my confidential files!'

'Yes.' He leaned against the worktop, folded his arms, his arrogance driving her fury. 'I found out all sorts of things…'

Grace rapidly ran through her emails in her mind, and then realised that her work shell had been linked to her phone. Information would have gone both ways. Dan would have seen messages that Remy had sent to her phone…

You know where to find me.

I really need you.

She paused for a moment, wondering to what degree she could explain some of this away. Then she wavered. What was easier to hear? That she was having an affair, or that she'd lied to him all along about some of the most fundamental things – who she was, where she came from, not wanting a child.

Which seemed worse, lying or cheating?

'Is that why you don't want a baby, Grace?'

'What? No...'

'Yes it is! You don't want a child with me because you want to be with someone else.' How could there be contempt and sorrow in his eyes at the same time? 'I loved you...' His voice trailed off.

Loved? The ice shifted again beneath her, about to crack, open up and swallow up the beautiful life she'd fought so hard to build.

'I blamed myself for not being able to give you a child, and instead I find that you've been lying to me...' He tucked his fingers into his pocket and threw a small, empty pill packet at her. 'Scared of getting caught with your lover's baby?'

She should tell him the truth, how difficult her start in life was, her worries about having a baby, the nature of her relationship with Remy.

But instead she just stood there, mute.

'Nothing to say?' Dan demanded.

But then Gracie emerged, pushing to the front of her mind, angry, defensive.

'Well, you got your story, Dan! You hit the big time and I've lost my job. You've beaten me. You're better than me. Do you feel like a real man now?'

He looked up and let out a lungful of air.

'I've tried, I really have, Grace,' he said walking towards the door, 'but I can't go on like this. It's over. I'm going out. When I get back, I want you gone.'

–

'Tell me everything again. From the start.'

Sarge sat with his feet up on the desk, eyes closed.

Bizzy cleared his throat and began. 'So, as you know, we got the call and we knew it was the moment we had to strike...' Mal hated it when Biz over-embellished, talking like he was in a spy movie. 'Mal put on the Janus uniform...'

'And that came from the same source as the phone call?' Sarge interrupted, opening his eyes.

Bizzy nodded in corroboration.

Mal sighed. Sarge already knew this.

Bizzy went on. 'My work on cracking their cyber-security paid off because...'

Sarge waved his hand to dismiss Bizzy, pointed at Mal and said, 'Continue.'

Mal ignored Bizzy's glare. 'There was a demo going on outside. I grabbed three young lads. Once I'd shown them the cash and the fake uniform, they were up for it. I told them to create as much havoc as possible and away we went.'

Sarge nodded slowly. 'Good work, boys.'

Biz scowled at Mal.

'Wouldn't have been possible without Bizzy's tech work,' Mal added. 'There was no way we could have got through the maze of corridors or all those bloody security doors without him.'

'That and a bit of inside info goes a long way,' Sarge agreed. 'And Grace didn't recognise you, Biz?'

He shook his head. 'I was totally covered and there was too much going on.'

'And he's safely in Tier Four?' asked Sarge.

'There's no way that fucker is going to talk again,' said Bizzy.

'Good work, boys,' Sarge repeated, sounding satisfied.

A feeling of relief washed over Mal. Maybe this had made up for his fuck-up in the big house and Sarge was going to let him off. But then he remembered his weakness in the library when he'd been disloyal and a coward. It seemed to him that the more Grace appealed to him, the more he realised what Sarge was becoming.

You're not the sharpest tool in the shed his father had often said, but Mal knew that he had good intuition and he could feel something bad coming, a point of no return, a crossroads where he would have to prove his loyalty.

'I'm just sorry that we couldn't have killed him,' said Bizzy.

'Then they would have guessed we weren't protestors!' snapped Mal. 'Protestors don't kill people.'

'They've committed arson and violence. It's only one step after that...' Bizzy said.

'We don't want to draw attention to ourselves,' insisted Mal. 'This way is much better. Everyone thinks it was just a protest and Remy's been silenced. Job done.'

'You're such a coward, Mal.'

'Boys, boys,' said Sarge, 'this is *done*. It's over. We did it our way and we stuck to our rules. Remy's never getting out of biostasis. It wouldn't have been our style just to go up and take him out. And let's face facts, there was no way we could have got away with killing him and getting out of there. If we'd done anything different then someone would've suspected there was something amiss.'

Bizzy hung his head for a moment.

'I know you're disappointed, lads. I want Remy dead too. But as it stands, it's as good as. He's where we need him to be. You did good.'

'At least we can keep an eye on him,' agreed Bizzy.

'Worse than death from what I hear.' Sarge stood up and stretched to his full height. 'Got to deal with that Gunnarsson bitch now.'

Mal felt himself hurtling towards the terrible crossroads, where decisions would have to be made.

'You managed to get a stash of drugs from the clinic?'

Bizzy nodded. 'Paid one of the kids extra to get them. I picked the smart one who didn't get caught.'

'Good, so now we can think about the other half of our knotty problem. We're going to make it look like Grace died taking an overdose of drugs that she'd been stealing from the clinic.' Sarge turned to Mal. 'Biz killed the last one. This time you have to do it.'

Mal stood at the centre of the crossroads. Whichever direction he took, it was going to lead to hell.

CHAPTER THIRTY-THREE

Grace pulled into the Agrarian after a journey that was fuelled partly by anger and partly by grief. Dan had been adamant they split.

She felt a degree of relief – relief it hadn't been her who called it, and relief that she no longer had to keep secrets about who she really was.

She'd called ahead, given Shannon a brief summary of events and asked for a place to stay that night.

Shannon's house was in a walled compound behind the main office. Grace pulled up outside the gate and sat for a moment in the silence of the car, turning over the keyring photo of her and Remy in her fingers – Funland, the two of them laughing.

Grace got out of the car when Shannon appeared at the gate, and was swept up in a hug and bustled into the house. In the living room, the two older kids and Shuggie were playing a game on the main screen, the three of them shouting. Grace didn't know if it was at the screen or at each other, but it seemed good-natured enough. The youngest two were sitting at the table nearby, eating toast and watching something on a small shell propped up in front of them.

When he saw Grace, Shuggie smiled and said, 'Right, kids, that's enough for today.' They groaned, but he switched the screen off and the older ones disappeared. 'Come on, you two,' he said to the younger kids. 'Mum's going to have a chat with Aunty Grace.' He herded them up the stairs. Grace watched her friend smiling after them and felt a brief, sharp stab of loss and longing.

The sounds of Shuggie putting the kids to bed gradually faded as the two women sat drinking AltCon on the sofa.

'So it's my fault that Remy is where he is, and that Dan's kicked me out,' she finished. She leaned into Shannon's embrace and let herself sob.

When Grace lifted her head again, she said, 'I've lost it all, Shan, everything. I can't help those poor people at Tier Four and I can't even come back to Tier Two. What am I going to do?'

'You'll find another job, doll,' Shannon said kindly.

'My mum...' Grace said, trying to catch her breath. 'My mum...'

'What about her?' Shannon asked gently.

'I couldn't help my mum... I couldn't save her.'

Shannon put down her glass. 'What do you mean?'

'My mum, she... died in prison. I was with her. It was back when they used to lock kids up. They didn't have places like the Agrarian then. She stole some money... addict... but she was a good mum. She loved me...' She clenched her fists.

Shannon shook her head. 'You never told me any of this.'

'If people knew, then they would judge me, they wouldn't let me work in the system. How could I ever have got a job with the Department of Justice if I'd admitted that? And Remy... I couldn't tell Dan, because...' She sniffed hard.

'Why is Remy so important to you?'

Grace took a moment to calm her breathing.

'Our mothers were best friends. When my mum died, Remy's mum took me in and brought me up as her own.'

'Oh, Grace...'

'And now Dan thinks I'm having an affair with Remy.'

'But you're not?'

'No! We grew up together. It's not like that.'

'Oh God, Dan rang up the other night looking for you. He said there was some emergency at work and asked if I knew where you were. I told him I didn't. I'm sorry.'

'You weren't to know.'

'Why can't you just tell him what you told me? He'll believe you,' Shannon said. 'Tell him. He'll understand.'

Grace wasn't sure she needed Dan to understand her any more.

'I don't think he will. He thinks I don't want a baby because of Remy.'

Shannon's eyes searched her face.

Grace paused before she finally said, 'I had a termination when we were first married. I didn't tell Dan because when I found I was pregnant, I wanted to check everything was okay first. We hadn't planned it. I was going to get balloons and make a card out of the scan to show him when he returned, because even though I was afraid, I knew he'd be so happy. Anyway, I went to the screening clinic and I found out' – she swallowed hard – 'that my baby had the violence pattern genes.'

Shannon sighed heavily. 'I get it now.'

'How could I bring a child into this world, knowing what would happen to him or her if that violence got out of hand, knowing now what happens in Tier Three? It's even worse than I imagined. So many conditions can be managed with gene therapy and manipulation, but not that one.' She sniffed hard. 'You know what's expected. The doctor assumed I wanted a termination. I knew what could happen to my child when he grew up, so I went along with it.'

'Oh God, I'm so sorry, Grace.'

'I couldn't tell him, Shan. I thought I loved him too much, but now I think I was just protecting myself.'

'You could get pregnant again and the baby might be fine...'

'I can't. I can't go through that again. And my mum... I felt that she'd abandoned me... left me all alone in the world. It messed my head up...'

'Look, you have to tell Dan all of this. He'll understand. He loves you, Grace. He'll get it.'

'I don't want to! I don't want to tell him anything! He doesn't love me. He's gone snooping in my work, he doesn't trust me

289

and he's put my safety at risk for a bloody news report.' She wiped her eyes. 'How can I talk to him about Remy without telling him about my whole past? He has no idea who I really am. How can he love me if he doesn't *know* me?

'Look at me, Shan. I've lost my job, which gave my life meaning. I've lost my husband. Even Remy, who did so much for me when we were kids, is lying in biostasis, some reel of a horrendous crime playing over and over in his head and he's not even guilty...'

She stood up. 'I've got to do something.'

Shannon stood up too, a concerned expression. 'It's getting late, Grace. Have a drink and a rest. There's plenty of time to deal with this tomorrow.' She rubbed her friend's back. 'Stay here, I'll put the twins into one bed. They won't mind, they usually get in together anyway.'

Grace glanced at the wall clock. It was nearly ten o'clock. At midnight, the security systems would automatically update and her bio-security wouldn't work any more. She had to reach Janus before then. 'I need to go to him...'

Shannon smiled and nodded. 'Yes, that's a good idea. Go to Dan. Go and sort it out. He'll listen, he'll understand...'

'No, I don't mean Dan. I mean Remy.'

Five minutes later, Grace was driving out of the compound and back to London. She sped down the dark country roads, past the wind turbines which loomed over the dark fields like ghostly sentinels.

She had no idea how she was going to get Remy out of Siberia. She'd have to figure it out when she got there. It would be quiet in the clinic now. She was pretty sure she could get past the security guards on the doors, and once inside, there wouldn't be many members of staff. But it would only be a matter of time before it was widely known that she wasn't welcome any more, that Conrad had sacked her. God, just the idea shook her up. Sacked? All that effort she'd made to better herself, to get away from her past, rise up out the mire.

Part of her past had come back and ruined everything that she'd worked so hard to build up. And now it was time to deal with it.

–

Abigail stood by Remy's bed, gazing down on him. He was good-looking, his square jaw and Roman nose with high cheekbones gave him a strong look. She didn't feel creeped out by Siberia like other members of staff claimed they did. The sound of the beds rolling and the gentle lighting calmed her. In fact, for Abigail, it was the perfect place to think.

She'd finished shaving his head and replaced his mask over his eyes. People's eyes fascinated her. She often wondered what was going on behind them, what made people tick, why they felt the way they did about things. Humans were so fascinating.

For instance, Grace Gunnarsson – why was she so obsessed with him? Why had she chosen him over all the other possible offenders? What was it about Remy, about Grace? She couldn't understand it.

She turned to go. She'd been at work long enough for one day, but Conrad seemed grateful she'd cleared up the mess in the clinic. The cleaners had done a lot, but they wouldn't be able to figure out where the various items of medical kit belonged. Nor would they be able to ascertain if anything had been stolen. She wasn't certain yet, but the drugs cabinet seemed less full than it had been that morning.

CHAPTER THIRTY-FOUR

Grace held her breath as she drove up to the entrance of the underground car park at the Janus Justice building. The roller-shutter automatically began to rise and she exhaled, relieved that the security system had not yet deactivated her access. Guards were stationed on all the external doors and gates. They were all new and, once they'd seen her lanyard, nodded at her as she made her way up to the top floor, unaware she was no longer employed there. The grind of the lift mechanism meant the bio-security pad had responded to her fingerprint, but she still wasn't home and dry.

As the lift rose, her heart rate rose with it. It stopped with a judder and the doors opened. She hovered for a moment on the threshold – Grace afraid of being caught doing something wrong, Gracie agitated that she might not get what she wanted. The corridor was empty and silent, the lights strips of soft luminescence along the ceiling, turned down for the night. She angled her face away from the security camera – just another employee doing her job.

She found a wheelchair by the empty guard station and pushed it towards Siberia ward. The door opened before she got there.

Her breath caught in her throat.

George appeared, his large shoulders slumped, regarding her with his soft brown eyes. 'Evening, Doctor G. You're working late. I thought you'd gone already.'

'Hi, George. I'm on call. It's an emergency, one of the patients having fits, apparently. I'm going to pop him down to

292

the clinic and check everything's okay with his reel.' She pointed to the wheelchair as if it somehow explained everything.

'Well, don't stay all night, they might think you're one of the patients and put you in a bed.' He chuckled.

'I won't.' She forced a smile and he continued on his way.

Grace peered into Siberia ward. It would only be a matter of time before another member of staff came along. She quickly pushed the chair over to Remy's bed without looking at the other offenders.

Putting the brake on the chair, she detached his fluid lines with shaking hands and paused briefly before removing his headset. What if snapping him out of his reel caused him to freak out? His closed eyes looked sunken into his pale face, lines from the frame imprinted onto his skin.

Taking a deep breath, she put her hands under his armpits and tried to lift him, but he was heavier than she'd expected. Approaching from a different angle, she pulled his legs across the bed towards the chair, wondering how the hell she was going to get him onto the chair without him crashing to the floor. It was warm on the ward and sweat prickled her skin.

'I would've done it for you if you'd asked.'

Startled, Grace turned around to see George again. He lumbered towards the chair and rearranged Remy's dead weight easily. He said, 'If you're taking him for more than an hour, you're going to need to sedate him, because otherwise he'll wake up with the Scaries.'

'The Scaries?'

'Yeah, you know, when you wake up out of a horrible dream and you don't know where you are and you're not sure if the dream is still going on. We call it the Scaries. Happens sometimes.' He rummaged in his pocket, brought out two nasal sprays and held them out to her. 'These can be pretty useful in tricky situations.' Grace took them and put them in her jacket pocket.

'Thanks, George.'

'You want me to take him somewhere for you?' He reached out to the handles.

'No, no, that's fine. Thanks, you've been very helpful.'

George considered her for a moment, then said, 'Doc, I don't know what you're doing. But I do know I owe you. I owe you for my sister's life.'

Grace nodded, biting her lip.

'I tell you what,' George said. 'I'll just push him to the lift for you.' He started moving Remy towards the door.

'I'll follow, I just need to get something.'

Quickly, she pushed at panels behind the workstation that sat by the entrance to the ward. A couple of minutes later, she found what she was looking for – drugs that would reverse the sedative quickly. She suspected that she was going to need Remy alert as soon as possible.

Grace followed George out into the corridor, feeling a growing sense of excitement. Maybe she was going to get away with this.

Safely in the lift, the doors began to close on George and he raised a large hand in a childlike wave.

Grace put her hand on her heart and whispered, 'Thank you.'

George nodded before the doors shut firmly and the lift moved down.

Remy was wrapped only in his white sheet, like a toga. She wished she'd brought something more substantial for him to wear. Just a few more floors to go. She peeled open a sterile hypodermic packet, filled the syringe with the clear liquid from the bottle, held it up and cleared the bubbles and injected Remy in his bicep.

The lift doors opened to the underground car park. There was no point in trying to conceal her activity from the CCTV. She would already have been recorded in the corridor and the lift. George knew she'd taken Remy from Siberia, that she was the last person to see him. It was only a matter of time before the police were onto her.

There was no way she could go back to the life she'd worked so hard for.

Two security guards stood chatting by the roller-shutter to the car park. Grace wheeled Remy behind a car so they wouldn't be able to see him and then ran over, shouting, 'There's an intruder up on Floor Three!' They immediately ran to the lift and when they had gone, Grace moved Remy to her car.

With the car door open to her left and Remy in the chair to her right, Grace geared herself up to getting him into the passenger seat. The drugs she'd given him to combat his sedation appeared to be working as he was beginning to stir. His eyelids flickered and his arms twitched. 'Come on, Rem. We need to get out of here.'

Lifting his arms over her shoulders, she tried to pull him up. It was hard to get a good grip on him that would allow her to lever him up. He was a dead weight, still not come round enough to move himself. How had she imagined she could do this?

As she struggled, she didn't hear the roller-shutter come up. By the time the car had pulled up behind her, its tyres squeaking on the eco-tarmac, it was too late. She turned around as Remy fell back into the wheelchair with a groan.

Conrad jumped out of his sleek black car, leaving the engine running. 'What the hell do you think you're doing?' He whipped his phone from his pocket. 'I'm calling security.'

Grace looked around in a panic and was about to run away, when Gracie suddenly took charge. She took a step towards him.

'No, you're not going to call security, Conrad.' She ducked towards him, snatched his phone and flung it to the far side of the car park. The sound of the crack reverberated around the walls.

'The hell...?' he said, staring after it. He turned back to her, outraged. 'You fucking mad bitch!'

'You're not going to call security, and you're not even going to stop me leaving.' She was amazed by the confidence in her own voice. 'Because you're in enough trouble. It's very late. I suppose you're here for some kind of emergency meeting about the protestors and the hackers?'

'Yes, I am!' he barked. 'And any minute now there'll be the head of security, board members, and a number of other people turning up.' He looked over to Remy, slumped in the wheelchair. 'You won't get away with this, Grace. You and him, you're both going down. What the hell has gone wrong in your head?' His expression was one of disbelief and contempt.

'Oh, I'm going to get away with this, Conrad,' she said confidently. 'You're going to let me leave, with Remy. In fact, I'm going to go further than that.' Her voice was low and menacing now. 'You're going to help me get him into that car. If the guards come back, you're going to tell them it's fine. You're not going to say a word to anyone else and you're going to delete the security video too.'

His laugh was strained and high-pitched.

'And what do I tell the Department of Justice? That I lost an offender?' Sweat began beading his forehead, reflecting the strip lights above.

'Remy was never here officially,' Grace said calmly. 'I brought him in. He was never arrested. No court orders, no papers were signed. He's a ghost.'

'You're mad if you think—'

She grabbed him roughly across the face, digging her finger-nails in hard.

'Yes, I am fucking mad!'

Conrad's eyes widened. She clutched at his face, her nails causing tiny moons, and through gritted teeth said, 'I have enough dirt on you to destroy you. I've got all the files, photos, videos. I know what you do in Siberia, the torture that goes on in Tier Three, the unlicensed drugs you use. I have evidence for all of it. I know all about your friend in the Department of Justice – your minister and your dirty little dealings.'

The hint of a smile came to Conrad's lips. Did he realise she was faking it?

'You don't know shit,' he said.

'Don't I? It wasn't hackers, it was NewsFlex who got into the computer system and found all the information. They've seen everything.'

His eyes lit up at this. Was he falling for her bluff?

'I know plenty, and if you don't let us go my husband is going to lay all your dirty laundry out there for the world to see!'

Conrad's smile disappeared altogether.

'Dan knows the whole story. One call from me and your shitshow is over. I'm pretty sure your minister is going to deny all knowledge and what's going to happen to you then? So you're going to do things my way, aren't you?'

His face had drained of colour. He nodded.

'So who's the bitch now?' she whispered and let go of him.

'You're going to give me my job at Tier Two back. Then you're going to destroy the security footage of this,' she waved her hand around. 'But first of all, help me get him in the car.'

'Jesus Christ...'

'You're going to do this or, I swear, I'll destroy you, your reputation and your company. You do things my way and we both walk away with what we want. No one needs to suffer, Conrad.' She knew his sense of survival, his ego and his desire for money would win out over doing the right thing.

She wasn't going to beg.

Not long later, Remy was sitting in the passenger seat, the wheelchair empty next to Grace's car. She sat in the driver's seat, the door shut but the window lowered. Conrad leaned over the car, one hand on the roof, his face almost level with hers.

'You realise that this means we have a hold over each other?' he said, wiping the sweat out of his eyes. 'I'll let you go now, but I'm not going to destroy the security tapes. They're my insurance. We're trapped in this agreement. Both of us. One step in the wrong direction and I'll have you.'

She started up the engine, and before she pulled off, she said, 'So be it.'

CHAPTER THIRTY-FIVE

Central London

11.17 p.m.

A large-scale protest here outside the building earlier today is believed to have been provoked by the arrival of Remy James Wilson, a convicted offender who has already been treated in Tier Three. In a shocking allegation, Wilson is rumoured to have reoffended, a claim which is strongly denied by Janus, who insist that the therapy here is effective and infallible. CEO Conrad Becker has so far declined an interview.

Wilson's alleged reoffending has called into question the dubious methods rumoured to be used by Janus. Many protestors argue that the therapy used here is against human rights, conspiracy theorists even going as far as to imply that Janus tortures the offenders in one of these clinics behind me.

Police officers investigating a break-in here this afternoon have confirmed that a large quantity of drugs was stolen, suggesting that theft, rather than genuine protest, was the motive for an attack that caused thousands of pounds' worth of damage to the Tier Three clinic. However, an insider who does not wish to be named has informed NewsFlex that a high-ranking psychiatrist has left the company out of the blue. There had been suspicions before now about her drug use and even possible dealings in the illegal drug trade.

–

Dan left the rest of the crew packing up the kit after filming the protest outside the Janus Justice building and made his way to the nearest Tube station.

He hadn't called Grace to ask if she was okay after the attack. Was that how bad things were between them? Only a week or so ago life had seemed perfect. It could have stayed that way but for Grace's deceit and pigheadedness.

Even reporting on Remy bloody Wilson boiled his piss. Maybe the protest had been caused by his article about Wilson, and yes, the protest had gone too far, but it was his job, wasn't it, to report the news, to show how things actually were? It wasn't really his fault that Grace's clinic had been targeted.

His eyelids flickered against a light rain falling from the dark sky.

But to think that she was involved with someone else… How could Grace take him for such a mug? He turned down a side street, pushing his hands into his pockets as he walked.

'You're that news fella, aren't you?' a man's voice came from behind him.

He sighed deeply. He wasn't in the mood for this. It happened sometimes, people stopping him in the street, recognising him.

'I saw your report about that Remy Wilson fella.'

'Yeah, yeah…' said Dan, walking on a bit, hoping the bloke would just go away.

'And those copycat crimes.'

The rain was going down his collar. He just wanted to get home and go to bed.

Copycat? No, he'd only reported on possible reoffences.

Dan stopped still.

'Your wife's called Grace? She works at Janus, doesn't she? Not difficult to guess where you get your info...'

The hairs on the back of Dan's neck stood up now, but it wasn't because of the cold rain.

He turned around slowly. A man, about his own height, dressed in black, stood in front of him, head cocked to one side. They were alone in the dark street. Was this going to get nasty?

'You want to watch what you report on,' the man said, his dark eyes narrowing. 'You could get a whole lot of people into trouble with your rumours.'

'Look, mate, I don't know who you are,' Dan said, taking his hands out of his pockets, 'but I've had a long week...'

'No worries, though,' the man interrupted. 'You won't be able to report on anything after I've finished with you.'

Dan didn't see the first punch coming, hardly felt it as the shock kicked in.

But by the fourth or fifth, he knew he was in serious trouble. His last thought before he lost consciousness was of Grace.

–

By the time Grace reached the Agrarian, the drugs she'd given Remy had done their job and he was conscious but distressed and confused. *The Scaries*, George had called it. Grace had been scared herself for the last few miles as Remy had been lashing out, fighting an invisible enemy. It had made for difficult driving. She'd tried to use one of the sedative sprays but couldn't wrestle with him and drive at the same time. Her cheek still throbbed from her attempt. The more awake he became, the more disturbed he seemed.

It was almost one in the morning when she pulled up to the compound gate. She got out of the car and shut the door, leaving Remy wild-eyed and slamming his palms against the windscreen inside, while she approached the intercom.

'Shannon!' she cried. 'I'm at the gate. I need help!'

The camera on the gatepost clicked and swivelled around, no doubt taking in the sight of a man, naked but for a white sheet, trying to fight his way out of the car, and Grace standing helpless nearby.

'What have you done?' Shannon's voice sounded tinny. 'Stay there.'

The gate started to open slowly.

'Remy, it's me, Gracie!' she shouted desperately through the car windscreen. His hands flapped at the door handle, unable to connect, leading to frustrated animal roars.

A few minutes later, Shuggie appeared, leading a group of men down the drive towards the car. Her protective instincts flared. 'What are you going to do?' she cried as one of them gently moved her out of the way. 'Don't hurt him!'

Shannon hurried down the drive after them and made straight for Grace, putting her arm around her shoulder in a gesture of comfort and restraint.

'Stand back, Grace,' Shuggie commanded. 'We know what we're doing.' The men took Remy roughly from the car, grabbing his arms and legs as he fought and writhed against them.

Shannon held her by the shoulders and turned her away from the spectacle. 'They're going to look after him now, doll. You just leave it to the lads. They see this kind of thing a lot...'

'Where are they taking him?' she whispered as they stood in the beam of her headlights, a fine rain catching the light in tiny dots that looked like snowfall.

'To the cooler,' Shannon said.

'What's that?'

'It's where they take the other lads, the soldiers, sometimes when they're suffering from PTSD – a quiet place, soft, he won't hurt himself and he'll calm down. He'll be fine,' Shannon soothed, 'just fine.'

Once the men had disappeared from sight, Grace and Shannon walked slowly up the drive, arm in arm. Grace was relieved she wasn't alone. Once in the house, Shannon sat her down on the sofa, wrapped a fleece around her, more for comfort than warmth, and poured them both a calming AltCon drink.

'Grace, love, I don't know what the hell is going on,' Shannon said, sitting down next to her, 'but what on earth are you doing?'

Grace drank quickly, half as a cure for the extreme stress she'd suffered and half in celebration of the relief she was feeling now that Remy was safe, at least for now.

'What are you playing at? You can't leave him here... they'll come for him.'

'Conrad caught me trying to take Remy.'

'Christ, Grace!'

'It's okay. He's not going to do anything. He said I can keep my job here, at Tier Two.'

Her friend's mouth fell open. 'How the hell did you manage that? What you've done is gross misconduct... It's more than that, surely – it's assisting an offender, jail term for abduction...'

'I'm blackmailing Conrad. Remy wasn't officially signed in.'

Shannon sighed deeply.

'Can I stay here? Just for a while...'

'Of course, but what about Remy? Are they going to put him in Tier Four?'

'Conrad says he can remain here.' Grace registered Shannon's expression. 'He's better off here than in Tier Four, Shan.'

There was a long silence before Shannon finally said, 'I don't like this, doll. Not one bit. I'd do anything for you, you know that. But is this right?'

Grace nodded gravely. 'You have to trust me, Shan.'

After drinking more AltCon while Grace explained about the brain scans, Shannon seemed more understanding about the situation. 'So it looks as though someone has set him up.'

Grace nodded. 'Are you sure, I mean about me staying here, with Shuggie and the kids and everything?'

Shannon put her hand on her friend's. 'Listen, you can stay as long as you need. And Remy… well, I don't know what will happen to him, but if Conrad says he can stay here, then I'm only following orders from the boss.' She gave a mischievous grin.

'Oh God, thank you, Shan, thank you.' Grace grabbed her friend into a hug and then released her. 'Remy will be safe?'

'Can't think of a safer place than with those lads.'

'I don't know what I'd do without you.'

Grace leaned back on the sofa, finally giving in to her exhaustion.

'There's a cabin, not far from this house,' Shannon said. 'It's nice and secluded, needs a bit of a fix-up, but it will give Shuggie and the boys something to do. Why don't you stay there until you get yourself sorted? Give you a bit of privacy and peace away from this madhouse.'

Grace nodded slowly. 'Sounds like a plan.'

Right now all she wanted was somewhere to rest and a chance to get back into her work, to find meaning in all the chaos.

Should she tell Dan the whole truth?

Screw him, he made his choices.

'I know what we need,' Shannon said, hoisting herself off the sofa. She disappeared into the kitchen for a moment and returned carrying a bottle of colourless liquid and two glasses. 'Hooch, made by the lads,' she said with a wink, pouring it liberally. She passed a glass to Grace and they clinked them together.

'To whatever the fuck happens next,' Shannon said and downed the lot.

'Amen,' said Grace. The liquid warmed her insides immediately.

Shannon refilled Grace's glass before she had a chance to put it down. 'Jesus, doll, that was nuts! You just kidnapped him,' she said, her face morphing from an expression of shock to one of hilarity, and she suddenly roared with laughter. 'You bloody kidnapped him! And you got away with it!'

'I guess I did,' said Grace, welcoming the fuzzy feeling that was beginning to wash through her. She emptied her glass again and reached for the bottle.

—

It was late in the afternoon when Grace awoke in a small pink bed with her face squashed up against a huge teddy bear. There was a fire raging in her throat, her stomach felt stripped of its lining and her head throbbed. She hadn't had a hangover since she'd been a teenager.

She shuffled downstairs and into the kitchen. The light was too bright, and the noise from the kids playing outside made her head hurt.

'You look as bad as I feel.' Shannon grinned as she stood chopping vegetables. 'But I had to get up with the kids. I've eaten and I'm picking up a bit now.' She threw the vegetables into a pan. 'You want something to eat? There's toast and cereal.'

Grace closed her eyes in response and when she opened them again, a glass of water sat in front of her. She gulped some and immediately regretted as she had to swallow hard to keep it down.

'That bad, huh?'

Grace nodded and squeezed her lips together before asking quietly, 'Is Remy okay?'

'Shuggie's been keeping an eye on him, says he's much calmer now.'

'I'm going to get some fresh air, walk over and see him.'

'You sure? You don't want to wait until you feel a bit better?'

She shook her head and again, regretted it.

'At least have some coffee and painkillers.'

Shannon put them in front of her, smiled and turned back to her vegetables. 'Shuggie says Remy spent a few hours in the cooler and he seems to be doing okay. He's had a hot shower and a good meal. The lads have taken him under their wing. They're going to wait till he's feeling stronger and give him some work to do, chop wood or paint fences, or something...'

Grace knew how healing simple work could be. Remy would feel at home here. He would belong.

'Shuggie thinks he'll do great here. He's one of them. They all fought in Africa, got a lot to talk about. Sounds like you got Conrad off his back. No one's going to come looking here for him, are they?' It was more of a statement than a question.

But images of Diros rose in Grace's mind. Remy might be in a secure compound, surrounded by combat-proficient, military-trained men. But whatever her friend said, Grace knew that Diros would always be looking for Remy, and once they found him, who knew what they would do to him?

CHAPTER THIRTY-SIX

Regardless of the way her life had unravelled, as she walked around the Agrarian Compound, Grace had an overwhelming feeling of gratitude to be back at Tier Two. This was where she belonged.

As though the universe was trying to reinforce this idea, a smiling woman carrying a baby and holding hands with a toddler walked past her as they made their way to join other mothers and toddlers picnicking on blankets in the warm sunshine. Grace recognised the mother as Nikki, the woman she'd brought here just a few weeks before. It was almost as if the two women had swapped places on the well-being scale. Nikki had already put weight on and her face was rosy and relaxed. Grace briefly returned the smile, feeling relief and satisfaction. But then her smile faded.

She made her way into the soldiers' enclosure with a temporary security pass that Shannon had given her. The smell of cut grass mingled with the aroma of cooking. A group of soldiers sat around a makeshift barbecue, occasionally poking at sizzling meat on a grill with long-handled forks. Grace's stomach roiled.

Their conversation and laughter halted as she approached. Remy was sitting in their midst, pale, but smiling, dressed in the white vest and cargo pants that the lads had adopted as a uniform. Immediately she saw him in another life.

His face fell as he turned to look in her direction. He made his apologies and walked over to her under the curious watchfulness of his newly adopted brethren.

They walked for some minutes in silence until they reached the shade of a copse of trees. She turned to him. 'Are you okay?'

He didn't reply. With his head shaved his grey eyes looked bigger – more like the child she'd once known.

'You'll be well cared for here. You need to get some rest, take some time. You've been through a lot.'

'I asked you for help!' He spoke quietly, but with venom. 'And instead you put me in Tier Four!'

'Remy, please, listen to me...'

'Do you know what it's like in there?' Spit flew from his lips as he spoke.

'Yes... I've been in there.'

'Oh, you've been in there!' He turned away angrily, caught his breath and turned back. 'You've got no idea! It's hell, watching yourself get beaten up and stabbed over and over again, actually believing it's happening to you... not being able to do anything about it...'

'You weren't supposed to be there. It was a mistake!' She briefly explained about the protest, the man trying to take Remy, and how she blackmailed Conrad into letting them come to the Agrarian.

'Mistake? Diros don't make mistakes,' Remy said.

'It was chaos. We had to get you somewhere safe.'

'Am I allowed to leave?'

'You're not here in an official capacity. You can go whenever you like. I just thought maybe you needed somewhere to be for a while.'

'Who the hell are you, *Grace*?' He stressed her name. 'The Gracie I knew wouldn't have worked for the authorities, wouldn't have put me in a place like that.'

'Remy, for Christ's sake, you were either going to be killed by Diros or go to Tier Four. I was trying to help you, getting you into the clinic was the only way I could fix your brain.'

'There's nothing wrong with me!' He punched the air in frustration. Some of the soldiers looked over in their direction at his raised voice.

'I know that now!' she hissed in frustration. 'I know you're angry and hurt, but please believe me, I was trying to help. I believed the scans instead of trusting my own instinct, my own experience. I know I've messed up, but look, we're here now. I got you out, didn't I? We're safe here. But you're right, there's nothing wrong with your brain. Someone swapped those scans, but I only found out just before those people broke into the clinic. It must have been Diros, but how the hell did they get access to the scans?'

'They've got connections, insiders… I think they…'

The sound of an engine approaching got their attention.

Shannon pulled up in her jeep. 'I'm sorry to interrupt, but you really need to see this.' She held out her shell to show a NewsFlex report on pause. Grace took it from her, a sense of dread rearing. 'I've got to get back to the kids. I'll leave it with you.' She nodded solemnly at Remy and drove off, waving to the other lads as she passed them.

Grace hit play. Dan stood outside the Janus Justice building, the large blue double-faced god above him, looking to the past and the future. It was dark, so it must have been late the previous night. She felt furious and hurt at the same time, confused, even. He knew she wasn't on drugs! Why was he even saying these things? She knew he was coming from a place of hurt, but the betrayal stung.

'I know what this is. Conrad's using me as the scapegoat. He's told Dan that I stole the drugs!' Grace looked up from the screen. 'He's punishing me because I dared to blackmail him.' She shook her head. 'We were nearly home and dry – me back at Tier Two, you with somewhere safe to stay, and Conrad could keep his dirty little secret. Now everyone thinks I'm a bloody dealer and they'll never believe a word I say.'

Of course Conrad would do this – there was no way he was going to let her get away with it. His ego wouldn't let him.

'It's not Conrad, it's Diros. Don't you see, Grace?' Remy took the shell from her hands. 'They're setting us up. Perfectly.

You look as though you're stealing drugs. I look like I've killed a drug dealer. They're going to get to us. They're going to find us and make it look as though I killed you – and everyone is going to believe it. It's what they do.'

'But why would they set us up like this if they think you're still in Tier Four? I think this is just about discrediting me.'

'Diros are very thorough, Grace. They'll protect themselves at all costs.'

'So why didn't they just kill you when they were in the clinic?' Grace asked. 'They had you in their hands! Why didn't they just kill me too, if they wanted rid of me?' She shuddered thinking about it.

'I don't know. Maybe it was too tricky. They want us both out of the way. If they'd killed us there someone would be looking for suspects, and that's the last thing they want. They hide behind other criminals' actions. It's what they do. Hiding a crime within a crime.' His shoulders dropped and he leaned against a tree, looking tired and defeated. 'They're playing with us, Gracie.'

After a few minutes, Grace said, 'Let's get them arrested. We'll go to the police. I'll tell them about the scans and how it was all faked.'

Remy laughed, a sad, hollowed-out sound. 'The evidence all points to the original offenders that Diros copied, so the police aren't going to believe it. We don't have any credibility now that I look like a two-time killer and you look like a drug-dealing addict.'

The sound of laughter drifted over from the soldiers.

'Anyway, they have an insurance policy,' Remy added.

'What do you mean?'

'I didn't get the chance to tell you the whole story before. When we worked as bounty hunters, Sarge collected bio-samples from all of us. Told us it was so we could be identified by the police and eliminated as suspects. We were employed by the government, I assumed it was protocol.

'The next job that came in was to catch a drug dealer. Things got out of hand. The guy ended up in hospital, slashed with a knife across the guts. It wasn't me, Gracie. But I was there. One of us had to take the fall for it, Sarge said, so that we could protect the group.

'He chose me. I went along with it, thinking it was for the best, told the police it had been a street-fight that had got out of hand. Thankfully the guy didn't die. I had Aversion Therapy...' He shook his head.

'I trusted Sarge, so I thought all the jobs he set up would be kosher, official, but soon he started going rogue. When we caught offenders, they usually ended up at Tier Three, but Sarge was of the opinion that Aversion Therapy wasn't enough to punish anyone.' Remy laughed sadly. 'If only he'd known just how bad it really is. So he decided he wasn't going to take the criminals we caught to Janus any more. He was going to do to them what they'd done to others.

'Then the killing started. It was either stay with them and go down a very, very dark road, or take my chances and escape.

'I told Sarge I wanted out, that it wasn't my thing. I'd already found a small flat and started to think about getting a regular job and sorting my head out after Africa. I wanted to start a new life for myself, a quiet life. But he's not the sort of man to take no for an answer. He told me I'd have to prove my loyalty or he'd frame me for a crime.

'We often took footage to show the authorities or the contractor that we'd made the arrest above board, avoid any problems with the court case. When we were sent on a new case to catch another drug dealer, Biz killed him. We'd gone from bounty hunters to vigilantes to just plain killers.

'Biz killed the drug dealer to set me up, even planted my bio-evidence. He was a genius on the computer and, under orders from Sarge, he tampered with the bodycam footage and made it look as though I'd done it. They were trying to force me to stay, or get me put away for good.

'Of course, I tried to tell the police what had really happened when I was arrested, but they didn't believe me.'

'So you ran,' Grace said. 'I'm so sorry I didn't believe you. I didn't understand.'

He shook his head. 'It doesn't matter now.'

'But they've got away with it,' Grace said angrily. 'Those offenders that they framed, they'd done their punishment. They'd made a fresh start. They could have had new lives and Diros destroyed that.'

'Diros are corrupt to the very core,' said Remy.

'Which means they're never going to change. At least the contrite feel shame, there is a chance of redemption… but the corrupt…'

'I know,' Remy said, his face darkening. 'You can't fix everyone, Grace. Maybe some people are just bad bastards who want to watch the world burn.'

'They're not going to stop, are they?'

Remy shook his head.

'And they're not going to let you go free, are they?'

'No.'

Grace put her hand in her pocket and pulled out the Funland keyring. She pressed it into his hand.

He looked down and gave a sad smile. 'Where did you get this?'

'I found it in your bag at the library. I've still got mine.' Had they really changed so much? 'Remy, do you remember those kids who used to say stuff about Lottie? There were three of them. They were bigger than us. But we got them.'

He nodded.

'We can do this. I'll be bait. We'll lure them in and finish this once and for all.'

There was a brief flicker of anxiety on Remy's face. Then he said, 'There's the Gracie I remember.'

CHAPTER THIRTY-SEVEN

'So you don't know if the reporter is dead or not?' Sarge was interrogating Bizzy.

They had met in the library as soon as the sun started to go down.

Bizzy shook his head. 'No, Sarge, I had to make a run for it. There was a couple walking their dog, came from nowhere.'

'This' – Sarge said loudly, startling Mal who was sitting in the corner, taking everything in – 'is what happens when you don't follow the plan!'

'But Sarge, I—'

'No, Biz – you went out there because you were riled up. Bloodlust, that's all it was. Insubordination and lack of discipline!'

'I stopped Dan Gunnarsson getting to the heart of his story,' Bizzy insisted. 'We don't want anyone thinking too much about things and putting two and two together.'

'Don't try to make out you did this to protect us, Biz,' Sarge said, his eyes screwed up, one finger pointing in the air. He opened his eyes, lowered his hand and moved closer to Bizzy. 'If you were trying to protect us, then Dan Gunnarsson would be dead now. Instead, he's going to be able to give the police a description of you. If the fucking couple with their fucking dog haven't already!' Sarge picked up a can of cola that was sitting on the desk and flung it across the room, its contents spraying in an arc as it went. 'No, you attacked Gunnarsson because you wanted to kill someone because I said you couldn't kill Remy in the clinic...'

'If I'd done Remy like I suggested,' Bizzy said, 'then he wouldn't be fucking out and about now, would he?'

Sarge launched himself at Bizzy, grabbed him by the throat and pressed him hard against a wall. 'You're a liability, Biz,' he snarled.

Mal shrank in his chair. He knew now that he'd made the right decision to leave. Why had it taken him so long? He should have gone with Remy, left these two psychos behind back then. He just had to keep his cool for another twelve hours, when his bus would leave from Victoria Coach Station. He wished it was him and Layla going together. She'd be proud of him for making the break. He could feel it. This time tomorrow, he'd be up in Scotland, looking for somewhere to sleep for the night and making plans for a whole new life. He ran his hand over the jacket pocket which held his ticket, double-checking it was zipped up tight.

'You're not always right, Sarge.' Bizzy spat the last word.

Mal's eyes widened.

Sarge hit Bizzy across the face and yelled, 'You got a fucking death wish, soldier?' He took out his gun and pressed it hard into Bizzy's face. Bizzy winced against it, trying to turn his head away, but it was jammed between the gun and the wall and Sarge pressed harder.

Mal waited, eyes averted, until Sarge had regained his composure. 'Enough of this,' he said finally, removing the gun from Bizzy's face where the muzzle had left a red circle.

'Enough!' he repeated. 'Kill him if you want to kill someone.' Mal cringed, looking up slowly, expecting to see a gun pointing at his head.

Instead, Sarge directed his finger towards the large, slouched figure sitting on the chair next to the librarian's desk, his hands taped behind his back, a steady stream of blood dripping from his face.

'Do you hear that?' Sarge turned rapidly and went down on his haunches in front of the man in the chair, jabbing his gun towards him.

The Janus clinic porter turned his head slightly towards Sarge. His face was a grotesque mask of bruises and swellings, his eyes swollen, the skin around them stretched shiny and purple.

'If it wasn't for you, George, Remy would still be in Tier Four. He was your responsibility. You didn't do your job. So that's why this is happening.' Sarge waved the gun in a circle. 'And you still insist you don't know where she was taking him?'

George lifted his head very slowly. 'Fuck you,' he said, flecks of blood spraying from his lips.

'You're no use to us.' Sarge stood up, looked at Bizzy and nodded.

Mal couldn't understand these two any more. Only a few minutes ago they'd been at each other's throats. Whatever it was that bound them together, he didn't get it. It convinced him that he was making the right move. He had to keep his mouth shut and his eyes open – stay out of trouble, just until the morning.

Mal turned away as Bizzy took a piece of wire from his pocket and approached George from behind. Mal only wished he could have closed his ears to the monstrous sounds that came next, sounds that he knew he'd struggle to forget for the rest of his life.

A few moments of silence passed before Sarge spoke again. 'Call her.'

Mal turned back to see Abigail on the chair opposite George, her face pale and her eyes wide and unblinking as she watched the pool of blood slowly spreading at George's feet. She didn't move as Bizzy took her phone from the desk where it was sitting in front of her, just out of her reach. He winked at her before finding a number and hitting dial.

–

'We can't use you as bait, Grace,' Shannon said, horrified.

The two women sat opposite each other at the small table in the cabin that was to be Grace's new home. It was small but solid, and the smell of wood was comforting. The stove was warm still after Shannon had shown her how to heat water for tea.

'We're going to have to,' Grace replied. 'We'll let Diros think I'm hiding out in the library because I'm on the run. I'll wait in the woods, and when I see them arrive, I'll call the police.'

'Are you sure Diros'll come?' asked Shannon. She looked over to Remy and Shuggie who each sat on one of the twin beds either side of the door.

'They think I'm boxed off in Siberia, but Grace is still a threat because she's the only one who knows the truth,' Remy said. 'They want her gone.'

Gone. The word sent a shiver through Grace.

'I don't like it,' said Shuggie, 'but I agree with Grace, it's the only way we're gonnae get them. After what you've told me this afternoon, they sound like a bunch of bad'uns who know exactly what they're doing.'

'Diros have hidden all their crimes. The police aren't looking for anyone else. So how are you going to convince them that these are the real perpetrators?' asked Shannon.

It was a good question.

'I'm going to contact the police and tell them all the information we have on Diros so far. Remy, have you got that list?'

Remy sighed, resigned. He reached into his pocket and pulled out a small scrap of paper. 'I wrote down as many as I can remember. Tell the police if they look in more detail at these attacks, they should find evidence to prove that Diros were involved.'

Grace imagined him sitting up all night at the campfire, trying to recall the actions of those three men.

'It's not all of the crimes, because I wasn't with the gang when they did the others,' he added.

'I'll tell them to look at the reoffences,' said Grace. 'And Myriam's death and the Payback couple.'

'Are you sure you want to do this?' Shannon asked.

'It's a risk I need to take or Remy and I will never be safe. This way, Diros are arrested and Remy and I have our names cleared.'

'What if they find you before the police get there?' Remy asked. 'They'll be armed. Is there any way we can get a gun?'

Shannon nodded. 'We have two under lock and key in the office, just in case anything goes off in the compound.'

'So how do we get them to meet us at the library? We don't know how to contact them,' said Remy.

'Shannon and I have already talked about this. Shan's going to ring—' Grace stopped talking and bit her lip.

'I'm going to ring Dan,' Shannon continued, 'and tell him that Grace has gone missing and ask him to report on it, in the hope that she'll be found. I'm going to drop a subtle hint about where she might be, the library, and hope Dan runs with it.'

'What do you mean a subtle hint?' asked Remy.

'I'll say Grace told me about a library from when she was a kid, keep it vague, but suggest she might be hiding there.'

'Do you think Dan will try to find her himself?' he asked.

'No, because he doesn't know anything about the library,' Grace said. 'He doesn't know anything about my past, so he won't be able to find me. It's a coded message for Diros. They'll know exactly where it is.' Her shoulders dropped. 'Dan wouldn't come anyway and I don't want him to.'

Shannon tapped Grace's hand briefly across the table and Grace sat up straight and sniffed.

'And you're sure Diros will be watching NewsFlex?' asked Shuggie.

'Yes,' said Grace with certainty. 'They want to find me and they know Dan is my husband.'

'I still think I should go with you,' Remy said.

'No, it's too risky. If Diros see you, Remy, you're dead.'

'So are you!' he replied.

'Yes, but if the police see you, then you'll be back in custody. Diros will convince them, will be able to *prove* to them, that you're in their gang. You said it yourself, they have evidence.'

'She's got a point,' said Shuggie and then turned to Grace. 'I'll go with you.'

Remy sighed heavily and nodded.

'And there's no way we can get the lads from the camp there?' Shuggie asked Shannon. 'I mean, four or five of them. The lads will be able to hold them until the police arrive. I'm not sure us four are a match for the three of them.'

'You know we can't, Shug,' Shannon told him. 'The lads are all bio-chipped. So if they go missing from the Agrarian, it'll only be a matter of time before they're found. They'll all be sent to eco-labour camps and we'll be arrested for assisting offenders. It's not fair to put them in that position. We're taking a risk with just you coming along.'

Shuggie looked frustrated.

'Can't you take the chips out, Shannon?' asked Remy.

'Look, I really want to help, but I don't want to lose my job. This is my life here, my home, the kids...'

'Of course, I'm sorry.' Remy's eyes darkened. 'I wish we could just kill the three of them and leave them there.'

'You slept there for God knows how long,' Grace said. 'Your bio-evidence is all over that place. Go ahead and kill them, but I guarantee you'll get done.'

'Kill them and dump the bodies then,' he said angrily. 'They'd kill us given half the chance. Think of all the people they've murdered!'

'Then they'll have turned you into exactly what they wanted you to be and exactly what you don't want to be – a cold-blooded killer,' Grace said. 'Remy, you have to be as far away as possible before the police get there, otherwise this will all have been for nothing.'

'You can stay here as long as you like,' Shannon told Remy. 'Stay here, hide in plain sight until your tattoo has worn off. Maybe we can get you out of the country for good then.'

'It's for the best, mate,' said Shuggie.

'Okay, let's do this,' said Shannon, taking her phone from her pocket. 'I've got Dan's number from the other night when he rang looking for you.'

Grace felt a jolt of regret.

Shannon sat waiting for an answer, staring at the others as she listened. Finally, someone answered.

'Dan, it's Shannon, listen, Grace...' She stopped speaking, her eyes moving from side to side as she listened.

'His name is Dan Gunnarsson. He's a reporter with News-Flex,' said Shannon.

Grace felt her chest tighten.

'I'm here with his wife, hold on.' She held her phone out to Grace. 'Dan's in hospital.'

The hairs on the back of Grace's neck stood on end as she took it and put it on speakerphone. 'This is Dan's wife.'

'I'm sorry to have to tell you this, but your husband was attacked late last night,' came the voice down the line.

'Who am I talking to?' Her chest felt so tight she could hardly make herself heard.

'I'm Leon, one of the nurses on the critical care ward. I'm here with Dan now.'

'Critical care? Is he... is he okay?'

'He's stable. He's in a much better place than when he came in,' Leon said pleasantly. 'However, there is some swelling on the brain, so he's in an induced coma...'

'Oh God.'

'...He's in the best place and we're taking good care of him. At least we have a name now,' said Leon cheerfully. 'He didn't have a wallet or any ID on him, so the police suspect it was a mugging, but it was pretty vicious. The paramedic said it could've been much worse, but a couple disturbed the attacker and he ran off.'

'Do you know who attacked him?'

'Ah, you'll have to speak to the police, love. I don't know about things like that.'

'Can I come and see him?'

'Of course, but as I said, he won't be conscious for a few days.'

Leon gave her the details and she ended the call.

'A couple disturbed the attacker,' she repeated, her voice choked with emotion.

'If you need to go to him, then we can do this…' said Remy. His words were resigned, but there was something in his voice that steeled Grace. Her old life – it was over now.

'No. He's in a coma but he's stable. He wouldn't even know I was there.'

'You don't know that, doll. He might be able to hear you,' said Shannon.

Grace shook her head. 'This was Diros's doing. Dan's lying in hospital, out of it, vulnerable… We have to get to them before they find him and complete the job they started.' Whatever the state their relationship was in, she wasn't going to let Dan be murdered.

Shuggie nodded. 'She's got a point, Shan.'

'But how the hell are we going to find them now?' asked Shannon.

At that moment, Grace's phone rang. She took it from her pocket. No caller ID.

Her mouth went dry. 'They might have found us.'

She switched on speakerphone again and answered. 'Hello?'

There was a strange gasping sound on the other end of the line.

'Hello?' she repeated.

'G… Grace!'

'Abigail?' Grace cried. 'Abigail, what's going on? Where are you?'

'They know…' Her voice was slurred. 'They know he's out… of Siberia…'

Anxious glances passed around the cabin.

'Grace…' Her voice was plaintive now, but then she started a low, moaning cry.

'Abigail, where are you? What's going on?'

'They… they've… killed George.'

There was a smacking sound on the other end of the line, and Abigail cried out.

'Abigail! Abigail!' All they could hear on the other end was her heart-wrenching wails.

'Bring Remy to the library now, or she dies too.'

It was Bizzy's voice. Grace felt her skin crawl.

The line went dead.

'They'll kill her,' Remy said definitively.

'They know you're coming,' Shuggie said. 'You can't just hide in the woods now.'

'We can't let her die,' Remy said.

'Can we call the police?' asked Shannon.

'No,' Remy told her. 'One sight of them and Diros will kill her and run.'

Grace stood up. 'Looks like this is on us.'

CHAPTER THIRTY-EIGHT

Shannon parked the jeep in the trees not far from the railway line. The sun was nearly down, the air cool and still.

'You're staying here, Shan,' Shuggie said for the third time. 'I'm not putting you in danger, hen. There's the kids to think about.' Shannon's face creased for a moment. He planted a quick kiss on her forehead and said, 'Do not get out of this car, no matter what happens, no matter what you hear or see, okay?'

The reality of what was about to happen was becoming all too stark to Grace. Her heart was hammering in her chest. Her mouth was dry, her limbs shaky.

Remy had gone very quiet.

Grace and the two men got out of the jeep and spoke in whispers even though they were some distance still from the library building. Shannon lowered her window so she could join in.

'As soon as we get Abigail, we're going to send her out to you,' Grace said. 'When she's in the car safely and you know the police are on the way, call me. We need to get Remy out as fast as possible.'

'Shuggie, you stay outside for now,' Remy told him. 'We don't want to spook them.' He handed him a gun. 'They expect me and Grace, but we might need an element of surprise.'

Remy checked the other gun and tucked it in his waistband.

Shuggie nodded, and halfway between the jeep and the library he ducked behind a thick clump of trees.

'You ready for this?' Remy asked Grace.

She nodded.

The back door of the library grated against the concrete, heralding their arrival.

Grace and Remy walked into the main body of the library. The three men looked up casually. Bizzy leaned against the reception desk, chewing gum. Sarge sat on a chair, his feet up against a wall as he flicked through a half-torn book. Only Mal looked anxious as he paced by the main door on the far side of the room.

A couple of army lamps lit the gloom in places, silhouetting George's slumped body.

Grace couldn't tear her eyes away from her friend until a groan caught her attention.

She turned to see Abigail sitting on a chair in a dark corner, her hands behind her back, her face streaked with tears. Grace mouthed, 'It's going to be okay.' She wished she felt confident about that.

Abigail whimpered in response.

Sarge dropped his book, stood up and moved towards Remy as though he was going to shake his hand. Grace felt herself tense. She couldn't tell if he was armed.

'We've been looking for you, Remy,' said Sarge calmly. 'Absent without leave.' He grinned. 'Check them over, Biz.'

Biz stood upright and ambled over to them. Grace glanced at Remy. His face had turned very pale. He took a step back and pulled out his gun. Bizzy mirrored him and the two stood facing each other, motionless.

Mal looked away and continued pacing up and down by the door, running his hand over the top of his head in a repetitive motion.

'Mal!' Sarge barked and immediately Mal stood still.

'Give Bizzy the gun, Remy,' Sarge said in a bored tone.

When Remy didn't respond, Sarge took out his own gun and sauntered over to Abigail. She yelped when the barrel made contact with her forehead.

'Give him the fucking gun!' Sarge repeated.

Remy's shoulders dropped, he turned the gun round and passed it to Bizzy, who tucked it into the back of his belt.

What was he doing? Was that it – they were just going to give up? Shuggie was outside. It wasn't over yet.

'You could've just let me go, Sarge,' Remy said boldly, as Bizzy patted him down. 'I wasn't going to tell anyone, not before you started attacking my friends.' He looked over at Abigail.

'You know me, Remy. I'm not risking my troop's safety.' He put his gun down on the desk and leaned against the wood.

Bizzy began patting Grace down, running his hands over her body, checking in unnecessary places. Her skin began to burn as revulsion rose in her.

'As for you' – Sarge pointed at Grace – 'you're part of the system that I'm destroying. The lie that is Janus Justice. And that husband of yours… someone had to shut him up.'

Grace pushed Bizzy away from her in anger. He laughed and moved so close she could smell his minty breath. He continued his invasive search, took her phone from her back pocket and threw it on the desk. It lit up briefly and she felt reassured that when Shannon rang she'd be able to see. It wouldn't be long now… if they could just get Abigail out.

She'd seen Remy do this before, get the opposition to show their hand, act vulnerable and then go in for the kill. But somehow she couldn't see how his plan was going to work this time.

That's when it occurred to her. Maybe Remy didn't have a plan.

Maybe he didn't expect to get out of there alive.

'You should've killed me in the clinic when you had a chance,' Remy said.

'There's plenty of time for that now,' Sarge replied.

'Let her go first,' Grace said. There was no way she was going to let them take Remy without a fight, whatever stupid ideas he might have. But they had to get Abigail out.

Grace glanced in George's direction again. These people didn't care who lived and who died. 'You said you'd let her go if I brought Remy.'

Sarge nodded.

Bizzy made his way lazily over to Abigail and released her. She stood up and ran over to Grace, who immediately put her arm around Abigail's shoulders and moved her towards the door.

'No,' said Sarge.

Grace turned back slowly.

Mal came a little closer now, curious as to what was going to happen next.

'I said *she* could go,' Sarge said. 'Not you.'

He'd underestimated her if he thought Grace was just going to walk out and leave Remy behind. She knew he wouldn't be able to see past the middle-class, do-gooder doctor, not imagining for one moment the street-child scrapper at the heart of who she was. She still had some fight left in her. She was going to get Abigail out of there and then she was going to get Remy too. She'd lost too much in her life.

No more.

'My friend, she's waiting in the car just along there,' she whispered to Abigail. 'You walk out of here and keep going straight, you'll get to her. Run. Do you hear me?'

Abigail nodded.

Was Sarge really going to let her go? After she'd seen their faces, seen what they'd done to George? Grace felt a creeping fear.

'When you get to her, she'll call the police and then everything's going to be okay,' she said, her voice the faintest whisper.

If only Grace herself could believe that.

Abigail gave the slightest flicker of a smile and left.

Grace turned back to Diros, not sure if anyone else was going to get out of there alive.

'You've got me now,' Remy said. 'Let her go.'

'I don't think so,' Sarge said. 'She knows too much.'

Mal started to get twitchy. He could feel the pressure in his head, things moving to their final conclusion. This would all be over and done within the space of half an hour. They'd probably go and have a few AltCons in a shitty bar somewhere and he'd have to pretend that he was okay with what had gone down at the library.

Christ, he couldn't wait to get away.

He knew he wouldn't sleep. Sleep would wait until he was on the coach in the morning. He hadn't bothered packing much, so the other two wouldn't suspect he was going anywhere. He had learned to exist with so little when he was on the street, to make everything count, to be grateful for whatever he could get. He was going to have a better life from now on. He just had to get through tonight.

'Well, get it over with,' Remy said.

What the hell was Remy thinking?

The loud crack of gunfire rang through the trees outside. Two shots. Grace and Remy looked at each other, but the other three didn't flinch.

Was it the police already? Grace looked to her phone but the screen was dark. Maybe this was Shuggie, coming in to rescue them?

Abigail walked back into the library. What the hell was she doing, coming back? She should be in the jeep with Shannon by now!

Grace searched her for any sign of injury, but she appeared unharmed.

'Abigail, I told you to run!'

But Abigail ignored her. Instead, she waved a gun at Sarge. 'I sorted it,' she said simply. Grace looked to the desk. Sarge's gun was gone. Abigail must have picked it up on her way past.

Sarge nodded in her direction. 'Good job.'

'What the hell is going on?' Grace asked.

Abigail approached her. 'You seem to know so much about psychopaths,' she said, her golden-orange eyes locked on Grace, unblinking. 'It's such a shame you didn't recognise one out in the wild. I've killed your friend in the car. So the police won't be coming after all.'

Shannon!

'Why?' was all Grace could manage to say.

'You said it yourself, in the clinic,' Abigail said. 'Psychopathy has its upside. We're not always killers.' She paused. 'Well, I am now, but you know what I mean.' Was that a smile? 'We can often function normally in society, under the radar. But we also like to get what we want.'

'I know you,' said Remy, staring at her.

Bizzy refocused his gun on him.

'You were at the clinic in Manchester,' Remy said.

'I'm flattered you remember.' She cocked her head to one side.

'The scans…' Grace shook her head. 'It was you. But why?'

'This…' – she indicated Sarge and Bizzy – 'this isn't my scene at all. But I do like to make money.'

'You work for them?' Grace asked, astonished. How could she have got this so wrong?

'How do you think they get all the information about the crimes? Those court reels are very interesting, so much… detail. And there's no way the boys could get their hands on the police documents, even though little Mal there does a sterling job on the evidence.'

Mal looked up on hearing his name.

'I mean it's no easy job, making those videos,' Abigail continued, 'but as you said yourself, psychopaths are more curious than anything else, and if I can make a bit of money on the side…'

Grace looked to Sarge, who nodded. 'Worth every Penny.'

The pressure was increasing in Mal's head. He couldn't stand that ginger-haired bitch. Patronising, greedy snake that she was. He was tired of Bizzy taking the piss and putting him down. He was tired of Sarge's constant demands. He just wanted it all to go away.

'Hold on, hold on…' he muttered to himself. 'Just a few more hours…'

He imagined Layla standing in the library, peeping from behind one of the bookshelves, smiling at him. If only they could have gone to Scotland together. Got married in Gretna! She would have loved that, probably would have worn flowers in her hair. He felt his eyes begin to prickle.

He snapped out of it when he heard Sarge say, 'Give Mal the gun, Biz.'

Bizzy slowly held it out, like a child reluctantly sharing a toy.

'Take it and point it at her, you fucking moron!' Sarge barked at Mal.

Mal had had enough of Sarge's shit. He did as he was told, took the gun and pointed it at Grace, but scowled at Sarge behind his back. He looked over to the bookshelves again, imagining Layla there, holding a posy of flowers.

Remy coughed, getting Grace's attention. He looked down and as she followed his eyeline he was holding out three fingers and then made a trigger-pulling gesture with his thumb and two fingers.

Three guns.

Abigail held Sarge's gun. Mal held one, and Remy's was down the back of Bizzy's belt.

'I'm tired of this. Mal, kill her,' Sarge said flatly.

Remy moved towards Bizzy, but Sarge took him down with two vicious punches to the back. He hit the floor and curled up, groaning.

'Mal?' said Sarge. 'What are you waiting for?'

Mal felt everything go quiet around him, as though he was standing in the eye of a storm. The coach, Scotland, a new life… it was so very close. But Sarge was forcing his hand. He had to do something, and do it now.

But when he looked at Grace, he felt sorry for her, sad that her life would end in this way, in a derelict, forgotten building. Sad that, in her innocence, she had come here to rescue Abigail – of all people! – Abigail, who didn't give a damn whether anyone lived or died, or hurt children, or burned innocent women in their beds.

'Bizzy, if he doesn't do it, kill him and then kill her,' Sarge said.

'With pleasure, Sarge.' Bizzy grinned.

Sarge stared at Mal. 'What's it going to be then, eh?'

Mal focused on Grace. She turned her attention from Remy lying on the floor, to meet his gaze. 'I've spent years analysing people,' she told him gently, 'and I don't think you want to shoot me.'

In the half-light of the library, Mal saw not Grace's face, but Layla's. She stood before him, vulnerable, fragile. Behind her, a pack of men, animals, ready to brutalise and destroy her, to take all the goodness, the joy.

Mal's gun swerved from Grace to Bizzy.

'Eh, big fella! You gonna be the hero?' Bizzy teased him. He grabbed Grace around the neck and swung her in front of him. 'Careful, you might hit your girlfriend.'

'Just shoot her, Mal,' Sarge growled, giving Remy a vicious kick as he struggled to get up. Remy went straight back down again, his body tensed in agony.

Bizzy's hands moved up and down Grace's body as he taunted Mal. 'You've fallen for her, haven't you, you *pathetic little bastard*!'

Mal shook his head and squeezed his eyes shut for a moment, trying to get Bizzy's words – ones that he heard in his father's voice – out of his head.

'Just shut the fuck up, Bizzy!' screamed Mal. 'Just shut the fuck up!'

'You haven't got it in you. I've said it all along,' teased Bizzy. 'Once a chickenshit, always a chickenshit.' He started laughing, a horrible, grating, wide-mouthed laugh.

Abigail stood watching, gun in hand, unblinking.

'Lads!' Sarge said, irritated. 'Stop fucking about! Do it, Mal.'

Mal fired.

The bullet clipped Bizzy on the shoulder and he cried out.

He let go of Grace, but she remained rooted to the spot, caught between Mal's and Abigail's guns.

'What the fuck, Mal?' Bizzy said, looking down at his shoulder, the material of his jacket torn by the bullet, a spray of blood on his cheek. 'You shot me!'

'I told you to shoot the bitch!' yelled Sarge.

Bizzy pulled Remy's gun out from the back of his belt.

'You fucking shot me, Mal!' he said in disbelief.

Mal faced Abigail now. 'It's your fault that woman was burned in the bed with Begbroke,' he said. 'She was innocent. She shouldn't have died. She'd still be alive if you hadn't met Begbroke in that bar and brought him back to the house. You knew what you were doing. You ruined everything.'

He absent-mindedly put his hand up to his pocket to check the zip was still closed tight. He turned to Grace, gun still pointed in Abigail's direction. 'I can't make up for the things I've done wrong… but I want to. Maybe if I save you, that means I've done something good… something right.'

Grace nodded slowly.

'Even if that means I have to do something bad,' he said sadly.

Grace held her breath as Mal seemed distracted momentarily by something she couldn't see in a dark corner of the library, his shoulders dropped, his lips moved, but she couldn't hear his words.

Then, suddenly, he refocused, took a strong stance, trained the gun on Abigail and shot her three times. The sound was deafening. Everything in the library seemed to freeze, even Abigail stood motionless for a moment, her face a picture of shock and outrage before she fell to the floor, her head bouncing as it made contact, her gun skittering over the floor towards Sarge and Remy.

As they dived for the gun, Grace turned to Mal. He stood still, gun pointing towards where Abigail had been standing. He was staring into space.

There was a scuffle as Remy and Sarge fought for the gun.

Bizzy turned his gun from Mal towards Remy but was struggling to get a clear shot as Remy and Sarge rolled around the floor.

Grace saw Abigail writhing. She was hit in the legs and stomach. She was still alive, but bleeding. Grace knew the second he had a clear shot Bizzy would kill Remy. She looked around for something to hit him with. Behind him, George's body caught her eye. His words came back to her. *These can be pretty useful in tricky situations.* Bizzy had been so busy trying feel her up when he'd done the body search that he hadn't checked her jacket pocket. She reached in and pulled out a sedative spray. With his focus on the two men, Bizzy didn't see it coming.

She jumped onto his back and although he fought it, she managed to apply the spray. Moments later, he slumped to the floor. His fingers were curled loosely around the grip of the gun, his eyes glazed. Grace stood on his wrist, grinding her heels on the bone, stooped down and took the gun from him. She stood up and kicked him hard in the groin, all her anger focused on the one spot. He groaned and rolled over before appearing to pass out.

Grace turned back to the fighting men. Sarge held the gun in the air with one hand and with the other delivered a savage blow to Remy's face. Remy reeled backwards.

Sarge stretched out his arm, pointed the gun in Mal's direction and fired twice.

Mal fell to the ground.

Remy had righted himself and was coming back for Sarge, who immediately turned his gun on him.

Grace fired at Sarge until the chamber was empty. Some of the bullets missed, hitting bookshelves and breaking windows, but some made contact. His leg, his shoulder, his jaw—

He crumpled on the floor, his face a mess, blood soaking his clothes.

Remy took the gun from his limp hand and held it up, breathless, to show Grace that they were out of danger. She leaned over, hands on her knees, and tried to catch her breath. From the corner of her eye, she saw Mal on the ground, a spray of blood as he coughed.

She moved across to where he lay amidst scattered book pages now soaking up his blood. Kneeling down next to him, she took hold of his hand, which rested on his chest above two dark, pulsing stains.

His eyelids flickered.

'You saved me,' she said softly. His hand felt cold and for a brief moment she was reminded of her mother.

'Layla?' Mal said, blood bubbling on his lips. 'Layla?' he repeated. 'Scotland,' he managed to say, his other hand resting on his zipped-up pocket.

'It's Grace,' she said. 'You saved me. Thank you.' She didn't feel the tears, but she saw them as they fell onto his chest and mingled with his blood. He gripped her hand tighter, fear in his eyes now.

From a distance, Grace could hear sirens, the high-pitched urgency of police cars and the plaintive wail of ambulances.

'They're coming,' she told him. 'Hold on.' But she could tell they wouldn't arrive in time. His breaths, shallow and staccato, stopped suddenly and he was motionless.

Grace placed Mal's other hand on his chest and closed his eyes. She stood up, took one last look and turned away.

'Remy, they're coming. You've got to go, before they get here.'

They quickly made their way out of the building and ran to the jeep. They saw Shuggie first, leaning over Shannon who was slouched in the front of the car. The windscreen had two bullet holes in it.

'All clear, Shuggie,' Remy said.

'Thank God you're okay,' he cried, but it was clear Shannon was in a bad way.

'Some one came out… I heard the shots… but I was way over there—' His voice was tremulous, there was blood all over his hands, all over Shannon's chest. 'I didn't get to her in time—'

'Help's coming,' Grace reassured him.

'I'm sorry, I couldn't help you,' Shuggie said, his eyes locked on Shannon. 'I had to stem the flow of blood.'

'It's okay, we got them… it's okay,' Grace told him as Remy looked gravely on.

Shannon looked very pale, her eyes closed.

The sirens became louder as Shuggie whispered comfort and encouragement to Shannon. Grace turned to Remy. 'You've got to go. I'll take it from here.' He grabbed her very briefly in an awkward hug, before turning and running.

She hurried to the gap in the fence. She bent over to climb through the gap, pausing to look back. Remy stood by the railway line, looking in her direction, nodded once, and was gone in the darkness.

Grace emerged on the other side, where blue and red lights blinded her, waved her arms wildly above her head and shouted, 'We're here! We're here!'

CHAPTER THIRTY-NINE

Siberia was nearly empty, just three occupants.

Grace stood still at the door, letting her breathing slow down so it was in rhythm with the rolling sounds, imagining she was standing on the shore, listening to the sea. She was glad that Mal wasn't in one of those beds. She'd been the only person at his funeral.

Sometimes, she could still feel his hand in hers.

Once the investigation began into what had been going on at Janus, it wasn't long before Conrad was arrested. It was what Grace expected. Someone had to take the fall and the minister had made sure that Conrad's version was dismissed out of hand. Grace felt relieved he was gone, along with his unscrupulous ways, but also a little sorry for him. She hoped they were kind to him, wherever he was now.

Conrad had always known her Achilles heel.

Dan had been surprised when she told him that she was returning to work at the Tier System, but it seemed the best way to clear her name and to get back to doing what she loved, what gave her life meaning. Sometimes it was worth getting back into the fight to get what you wanted.

Gracie knew that.

She'd spoken to Dan occasionally while he was healing physically and mentally from the attack, but that part of her life was over and she rarely spoke to him now.

The new psychiatrist would be in at two o'clock. She'd smile and give him the tour, show him the ropes. She'd teach him, like Abigail had once taught her, how the clinic worked, but now, instead of Aversion Therapy built on fear, there was something kinder in its place.

It was her treatment, but she didn't feel jealous or resentful or possessive. She didn't care who was in charge, as long as they used her new treatment.

She just didn't want to be at the Janus clinic any more. Too many bad memories.

The minister from the Department of Justice had been in charge of the investigation. He'd called her into Conrad's office and they'd struck a deal. Grace would remain silent about Siberia if she could run the Agrarian and choose the right people to run the new therapy.

She would be Shannon's replacement.

When her friend came to mind, she felt her heart clench. It was still so painfully raw, even after four months. It had taken a while to settle into Shannon's house on the Compound. Grace found herself standing in various rooms at different times crying. She'd cried with loss after Shannon's sister had come up from London to collect the children and she'd found a toy left behind. She'd cried with guilt seeing Shuggie through a window out in the fields looking bereft. She'd cried when Remy left the Agrarian, the night after Shannon's funeral. She wondered if he'd gone because he too couldn't look Shuggie in the eye.

She'd probably see Remy again someday, wouldn't she? She had lost so much, a hollow victory.

Who knew what the future held? But for now it was enough to know that she was back where she should be. Helping, healing, rehabilitating.

This was the last time she would come to this ward before it was closed for good. She wanted to see with her own eyes the three people who had caused her so much trouble, who had changed her life so drastically.

Bizzy was in the first bed she came to, lying prone, inert, innocuous.

Her skin crawled.

Moving along the ward to the next bed, Grace looked down at Sarge, the powerful, unused body wrapped tightly in the white sheet, his damaged lower face hidden by medical dressings, the scar on his arm looking almost maroon under the soft lights.

And in the corner, there was Abigail.

The ward would be shut down in a few days, just as soon as the minister had made a decision about their fate. Who knew what would happen to them then? Grace tried not to think about it. It wouldn't be her problem any more. But the minister had agreed to her demand that this was where the three should be kept until then.

She walked over to Abigail's bed and stared for a while – all her strawberry red hair gone, her bone-white skin, the marmalade eyes hidden behind the headset.

How could Grace not have seen the signs? She reassured herself that anyone could fall for a psychopath's manipulation. She was only human.

On the wall above their beds she could see projected the reels that were being pumped into their brains. They were getting the whole hit. Everything they'd done to others they now experienced being done to them. All the crimes they'd organised and carried out, with the added ingredient of synthetic empathy to really drive it home.

Grace wasn't sure if she believed in Hell. But maybe this was the closest it came.

She couldn't save everyone. She knew that now. You couldn't always cure people with kindness, but sometimes people needed to be punished before they could move on, to come to terms with what they'd done so that they might face redemption.

Before she turned away and left the ward for good, Grace pulled something out of her pocket and placed it into Abigail's limp hand, wrapping the long, pale fingers around it – a brightly coloured plastic keyring photo frame, the word FUNLAND, each letter a different colour, an image of two children, Grace and Remy, on a rollercoaster ride, the pair of them laughing, really laughing.

ACKNOWLEDGEMENTS

It takes a village to raise a book but this particular novel was written in the isolation of lockdown. With a subject as complex as the human brain, I was in no way qualified to write about it, so the support I received was like home schooling by Zoom where I met some brilliant people who educated me enough to look like I know what I'm talking about!

My particular thanks goes to Dr Jayne Martlew of the Walton Neurological Centre in Liverpool who very kindly agreed to meet with me over the internet to discuss the brain and types of empathy, that most beautiful human quality. Together we went on a journey of discovery and, I'm very glad to say, became friends.

I have more clever people to thank:

Dr Julia Ravey, with her expertise on Neuroscience.

Dr Nauman Butt from the Clatterbridge Cancer Centre, Dr Maria Safar from Aintree University Hospital, Dr Matt Wedlich and Dr Michael O'Brien – all of whom gave me advice about medicine and its effects on the body.

Professor Thomas Fischer from the University of Liverpool School of Environmental Sciences for his help on plastic pollution in the oceans.

Paula Storey-McCann for her knowledge on early childhood experiences and empathy.

It sounds like I contacted all the brain-boxes on Twitter for my research but amazingly I know all these people in real life!

Thanks also goes to Jessy Minney Ph.D from the Health Foundation for Western and Central New York for her thoughts on the 'empathy switch', and Forensic Science Lecturer Jennifer Rees for a talk she once gave in a pub in Liverpool about psychopathy, the empathy switch, the temporoparietal junction and the effects of magnets on the TPJ. She blew my mind and the ideas never left me.

Then there is the Crime Writing community – the loveliest people on the internet – and in particular Trevor Wood. In lockdown he introduced me online to the Northern Crime Writing Syndicate, and the Debuts 2020. Later, in real life, he invited me to Newcastle Noir and Bay Tales where I met lots of other writers that I feel lucky to know. Trevor, you've been an absolute blessing. I wouldn't be where I am without your support.

My gratitude also goes to:

My other writer friends and first readers. Victoria Dowd, Philippa East, Heleen Kist, Rob Parker, Rob Scragg, John Thompson, Stuart Turton, Vic Watson. Thank you for the advice, kind words, laughs, quotes and general shenanigans.

The Debuts 2020 and the NCWS.

The Wordsmiths – Stanley, Neville and John for critiquing the early draft.

Caroline Maston of the UK Crime Book Club for her valued support.

Podcasters and book bloggers – where would us scribblers be without you?

Huge thanks go to my agent Ed Wilson for the support, encouragement, confidence, and knowledge of the arcane ways of the publishing industry!

The dynamic team at Canelo – Kate, Thanhmai, Claudine and Nicola – who are doing all they can to get me to where I need to be.

And of course, my brilliant editor, Kit Nevile, who understands what I am trying to do and helps me to be the best I can be! Thank you so much for the opportunity.

Love and thanks go to my cheerleaders and the people who keep me going – Mum and Dad, my cousin Frank, Marie,

Sarah, Julia, Mary Rose and the Wise Women – Susi, Cate, Emma and my oldest and dearest pal, Maggie.

In memory of my lovely friend Gill Power – I think you would have liked this one.

For all those who are trying to get published... keep going! Aim for the stars, you might land on the rooftops – the view's pretty good from here!

But most of all, thank you to Seán, Paddy and Tadhg – the loves of my life.

You're what makes it all worth it.

If you would like to know more please look me up at www.sarahmoorhead.com

CREDITS

Canelo would like to thank everyone involved with the publication of *The Treatment*

Editor
Kit Nevile

Copyeditor
Kate Berens

Proofreader
Vicki Vrint

Cover Designer
Andrew Davis

Editorial
Hannah Taylor

Production
Micaela Cavaletto
Nicole Abel

Sales
Claudine Sagoe
Thanhmai Bui-Van

Marketing
Nicola Piggott

Publicity
Kate Shepherd